THE POISONED ISLAND

LLOYD SHEPHERD

**SIMON &
SCHUSTER**

London · New York · Sydney · Toronto · New Delhi

A CBS COMPANY

1 3 5 7 9 10 8 6 4 2

Simon & Schuster UK Ltd
1st Floor
222 Gray's Inn Road
London WC1X 8HB

www.simonandschuster.co.uk
www.simonandschuster.com.au

Simon & Schuster Australia, Sydney
Simon & Schuster India, New Delhi

A CIP catalogue record for this book
is available from the British Library

ISBN Paperback 978-1-47110-036-9
ISBN E-book 978-1-47110-037-6

Typeset by M Rules
Printed and bound by CPI Group (UK) Ltd, Croydon CR0 4YY

For Jack and Lily

ONE

She comes! – the GODDESS! – through the
    whispering air,
Bright as the morn, descends her blushing car;
Each circling wheel a wreath of flowers entwines,
And gem'd with flowers the silken harness shines;
The golden bits with flowery studs are deck'd,
And knots of flowers the crimson reins connect.—
And now on earth the silver axle rings,
And the shell sinks upon its slender springs;
Light from her airy seat the Goddess bounds,
And steps celestial press the pansied grounds.

Erasmus Darwin, The Botanic Garden', 1791

TAHITI, 1769

Near the foot of great Tahiti Nui, in the shadow of the dead volcano and beneath the hungry eyes of ancient gods, the young Englishman chased his princess through the forest, despite the best efforts of the forest to stop him. The dipping branches of trees slapped his face and arms. Damp leaves, drenched in the mountain's tears, were heavy on his face, like wet green clothes hung out to dry. The sun had come up after the rain storm and joined the gods to watch proceedings. The air was warm and liquid.

The Englishman's breath was loud but steady in his ears, strengthened by countless rope exercises on the deck of his ship, just one of the many ways he'd filled the endless empty days of his voyage. His bare feet, strong and leathery after weeks on the island, felt solid and sure on the slippery earth. He had stopped concerning himself with the crawling and slithering creatures underfoot.

The princess (favoured by the gods) said nothing as she ran, and neither did he. Both of them breathed and breathed and breathed, their lungs in counterpoint, three of her inhalations to two of his, her waltz to his march. On every third breath, she exhaled a little sigh, and the gods sighed with her.

The chase was in its final stages. It hadn't started in this grim silence punctuated by sighs. When she had first leapt up and started to run from him she'd squealed the same delightful girlish squeal he'd heard so many times before. She'd bubbled with laughter and he did, too, as he'd set off after her. The other Englishmen and the island women seated around the tents had laughed along with them, the men cheering heartily as he crashed into the green wall of trees to follow his escaping quarry. Her laughter had seemed to fill the forest, as if the island itself was joining in on this tremendously spirited romp. Above them rose mighty Tahiti Nui, its smoke long extinguished but its memories as enduring as the sea.

She'd shouted to him a few times as the chase began, and he'd recognised several words in the local tongue, with which he'd made pleasing progress. *You cannot,* he thought he'd heard. *I am fast* he was sure about. And *No no no* was as clear as day, and he'd laughed at that again, laughed at her games and her delightfully arch modesty. He knew it to be a masque. Was it not just what those charming London courtesans had said on that cherished fishing trip with his Lord S—. They too had lifted their skirts and run away, ankles dappled with mud, eyes sparkling and full of hidden knowledge, the game all part of the essential transaction.

In any case, this coquettish flight was certainly not in keeping with the island's delicate intimacies. He was *sure* of that.

They ran like that for some time, laughing and shouting at each other, but at some point the nature of the chase had changed. Her laughter had died. His continued for a while, but it became forced and then it too ebbed away, replaced by the grim metronomic breathing, the liquid trees, the slapping, muddy feet, the little royal sighs of the princess. Then they were only running, breathing together, the wet sound of their bodies crashing through the undergrowth silencing the forest creatures around them.

And as the Englishman ran, his certainty grew.

No more. No more of this. No more teasing and cajoling. The other women of this island have given themselves freely and often, both to me and to my men. They have moaned and sighed and stroked and played, while this one has shared only caresses and the occasional chaste kiss. She knows I want her. I believe she wants me. What is this escape, but the need to find seclusion and privacy for our final consummation? She wishes to be hidden from the eyes of her retinue. Well, let her have her ways. And let me have mine.

His self-assurance grew. So did his desire. He felt he could chase her all the way to Venus.

The ground began to climb, and even with his heart pumping in his chest and the sweat bursting through his skin he knew where they were. They were running south, into the heart of the island, where water cascaded down into pools and birds circled. The trees would start growing ever thicker as they climbed away from the human places and into the green jungle, the place where only priests and their adherents ever went. The place where, the Englishman had been told, the Arreoy sanctified themselves with the blood of babies.

Her breath, he could hear, was beginning to sound ragged, and almost without thinking he slowed down. His arousal was by now at a delicious plateau. There would be no refusal. But the pursuit was pleasant and he wanted it to last.

A sound of water close by. They were near one of the many falls. Up ahead he heard a shriek and then a splash, and then he was into the water, and he had her.

She wriggled and scratched like a fish with claws, and for a moment his certainty faltered. *Why so steadfast? Does she not indeed want this? Perhaps whatever faith she has precludes it?* He considered this for a moment, even as he held her around her middle and felt the sharp angular rocks at his feet, one of them biting into his ankle and tearing the skin. He felt his blood in the water and the water in his blood, and he laughed and shouted because of the magnificent feeling of being *alive* that now encased him. Like a bear with a salmon he climbed up the other bank and onto the shore line, where she collapsed onto the ground and he began to unbutton his fine Covent Garden breeches, stained green and brown with his time on the island.

She said nothing for a moment, watching him. Her fine colourful robe, the mark of her nobility, was wet against her skin, and her dark shining hair was flat against her head. The flowers with which she'd decorated herself were gone, washed away down the mountainside by the stream. Her skin – *my God, her skin* – glowed like butter before a fire, wet and bright and alive. He congratulated himself on his refusal to accept *no* as her answer. Every pore of her, every fibre of her hair, every shining droplet of water on her hot, soft skin, spoke of desire. But then, as he stepped out of his breeches and prepared to lie on top of her, she spoke, in his own tongue.

'No, Joseph. No.'

The words were flat and shockingly tuneless, with none of the melody of the local tongue in them. He noticed her breathing, how it was still dancing along in three-quarter time with that persistent little sigh. There was, for that moment, no doubting the woman's meaning. For a second time he hesitated and his rational self seemed to emerge from the wet trees to find him there, his fine breeches round his ankles and his gentleman's cock high in the air. That self shouted at him, pleaded with him, and its voice was the voice of his mother. He could almost smell her old perfume, and hear her high, tissue-thin voice, and it told him to stop, now, stop, before everything changed forever.

But there was never a chance of that. This was a man of action, of determination and most of all of will. This was, above all, a *young* man whose appetite for women was already the subject of scandalised rumour in the drawing rooms of England. He roared like a bear again, laughing delightedly at the princess lying on the ground (who must, after all, desire him for she did not struggle, only breathed that odd little rhythm), and he fell on and into her.

She had made no new sound as he'd taken her, other than that precise little pattern of breathing and sighing. When he rolled away from her she did not move. Her eyes looked to the sky. Her chest rose and fell. He stroked her face, smoothed her hair and kissed her forehead, frowned in irritation and mild concern at her silence, and then he slept and dreamed. In the years that followed and across the thousands of nights in which she haunted him it became impossible for him to unpick the real from the dream.

In his dream she stood and walked away from him, her damp robes falling to the ground, her black hair unrolling down her back as she went. His dream-self woke up and followed her close behind, respectfully this time, although even here the desire was still present, impossible to ignore. It was as if their previous relationship of visitor-and-monarch had been restored. She walked along the side of the pool, then she climbed – or rather, in this dream state, she seemed to *float* – up the rocks which lined the waterfall. He clambered after her, heavy and clumsy and lumpen (he would grow heavier and clumsier the older he got, the years fattening him as his belly grew as enormous as his reputation, but the dream would stay with him). By the time he reached the top she was already disappearing into the trees. He followed her once more, occasionally glimpsing her as he struggled to keep up.

And then, she began to sing.

He recognised neither the words nor the melody, and he'd made a careful study of the islanders' music. What she sang sounded different from anything he'd heard, a complicated melange of tones and whistles, and after a moment birds began to sing in the trees around them. And here was something to thrill the heart of a voyaging explorer: the birds were singing along with her. They harmonised, they made counterpoint, they embarked on thrilling little rills which ran through and around and into the princess's own song, like crystal water flowing into a blue pool.

He came upon the hilltop clearing suddenly, emerging from the green just as she stopped singing and the birds, one by one, ceased their accompaniment. He picked up his pace now, some new urgency coming over him, but she stopped, finally and completely, her glorious back to him.

There was a crackling wooden sound then, and the ground around her came to life. Tendrils of green burst upwards and wrapped themselves around her feet, her calves, her thighs. Her hair burst open with green light and fire, and her back began to elongate and spread itself up towards the fresh sunlight. Her fingers twisted into twigs which curled out from the branches of her arms. Shiny ovate leaves appeared all around these branches and twigs and then, with a final crunch of wood and bark, her shape disappeared within the new-yet-ancient body of a small, elegant tree, perhaps fifteen feet high, its canopy a neat, shining triangle which caught the brilliant sun and reflected it in a symphony of green, her legs fused into a single straight trunk.

He woke up beside that Pacific waterfall. Only Tahiti Nui, its gods and the sun remained to watch him as he stood and dressed. The princess was gone.

THE THAMES

A nondescript ship containing wonders arrives at the mouth of the Thames estuary on a dull June morning in 1812. England is not looking her best to welcome the ship home. The estuary is certainly capable of splendour, if the time of day is right and the sunlight hits the damp air at the correct angle to split itself. An artist might perform miracles at such times. If the Navy was mustering on the Nore, well then, such an artist might even see something transcendent.

Not today, though. Today, the edges of Kent and Essex are indistinct things, and though the day is warm the air is heavy and damp. An artist wishing to paint today would need bring only browns and greys and an air of disappointment.

The new arrival is called the *Solander*. She takes her name from the Swedish botanist Daniel Solander, who charmed London in the last century with tales of his great voyage to Otaheite. Solander's loyal friend Joseph Banks had given the ship her name and had sent her away to follow the same track he and Solander and their captain James Cook had sailed, back in the mists of legend.

Given her distinguished name, the *Solander*'s wonders are of an appropriately botanical kind. Hundreds and hundreds of plants from the paradise island of Otaheite have been planted in pots and barrels throughout the ship; her insides have been refashioned to accommodate them, and even the captain's great cabin and his quarterdeck have had to make room for gardeners and their tools. Every spare surface and rail and cubbyhole contains some kind of South Seas plant life, either as seeds or bulbs or seedlings wrapped in linen (which must be kept constantly damp) or small plants in soil inside half-barrels secured by the carpenters to ensure they are not disturbed by rough seas. The quarterdeck has itself been taken over by a kind of plant house, constructed specially for the voyage. Captain Hopkins has made one thing very clear: each plant is to be cherished as if it were a human member of the crew itself, and the expiry of any flora through negligence will be punished by the lash. Hopkins is a hard man, though not a cruel one, and his order is observed with due attention.

As for *why* the plants have been brought back to London, most of the crew could not care one way or another. They are being paid well (*very* well, truth be told), and most of them are returning with tales of the delights of Otaheite which will make their women cringe with jealousy and rage for years to come. These women may soon be cringing for rather different reasons, as the infections of Otaheite return to Europe. Most of the men on board are carrying some kind of venereal disease, the blighted fruit of dalliances with the women of Otaheite who were themselves blighted by contact with European sailors. Who carried these afflictions to the island is still the subject of nationalist conjecture. The English say the French infected the islanders on their first visit, while the French say the reverse, nodding in a knowing fashion at the widely published accounts of Sir Joseph Banks himself, who fearlessly and scandalously described his own dalliances on the island.

The crew of the *Solander* know nothing of such historical debate. They know that Otaheite presented them with experiences which had been previously unimaginable. They know that they are beginning to itch. They know that the treatment will be unpleasant. They discuss these matters only obliquely, each man an island of secrets.

Sam Ransome is a not-quite-stupid seaman who is seeing the muddy and featureless estuary seascape for the last time. He carries his own Otaheite secret, as do several other men in the crew. He is up on the main yard, his slow head still full of the wonders of southern oceans, where blue-green summits had sprung up over endless horizons after the yawning weeks of waiting. Beneath those summits he had found golden beaches, blue seas, willing women and intoxicating draughts. Otaheite had risen clearly and spectacularly from the blue Pacific, its peaks shrouded in a pearly mist which only emphasised the resolute edges of its green tree-shrouded hills. At the other end of that memory sits his immediate future: a scruffy boarding-house room, a fat woman the wrong side of forty and the constant threat of impressment or penury. Yet he aches for home, his hunger for it driven by an unquenchable thirst which has grown with every nautical mile.

For most of the crewmen, the remembered magic of home will be a short-lived thing; it barely lasts beyond the first night back on domestic shores. Within the week most sailors will be sniffing the air in a particular way and strolling down to the wharves in a meaningful fashion. The truth is that home is complicated and seafaring is simple. Hard, but simple. You do what you are told, you sleep when you are allowed to, and no one (particularly no one of a *female* nature) gives you unclear instructions with unknown consequences.

Next to Sam, Bob Attlee has started whistling a merry London tune which Samuel half-recognises, while Attlee's great friend Tommy Arnott scowls into his work, his silence encasing him like a shroud. On the *Solander*, as on all ships, there are two types of seaman: the overweight and the skinny. Each thrives on the same rations, to the consternation and puzzlement of the other type. Attlee is fat and red; his silent friend Arnott is thin but as brown as an old shoe. Sam, for his part, is comfortably padded.

Attlee winks at Sam when he sees him looking, a theatrically knowing wink which is instantly noticed by the fourth member of the main yard crew, a despicable little Geordie called, much to the delight of his shipmates, Craven. For weeks now Attlee has been torturing the Geordie with intimations of a great secret. Sam wishes, with all his heart, that Attlee would desist; each one of those jokey winks feels like a warning shot from a marine's gun. Craven cannot help himself, and rises to the bait.

'Will ye be headed anywhere in particular when we get ashore, Sam?' he asks, his disappointed eyes hungry for information. Attlee's mouth is carved with contempt, and Sam feels the same, toying with the idea of shoving Craven off the yard and down to the deck below.

'Away from *you*, Craven, is all,' he says, and Attlee laughs at that. Even Arnott smiles.

The banks of the river close in on the *Solander* as she makes her way upstream. Tilbury and its Fort go by on the north shore, guarding the empty and windswept Essex marshes, where only birds keep watch. Gravesend is to the south, the Kent hills rising behind. At least a dozen ships have accompanied them into the river: laden colliers, a cutter on official River Police or Customs business, and a pair of substantial Indiamen headed slowly for the new docks.

At Woolwich the military river begins. Men in uniform look down onto the deck of the *Solander* from mighty warships, like gods gazing down on their congregation. The crew resist the temptation to shout something disrespectful up at them, lest Captain Hopkins hear them and unleash his own wrath.

The river is crowded with vessels now. They pass Galleons, and off to starboard Samuel can see the great new West and East India Docks, crammed with ships as big as cathedrals. Each of those enormous floating leviathans will only ever make three return journeys before the tide and the wind break them down. Sam's imagination grapples with the idea that money should be so great that a machine like an Indiaman becomes itself disposable. It is a fearsome thought, the size of which is too much for Sam's conception. His hand moves from the main yard to his side to feel for the pouch which sits there beneath his old cotton shirt. Attlee sees the movement and smirks. Craven sees it also, and files it away in some dark little place for when Opportunity presents itself.

The order comes from the officers to prepare the ship for mooring, and for the next hour the seamen on the main yard have little time to talk, their hands busy with the mindless repetition and urgency which accompanies any change in the state of an oceangoing ship. They pass the Hospital at Greenwich and then the Dockyard at Deptford, where more military vessels glower down at them. The ship's sails come down one by one as they approach their mooring, on the chain in the river just downstream from Rotherhithe.

It takes a couple of hours to make the *Solander* ready for a lengthy stay; the officers bark commands, and the men work harder than they have for weeks, keen to get the work finished. Samuel works as hard as anyone; this is a rarity, for Sam Ransome is a recognised expert when it comes to avoiding hard work. The pouch inside his shirt bounces against his chest, an incessant signifier of pleasures postponed. The serpent in his belly which has been his shipmate since leaving Otaheite tightens itself and hisses, desperate to be appeased.

A flurry of lighters, wherries and barges comes alongside the ship as she is finally moored to a chain. The botanists, who have emerged from the quarterdeck plant house like moles unexpectedly surfacing into daylight, are supervising the transfer of the first tranche of plants from the ship to two waiting barges, which will carry the specimens down to Kew.

Around half the crew are discharged immediately. There is a crush of bodies as these men are given their papers and their pay. Samuel, Arnott, Attlee and Craven are all part of the mêlée. Sam tries his best to remain patient, but the buzz of desire within him is growing, and he can see it in the faces of Arnott and Attlee as well. They collect their belongings from below – Sam's in a sea chest, Arnott and Attlee's in ancient but sturdy kit bags – and then they are ready to leave the ship. Three other men join them at the gunwale: seamen Elijah Frost and Colby Potter; and Jeremiah Critchley, the carpenter's mate, as blonde as a Viking, whose brown arms and enormous hands should be clutching an ancient hammer rather than the tattered little scroll which contains his discharge and the canvas bag which contains his pay. Around a dozen wherries have appeared round the ship ready to take men ashore, and the discharged crew are clambering down to them. But these six men hang back for a moment, their faces pinched with the same thirsty desire which marks Samuel. Craven attempts to join the little group, but he is shoved away by Critchley.

'Fuck off, Craven.'

The little Geordie attempts defiance.

'Fuck off yourself, Critchley. I've every right to go ashore with whom I choose.'

The tall man says nothing. All six of the men in the group glare at Craven with their suspicious eyes. Craven gives way, slouching off to find another wherry.

Samuel watches the Viking Critchley, the unelected leader of their clandestine group. He sees the tension in Critchley's face, the same tension they all feel as they wait their turn for a boat to take them to shore. Finally it is their time and the six of them climb down, each with hidden pouches bouncing against their sides. The boat takes Attlee and Arnott to Rotherhithe first, on the Surrey shore, and Critchley speaks to them before they climb out. Then the wherry turns and takes the remaining four men a little upriver and across to the stairs just below the River Police Office at Wapping. For the last time in his life, Sam Ransome scrambles up onto English land. Critchley speaks to Colby and Potter and then they too disappear like the rest of the *Solander*'s secrets, botanical and medical, into the anonymous chaos of the metropolis. They have a favourite boarding house in Ratcliffe, while Critchley and Sam plan to seek lodgings in Wapping.

Sam and Critchley walk up Wapping Street for a while, Critchley warning Sam to keep his peace and avoid any suspicious behaviour, just as he had warned the others. Then Sam leaves Critchley for good, turning up Old Gravel Lane and away from the waterfront, the disquieting walls of the London Dock pushing him east and north. His sea chest is heavy and he is very tired, but he walks with unfamiliar swiftness, a lazy fat man hurrying to a much-postponed assignation. He turns right off the lane into a side alley and goes through the door of an ancient, nondescript boarding house. Inside he speaks to an equally ancient and nondescript landlady, who recognises him but greets him with contempt anyway. He takes out some of his pay but before handing it over he demands she fetch him something. She becomes annoyed and demurs, but he insists, holding the coins away from her, and at last she surrenders to her own need for money and goes to find an iron kettle from her kitchen. He takes it off her when she comes back, almost snatching the thing away despite its weight, and heads up the stairs.

His room is empty apart from a bed and a chair, but as promised there is wood in the fireplace. He spends twenty frustrating minutes trying to light the fire, his hands shaking, his stomach now as clenched as a hand on a sword, sweat smearing his face even though the room is disgustingly cold for June. Eventually the fire takes, and he remembers the kettle is empty. He goes out of the room and down to the kitchen to fill it with water. The old boarding-house woman looks at him from her perch at the kitchen table as if he were a particularly nasty form of cockroach which had introduced itself to her residence, but he ignores her. The iron kettle and the water inside it are heavy, but even so his hands shake as he climbs the stairs again, goes into his room and puts the kettle on the fire.

It takes an eternity to boil, months and years and decades of waiting. He takes a primitive-looking wooden cup from his sea chest, and then he takes the pouch from around his neck and opens it. A foreign, pungent smell instantly engulfs him, a smell full of sun and sand and trees. He tells himself to be calm, to be steady, and with struggling care he empties some of what is in the pouch into the wooden cup. He tightens the pouch back up again and places it in his sea chest, along with his bag of pay, and pushes the sea chest under the bed. The kettle is boiling, at last, and he pours the hot water onto the dried leaf inside the cup. The smell that had sprung out of the leather pouch now deepens and spreads throughout the room, and every one of Sam's senses is ringing; he can even hear the noise of a woman laughing, presumably from out in the street. He sits on the bed and finally, deliciously, succumbs to months of waiting, pouring the hot tea down his throat and crying out as it scalds his mouth, his tongue, his lungs. But the pain lasts only a moment, and then a familiar light opens up inside his head and he lies back on the bed, a smile of bliss already slashed across his face.

WAPPING

Many hundreds of pairs of eyes watch over the river. Shipowners and insurance agents cluster at the windows of offices and warehouses to keep an anxious watch on the precarious states of their investments. Old sailors cast mournful gazes and half-remember, half-invent former, brighter days. Boys with the rage of mothers hard in their ears see the masts and picture far-off coasts glittering with adventure, while their mothers look up tiredly from their laundry when they have the strength to do so and curse the river for being so much more attractive to their husbands than they.

One pair of eyes watches with a particular intensity. John Harriott, the resident magistrate of the River Police Office, looks out from his office on the second floor of the Police Office building in Wapping, which has stood looking out over the wharves and between the warehouses since the end of the last century. The building would not be out of place among the new avenues of villas at the fringes of Middlesex and Westminster. Out here among the dingy and ancient wharves and in front of the crowded untidy foreshore, the Police Office looks as out of place as a dainty missionary bringing the word of God to a town of sullen thieves.

Harriott was the Police Office's founding magistrate and has indeed felt like a missionary himself at times, sent down to the river to deliver a message of Law and of Order to a community which had taken pilfering to levels which threatened London's very status as the richest entrepôt in the world. His officers and waterman-constables have been given the power to board any ship in the river and to *watch* it: to see that its cargo is loaded and unloaded according to its manifest and to confirm that, as far as is possible, none of the items in its hold finds its way into a sailor's pockets.

In Harriott's time as magistrate the river commerce has been drastically altered by the coming of the docks: the East and West India Docks in the Isle of Dogs; the London Dock behind Harriott's Police Office ; and a new dock system on the Surrey shore around the old Howland Dock. Harriott does not concern himself with whatever criminal activity occurs within these docks, which are owned by private companies responsible for their own security and answerable to none but the Customs and the Crown. His domain on the river remains a vibrant, noisy, crowded place, despite the arrival of these mercantile cathedrals. Some had imagined that the river trade would die out with the coming of the new docks. They were quite wrong. London's trade continues to grow at an astounding rate, even in the face of the obstructive little Emperor's attempts to strangle it. Britain is at war, and no one is more aware of the importance of commerce to that effort than John Harriott, a bristling patriot who has served in the Royal Navy, the Merchant Navy, and the East India Company. Now sixty-seven years old, he has buried two wives and reached an accommodation with a third, and his sons are full-grown and leading mercantile lives of their own. His energy is notorious, his bulldog stubbornness resented, his commitment to his duties fearsome.

Harriott has been watching the water to see if he can catch a glimpse of today's celebrated arrival. The *Solander* is a rare thing on the river: a ship arriving from far-off climes preceded by its own reputation. She is something of a throwback to the great days of discovery of Harriott's youth, when ships with names like *Endeavour* and *Resolution* set out onto the white expanses of the charts and brought back tales of lands formed from ice, islands of sun and enchantment, cannibals, canoes, spears and serpents.

Harriott has his own particular reasons for wanting to witness the safe arrival and mooring of the *Solander*. The vessel's main backer, the Royal Society President Sir Joseph Banks, has asked that Harriott in particular take an interest in the ship's security; word has got back to Harriott that Sir Joseph has described him as a 'singular man, one who can be trusted with the Treasures of my returning Ship.' This does not flatter Harriott; rather, it has only served to make him resentful but determined. Resentful, for Harriott has reasons to distrust Sir Joseph, reasons that lie within recent events in Wapping. Determined, because he wishes his relationship with Sir Joseph – such as it is – to be one of unblemished achievement on his side, and guilty reliance on the part of Sir Joseph.

The ship in question had arrived on the morning tide, and she is now moored to the chain in the river, just upstream of the new entrance to the Surrey Canal system. She is hard to spot around the bend in the river, in amongst the busy shipping which, day and night, turns the Thames into a floating city of wood and rope. Harriott knows what to look for, though, and he does indeed spy her. She is not, truth be told, much to look at, but Harriott knows his maritime history and knows that her predecessors, from the *Endeavour* on, were all very ordinary-looking vessels. Like the *Endeavour* and the *Bounty*, the *Solander* is a Whitby collier, broad-beamed and square-bowed, squat and practical, made for the repetitious carrying of coal across the unyielding North Sea. There is no romance to look at her, unless you know something of where she's been and what she brings back. Knowing that, an old Navy man like John Harriott cannot help but find the romance in her irresistible.

It is now the afternoon. Looking up once again from his work to gaze out of the window, Harriott thinks that he can detect a wherry rowing away from the *Solander* and heading upstream towards him. Years of looking at the river have given him the ability to pick out particular activity, even among the clamour of barges, whalers, luggers, packets, brigs, ferries, dinghies and lighters. Wherries have been making their way from the *Solander* for some time now – indeed, one discharged several seamen at the Wapping stairs just below his office only a quarter-hour ago. But this particular wherry carries only one passenger, and as it rows closer Harriott is convinced it must be the captain.

Harriott is seated in his ancient leather chair, saved from the rushing Essex waters during the inundation of his island farm years before he came to Wapping. The chair can swivel through a full circle, allowing him both to watch out of the window and work at his desk without standing on his lame and increasingly pointless leg. He turns the chair back to his desk and away from the window to await the man, checking the letter from the resident magistrate at Bow Street, Aaron Graham. It is this letter which introduces the captain and asks Harriott to receive him. Thomas Hopkins was made post-captain five years ago, is now almost forty years old, and has a solid Royal Navy career behind him. He has commanded the *Solander* as a particular favour by the Admiralty to Sir Joseph.

The letter does not reveal what Harriott understands to be the truth behind this odd arrangement: that the Admiralty had refused to fund the *Solander*'s mission, even though it had funded other similar voyages, but as part-compensation had thrown a decent captain Sir Joseph's way. Harriott wonders what this says about the capacities of Captain Hopkins, or at least the Admiralty's view of him. Is he not needed for fighting, or is he seen as someone reliable? Hopkins has a wife, lives in comfortable surroundings in Putney, and (rather to Harriott's dismay) is Welsh.

Though not one for society gossip or even daily news, Harriott is aware that the arrival of the *Solander* is a significant matter to the social and cultural cognoscenti of the metropolis. It has been much discussed in the capital's newspapers over the last two days, and Harriott perfectly understands why. What could be more romantic than a deliberate re-enactment of the first journey of the *Endeavour*? It has been forty years since the working man's son James Cook extended England's dominion into the southern seas, coming home with tales of beautiful native women, strange flora and fauna, treacherous reefs and adventure. Those tales spawned thousands of inches of newsprint, and hundreds of volumes, both learned and scurrilous. Also, more to the immediate point, detailed charts and new names for far-flung islands, shores and seas bloomed from Cook's voyage. New *English* names.

This new ship, the *Solander,* seems all of a piece with that brighter, clearer time, when an Enlightenment England was still thrusting out into the world, when America was still a brother and not an enemy, when fighting France meant fighting another King, not a bunch of shouting zealots whose revolutionary prognostications seem to cut at the heart of statehood itself. Those were the long-ago years when Harriott himself had been at sea, joining the Navy at thirteen and the

East India Company at twenty-three. Adventure had been in his heart then, much as it had been in England's. Now his heart is old, and England's great dreams of discovery are, if not quite over, then certainly grown old and cynical. These voyages are now about acquisition rather than discovery, and acquisition is a drier thing, more for clerks and accountants than captains.

Of course, it had been Cook's journey on the *Endeavour* which had embedded the extraordinary personality of Joseph Banks in the English imagination. Cook had returned with charts; Banks came back with tales, scandalous tales of sexual encounters beneath beached boats and in forest tents, drenched in descriptions of dark ritual and human sacrifice. Caricaturists and satirists had dined magnificently on the public body of Banks, while the man himself accrued vast influence, including friendship with the King and the presidency of the Royal Society itself.

Now Banks – old, fat and politically weakened by the recurrent illness of his great royal benefactor – has with characteristic theatrical flair dispatched a second ship to Otaheite, that strange Pacific paradise which has infected imaginations for decades, with its waterfalls cascading down from green hills to wash the backs of sultry, willing natives. The *Solander*'s voyage was primarily intended to stock the hothouses of the botanical garden at Kew, which Banks has championed in countless editorials and speeches but which now faces the noted indifference of the aggressively non-horticultural Prince Regent. Every Briton who reads a newspaper knows what Banks has long claimed for Kew: that by owning and adapting the natural world to its own ends, Britain will shape the future of the world. For Banks, the transport of plants from one place to another is an Imperial undertaking, the whole globe merely a market garden for the English, with Banks as head gardener and

Kew as the hothouse, the place in which English horticulture is fused with British ambition.

It is a weighty narrative to rest upon an ordinary Whitby collier, but it was magnificently told by Cook and Banks forty years ago. And now Cook's successor, Captain Hopkins, is on his way.

Twenty minutes after Harriott's first sighting of the captain in the wherry there is a knock at his door, and one of the servants lets Hopkins into his office. The man certainly looks Welsh – short, barrel-chested, his face round and red with that familiar sheen of sweat to which a sea-captain carrying a comfortable load around his stomach is prone. He wears a naval uniform of white breeches and blue coat, and looks rather annoyed to be here.

'Captain Hopkins,' says Harriott. 'Welcome to the River Police Office. Please be seated.'

Hopkins takes a seat opposite Harriott, his hat in his lap, and looks around the trim office and out to the riverside window.

'Your office reminds me of a captain's cabin, Harriott,' he says. 'Though on a far bigger ship than mine.'

Harriott frowns slightly at the familiarity in Hopkins's tone, being used to deference even from captains. But this man is a senior officer and, Harriott thinks, has earned the right to some familiarity with a magistrate, particularly after a circumnavigation.

'All is well with the *Solander*?' he asks, which, after all, is the only question required.

'Very well, Harriott, thank you. Although I am confused as to why the Police Office is interested.'

The man is fierce and impertinent but also charming. His irritation is manifest, but so is his bonhomie. He sits in the chair with enormous relish, as if sitting in this particular chair is the most important thing in the world. A man with an appetite for life, Harriott decides.

'I take an interest in all shipping arriving here, Captain.'

'But I'll wager you don't call in the captain of every lugger and whaler which comes to London, Harriott. There'd be a queue of salty individuals down the stairs if you did.'

Harriott smiles at that.

'No, indeed. But you are obviously aware of the special status of the *Solander*. Sir Joseph has asked me personally to welcome you and to ensure you have everything you need, and are secure on the river.'

'Are you a friend of Sir Joseph's, Harriott?'

This with a smile, drawing the old magistrate in.

'More of an acquaintance, Captain.'

'Well, Sir Joseph's *acquaintances* are said to run Britain, Harriott, so I will take you as a man of importance and standing, and will thank you for your kind attention. My ship's in good heart, I would say. She is tired and in need of some loving care, but has performed admirably, as has her crew. I've discharged about half of the fellows, and many of them have already left. Those who remain are either preparing her for the dockyard, where she's going to need some repairs, or else they're looking after the cargo.'

'Ah yes. The cargo. The plants survived the passage?'

'A great many did, Harriott, a great many. I am taking the first consignment – two barges of it – down to Kew tomorrow morning, where I understand a small welcoming committee is to be assembled. How they've done that when we only arrived today is a mystery only Sir Joseph can answer.'

'We received news of your arrival some days ago. You put in at Portsmouth, did you not?'

'We did indeed. I do hope Sir Joseph hasn't had a crew of lords and ladies huddled by the riverside since then.'

Harriott smiles broadly at that. He does not doubt that Banks has almost certainly done exactly that.

'So there is nothing you need of me, Captain?'

'No indeed, Harriott.'

'I would be happy to supply a waterman-constable or two to keep watch on the ship.'

'That will not be necessary. I have my own men to secure the ship, and they're more than capable of sorting out any London mudlarks who try and get over the side.'

'Well, then. All is well. Welcome to London, Captain Hopkins.'

WAPPING

Charles and Abigail Horton are walking down Old Gravel Lane in Wapping, at the point where the gleaming new constructions of the London Dock give way to what remains of the ancient labyrinth of streets which used to vein the whole district. The Hortons have been on a rare trip into the West End, and for an equally rare event: the final lecture at the Royal Institution by Humphry Davy, newly married and newly knighted by the newly minted Prince Regent. Abigail is a regular and enthusiastic attendee at the Institution, and Davy had not disappointed her. His lecture, like his newly published book, *Elements of Chemical Philosophy*, was a summary of his last decade of speaking and experimenting and was (or so Abigail explained to her polite but glassy-eyed husband) nothing less than a Bible of the hidden world, a set of instructions for building Everything. Abigail's eyes shine when she speaks of these things, while her husband characteristically frets that these enthusiasms, so odd for a woman of Abigail's background and class, can only be explained by their failure to produce children. His wife's profound intelligence, an intelligence which can scare him as much as delight him, must find its own outlet in the experimental observations of the Royal Institution and its older, grander sibling, the Royal Society. In the past he has joked that she must take up with a natural philosopher in need of an intelligent assistant, a Caroline to a William Herschel, but Charles Horton never really jokes, his every word laid out carefully on a bed of acute seriousness, such that this remark caught in his throat as he said it, and Abigail squeezed his arm as if in forgiveness of his mild lack of taste.

The Hortons live in Lower Gun Alley, just off Wapping Street, between the Dock and the River and close to Charles Horton's place of work, the River Police Office. This riverside district, laced with penny-a-night lodging houses and stinking permanently of an unwashed humanity, is in marked contrast to the elegance of Albemarle Street where they have spent the evening. Horton is, on paper at least, a waterman-constable, one of dozens employed by the magistrate John Harriott at the River Police Office.

They make an attractive if not particularly noticeable couple as they walk down the old street. Horton is a tall quiet man in his late thirties, some years older than his wife. If your eyes were drawn to them, it would be to Abigail that they'd be attracted, not so much by the prettiness of her face or the cut of her clothes (though these are by no means unremarkable) but by the energetic enthusiasm which bubbles out of her as she talks her quiet husband through the latest theories of natural philosophy. Charles Horton you would barely notice, and this is how he would want it. All you'd be left with is a vague sense of having been measured by somebody, though to what end you would not be able to say.

They had taken a carriage to and from the West End, a luxury they can ill afford. Horton insisted on the treat, determined to make the night a special one for Abigail, and in one of the unspoken transactions which oil their marriage she volunteered to walk the last part of the journey home. She knows how much Horton likes to hear and smell the streets before retiring, to listen for anything out of kilter in the apparent chaos of the neighbourhood. So there they are, the two of them, she chattering cheerfully of chemical matters, he listening as carefully and assiduously as ever while at the same time taking in the air of the Wapping streets. Horton's capacity for listening and observing is enormous, as is his ability to make himself imperceptible. It is a skill bought dearly over the last fifteen years, as he has carefully rebuilt his life after leaving the Navy in murky circumstances at the end of the last century.

Abigail has just begun outlining the new debate in botanical classification sparked by the work of the French genius Jussieu, which Davy had alluded to in his lecture.

'So, you see, what is being suggested is a synthesis between two systems: the natural system of Ray and the artificial one of Linnaeus,' says Abigail, her hand gripping her husband's arm, her eyes facing forward but also outward into a natural world of wonder and discovery.

'Being suggested to whom?' inquires her husband. 'Who is it that decides these things? The King?'

'Of course not the King, Charles. Although he has long been interested in such matters.'

'Well, I'm confounded by it. All these so-called *natural philosophers*, hustling around and arguing with each other, and they cannot even decide what to call' – he bends down, and pulls up a weed from between two cobblestones at their feet – 'what to call *this*.'

'But why should naming a plant be a simple matter? Surely it's a profound thing, everyone agreeing, whatever their language, that you've picked up a kind of burdock.'

'Have I?'

'Yes, husband, you have.'

'So, there you have it – you have told me what I have picked up.'

'But how to describe it to a Frenchman, or an Italian?'

'Well, surely they have their own words?'

'Well, exactly, Charles. But how do I know when we are talking about the same thing?'

'Why do you need to know? If a Frenchman is shouting at his horse even now in Paris, why do I need to understand?'

'What if he was shouting at his horse in a new way, and if you understood it you would be able to shout at your own horse more effectively? Wouldn't it be good to understand what he had learned so you could learn from it?'

'The Frenchman is just as likely to eat his horse as teach it in a new way.'

'And you, Charles Horton, are impossible. You understand me perfectly.'

'Because, dear wife, we are speaking the same language, one we have grown up with, not one argued over by Swedish professors and French gardeners, and—'

A woman's scream breaks across the dark street, coming from a small alley running off the east side of the Lane. For a moment everything is still, as if the old place had heard something it didn't recognise and was now waiting for some confirmation. Another scream, and that spell is broken.

Horton moves immediately towards the sound, but then looks back at Abigail, ready to apologise for the disruption and to shrug in that familiar *ah, well* way which always precedes his disappearing into the night on another 'bit of investigation', as Abigail is wont to call it. But she is moving towards the sound too; they are still holding hands, even. He feels an incongruous stab of affection, and after a moment the two of them are standing in front of one of the shabbiest of the little street's shabby buildings. The ugly place presents a confusion of windows at different heights and doors in irregular positions. This building, like many of those around it, has been blackened by coal smoke and yet retains a kind of mongrel vigour. It seems to have been assembled from the discarded parts of a dozen other dwellings. The screams come from inside. Like a river with a huge rock chucked into it, the stream of people in the Lane has already changed direction, and there is now a little eddy washing into the side street.

'Keep your distance!' Horton shouts at the crowd, and some of them stop immediately. Horton's voice can carry a weight of authority when he so wishes, a skill he has learned from his bulldog magistrate John Harriott. Horton turns his back on the locals while they are quiet, and knocks on the door. He has dropped Abigail's hand now, but she has placed one of hers onto his shoulder, and stands just behind him.

An old woman answers immediately, her head covered in a dirty brown bonnet, her skin cracked and dry like a neglected hull. She starts to speak, but Horton interrupts her as he pushes into the house, his wife still attached to his shoulder and swept along with him.

'Charles Horton, madam. Constable of the River Police Office.'

He has no real authority to enter the house without a warrant from a magistrate, but such niceties are rarely observed in Wapping at times such as these. He is in the hall in an instant, and Abigail follows, turning to close the door behind them in another out-of-kilter gesture, but the old woman has already done this and now has her back to the door. She turns on them, the old dry face angry and spitting.

''Ow *dare* you! 'Oo are you to come in 'ere without me invitin' you? This is my 'ouse, this is. It's a bloody—'

'Madam!' She shuts up at that, just as the crowd outside her

31

door had shut up when he shouted at them. She scowls at him but says no more. 'There is a woman screaming in this house. You cannot have failed to hear it. Now, I am here to—'

A loud wail breaks out from upstairs, tailing off into a broken sobbing rattle. It is a theatrically awful noise. Horton breaks off from scolding the old woman and turns towards the stairs, or at least to where he imagines the stairs to be. The hall of the house is dark. The window at the far end is opaque with dirt and lets in almost no light, only a smoky radiance from what little illumination there is outside. He locates the stairs somehow, and now feels his first stab of anxiety for the well-being of his wife. The stairs are crazy and unsteady, and Horton entertains a momentary vision of Abigail tumbling down into whatever dark and dingy Hades lies beneath this disgusting old residence. He almost decides to ask her to wait downstairs, but then she passes him and reaches the upper landing first, moving steadily towards the source of the screams.

It is somewhat lighter on the first-floor landing, but not much. The walls are bare and the naked wooden floor creaks like the masts of the ship in the Dock to the back of the house. There are four doors giving onto the landing, each of them closed. Abigail walks up to all of them, as it is not immediately obvious which one contains the screaming woman, but then there is another drawn-out shriek of anguish, and she opens the correct door and goes into the room beyond, her husband following her quickly and now with mounting concern, as his old fear at Abigail's being exposed to the darkness of his world fills his chest.

The small room contains a single but decent-sized bed, a misbegotten armchair and a fireplace which is little more than a void in the damp wall. A fire has been recently lit, Horton sees, and a kettle sits on the floor in front of the hearth. Above the fireplace is an horrendous seascape of a ship coming to grief in a storm, and the single window looks out onto the street beyond, or rather would look out if it had ever been cleaned.

There are two figures already in the room. One, a rather fat man, lies on the bed, unmoving. The other is a middle-aged woman in a careworn dress, wearing a filthy bonnet which would make a perfect companion piece to that worn by the landlady downstairs. The woman sits in one of the two chairs, her eyes to the ceiling, clutching a dirty handkerchief to her face while she sobs into the air above her. The scene is like something from a Drury Lane melodrama, staged and artificial.

So loud is the noise the woman is generating, so engrossed is she in her grief, that she does not hear the Hortons enter. But there is nothing to hide behind in this little room and their movement soon distracts her. The wailing ends abruptly like a switched-off faucet, much to Horton's relief, and she stares at him, and then Abigail, wide-eyed and scared.

'*'Oo,*' she says, '*are YOU?*' If anything the question is louder than the caterwauling which preceded it.

'Madam,' he says. 'You must calm yourself. My name is Charles Horton, and I am an officer of the Thames River Police. We heard your screams from the street, and came in here to see if you need assistance. The noise is causing some disturbance.'

She leaps up at that and runs to the window to look into the street, rubbing it with the damp handkerchief to get a better view, and smearing her tears and snot over the lumpy glass. She yelps at what she sees down there, and Horton wonders if he sees a flavour of delight in her expression. She makes as if to open the window but then thinks better of it and turns back to him. The handkerchief is back at her breast. Abigail moves towards the figure on the bed.

'Oh, Lor', sir. Oh Lor'. Did all those people out there 'ear me 'ollerin' and ravin'?'

'Madam, I believe they did. Now, is this man—'

His glance towards the bed sets her off again, even louder than before. She collapses into the chair, with no little dramatic flair. There is an audience now, both in the room and out in the street.

'Dead, sir! Dead! I found him like this just now! Dead as them burnt out logs in the fireplace!'

She follows this with a long painful moan which is just loud enough to penetrate the window to the crowd outside. Then she collapses back into quiet sobs. She looks exhausted by her performance.

Abigail is leaning over the man, her face white. She has taken a small mirror from the side-table and is holding it over the man's mouth. Horton marvels at her forensic calm but is distressed to witness the slight shake in her fingers. He steps to the bed and gently moves Abigail's fingers away, taking the little mirror from her. She puts her hands behind her back, and stares at him with a kind of awe in her face.

The man is laid out as if for a coffin, his hands clasped over his stomach. Horton marks him for a sailor instantly, and one recently returned from sea. The face, even in death, is deeply tanned and lined, though his thick, dark hair and smooth ears speak of a rather young man. The tan extends down to the open shirt, but even so the bruises which circle the man's neck are vivid. He has been strangled. He is dressed as a sailor, too – rough, heavy trousers, an ancient-looking white shirt which has been opened almost to the navel, and a thick, pockmarked leather waistcoat. Without thinking, Horton glances back at the door and there, hanging from a rusty nail, is the inevitable sailor's pea-coat. Like Abigail, he holds the mirror over the man's mouth, and then turns it to look. It is clear. He places a hand over the man's chest. It is still.

Beside the bed is a sea chest, the final evidence of the man's profession. Horton kneels down to inspect it. He has seen these chests all over Wapping, filled with the entirety of itinerant men's lives. They sleep with these chests at their feet or beneath their hammocks while at sea, and on land guard them with more care than a prized wife or cherished dog. Next to the chest, on the floor, is a wooden cup, which he picks up. It still has a slight warmth to it, and there is the residue of something like tea at the cup's bottom. Horton looks into the sea chest, which has obviously been ransacked. A small canvas bag sits within a pile of old clothes. Horton pulls it out; it is full of coins.

'My God, Charles,' whispers Abigail. 'His *face*.'

'Yes.'

The face is confounding. The man is smiling. He must have been smiling even while he was strangled.

''Oo did you say you were?' asks the tatty woman in the chair. She sounds suspicious and perhaps a little annoyed at Horton's peremptory tone and manner. She may also be exercised by the presence of another woman in the room. More than anything, thinks Horton, she is bothered by the attention he and Abigail are paying to the dead body. He wonders if this woman is capable of feeling any emotion for more than a minute or two.

'Horton. I work for the River Police Office.'

'What, for that old rogue Harriott? The man as what stole bread from the mouths of honest river folk?'

The statement places her age more precisely. For her still to be arguing the debates of the late 1790s makes her between thirty and forty.

'You say you found him like this?'

She nods, with some hauteur.

'When?'

'I come in ten minutes ago.'

'Who is he?'

'His name's Ransome. Samuel Ransome.'

'And you are?'

''Annah. 'Annah Crabtree.'

'And how did you know this Ransome?'

She blushes, almost coquettishly, and looks down at her blotchy décolletage and then up at Abigail. Her manner has changed again. Gone is the inflamed matriarch, replaced by a naive little innocent.

'We was in love, sir. He proposed to me before he set off on his travels.'

Her eyes are becoming watery again and the hands look dangerously close to springing into a new pose. Horton hurries to move things along.

'When did you last see him?'

''Oo, Samuel?'

'Yes, madam, Samuel. When did you see him last?'

'Afore 'e left. I've been waitin' for 'im to get back. I 'eard from a woman in a shop over by the Prospect that Sam's ship 'ad come in, and 'im nowhere to be seen! I was proper annoyed, I was, 'im gone for months and me with nothin' to do but wait until 'e showed 'is face again. Soon as I 'eard the ship 'ad arrived I came over 'ere to give 'im a piece of me mind, but 'e was ... 'e was ...'

Her chest is heaving again, like a Whitby collier cresting a wave. Horton jumps in to stop the onslaught.

'He was like this when you found him?'

'Like what?'

'Lying on the bed, like this?'

'Well, I 'ardly moved 'im, did I? Weak woman like me?'

She sounds petulant again now, and Horton thinks that perhaps he has located her genuine register.

'And you got here ten minutes ago, you say?'

'That's right. Give or take a bit.'

'He was a sailor?'

Her eyes widened.

''Ow did you know that?'

'So he was?'

'Yes.'

'Recently returned from sea?'

'Did you know him, or somethin'?'

'You just said he proposed to you when he set off on his travels.'

She says nothing, looks a little irritated.

'Where was he sailing from?'

'He's been round the world, he has. Proper adventurin' voyage. He's a proper British 'ero, is Sam.' This more to Abigail than to him. Horton realises he will get little more information out of this woman. And in any case, he has little right to pursue an investigation into this matter, even if there is anything to pursue. Jurisdiction is an issue here, as it so very often is. The river is his official realm, not the shabby streets which sit behind it, and not even the gleaming warehouses and wharves of the new Dock. The Shadwell magistrates will claim this crime as within their jurisdiction, and the last thing magistrate John Harriott needs is another clashing row over who is responsible for what. The lines of policing in the metropolis are both new and ancient, and are everywhere profoundly blurred. A man of Harriott's impatient character inevitably has the imprint of other men's toes on the soles of his shoes. It is one of the many things Charles Horton strongly admires about his magistrate.

So, a matter for Shadwell, almost certainly. But there is much here to interest the inquisitive. The ransacked sea chest, still with money within. The cup. And the man's face in death.

Why does he smile like that? How could he smile while being strangled?

But these are questions for the coroner, not a waterman-constable. He turns back to the actress in the chair.

'Madam, one more thing before I go and retrieve some men so this sad affair can be looked into. His ship, please. Its name, and where it came in from.'

She sniffs and wipes her nose on the appalling handkerchief, reminding him that she is also holding a letter.

'The *Solander*. Under Captain 'opkins. She's moored in the river off Rotherhithe, sir.'

The name of the ship puts all his previous considerations in a new light. A crewman from the most celebrated ship currently in London, dead on the first night of its return, in Wapping. He knows that Harriott has a particular interest in the *Solander*. He knows, too, that the old magistrate will not be able to refrain from involving himself in an investigation into this latest death. He can imagine him bellowing even now: 'Jurisdiction be *damned . . .*'

So, the coroner must be called, and he rather thinks he will tell his own magistrate of his discovery before he informs Shadwell. But the oddness of this death, so soon on the man's return to London, strikes him with some force, such that he cannot stop himself asking a final question, even while Abigail's pale face urges him to get her out of this awful room.

'Did you disturb Sam's sea chest, madam?' he asks. Hannah Crabtree looks at him, then down at the chest, and she lets out a new shriek, this time one full of anger and outrage.

'Why, look! Sam's been bleedin' well robbed!'

TWO

The greatest service which can be rendered any country is to add a useful plant to its culture.

Thomas Jefferson, *Memorandum of Services to my Country,* 1800

TAHITI

The young prince waited on the beach for his brother. He was becoming anxious. His brother was still not in sight, and the appearance of great white pieces of cloth unfurling along the branches and trunks of the great vessel in the harbour was a clear sign that it would be leaving soon.

Perhaps the British intended to kidnap his brother? It had happened before, the prince knew. His father, the chief of this part of the island, told stories of how the British captain Cook had kidnapped a great prince of the island when he first came to Tahiti, and had later kidnapped a chief and a princess on the sacred island of Ra'aitea. This, said his father, would have angered the great god Oro beyond all reckoning, for it was on Ra'aitea that Oro had been born of the god Ta'aroa, and it was on Ra'aitea that the most sacred of all the *marae* had been built, at Taputapuatea. The prince's father was a devout man, with his own *marae* and priests, but he did not have the respect of his sons, particularly the eldest, that same brother who was now on the British ship. The eldest son had proclaimed loudly and often that custom declared that he should be the chief, that his father

41

was only a regent and that the chiefdom had passed down the family line the moment he was born. The younger prince understood little of these arguments, but there was something in his father's eyes, and in his reluctance to discipline his eldest son, that suggested the chief believed the boy had a point.

Whatever the stories his father told him, the young prince found the idea of British perfidy puzzling, because so many of the islanders – including his own brother – spoke longingly of going onboard a British ship and travelling far, far away from these islands. Even at the age of eight the prince had some of the same dreams, but only because he wished so much to emulate his older brother. The idea of actually climbing on board one of those wooden giants was as otherworldly to the prince as were the odd lectures of the British missionaries, who travelled the island and tried, in their broken version of the island language, to tell the stories of their own god. The prince understood almost nothing of these stories. His young head floundered on the missionaries' assertion that there was only one god, who ruled over everything that was. The impossibility of this yawned in the prince's mind and had, on one occasion, actually spawned nightmares. On that occasion the story of the One God had been told to him by the young man who lived with the missionaries, the one who had an English father and an island mother. Many of the children had been told by their mothers that this man was not to be trusted, that the English blood in his veins had made him mad, that his father had been an evil man who had betrayed his chief. Most of the children didn't listen to these tales, and had actually spent many happy afternoons taunting the young man for his dark European clothes and puzzlingly pale face. But the young prince's imagination was a wild thing and the tales of the women had lodged within it, such that when he had come across the strange half-breed boy on the beach, and when the boy had begun preaching to him with a vibrating zeal and passion which set his eyes alight, the prince had become so terrified that he'd run away to the arms of his mother and had kept his whole family awake several nights with his shrieks.

The prince stood up with relief. A big war canoe, its prow colourful and ornately carved, was pulling away from the ship. His brother had told him the foreign ship was called the *Britannia*, like the country it came from, and that she was used, wonder of wonders, to hunt whales. The prince had no conception of a whale, other than its vast implausibility, and the idea of hunting them seemed ludicrous. His brother was sure to be in the canoe, and the prince's nerves calmed a little. He would not have blamed his brother for going with the British – but he would at least have wanted to say goodbye.

The canoe got bigger and bigger and, as it approached the shore, men started diving off it and swimming to the beach. One of them, to the prince's delight, was indeed his brother. Strong and brown and gigantic, he rose from the waves, the seawater beading on his skin, pushing his long black hair away from his forehead and waving to the younger boy, who ran into the surf and greeted him with a very un-noble embrace.

The brothers walked out of the sea, and the younger's questions began to flood over the older like an endless waterfall.

'Did you see guns?'

'Yes, Raanui. A great many guns. Some of them bigger than you.'

'Guns bigger than me? How do they lift them?'

'They don't lift them. They are on wheels and they fire great lumps of iron into their foes. As much iron as you've ever seen in every shot.'

'Their country must be *made* of iron! Was there a whale?'

'No, Raanui, of course there was no whale. A whale is as big as their boat.'

'As big as their boat!'

'Yes. When they kill one they tie it alongside and bring it to shore. Or they cut the meat off the bones and leave the carcass in the ocean.'

'Were there British women?'

'No, only men.'

'Were any sickly?'

'No, they were not sickly.'

'Did you eat?'

'No, Raanui. They only have their own voyaging food. That is why they are here, to collect provisions.'

'Did you speak about leaving with them?'

Pause.

'No, Raanui, I did not.'

'But you still plan to leave?'

'To leave would be a great adventure. There are too many dying here.'

'Will we die?'

'Who can tell? Who knows why we die?'

'The missionaries say it is because we do not follow their god.'

'And the priests say it is because we have angered our own. No one knows the truth, Raanui.'

'Some say the British brought the disease.'

'Yes, some say that. Others say the French. Or the Spanish. Or the seagulls.'

'The seagulls!'

'Yes, Raanui, the seagulls. Now go and play with your little friends. I must speak to Father about what I have seen.'

'You wouldn't go to Britain without saying goodbye, would you?'

'No, Raanui. Now run and play.'

KEW

It is mid-morning the next day when the plants from the *Solander* arrive at Kew. It the kind of June morning in England which even Scottish eyes must admit is magnificent. The sun is shining on golden water, there are fresh leaves on the trees and the pollen in the air is like stardust, although this particular pair of Scottish eyes are somewhat inflamed by that ethereal flower dust. Robert Brown is feeling positively rheumy in the face of England's summer splendour, which is unlike him. Almost two decades of collecting and investigating plants have turned him into a botanist and have inured him to most allergies of this kind. There must be something particularly pungent in the air this morning.

Being Scottish he is dressed entirely inappropriately for an English summer's day, encased in dark clothes tailored by cold men in draughty cellars. But he is by no means the only man who has come to Kew in the wrong kind of clothes. Much of the crowd is wearing something which is inappropriate for one reason or another. He has been amusing himself as the great classifier Linnaeus often did, by categorising the crowd which stands beside the small jetty behind Kew's Dutch House.

First of all, he carefully notes the Family of the crowd, which is undoubtedly English, not Scots or any of the European families. It is well-mannered, of course, which he supposes would be a natural mark of Englishness, although the manners on display this morning are peculiarly affected, as he has come to expect of crowds made up of London's more fashionable specimens. This crowd seems to be aware that people might be watching, and so it puts on its manners rather in the way an actress might put on face paint. The ladies are dressed in the most fashionable style, some of them with breasts quite alarmingly close to falling out of their dresses, which would be by no means acceptable in a Scottish setting. Indeed, Brown thinks that even English eyes must find it somewhat distressing to see such décolletage on display during daylight. This kind of exposure is normally only appropriate under candelabra, with charming music playing in one corner of a ballroom.

There are two distinct Genera of men within the family, and these are easily separated by their habit. First are the men who are, like him, dressed for winter weather on a summer's eve, sober and yet still potentially excitable. These are the Royal Society natural philosophers, some of them clergymen, all of them pious in their own way. The second Genus consists of gentlemen and nobles, who for the purposes of today are most definitely here on Aristocratic Business (i.e. to be seen and to be admired), and are therefore dressed with seasonal and sartorial precision and flair.

Despite the differing levels of flamboyance and motivation, Brown is well aware that both these groups of men present a common problem of classification: same family (*Angloeae*); different Genera (*philosophis* or *aristocrasis*); yet they also fall into a common Set, as almost all these men are also Fellows of the Royal Society. Thus in miniature, Brown notes, they encapsulate the Society's Janus-like nature: a scientific foundation, certainly, but also a plaything for rich men who want to appear clever and curious. Perhaps Royal Society membership should be considered a *variety* of some kind, cutting across Species and Families, uniting different creatures in a common undertaking? He ponders on a binomial. *Homo experimentalis*, perhaps.

He smiles at his own whimsy, a small Scottish smile which would be imperceptible to the showier members of the Kew fraternity currently gathered. He understands that, like flowers seeking the attentions of insects, all these creatures are here to make appearances. Even the most dedicated natural philosopher must be seen to be philosophising. Much has been done to banish ignorance, and much of that has been done to avoid being ignored.

This is sadly ironic, realises Brown, for the personage whose attention is most craved will not be present. The King is still indisposed, as it is said, and is thought to be at Windsor. He has been there since the return of his illness last year (it is only ever called his illness, partly out of politeness, partly out of complete ignorance as to what the illness actually is). His Majesty is here in spirit, however, for a little further upstream from the crowd on the jetty loom the doomed, Gothic and silly towers of George's Castellated Palace: unfinished, bankrupt, and still wholly inappropriate for a royal dwelling. The palace's insane architecture and recent abandonment are now only metaphors for the King's departed mind.

Prior to his illness, the King would certainly have been here. Kew is his favourite place. The man who would have been a philosopher-king has turned out to be merely a royal gardener, and Brown thinks there is no shame in that. Like all those here tonight, Brown feels a sharp anxiety about the wishes and ambitions of the King's son, now the Regent, who shows no interest in the science of horticulture while maintaining a massive appetite for its fruits.

So the royal family is unrepresented, but in its place is another who can claim a good portion of regal authority over this blessed plot. He sits, a massive bull of a man in a wheelchair of his own design, his head as large as one of the marrows in the botanical garden. His enormous belly is bisected by the bright-blue sash and the glittering yellow star which he wears everywhere in public. And something else, something only a man with the searching eyes of a botanist would notice: his knuckles, white and shaking, gripping the worn leather armrests on the splendid old wheelchair.

Thus Sir Joseph Banks, President of the Royal Society, awaits the treasure from the other side of the world, attended by his librarian, the Scottish botanist Robert Brown.

Now, a pinnace – a rather grubby thing which has clearly seen a good deal of the world – appears around the bend of the river towards Putney. Behind it are two Thames barges, flat and black in the water, like dangerous and near-invisible bodyguards to a St James's beau. The women in the waiting group chatter and chirp with excitement, and for a moment Brown thinks Banks will rise from his chair. His body tenses as if to do so, but then with a near-silent sigh he settles back to wait. His knuckles are still white.

The flotilla makes its way towards them, passing the village of Chiswick and disturbing the herons which rise from the riverbank as one and fly out and east, towards Hampton Court and Runnymede. The excitement in the crowd has been premature, because the river is playing games with everyone's sense of perspective and the flotilla has further to go than was thought. After a quarter-hour more it is nearly upon them. Brown can see the familiar figure of Captain Hopkins in the prow of the pinnace, standing firmly with his hands behind his back in that confident way all competent sea captains possess when they have delegated their tasks and now merely await their completion. Behind him stream the Thames barges, piled high with the treasures of foreign seas. The women and the gentry applaud the captain's arrival and his moment. Brown wonders at how much the English do love a sea captain.

Now the fat old bull in the wheelchair stands, solidly if carefully, and walks to the edge of the jetty as Hopkins's boat approaches. Brown goes with him, one step behind, and for the hundredth time finds himself resenting the way this makes him feel – a manservant instead of an amanuensis. And for the hundredth time he tells himself to trample on his silly pride. He does what he does in the name of knowledge and advancement. The occasional mild humiliation by Banks is a small price.

Banks bellows his welcome and applauds, the bull replaced by a huge hospitable bear. Hopkins salutes stiffly. Brown, a former Fencible, wonders if that is entirely appropriate, a military salute to a civilian like Banks, but reminds himself that Banks is a very particular kind of civilian. After only a few minutes of business in docking the pinnace, the captain is able to step up onto the jetty and into the outstretched arms of Joseph Banks.

Never one for decorum, Banks hugs the surprised Hopkins into his great stomach, and roars his approval. A few ladies gasp at his lack of manners, but most of the men roar along with their President. Brown adopts a face of social invisibility, and continues to observe.

'Captain Hopkins!' shouts Banks. 'We welcome you to Kew, and we delight in your cargo!'

'Mr President,' says Hopkins, carefully rearranging his tidy uniform. 'Your welcome is as one with your personality: large, unexpected and terrifyingly warm.'

The ladies laugh at that. Why, a sea captain with *wit*. And Welsh! Such a delightful creature! Sir Joseph's bonhomie can be rather exhausting, after all.

The barges are now fixing themselves just off the jetty, the men on board tying the vessels together to stop them being jostled away from each other by the stream. The men then work to remove tarpaulins and untie ropes, and before long (with a gratifying moan of pleasure from the crowd) the cargoes of the barges are revealed to the hungry eyes of those watching.

As the tarpaulins are removed, the barges burst into flower. It is, thinks Brown, the only possible way to describe it. Within are such riches, such beautiful clusters of colour and shape, that the barges themselves seem to spring into life, touched by some green flame. Even Brown finds himself sighing with the wonder of it. The plants in the barges, which have been growing for months as they travelled around the globe, spring up into the sunlight with hungry speed and transform the two barges into floating pleasure gardens. Greens and browns redecorate the dirty black hulls of the barges and, for a moment, compete with the trees and bushes of the riverbank for pre-eminence. While the ancient riverbank can boast of its elegance and history, it can say nothing against the alien magnificence of what lies in the barges. Strange flowers, surprising bushes, exquisite little saplings, and from the whole a cloud of strange new pollen which rises up into the air like a benediction from distant civilisations, mixing with the golden Kew stardust already in the air and inflaming, once again, the watching Scotsman's eyes.

Banks, one arm still on Hopkins's shoulder, gazes upon the sight. It will be later reported that tears sprang into his eyes, to which Brown will remark that it was perhaps the alien pollen. For a moment, the crowd on the jetty has forgotten itself: forgotten to think, forgotten to plot, forgotten to pose. It is held, magnificently, inside a moment of natural awe.

The courtly ladies remember themselves first, and one – a young, tall, stunning redhead whose décolletage had been the most wondrous thing about the morning, prior to the arrival of the barges – exclaims: 'Sir Joseph, England is enchanted by this gift!' And with that, all of those on the jetty compete with each other to craft the most memorable aphorism.

The President recovers his famous bonhomie, which persists in the galloping face of the gout that has consumed his frame this last decade. He turns away from the miraculous barges and towards the crowd behind him, which for a moment stops competing with itself and waits to hear what he has to say.

'Gentlemen! And ladies! In the name of the King, whose condition I regret but in whom I will always place my loyalty and my friendship, I give you – the cargo of the *Solander*!'

After several more acclamations, the crowd moves away from the jetty and towards a marquee that has been placed on the lawn in front of the Dutch House for a celebratory luncheon, leaving the lightermen to unload the precious cargo from the barges, under the watchful eyes of Banks, Brown and Hopkins. The plants are carried, one by one, into the Gardens, where a team of gardeners and botanists are waiting to catalogue them and prepare for their planting, either in the grounds of the Gardens or in the enormous hothouse, the Great Stove.

Brown can see the true fire of excitement in the old fat face of Sir Joseph Banks. That riveted greed in the eyes, that expulsion of all external elements in the cause of *investigation* – it is plain to the librarian that Banks is being transported as the plants are carried from the barge into the Gardens. Occasionally, the older man will rattle off a little fragment of Latin, presumably naming the plants to himself as they appear. This is a feat beyond even Robert Brown, whose knowledge of botany is as broad as anyone's; for the past year Brown has been responsible for Banks's library and herbarium, which records the old man's unquenchable collecting. These new plants are profoundly exotic, the products of a strange, alien island in the middle of a great ocean, which have only survived the journey to England thanks to techniques pioneered by Banks himself.

Before long, Captain Hopkins takes his leave, saying he has business in town that cannot wait. Banks is back in his wheelchair, exhausted by his efforts, and the botanists bring him individual plants in their heavy wooden pots for him to investigate, like wise men presenting gifts to a prince. Banks observes each one, closely, and mutters in his occasional Latin, before passing it back and advising where it should be planted. Brown finds himself wondering whether Banks can remember these plants from his own visit to Otaheite. Can it be that he has carried the image of them in his head these past forty years?

Brown picks up one of the smaller pots, containing a sapling with no more than a dozen small, bright-green oval leaves. He recognises it immediately: breadfruit, the strange treasure of Otaheite which, even now, is growing with impertinent relish in Jamaica to feed the slaves who still work there. It is such a commonplace thing, in fact, that he almost hands it straight to one of the attending botanists, who will know without any advice from him how to deal with it. But Banks barks at him, and Brown hands the sapling to him instead.

It is about ten inches tall. The pot it sits in is light, the soil having dried out quickly despite the obvious care taken by the *Solander*'s crew to maintain it. Banks snaps his fingers at one of the gardeners, who brings a small watering can, and Banks slowly dampens the soil, with the infinite care of a mother washing a baby's face. Brown imagines he can see the little sapling actually grow a little straighter, two or three of its leaves almost touching the face of the President, before telling himself he has been spending too much time alongside fanciful fools and the women of court.

This odd scene is broken by the crashing sound of a carriage approaching, at speed, from the gate at Kew Green. The sun sparkles on the gold inlay and the brocade at the windows of the carriage, and on the exotic costumes of the attendants. The noise and the exoticism of the carriage cause even Banks to look up, and then his eyes darken as he realises who is about to arrive. His botanic enthusiasm is, for now, switched off. Banks stands up from his chair, still holding the pot with the sapling in it, as if it held some kind of totemic force.

The glorious carriage comes to a stop on the grass itself, gouging heavy ruts into its immaculate green surface, and several attendants climb down. Steps are placed, doors are opened, and a succession of increasingly expensively dressed men and women begin to climb out of the obviously cavernous interior. Eventually two men step out and aid an enormous beau down the elegant steps (which, Brown notices in passing, have been reinforced with carefully contrived struts and beams). The man is dressed with insane magnificence, as if fashion had been taken to a point of theatrical satire. The Prince appears like some globular sartorial moon, his powdered wig sending up little clouds of dust into the golden air. He is handed a stick and then, with the small crowd of noble men and women following him, he totters across the grass towards Banks and Brown, who bow deeply.

'Your Royal Highness,' growls Banks, looking down at the grass, so that his expression is impossible to read. 'Your presence is as welcome as it is unexpected.'

The fat man says nothing, and fiddles with his wig for a moment before turning in exasperation to an attendant, who fiddles with it some more before the fat man is satisfied.

'Is it all here?' he asks, his voice surprisingly squeaky for such a frame. Banks looks up to reply, his face composed.

'More than we can possibly have hoped for, your Highness.'

The fat man looks without interest at Brown before turning back to Banks.

'Then I take it this hugely expensive folly of my father's can be judged to have been a success?'

Banks's face stiffens a little at that. Brown tries not to show surprise at the inference – that the mad King, and not his old friend Banks, had paid for this voyage.

'Your father can be assured that we have done everything we hoped to do, and much more. The Gardens will eventually have a new Pacific hothouse where we will attempt to transplant much of the fauna from Otaheite. It will be a wonder of natural philosophy and of botany. I hope your father will improve such that one day he may enjoy it.'

It is the fat man's turn to look slightly put out.

'It is a hope we *all* share, Banks. Do not assume any individual merit in your concern for my dear father. I more than anyone understand the anxiety his condition engenders in the People.'

'Indeed, your Highness.'

'When will this new hothouse be ready?'

'Not for some time. For now the plants which cannot survive in the open will be taken to the Great Stove, which is insufficient as a permanent home but will pass muster for now. There they will bloom, I am sure. Within weeks I anticipate wonders.'

'Within weeks. We have already waited months. Even years.'

'Nature will not be rushed, sir. We will do all we can to encourage her along.'

The fat man looks down at the pot in Banks's hands, as if gazing on a hungry dog lying dead in the dirt.

'And this thing you are holding? What wonders does it contain?'

Banks looks down at the sapling, almost as if in surprise.

'This, your Highness? This is a particular species of one of the most useful trees in Paradise. I am taking a personal interest in its cultivation.'

WAPPING

The morning after he and Abigail discovered the dead body and its melodramatic attendant, Charles Horton is in the office of his superior, John Harriott. Harriott is seated in his ancient chair. Right now, he is facing out to the river, pondering what Horton is telling him about the death of Samuel Ransome.

The river is busy on this bright spring morning, but then the river is always busy. Between here and the Surrey shore there must be a hundred boats visible from the Police Office window: larger ships moored on chains or making their way to the entrance of the London Dock or the legal quays up past the Tower; and the smaller lighters and wherries which service them, manned by men from ancient families with long pipes in their mouths, wearing misshapen, colourless clothes. The window is partly open, and the shouts of these men provide the background for Horton's precise narrative. The smell of the river creeps in through the window, too; a complicated aroma consisting of salt, shit and steel.

Ransome's body is still where Horton and Abigail discovered it. It is being watched by another constable of the Police

Office, ready for the coroner to visit later today. Harriott is (as Horton had been) immediately exercised by the question of jurisdiction. He has listened patiently to Horton's tale, and (like Horton before him) has assumed that the case will be handed over to the Shadwell magistrates forthwith, following its accidental discovery by a River Police officer. But as soon as Horton mentioned the *Solander*, Harriott realised this would be no simple matter. Like his constable before him, the magistrate sees immediately how a simple handover to Shadwell may not be in his best interests.

Not for the first time, Harriott finds himself regretting the limited powers he has to investigate crimes on the land, even when those crimes involve river activities. He has no one but himself to blame for this persistent annoyance. He had helped draw up the blueprint for the River Police Office, and thus had been one of the fathers of a system of policing which he now finds works only in the most limited fashion. There are magistrates in each of the seven new Police Offices which were established in the parishes around the City at the end of the last century. Within the City itself the role of magistrate is performed by aldermen. But these magistrates have little interest in cooperating with each other; indeed, they compete for success, and for the positive regard of the Home Office. Harriott has little time for most of them, and he harbours a particular contempt for the limited men who currently infest the office in Shadwell.

'Have the Shadwell magistrates responded?' he asks Horton.

'Yes, sir. First thing this morning. They will be taking over supervision of the body and will arrange the inquest.'

'I have heard nothing from Markland.'

'No, sir. No doubt you will.'

'No doubt. He is the only halfway-competent magistrate in the place. But the man is desperate for prestige in Whitehall.

An investigation into a murder linked to the *Solander* will look like a golden opportunity to one such as Markland.'

'I would agree, sir. And on the face of it, this is a straightforward felony. Ransome was killed and apparently robbed, though there was money left behind and it remains unclear what was actually taken. The old woman who runs the place confirms that she heard someone ascending to Ransome's room some time before I came upon the body. If only she were as diligent in keeping an eye out for murderers as she is for constables, we might even have a description of the killer.'

Something in Horton's voice causes Harriott to turn his chair around and face his constable. Horton is standing in his customary position in front of the desk, hands behind his back, eyes watching his magistrate closely, with that infernal quality of inspection which the man brings to everything he looks at. Horton is wearing his usual darkly bland uniform of charcoal-grey trousers and frock coat. Harriott is dressed in a more traditional manner, with breeches and wig, as is his custom when attending as magistrate. It is a costume increasingly out of step with the street clothes of Wapping and the environs of the dock. This is a fact which Harriott has magnificently failed to notice.

'You think it a mere robbery?' he asks.

'On the face of it, yes.'

'Horton, you are beginning to perform a merry little dance which I will soon find exasperating. Your voice and your attitude suggest you believe there is more to this.'

'Sir, I do not have enough information to describe to you any more than a sensation. A feeling that there is something going on beneath the obvious.'

'The source of this feeling?'

'The bag of money in the sea chest. If this was a robbery, why was it not taken?'

'What indeed?'

'The materials in the room – the cup, the kettle – suggest Ransome had imbibed something before he was killed. The look on his face, while hardly evidence, is indicative of something unusual. And then there is the timing.'

'Timing?'

'Ransome is killed the day he gets home from an ocean voyage. His sea chest is ransacked, but his pay is left behind. Was something else taken? And was that something related to the voyage of the *Solander*?'

It is extraordinary – only yesterday, the captain of the *Solander* was seated next to where Horton stands now. Harriott's breezy conversation with Captain Hopkins now seems poignant. The situation has quickly become complicated. Any investigation involving Sir Joseph Banks will be fraught with political dangers. Harriott has had dealings with Banks before. Six months ago he and the Bow Street magistrate Aaron Graham had investigated the terrible murders on the Ratcliffe Highway, an investigation which had ended with illicit undertakings into which Charles Horton himself had been dragged. Harriott believes that Horton knows little of the link between those dark events and the President of the Royal Society, but he now makes a rare (for him) political decision; he will not speak of Banks just now.

'The fame of the *Solander* may bring its own complications,' Harriott says, choosing his words as carefully as he is able. 'But the ship is in the river, and a member of its crew has died in circumstances which raise some suspicion. I have given personal assurances that the vessel will be properly watched. We are perfectly entitled to investigate. I want the *Solander*'s captain spoken to, and not by Markland. That will make matters even more infernally difficult.'

'Yes, sir.' Horton seems strangely delighted, as if eager to get on board the *Solander*. How much does he know of Banks's involvement in the melancholy transactions of the previous Christmas? For a moment, Harriott ponders pulling Horton away from the current case, for his own good. But it is only a moment. Horton is his best man, by far. Harriott will always choose immediate duty over distant sympathy.

'I have some information here on the captain.' He hands Horton the letter from Aaron Graham. 'His name is Hopkins. He came here yesterday to make his introductions.'

'And perhaps I should ask what kind of investigation this is, sir?'

Neither says anything for a moment, and Harriott deliberately turns his chair back to look out at the river. He sometimes feels vaguely and irritatingly angered by Horton's ability to ask the single question which exposes all the hiding places in which information might be concealed. For this is indeed the question. What exactly are they investigating? And how official are they to be?

Horton has more than any other man opened Harriott's eyes to the need for a different type of policing in London. When Harriott and his fellow magistrate Patrick Colquhoun had proposed the River Police Office almost twenty years previously, they had done so with the express intention of paying men – constables – to go on board ships and observe. This had been the basis of English policing for centuries: men watching other men both to prevent crime but also to witness it should it occur. Watchmen, in other words.

In the matter of the Ratcliffe Highway murders six months before, Horton had quietly and diligently pursued a different method. The crimes had happened. The killer or killers were unknown. What was needed was an investigation, and that strange word had spawned others: evidence, detection, theory, proof. Those words had seemed to the diffident magistrates of

Shadwell at best incongruous and at worst downright sinister; when Harriott had confronted them with Horton's ideas, they'd reacted with anger and a refusal to cooperate. But it had been Horton who'd identified the killer, and Horton who'd finally confronted him. The Shadwell magistrates had relied on witnesses and statements; had relied, in other words, on the watching of others. This had led them into a swamp of lies and dead ends. Horton had pursued clues and evidence and proofs. He had uncovered the truth – or, at least, part of the truth. Horton does not know in what murky depths the real facts of the Ratcliffe Highway case dwell. His magistrate does.

John Harriott is a man who has thrived, throughout his life, on innovations. He is himself an inventor, both of mechanisms such as the Police Office and of machines; he has patents for a ship's pump and for an engine for raising weights and working mills. So, in the six months since the Ratcliffe Highway case, John Harriott has been secretly funding his own clandestine project, an Investigative Unit, within the River Police Office. At the moment, the Unit consists of only one man: Charles Horton. But Horton has already broken three different but overlapping smuggling rings, has apprehended a group of Essex river pirates and has tracked down and captured a strange Portuguese waterman who had taken to knocking out his passengers halfway across the river, robbing them and then leaving them, tied up and gagged, at the door of the Police Office with an apologetic note.

With these successes John Harriott has regained enormous credit with the Home Office, and has also recaptured his enthusiasm for the work of policing. This enthusiasm had been waning as a combination of increasing years and decreasing responsibility had dragged a cloak of torpor over the old man's previous energies. All that changed with the Ratcliffe Highway case, and the old excitement is growing within him again for this new episode. Sir Joseph Banks is at the very centre of London social and political life. Like many self-made men, Harriott is both repelled and enthralled by nobility and privilege. Investigating the *Solander* will require him to limp through gilded salons once again.

Horton's question, then, is simply this: is this to be an *official* investigation, or are they to pursue it in secret? Harriott decides, for now, not to answer.

'We will proceed discreetly. Go and see this ship, in the name of the River Police, Horton. I will have some conversations of my own.'

THE THAMES

Horton sends a note out to the *Solander* to request a visit with the captain, and soon receives a note back to say Hopkins is currently at Kew, but is expected back in the early afternoon. He spends the intervening hours in Sam Ransome's room, watching a physician appointed by the coroner as he makes an examination of the body. Like Horton and Abigail before him, the doctor's eyes return time and again to the dead man's face and that extraordinary grin, which expresses gleeful delight at the departure of Sam Ransome from this vale of tears. As the physician finishes, Horton asks him for his judgement.

'It can wait until the inquest,' says the physician, but he is in a hurry to leave the room and that terrible smile, and he sees that Horton is prepared to make an argument over the matter. 'Oh, very well. He was strangled. The bruising on the neck makes that obvious.'

'And his expression? Could he smile like that while being strangled?'

The physician looks downcast.

'It is possible. But I only say that because it must have happened. I have never seen the like of it before.'

Horton lets the physician leave, casts one more look around the meagre room, and then leaves it for the last time.

By now it is time to visit the *Solander*. Horton is taken to the ship by a private wherry, avoiding the little fleet of Police Office boats. Harriott may have fudged the status of this investigation, but he was perfectly clear about the need for discretion.

The ship is just downstream of the Police Office, at the point where the river bends south around the Isle of Dogs. The *Solander* is over towards the Surrey side of the river. Horton's boat must navigate round two large ships which are waiting to get into the London Dock. Both are fully laden and low in the water and are being readied for towing into the dock, their sails down and their movement sluggish and stupid. Men shout at each other across the water, from ship to ship and boat to boat and barge to lighter to wherry, the constant argument and violent debate on a river made narrow and even solid by the sheer weight of shipping upon it.

The waterman takes the wherry over towards the far side of the shore. Horton looks back behind him to Wapping, seeing the top of the building in which he and his wife live peeping over the roof of the warehouses on either side of the Police Office. He is tired, having slept little, his arms tight around his wife as she slept. Abigail had been quiet when they returned from Sam Ransome's room, and had only nodded to his repeated questions about her wellbeing. He had marvelled at her calmness in the presence of Ransome's body, but then remembered her time as a nurse, and reminded himself that the cheerful bearing of his precise wife hid a coriaceous toughness. She had gone to sleep immediately, encased in the arms of her husband, who had counted her breaths and measured their depth in a doomed attempt to calculate her state of mind.

The old weight of responsibility had tugged him down, though not into sleep.

From the river, the *Solander* isn't easy to spot in among the vessels moored at the chains off Rotherhithe, but Horton has already identified her from Harriott's office window and has no trouble finding her. She is a plain-looking collier but she is also, thanks to the pioneering example of Cook, the very model for a sensible, careful round-the-world vessel. There is very little to distinguish her from other similar colliers in the river, some of which are now stocking up on gravel as ballast for their return journeys to the north-east. She is buff-bowed, her front rising almost square from the water. Her sails have been stowed in readiness for a long stay, and there is little activity up among the rigging of her three masts. She is a little less than a hundred feet long, by Horton's reckoning, and perhaps twenty-five feet across the beam. A pinnace is tied up at her side. If you did not know what she was, there would be no earthly reason to be interested in her, apart from one oddity: a square-shaped superstructure on her quarterdeck, which looks to Horton's eyes like a big shed, and which immediately disturbs the expected lines of the ship, lines which every London river dweller has become intimate with over the centuries. That shed-like structure makes the *Solander* look a little eccentric, like a single gentleman appearing at a party with a small monkey on his shoulder.

Horton calls up to the ship while the waterman comes alongside, and a face appears at the gunwale.

'River Police!' he shouts. 'Permission to come aboard and talk to Captain Hopkins!'

The face nods and disappears. After a few minutes, the face reappears and motions for him to come aboard. He tells the waterman to wait for him, and climbs up onto the ship.

Halfway up, his nostrils begin quivering with the shocking

aroma which pours out like liquid from the *Solander*. Stepping on board is like stepping through a curtain of smell. Before, the smells of the riverside commerce: oil, salt, tar and the pervasive, solid stench of the river. After, a *green* gas which seems to swirl through the air, dropping pollen and spores and vegetable matter, such that the *Solander* reminds Horton of a lady's bouquet held to her bosom against the smoke-and-ale smell of a public saloon.

The hold of the ship is open, and looking down into it Horton has an impression of flying over a compact, impossible jungle-garden. Greens and browns predominate but here and there is an outrageous splash of colour, as if whatever dwells below is captivated by the weak London summer sun. Horton breathes in several times, inhaling the pungent wash and remembering half-forgotten voyages. Beaches and rocks and palm trees on Caribbean shores.

He looks up from the hold, aware of a man watching him, silently but carefully. He does not speak until Horton looks at him, as if to allow the new arrival to take in the view.

'I chose not to disturb you,' says the man. 'You had the air of a man experiencing a kind of epiphany.'

His voice is educated, with a strong hint of Welsh about it. He certainly looks Welsh: short, stout, solid, with a dark barrel-chested melancholy.

'I thank you for that,' says Horton. 'It is not every day one gets to gaze down into a tropical paradise within the confines of London.'

'No indeed,' says the other man. 'And now I would ask your business on board my ship, sir.'

'I take it that you are Captain Hopkins?'

'I am.'

'Sir, I am Charles Horton, a constable from the River Police Office.'

'Indeed? I met with your magistrate only yesterday. I was surprised by his interest in my ship even then. A personal visit surprises me even more, constable.'

'I am here about one of your crew members. A Samuel Ransome.'

The captain scowls at the mention of the name.

'If we're going to talk about Ransome, we're not going to do it on deck. Come to my cabin.'

They walk back to the rear of the ship. The *Solander* is quietly busy and sprucely clean. About a dozen crewmen are in view, most of them occupied in transporting the remaining flora in the hold onto the deck and preparing it for loading onto two barges which lie alongside. The containers for the flora are mostly half-barrels of various sizes. All the men are tanned and healthy-looking, and a number of them look towards Horton as he walks with the captain, clocking the interloper and filing the intelligence away. They note Horton's ease on deck, and take him for a seaman. They also note the suddenness of his arrival, as if he'd popped into existence at the lip of the hold just in time for the captain, and they warn each other that here is a man upon whom a sharp eye needs to be kept.

An incongruous young man whom Horton takes for a clergyman nods as they pass and then stares, without embarrassment. He is holding a small book he has been reading while walking on the deck. He is dressed like a country vicar from the previous century. His skin is as brown as that of the crew, his nose broad and his hair as dark as his breeches. Horton almost stops, expecting to be introduced to the young man by Hopkins, but the captain does not even look at the clerical stranger, whose eyes follow the two men up to the quarterdeck with an oddly desperate intensity.

The quarterdeck is dominated by the strange shed-like

structure Horton saw from the river. There are glass windows all round its walls and looking inside Horton sees even more plants within. The shed is a hothouse, and the flora within quiver and sweat with an alien energy. Hopkins sees him looking through the window.

'Our plant house, constable. Constructed on this river over a year ago and now full to the brim with plants from Otaheite. Here, let me show you something.'

Hopkins pulls open the door to the plant house, and Horton is instantly assailed with an even more intense aroma and something more physical: a shower of dust which seems to be ejected from the plant house like the exhalation of some botanical dragon. It gets into his eyes and nose and causes him to want to sneeze. His skin, suddenly inflamed, seems to come alive.

'Vivid stuff, this Otaheite plant life,' he says. Then he does sneeze, a loud and wet explosion which causes some of the crew to laugh, though they fall silent when Hopkins glares at them.

''Tis indeed, constable, 'tis indeed. My poor Welsh constitution didn't know what to make of it at first. I sneezed and scratched my way back around the Cape, I can tell you. Now, see this.'

He closes the door of the plant house and then descends a ladder to the back of the ship, beneath the captain's and master's cabins. There is some light here from portholes that run the length of the ship on both sides. Behind them, in the hold, are the plants and flowers Horton first saw on coming on deck. But here is something even more extraordinary: dozens and dozens of half-barrels, each filled with flowers and plants, sit in the back of the ship, held within a false floor into which holes have been sawed to hold them. More barrels are held in holes down the sides of the ship. There is no noise in here, but something almost like a noise: a thick, stirring sense of quivering life, which once again begins to invade Horton's eyes and nose and causes him to weep, after a fashion.

'We call this the Garden,' says Hopkins, his voice hushed, and there is indeed something churchlike about the space. 'Bligh called it something similar on the *Bounty*. Though with less happy results.'

They stand and watch, Horton watching the plants, the captain watching Horton, smiling proudly at his cargo, but also careful. Horton is very aware of being observed, and of Hopkins's fierce intelligence. He is careful to compose his face in a mask of wonder, and nothing else.

'Now, so, come,' Hopkins says at last, and Horton follows the captain back up the ladder well and into a cabin which is as spruce, plain and businesslike as his ship. He is at a loss to understand the internal layout of the ship; the great cabin seems to have been removed completely, while the captain's cabin is small, barely more than a cupboard. He recalls Bligh's descriptions of his own accommodation on the *Bounty*, and wonders how similar this other captain's space must be.

Despite the lack of room, there are plenty of little books on the shallow shelves, and Horton looks at them carefully, his eyes clearing from the effusions of the flora below and around. Most of the books are botanical works, some of them in Latin. Horton notes the name Daniel Solander on one of the spines.

'The ship is named after the botanist?' he asks.

Hopkins smiles.

'An enthusiast, constable?' he asks.

'Not at all. My wife, though, is an avid natural philosopher.' He speaks the words drily, and Hopkins laughs for the first time, a deep rich brown-gravy sound which causes even Horton to smile.

'Ah, a wife who is a natural philosopher. Which would make

you a specimen for daily investigation, I'll wager, Constable Horton.'

'Indeed. More often than I care to imagine.'

'But a man of the sea also.'

'Is it so obvious?'

'Always.'

'I have not been on a voyage for some time. I have been on ships . . . but not on the open sea these past five or six years.'

'Were you on a merchant vessel, or a fighting ship?'

It occurs to Horton that it is he, not the captain, who is supposed to be asking questions. Particularly when the questions turn into the awkward byways of Horton's naval history.

'I was in the Navy. So, Captain. This Ransome. You can confirm he was one of your crew on the most recent voyage?'

The bonhomie departs from Hopkins's face like mud mopped off a deck, and he sits at the small table in the cabin, gesturing to Horton to sit upon the bed. This strikes the constable as unusual. The captain is clearly of a higher social standing, but the way he talks to Horton, and this invitation to sit, suggests that Hopkins feels no sense of superiority.

'Ransome is a lazy unappealing bastard of a crewman, Constable Horton. You'll have come across his like plenty of times before. Always complaining, always absent when hard work is needed, and always whispering behind his hand like a bloody old woman. I was glad to see the back of him when we docked. He took his pay and hopped off into Wapping at the first opportunity. I haven't thought of him once since he left. Got himself into bother, has he?'

'He's dead.'

The captain raises one thick black eyebrow and rubs his chin. He gazes in that appraising way at Horton.

'Now then. An interesting statement, Constable Horton. Dead when?'

'We believe yesterday evening. He was found dead by a female acquaintance, name of Hannah Crabtree.'

'*Found dead by a female acquaintance*. The kind of epitaph I'd expect for Sam Ransome. How did he die?'

'We believe he was strangled.'

Hopkins frowns and smiles at the same time, his face painted with disbelief.

'Strangled? Are you certain?'

'The appearance of his body suggests such a death. We believe he was killed and then robbed.'

'In his room? Extraordinary.'

Hopkins looks like a man half-amused, half-annoyed by Horton's story. He seems oddly unmoved by Ransome's death. As a former Navy man Horton feels a quick but fierce dismay that a captain should be so negligent of the welfare of his crew. But then, Sam wasn't part of Hopkins's crew when he died.

'Your magistrate must have some powerful friends, Constable,' says Hopkins.

Horton blinks at this.

'I do not understand your meaning, Captain.'

'Sending a constable out to investigate the robbery of a poor seaman. I knew the *Solander* was important, but I'm only now beginning to understanding how important.'

The captain looks at Horton and waits, leaving the constable to ponder how much to say. He needs this man's help, and just now the man seems disinclined to give it. He decides to be more direct than he would quite like.

'Some matters about Ransome's death are mysterious,' he says, after a moment. 'It may not be a straightforward robbery.'

'Ah. Now we come to it then.' The captain is smiling now and leans forward, suddenly interested. 'What are these mysterious matters?'

'Ransome's pay was still in his sea chest.'

'Indeed?' The captain ponders this with some care, as if he does not at first understand it. 'Would have been a pretty amount, too; he was only paid yesterday.'

'A pretty amount, as you say.'

'So what was stolen?'

'We don't quite know.'

Again, that disbelieving, amused look transforms the captain's face. Horton finds he doesn't like it.

'You don't know? Then how do you know there was a robbery?'

'The room was disturbed. Ransome's sea chest, also. Somebody was looking for something, and they killed Ransome to get to it.'

This is far more than Horton had intended to say, and he immediately wishes he could take it back.

'Pretty thin, isn't it, Constable?'

'The man was killed, Captain. His pay wasn't taken.'

'So, you need to find what this apparent killer was looking for, otherwise you don't know why any of this happened.'

'Could it have been something from the island?'

'Well, I've no doubt Sam brought something back from the island, but I'll wager it was in his breeches, not his sea chest.'

'You mean he carried an infection.'

'Most of the men do.'

'I have read of such matters. So has everyone.'

'Indeed. Many men have grown quite fat on tales of Otaheite.'

'Including the sponsor of this vessel.'

'Sir Joseph? If you like.'

'So you have no reason to think Ransome suffered particularly on the trip?'

'Oh, I've no doubt he *suffered*, Horton. Sam would make out he was suffering if he was lying in a hammock drinking fine wine and being stroked by native virgins. But no, this particular journey was nothing short of *blissful*, Horton. I've never been on a voyage like it.'

'So you can think of no one who bore a grudge against Ransome?'

'Lots of the men found him annoying. But not annoying enough to be done away with.'

'And you can't imagine what might have been taken?'

'No, Constable, I can't. My imagination is a poor, withered thing.'

The captain smiles at that, the Welsh charm transforming the cruel, amused expression. Enough, the smile says. We shall part as friends. Horton decides to surrender.

'My thanks, Captain,' he says. 'And the thanks of my magistrate.'

'My pleasure, Constable. Perhaps you could both leave me alone for a day or two now, hmm?'

KEW

The June twilight is quiet and the surface of the river is once again busy with insects and floating organisms which seem to glow with stored sunlight. On an evening like this it is possible to imagine that darkness will never fall on England. Sir Joseph Banks is in stolid, silhouetted stillness. Robert Brown stands behind the wheelchair and watches a pair of swans which are preparing to roost on the opposite side of the river. One twines its neck into the other, and they appear like a young couple preparing for a midsummer's snooze, bellies filled with wine and cake, hearts filled with possibilities. Then, with a wave and a grunt, Banks indicates that he wishes to be moved.

The President is a heavy burden. Brown pushes the wheelchair back along the path, up the bank and around the polite, austere decorum of the Dutch House, their way occasionally lit with candles glowing from the tidy pathways. Round the corner of the little house they see the enormous vacancy where the White House once stood, and to the left of that is the Orangery, dark and square in the twilight. They walk past the Orangery, until they see the hundred-foot-long glass-and-wood shape of the Great Stove. From within, dark shapes can be seen fluttering in an impossible breeze.

They walk up to the door of the Stove, the librarian now puffing with the effort. Banks does not notice the man's exertions. The park is quite silent now; the King is elsewhere, the Prince is back in London, and if there are staff still within the mess of buildings within the park, they make no noise. The botanical riches have been pored over and prepared all day long by a small army of attendants under William Aiton, the Director General of the King's gardens, as he has taken to calling himself. For some hours Brown has allowed himself to just wander and remember, thinking back to his own botanising on the distant shores of New Holland as the alien odours of the South Pacific dressed the bank of the Thames. But now he must attend on Banks again.

Robert Brown has been Joseph Banks's librarian for just over a year, and the post has brought him two things which are to be highly cherished: a fellowship at the Royal Society, and some measure of financial comfort. He combines his position with that of part-time librarian of the Linnaean Society, and the money is good for a self-taught Scot with an incomplete education. Nonetheless, he has been considering returning to a medical career in recent months. Banks has grown increasingly tiresome, and with each little humiliation Brown has found his mind wandering back to his time as a young Surgeon's Mate in the Fifeshire Fencibles. He has considered how nice it would be to have the quiet life of a country doctor, away from the frantic whirl of London and the whims of an old and occasionally insufferable old man.

But these are just fantasies, because the itch in his bones will always be there, the same itch Banks sometimes speaks of. It's there when he catches a whiff of saltwater from the river while attending Society lectures at Somerset House. It's there when he hears a seagull caw-cawing through the air and heading downstream towards the rich pickings of Billingsgate. Even the dry recorded memories of adventures which are the very skeleton of Banks's own great library are merely an academic simulacrum of something else, which can only be felt when your hands are on the ship's rail, when swell is splashing into your face, and when an undiscovered land rises before you like smoke from an eternal fire. Discovery stirs Robert Brown the way it once stirred Joseph Banks, and if that discovery must occur within the confines of a library rather than on the endless flats of an open sea, well, then, so be it.

It is over six years since he returned from his own great voyage of discovery aboard the *Investigator*, a journey which lasted five years. Before he'd left England, he was often ill, and had frequently been away on sick-leave from the Fencibles. He'd struggled with his own sense of himself when these illnesses struck, for they often seemed to be illnesses of the mind – great torpid clouds of melancholy which he characterised as indolence and struggled to put down, his father's rigid Protestant work ethic loud in his ears as if it were shouted from the top of a staircase. Banks at the time was often bedridden in Spring Grove, the gout galloping through his body, but he'd detected something in what he'd heard of young Robert Brown – the same botanical spark that had lit him up, decades before, and which had taken him around the world on the *Endeavour*.

So when Banks needed a botanist for an expedition to New Holland – and when his first choice, Mungo Park, said no – it was to Brown he turned. They'd dined together on Christmas Day 1800, haggling like a pair of old bankers before agreeing on a salary of £420 for the voyage. Six months later Brown was sailing south aboard the *Investigator*, and his fortune, for good or bad, was set. Now, he is a librarian, a botanist and, it would seem, a pusher of wheelchairs.

He steps from behind Banks's wheelchair and opens the door of the Stove, and once again finds himself astonished by the richness of the new odours which spring out from within. The plants which have been placed inside the hot-house have survived thousands of miles of travel, thanks to techniques invented by Banks and perfected by Brown. He may understand those techniques, and yet it still seems a miracle to him that these delicate exotic things have made it this far.

The door squeaks slightly as it opens, and for a moment the squeak sounds like the giggle of a girl, and the librarian pauses, wondering if a child of one of the staff has entered.

'What is it, man?'

The bark from the chair is familiar if unwelcome.

'I thought I heard someone, Sir Joseph.'

'In here? Don't be ridiculous.'

A pause.

'What did it sound like?'

'Like a girl laughing.'

Banks grunts.

'What would a girl be doing in the Stove, Brown?'

'I have no conception, Sir Joseph. Collecting flowers?'

Banks laughs at that, an intelligent and generous laugh which reminds the librarian once again why he loves this enormous man, with his curiosity and energy and spirit, despite his lapses into gruffness.

'Collecting flowers! We have done little else with our lives, Brown. So are we nothing more than girls ourselves?'

'Perhaps so, Sir Joseph. It might explain our occasional petty quarrels.'

Banks laughs even more at that, the joke from his librarian all the more valued because of its rarity. Brown pushes him into the Stove.

'Leave me for a while, Brown. I wish to renew my acquaintance with some of these treasures.'

So the old President of the Royal Society wheels himself into the hothouse, leaving his librarian by the door. Brown stands and watches him for a while, but Banks has already departed into a botanical world of memory in which no one else exists. He smells the air around him, as if comparing the odours.

'*Barringtonia asiatica*. It keeps its odour well. And *Triumfetta procumbens*. That was one of your triumphs, Sydney. The smell and the picture are as one in my head.'

He continues to move forward, pulling up next to a small pot which is waiting to be planted in the earth. He lifts it up, and holds it in front of his face. Brown thinks it is the same plant Banks had been holding when the Regent made his sudden and unwanted incursion into the Gardens earlier in the day.

'And you? What are you?' says Banks. 'Well, we shall see.'

He heaves himself out of the wheelchair, and digs a hole in the virgin earth which has been made ready. With infinite care, Banks plants the little thing into the soil of the Stove, and the librarian turns and makes his leave.

THREE

Thou knowest that the ancient trees seen by thy eyes
  have fruit;
But knowest thou that trees and fruit flourish upon the
  earth
To gratify senses unknown? Trees beasts and birds
  unknown:
Unknown, not unperceived, spread in the infinite
  microscope,
In places yet unvisited by the voyager, and in worlds
Over another kind of seas, and in atmospheres unknown.

William Blake, 'Visions of the Daughters of Albion',
1793

TAHITI

The prince's brother began moaning in his sleep a week after the *Britannia* had departed. The prince was the first to hear his brother's groans and sighs, as they slept side-by-side in the hut, but his mother came soon after and asked her eldest son what was wrong.

'My stomach hurts, that is all,' said his brother, embarrassed by the fuss, and affecting manly irritation. 'I was asleep. I didn't know I was making any noise.'

'You sounded *terrible*,' said the little prince, and his brother scowled at him. The prince felt bad, though he didn't quite know why.

'Drink some water,' said his mother, and something in her eyes scared the younger boy for a moment, because it looked as though she was afraid. But this idea – his mother, afraid – was such an impossibility that the prince forgot it instantly. His brother did what he was told, and they all went back to sleep.

His brother ate little the next day. The following night his groans were louder, and their mother came immediately, as if she'd never really fallen asleep. His brother claimed he was fine again, but then suddenly he leapt up and ran out of the hut. From outside they heard him throwing up, retching sounds followed by great shocking wet noises which made the prince think, somehow, of a fish eating. His mother followed the prince's brother out of the hut and they were both gone a long time. Eventually they came back and his mother laid her eldest son back down. The prince lay alongside him, feeling him shiver and hearing him moan the rest of the night.

His brother could not get up the next day, and their father came to see what was wrong. A look passed between their parents which the prince just about caught, but could not decipher. In the afternoon a great smell rose from his brother, and some men came and took him out of the hut and laid him on the ground outside, washing him down with water because he had soiled himself. His brother was shrieking now, even when he was sleeping, and all the little prince could think was *he went on board the* Britannia *and he came back ill.*

And then, after two more days of shrieking and vomiting and that terrible brown stinking excrement, came the end. His brother yelled one more time, a liquid yell of despair, and then he was silent.

The traditional mourning followed. The prince's mother was joined by other women from the district in a terrible wailing around the body of the elder son. The women beat themselves around the head with shark's teeth and conch shells, blood dripping down their cheeks from the wounds in their scalps. The men hung drapes made from *tapa*, the bark of the breadfruit tree, around the body, and soon joined the women in their mutilations.

Other men spent this time building an altar for the dead prince in the family *marae*. This altar was six feet high with a roof to shelter the corpse. On the third day the women stopped wailing and ceased their mutilations, and the prince's body was taken to the altar so that the public mourning could begin. For the younger boy the site of his mother's bloodstained face had been the stuff of nightmares, but this soon gave way to the appearance of a new horror: the *haiva*, an enormous monster with mother-of-pearl eyes, a tiara of red feathers and a vicious sceptre, lined with shark's teeth. The *haiva* ran through the district accompanied by a gang of young men and boys, smeared with mud, and as he ran he clattered together two mother-of-pearl shells in his hands as a warning of his approach, so that the district resounded with the snapping echoes of a wooden-footed demon trampling among the surrounding rocks.

The young prince buried his head at the sound of the *haiva*'s arrival, and hid himself even after the *haiva* had disrobed himself at the altar of his dead brother, revealing an ordinary man. The chase around the village was a representation of his brother's spirit, the prince understood, a spirit which was still in the air and the trees and the ground around them and which would not depart that place until it was satisfied with the mourning. Every night he told himself this, and every day which followed he fled into the hut again at the sound of the *haiva*'s approach, so full of terror that his bladder turned to water and his eyes ran.

Every day for a fortnight the *haiva* performed his manic masque, ending each day disrobed and eating calmly with the dead prince's family. Finally, after seemingly endless days of wailing and chasing, the body of the older brother was wrapped in *tapa* and taken up into the mountains, and the younger boy was given to understand that now, at last, his brother's spirit could leave the island along with the spirits of all the other dead, and be free.

WAPPING AND ROTHERHITHE

Charles Horton is prowling Lower Gun Alley, below the windows of the rooms he shares with Abigail.

Up and down. Up and down.

It is Saturday. The coroner's inquest into Sam Ransome's death is to be held on Monday. This morning, John Harriott received notice from the Shadwell magistrates that Charles Horton was no longer welcome to pursue the matter, which was formally under their jurisdiction. The Shadwell magistrate Edward Markland had added a postscript insisting on an interview with Captain Hopkins of the *Solander*. Harriott had expressed his surprise at Markland's aggressive alacrity, and Horton had seen how angry this had made the old man. Persistent battles are being played out, he can see, and he finds himself asking how any of this helps discover who killed Ransome, and why he died with that satanic grin on his face.

So now Horton walks. Up and down. Up and down.

Neither the coroner nor the Shadwell magistrates remarked on what he had noticed: the bag of money in the sea chest, left untouched. Nor had they yet spoken, as he had, to the boarding-house woman. This was how magistrates traditionally proceeded. There had been a death. Was there an obvious perpetrator? And was there anyone who wants the perpetrator prosecuted? If the answer to either question was no, the case was judged unimportant. If the answer was no to both questions, well then. There are other cases to pursue. Niceties such as evidence and even motive are too complex for a busy coroner and a trio of unimaginative magistrates. A poor, uneducated sailor is dead. Hardly unusual, and hardly dramatic. Samuel Ransome had been a seaman (able or otherwise) of no distinction in either his work or his relationships. A fat, lazy, unremarkable human being with few acquaintances and even fewer friends. There is certainly no sense whatever that the murder should be investigated because a wrong has been done. As far as the magistrates can see, the only victim in this case is dead. So on whose behalf would they pursue an investigation?

Up and down. Up and down.

Little dramas play out in his head, imaginings of possibilities. Sam in his room, straight off the ship, boiling a kettle, making tea, falling asleep. Being killed. But why? The killer, hunting through the sea chest, looking for something, ignoring the money. But why?

Start somewhere else, he thinks to himself. Start with a motive for a killing. Why might someone want Sam Ransome dead? The most important fact in this consideration is out in the river: the *Solander*. This has been the thing that defined Sam for the last eighteen months of his life. So, if there is a motive for his death, it either sat and waited in London for Sam's return. Or it was forged on the ship itself.

An oceangoing ship is, Horton knows, a crucible of murderous intent. Violent men spend months and months huddled together, and gossip and envy and deceit are distilled over the long ocean nights into something potent. Disagreements can turn into feuds, vengeful thoughts become vendettas. It is a great deal more likely that whatever killed Sam Ransome came back on the ship with him, and did not wait for his return.

Up and down. Up and down.

Her husband, notes Abigail, is prowling again. The sun is high and a warm breeze blows down Lower Gun Alley, and Abigail can look out into the street to see Charles marching up and down, up and down, as if wearing in a new pair of boots on the dirty, foul-smelling cobbles of the little street. Her window is open, and the noises and smells of Wapping fill the small first-floor apartment in which they live, fill it with such intensity that the tidy room she stands in actually seems to be getting dirtier before her eyes. She watches her husband for a while, smiling a smile which covers an enduring inner concern. Charles Horton is on the trail of another mystery, and she'll not get the benefit of those calm dark eyes again until the mystery is solved. She thinks back to her pleasant night at the Royal Institution, which ended so suddenly with the discovery of a dead body. The memory of this still makes her shudder, though not with the fear that her husband imagines. It is the memory of Horton's own body, broken and almost dead when it was brought into the hospital, that first time she'd laid eyes on him, which causes her discomfort.

She is dressed simply in a white muslin dress which is, despite its plainness, in the latest Empire style. She wouldn't be ashamed to be seen in it. The air is warm. She has nothing else to do today. Well, then.

A few minutes later, she appears in the street behind her husband, a shawl over her shoulders, a bonnet covering her blond hair, an old but perfectly serviceable parasol over her arm. When her husband reaches the end of his little march and turns, she is waiting for him, and even with his mind whirring on yesterday's scraps he stops short. Abigail realises she may have been mistaken in her previous thoughts, for those cool dark eyes do rest on her for some moments. They have a warm disbelief in them, as if she were something of another world.

'So, husband. You are exercised by Rotherhithe matters.'

He smiles and nods.

'And I neglect you,' he says.

'Aye, you do. And I crave some attention. So it occurs to me, I have heard much about the new constructions which are appearing on the other shore of our river. I have never seen them. Perhaps a walk in the sun on the Surrey shore would be a sweet way to spend our Saturday?'

Charles Horton's smile is broad now, and its appearance causes Abigail's heart to skip, for such a smile is a rare thing indeed on such a man, carrying as he does curses and guilts which she can barely fathom.

'To Rotherhithe you would go, madam?'

'Aye, sir. To Rotherhithe I would go.'

They take a wherry from the stairs beside the Police Office: an official boat, piloted by a waterman-constable named Peach, who says nothing during the crossing, only glares at Charles in a way which Abigail finds alarming and amusing in equal measure. When they reach the Rotherhithe stairs at the end of Love Lane, they turn to watch the angry Peach turn the wherry around and begin to make his way back to Wapping, through the crowd of ships and lighters.

'Your friend Mr Peach must be unwell today. He seemed rather quiet.'

Charles looks sad, and she wishes for a moment she had said nothing.

'Aye, he is not alone in disliking me. The other constables

resent my position with the magistrate. They see nothing of my work, and imagine I am a kept man with little to occupy my time. It is the price I pay for the work I do.'

He says nothing more, and they begin to walk along Rotherhithe Street, the thin strip of houses, wharves and warehouses which follows the course of the river. The houses are small and poor and, in places along the river, old and alarmingly ramshackle, stretching out over stairs and wharves and, in some cases, over the water and foreshore itself. The place has something of Wapping's sense of overwhelming narrowness and complexity, although it feels more open to the sky at those points where development is only just beginning.

They pass a timber yard, and then St Mary's church, which faces almost directly onto the foreshore. The street skirts round the church, but the two of them walk through the churchyard itself, staying as close to the river as possible. They walk past the old alehouse the Spread Eagle and Crown, and after another few minutes they come to the first evidence on the Surrey shore of the mercantile classes' new passion: the building of docks.

A great lock has been built at the river's edge, and behind it lies a body of water which is part canal, part dock. This is the new Surrey Canal, Charles explains to Abigail, which reaches only to Camberwell to date, but is still the subject of great schemes for development. Abigail surprises Charles by making reference to the great canal of Canute, which cut through Rotherhithe and allowed the old Dane to take London from the rear, as it were, by skirting round London Bridge. Charles decides his wife needs no instruction on dock-building. His wife smiles and turns her face to the sun. It really is a beautiful morning.

On the downstream side of the Surrey Canal lock are more shipyards and timber yards, and more riverside tenements and warehouses. Behind Rotherhithe Street have long been marshes and meadows, rope walks and tenter grounds, which are now being covered, yard-by-yard and year-by-year, with boarding houses and shops and storehouses and manufactories and brothels, the inevitable handmaidens of the docks.

As they head round the great bend in the river, which turns south here, the dwellings disappear on the right-hand side of the road and give way to open meadow and swampy-looking ground. Some hundreds of yards away the basin of the canal can be seen, and the north edge of the newly-extended Commercial Dock, the renamed and improved old Howland Wet Dock, where whales were once boiled down and men could be seen walking through the cavernous bones of leviathans. The old whale graveyard is now the oldest part of the emerging Surrey dock system, with its new canal and basin and its mass of warehouses and locks and wharves, paid for by entrepreneurs with their eyes on the same lucrative prizes already seized by the City merchants who'd subscribed to the new London, East India and West India docks. Abigail remarks how very different to Wapping the dock-building scheme is here, how few dwellings there are to be cleared, how flat and empty the land is. She asks the question which has been asked by hundreds of others before her: why did the dock get built in Wapping? Why force out so many thousands amidst such a wave of demolition and clearance, when all this land was available just across the river? Charles is pondering this question when, up ahead and clearly visible above the sketchy crowds which are making their way up and down Rotherhithe Street, he sees a familiar figure emerge from a wherry tied up at a wharf.

It is the strange dark-suited gentleman from the *Solander*. Looking out to the river Charles notices that they are almost alongside Sir Joseph Banks's ship, which is moored just off

Rotherhithe. She is quiet, her sails now completely stowed, only three or four figures visible up on deck.

The man from the *Solander* is looking up and down the street, his eyes gliding over Charles and Abigail without recognition. He is wearing the same dark suit Charles saw on ship, the clerical appearance at odds with his tanned face and its broad, almost Asiatic features.

'What is it, Charles?'

Abigail's hand is on his arm, but she is not looking at him – she has instinctively turned to look in the same direction as him. He keeps his eye on the dark-suited man while replying.

'Well, my darling, it is an interesting young man from the *Solander*. See, the fellow in the dark suit heading away from us.'

'He looks like a vicar.'

'Indeed. A vicar with a mission, it would appear. Abigail, I would very much like to see where that man is going. Could I call you a boat from the stairs beyond this yard?'

His wife is studiously ignoring him.

'Your young man is disappearing fast, though he sticks out somewhat like a horse amongst sheep. We will lose him. Hurry, husband. We will lose sight of him in moments.'

Her parasol over her arm and her shawl flowing behind her, Abigail follows the priestly figure along the riverbank, pursued by her husband.

They walk for perhaps ten minutes, and soon the newly minted Commercial Dock is to their right, clearly visible as, unlike the Wapping Dock, it is not yet surrounded by warehouses and walls. There are more houses here, some of them built quite recently in anticipation of an influx of money from the new dock.

The man from the *Solander* walks with his hands behind his back, stooped slightly, and the image of a country vicar strolling around his parish is overwhelming, though this vicar looks to have seen exotic shores and his parish is crowded, smelly and loud. Near the Commercial Dock he stops walking suddenly, before one of the newer-looking buildings, which seems to be part storehouse, part wharf, part tavern, part lodging, its hasty, tentative balcony almost poking over the foreshore. Charles and Abigail stop perhaps fifty yards away, stepping into a gap between two buildings (Abigail gasping, even giggling). The man eyes the building for a while, looking along the windows and running a hand through his dark, oiled hair as if steadying himself for an unpleasant task. After a minute, he steps into the building.

'Now what, husband?' whispers Abigail, and Charles, despite himself, smiles.

'I think you need not whisper, dear wife.'

She smacks his arm at that. He keeps an eye on the building.

'I think we should wait for a while. If he doesn't come out soon, I will make a note of the address and take the information back to the Police Office.'

'What has that young man done?'

'Nothing, that I know of. But I was struck by him when I visited the *Solander* about the . . . incident we came across the other day.'

'Ah.' Abigail goes quiet at that. The mention of the dead body drops like a shadow between them, and their little game of chase takes on a more melancholy character. Then the priest-like man reappears, darting back into the street, his eyes looking into the house he has just departed before glancing around like a squirrel surrounded by dogs.

After a final glance into the house, the man turns and walks towards them, much quicker than before, closing the ground in seconds. Charles steps out from around the corner of the building where they have hidden themselves, holds out a hand

and brings the man up short. The man looks brutally alarmed, though whether this is because of the appearance of Charles from around a corner or because of what he saw in that house Abigail cannot say.

'You . . . you were *following* me?' he says. Charles has a hold of one of his arms, and does not answer, but thinks: he recognises me. Is that not odd?

'You appear to be in a fearful hurry.' Abigail notes the hint of tenderness in Charles's voice, and notices for the first time how awfully young this priestly man is. She sees his face preparing to lie, the eyes starting to hood themselves.

'Oh, there's a woman in that house,' he says, and his attempted hail-fellow-well-met nonchalance would be funny were it not acutely embarrassing. '*You* know, Constable.'

He knows I am a constable, thinks Horton. A most informed young man. Abigail, meanwhile, finds it hard not to smirk at the uncomfortable fellow's attempt to lie. A romantic liaison for a diffident cleric? How fantastical.

'Well, then, let's go and see this woman,' says Charles. He starts to pull the arm he is holding back towards the boarding house.

'Oh, no, I don't think we should at all . . .'

'Come on.'

Charles has to virtually drag the jittery man back to the boarding house. Abigail follows. Several people had come out of the house when the young man made his escape, including an older man wearing only a cotton vest and a disgusting pair of trousers who is giving vent to a stream of riverside obscenities which Abigail attempts to ignore. There is a great confusion in the doorway of the boarding house, as if a wild animal had torn through the interior and out into the street. Charles pulls the captured young man back into the house, and Abigail follows them inside, where there are more people shouting, mainly women, most of them barely dressed, some of them with men (or *customers*, thinks Abigail) or small children, and miscellaneous dogs and cats running round at their feet. There is barking and screaming and mewing and cursing.

Charles ignores the mêlée, and shoves the man before him through the hallway and towards the back of the house, where another door gives out onto a wharf and several more rooms give out onto the hall. Charles is being rather rough, Abigail thinks, not liking what she is seeing in her husband, whose face looks grim and angry and determined and cold all at the same time. Charles surely cannot know where to go in this strange Bedlam. The dark-suited young man stops before one of the open doors, Charles behind him, and the younger man screams a girl-like scream, so horror-stricken that it silences everyone in the crowded little hallway. He screams again, and again, and again, and Charles shoves him aside, leaving the young man to fall back against the opposite wall and slide down it onto his haunches, weeping now like a woman in the terrible throes of childbirth. Abigail approaches the door, and catches sight of something red around the corner of it before her husband grabs her and holds her head against his shoulder while he turns away, and all she can hear is the terrible moaning of the young man behind her, who through his sobs is saying 'it cannot be … it cannot be … it cannot be' over and over and over again.

THE HINDOSTANEE COFFEE HOUSE

John Harriott heads for the West End in a rage which has been building since the previous day. The Shadwell magistrates are once again attempting to preserve their own dignity at the expense of discovering a murderer. Those who know him worry about these periodic rages and what they might one day do to him, as if he were an old steam engine pumping water from a tin mine, permanently suspended between functioning, exploding and expiring. The rages always blow out, often quite suddenly. At least he has the carriage ride from Wapping to Portman Square in which to calm down.

His destination does nothing to improve his mood. He is an old soldier and sailor who has nearly died at the hands of rebellious Hindoos and tigers, and he would prefer to be left in a room with either than with one of the slippery and clever denizens of Mayfair. Politicians, bankers and noblemen make him twitch and fret.

There is one notable exception to this prejudice. Despite his anger with Shadwell, Harriott is able to feel comforted that today, of all days, he should be visiting his one true friend in the salons of the west: Aaron Graham, the resident magistrate at Bow Street, and a most comfortable schemer and player of West End parlour games. Graham is smooth where Harriott is rough, accommodating where Harriott is brutal, and calm where Harriott is passionate. Graham, for his part, admires Harriott more than any man he knows. He cherishes the older man's spirit, his energy, his patriotism and his muscular honesty. They have some shared history. Both are ex-Navy men, with attachments to Newfoundland in particular, where Harriott had sailed on his first voyage and where Graham had served with distinction as secretary to Admiral Edwards and even, for a few years, as a sort of Chief Justice.

Even so, the warmth between the two men has cooled of late. There has been a shadow in their relationship – a tiger in their room, always ready to pounce. Aaron Graham's late entry into the Ratcliffe Highway investigations the previous December have permanently changed John Harriott's view of his charming friend. Blackmail and violence and something worse, something old and unspeakable, had come between the two magistrates, and it was taking the Devil's own time to lift. The resentment still festers and dances around every lunch, dinner and conversation Harriott and Graham have shared since that terrible time.

But they have kept up at least the appearances of friendship, maintaining those regular luncheons and occasional dinners. Today's luncheon is a long-standing fixture in both men's diaries. As his carriage makes its way towards Portman Square, Harriott ponders this latest coincidental conjunction of worlds, the affair of the *Solander*. He has been desperate to avoid such collisions since the Ratcliffe Highway affair. Now it must be faced. Aaron Graham is very close to Sir Joseph Banks. Indeed, the man was an investor in the voyage which the *Solander* has just undertaken. What is more, Banks has a strong hold on Graham. He is able to force the Bow Street magistrate into actions which Harriott strongly doubts can be seen as entirely ethical, at least in policing terms. Harriott has sometimes wondered if his friend is sometime guilty of dishonesty, such is Graham's readiness to preserve the good name of men like Banks. And as for whether he has always had Harriott's interests as his prime priority – well, that is the essential matter of the cloud that has fallen between them.

Today's luncheon venue is new and intriguing. The Hindostanee Coffee House is an establishment just off Portman Square advertising Indian cuisine, the *hookha* and the finest Chilm tobacco. Mrs Harriott would disapprove, for this smacks strongly of nostalgia for Harriott's distinguished service in India. She also knows something of the illicit intoxication by which even men old enough to know better are sometimes tempted.

Harriott's carriage emerges onto Oxford Street and makes its way down its full length, turning right before reaching Tyburn and then, after a block or two more, entering Portman Square, one of London's grander spaces. Large and refined houses enclose a fenced green space in the centre, filled with pleasing trees and shrubs. A few gentlemen and ladies are wandering and taking in the summer air.

The Hindostanee Coffee House is a block further north on the corner of George Street and Charles Street. The smell from the place pours out into the street, and Harriott's nostrils quiver in memory of elephants, tigers and Mahometans. His carriage comes to a halt outside and, with no little trouble from his lame leg, Harriott descends. As he does so, three gentlemen emerge from the coffee house, rather more rapidly than would be considered good manners. One of them is shouting. The other two appear to be chasing him.

'There is a crack in the sky!' shouts the first man as he races down the street, the other two following. Harriott watches them go, puzzled and a little amused. Intoxicated young men are hardly an uncommon sight in London or in Westminster, but there is something striking about this scene: the first man apparently terrified, the other two embarrassed and determined to catch him. He continues to shout as he runs. 'That's how the rain gets in! The sky is cracking!' They disappear around a corner.

Harriott looks back at the coffee house with renewed interest and goes inside. The interior is furnished with bamboo tables and chairs and vaguely Asian drawings on the walls. Some of these look Chinese, not Indian, and Harriott allows himself a moment's irritation at the owner's lack of precision. There is a separate drawing room in which Harriott can already see some well-appointed gentlemen puffing away on *hookhas*, surrounded by rich and various smokey odours: tobacco, certainly, but other things as well, including something very much like hemp, which Harriott had come across often in India. He wonders if this explains the erratic behaviour of the young man outside.

A harried young Indian boy greets him, and hearing the name 'Graham' rushes Harriott through to the main dining room. This is actually a smallish salon containing no more than a half-dozen tables and surrounded by pictures of tigers stalking through opulent jungles. Graham is already seated in front of a colourful variety of dishes, set off with several bowls of gleaming white rice. He looks, as ever, immaculate.

'I asked them to wait, my dear Harriott,' says Graham, rising majestically from his seat as if performing in one of his beloved Drury Lane productions. 'But these fellows do seem to be in an awful rush.'

Graham's attire is almost as spectacular as the food which surrounds him. He wears a purple cravat within a pink waistcoat and pink breeches, with yellow stockings and a pitch-black wig which startles and craves attention. He is holding an equally black walking stick, topped with an elaborate silver sculpture which, to Harriott's untutored eye, seems to be some kind of plant. He smells of gardens and galleries, even within the powerful aromas coming up from the food.

The old friends greet each other, and sit down to the feast, which they eat carefully and assiduously, conversing throughout. Graham in particular is possessed of that unique skill of the English gentleman, to eat and talk at the same time without ever missing his conversational cue or speaking with food in his mouth.

'Enjoy the meal, my dear Harriott. It may be the last chance you get.'

'How so, Graham?'

'This splendid place has recently been declared bankrupt. It's being kept going by the kindness of friends and clientele, but I understand it could disappear at any moment.'

'A great shame. It has a splendid originality. I saw a young gentleman running from here as I arrived, shrieking the most extraordinary things.'

'It's the *hookhas*. They put all sorts of things in them here, some of which you no doubt tried yourself while in India.'

'I was careful what I put into my mouth, Graham.'

'Indeed. The owner of this place, a certain Dean Mahomet, is an interesting fellow. Made his fortune shampooing the heads of the wealthy, I understand. But this' – he indicates the coffee house with a grand wave – 'was somewhat beyond him, and has become a terrible financial burden, I hear.'

'It is a shame.'

'That it is, Harriott, that it is.'

'And Mrs Graham does well?'

At the mention of his wife, Graham does something rather

odd. He puts down his fork and looks at Harriott directly and, Harriott feels, somewhat coldly. He frowns, and looks down at his meal again. When he looks back up, his face has been partly smoothed back into a mask of bonhomie.

'Sarah is *perfectly* well,' he says. He smiles at some private joke which Harriott does not understand. There is a bitterness in the smile which Harriott can detect but not decode. 'I see so little of her. I am always at the Bow Street office or at Drury Lane. And she has her own *interests*, as I'm sure you understand.'

He looks at Harriott directly again, his eyes slightly narrowed, that harsh smile still in place. For a moment, Harriott feels at a complete loss. The conversation's anchor has come away and he is drifting dangerously. He feels as he often feels in a West End salon – lost in a maze of secretive double meanings, as if every word had been detached from the thing it described. He struggles to find a word, but then Graham seems to shake his head, like a fastidious but damp dog, and the bitterness leaves his face.

'And Harriott, what do you think of this? My son has been made post-captain!'

Harriott roars at this, with pleasure and some relief but also with a stab of envy that the other man's son should be thriving so well. His own sons have made no such impact on the world. But this envy is beneath him, and is quashed, and under it lies the memory of that odd little moment of tension which followed his mention of Sarah Graham. They toast Graham *fils* with a fine claret which neither feels goes particularly with the food, but no matter.

Graham begins enjoying himself again. His eyes sparkle and there is obviously hope that, now, all will be well between them.

'So, what of Wapping? What news from the river?' he asks.

'The usual pilfering and thuggery, but I do have something interesting for you. An odd murder, of a man recently returned to London from a long voyage.'

'Ah! The details, then, if you please.'

Harriott provides the said details, including the apparent lack of motive for a murder (he uses the word *motive* as if trying out a new French word, so unfamiliar is he with it, despite Horton's apparent obsession with it).

'The man was strangled?'

'It would appear so. There are the clear marks of a man's fingers on his throat.'

'Or a woman's.'

Harriott glares at Graham, as if he were about to lash out at the man's flippancy. But there is nothing flippant about Graham's expression. He is concentrating, fiercely.

'Or woman. In any case, we find the circumstances most odd, Graham.'

'*We* find? Ah, yes – I can sniff the detective processes of your remarkable Constable Horton.'

'Indeed you can. He has been investigating further. But now Shadwell gets in the way.'

'Shadwell?'

'They take the case as their own, and have forbidden Horton anywhere near it. I swear, it is like the Marr killings all over again.'

'Perhaps I can have a word with Sidmouth. Though I fear he is rather keen on Markland; admires the man's polish, he says. But why such a fuss, Harriott? Why should a death in Shadwell's jurisdiction exercise the hopelessly busy magistrate of the River Police?'

'There is a further complication. I have not told you of the man's ship.'

Harriott rather relishes what comes next, which does him little credit, but it is not often he can out-manoeuvre his clever Covent Garden friend.

'It is the *Solander*.'

At the mention of the ship, Graham's expression changes from one of cheerful bonhomie to one of sudden and complete engagement. Something like apprehension passes across his face like the trail of wind on a smooth ocean surface.

'Extraordinary! Sir Joseph Banks's ship?'

'The very same. You know the captain, Hopkins?'

'Indeed. Splendid fellow. Reliable, imaginative, cultured. Somewhat unusual for a sea captain, I would say, but as you know I have little interest in salty matters these days.'

'I met the fellow when the vessel arrived. He visited me at the Police Office.'

'So, this dead fellow was one of the crew?'

'So it would appear.'

'And he died on the *day* of the vessel's arrival in London?'

'Indeed.'

'Well, Shadwell must be dealt with, of course.' Harriott notes Graham's sudden passion for dealing with Shadwell. The mention of Sir Joseph's ship has changed the shape of the problem, that is clear.

'I believe Horton should investigate this matter,' says Harriott.

'Horton? Yes. Very good. Horton's new ideas seem just the ticket for this ... situation. So, how do you proceed?'

'Carefully. The coroner will report on Monday, but I expect little to come of it other than an open verdict. The doctor who examined the body confirmed what Horton first thought – the man was strangled.'

'And Horton maintains his customary *investigative* air?'

'Indeed. The man is a ferret. He can sniff out hearsay and evidence like a French pig sniffs out truffles. But what of *your* involvement in all this, Graham? Do you know the ship well?'

'Alas no, old friend.' Something about that *old friend* sounds forced to Harriott's ears, too self-consciously emollient. 'I am merely an investor via my connections within the Royal

Society. The trip is the creation of Sir Joseph, who has, if I may say so, been a devilish irritating creature these past weeks as we expected the ship's return. Every detail checked, every slither of news pored over, fussing and fretting like a woman organising her daughter's marriage.'

Graham pauses, as if to go on, but there it is again: the shadow between them, the narrative which cannot be mentioned, whispered by Graham months before during a dark winter's night. Harriott flounders for something to say, but then finds himself.

'I assume the monies involved are very great?' he says.

'For me, not at all. Merely enough to keep up appearances. For the President, a great deal more. I understand even he has had to mortgage some estates in the Midlands.'

'And the purpose of the trip?'

'Entirely botanical. Firstly, to demonstrate the latest techniques in transporting flora over long maritime distances. Secondly, to bring back seeds and plants for the Gardens at Kew. Thirdly, to stock Sir Joseph's herbarium with even more materials.'

'And the trip was a success?'

'Almost a complete one. A great many plants survived the trip, thanks to Hopkins and the techniques sketched out by the President. And even more seeds were returned. Many plants died, of course, but the losses were well within those predicted by Sir Joseph. He mourns the deaths, nevertheless.'

For a moment, Harriott finds himself wondering on that word 'deaths'.

'But it is a trip of months, not weeks,' he says. 'It is a miracle any plants survived at all.'

'Indeed. But as he ages, Sir Joseph's glass is always half-empty, not the half-full measure to which he had been formerly accustomed.'

'Well, he is not alone in finding the world a harder place as age increases.'

'Indeed not, Harriott, indeed not.'

They have barely nibbled at the edges of the food on the table, delicious though it is, and this now craves Harriott's full attention for some time. His appetite, which remains strong but declines rapidly with his mood, is such that he feels he could eat all evening, and he attacks the dishes with gusto.

'So, my dear Harriott,' says Graham, whose own appetite seems somewhat to have declined. 'I will discuss the matter with Sidmouth, and we will see if we can pull Markland away. Is there anything else with which I can help?'

'Well, Graham, I was rather hoping to approach Banks.'

'Ah.'

Graham looks like a man who has just received some expected bad news, and is considering how to respond to it.

'That may be difficult,' he says at last.

'Would he not want to be kept informed?'

'Almost certainly. But – and this is indelicate – he surely does not bother himself with the details of a trip such as the *Solander*'s.'

'A man's death can hardly be described as a mere detail, Graham.'

The Bow Street magistrate does not respond to that. But the meaning of his silence is clear. The Bow Street magistrate's sangfroid is legendary in London, but now he is fidgeting like a boy caught stealing from an orchard.

'Here is what I would do. In the first instance, you could try Brown.'

'Brown?'

'Robert Brown. His librarian and I suppose his assistant. He goes pretty much everywhere Sir Joseph goes. He can normally be found at the residence of the PRS, in Soho Square.'

'Yes. I know where Sir Joseph lives.'

'Ah, yes. Well, of course you do.'

Graham looks miserable. Harriott is full – *as full as an egg*, as his second wife used to say – but Graham has barely touched his food since the first mention of the *Solander*. Harriott says nothing for a while, waiting for Graham to take up the reins of the conversation. Eventually, the younger man appears to force himself to say something to break the uncomfortable silence.

'You do believe – you are *certain* – that this fellow was not just the victim of a simple dockside robbery?' he asks.

The question is an odd one. Perhaps even an impertinent one. Graham, it seems, would somehow wish that this matter would go away. Harriott controls his temper as he answers.

'It remains a possibility. But if so, what was taken? The man's money was left behind. Horton is trying to seek out the *why* of all this.'

'He will no doubt be successful.'

'I trust so.'

'You have no thoughts yourself?'

'None at all. The man's neck was bruised, I am told, confirming the analysis of strangulation. But he had a confoundedly happy grin on his face, which struck Horton as most odd. He seems to have died happy, in any case.'

Graham, ruefully, looks at his fork.

'We should all like to die happy,' he says.

'Indeed. But what does an illiterate sailor with grim lodgings and a fat old mistress have to be happy about?'

'I sometimes think an ordinary life would be more desirable than the one I lead.'

Harriott stares at Graham. It is as if the Bow Street magistrate had just admitted to a sympathy for the Jacobin revolutionaries. Graham barely notices, and then speaks with unaccustomed urgency.

'I will do what I can, Harriott. But tread carefully. And I beg of you – do not approach Sir Joseph until you are sure of what you know.'

'I am no child, Graham.'

'Indeed you are not. But Sir Joseph is one of this nation's great men. He can snap a man's reputation as easily as a tiger chews on a bird.'

From the *hookha* room comes the sound of young men, giggling.

ROTHERHITHE

At first, before he starts thinking, Horton feels only a dull
anger with himself as he stands in the shoddy boarding room,
surrounded by the scarlet of violent death. Abigail is on her
way back to Wapping, leaving him here to dwell on the cataclysm before him and the fact that the one thing that is never
supposed to happen has now happened, for the second time in
days.

Abigail has once again seen things she shouldn't ever see.

Something has been broken between him and his wife,
although it may be a something of which Abigail knows nothing. His wife was to have been preserved and protected in her
own calm world, a place in which the visions of this terrible
room were at worst unfamiliar shades. Of course Abigail
knows that violent death is as much a part of London as the
abusive fishwives of Billingsgate. She is an intelligent woman.
But she is also a special kind of woman, believes Horton, for
she is a woman who has been willing to take him up and tend
to his wounds both physical and spiritual. In the careful project around which he has reconstructed his life, protection of

this special woman has long been the single priority. In this he has now failed. Twice.

Why had he followed the man from the *Solander*? Why had he pursued this awful coincidence? Wasn't it the truth that, from the moment he saw the man getting out of the wherry, he had forgotten all about his obligations to his wife?

For there can be no doubt that Abigail did glimpse what was inside that room, just as she had seen the dead body of poor Sam Ransome. In that awful moment when she had looked around the door, she had seen the two bodies on the beds, the cascades of red upon the walls behind them, and the fearsome ribbons which lay where their necks should have been. She also saw the way the room had been torn to pieces, the furniture (what there was of it) knocked about, the men's canvas bags ransacked, clothes and boots flung around as if by some enraged animal. And perhaps she took in, or perhaps she did not, the first thing that Horton himself noticed: the terrible stillness of the two bodies on the beds, the way their faces looked up to the ceiling and their arms lay by their sides. The way they were smiling.

Abigail saw some or all of this, even before Horton was able to drag her away from the door, even while the young clerical man from the *Solander* screamed and sobbed in the hallway behind them. Horton had folded her face into his shoulder as he'd pushed her away, pulling the door closed behind him, feeling a growing sense of panic. How was he to both preserve the evidence of the room and protect his wife, with all these people shoving and shouting? If he took her out into the street, no doubt some curious fellow would open that terrible door, and then another type of hell would break loose, the avaricious curiosity of the mob, and whatever evidence lay in the room would be destroyed.

These thoughts took barely a second to cohere, and within

that second Abigail herself answered his question. She pulled her face away from his shoulder, and the cold rage Horton felt with himself dropped in temperature even further when he saw her pale expression and the firm cast of her eyes. She looked shocked and appalled, but she also looked determined. She seemed hard at that moment, he remembered thinking. *And I have made her so*.

'I am calm, Charles,' said Abigail. 'I feel the terror of this place, but I am calm. Now, do what you must do.'

And she had turned and left the lodging house, her shoulders small and strong in the shouting throng. He remembered the way the back of her head had looked as she lay sleeping the night after they had discovered the body of Sam Ransome. His back to the door in that noisy Rotherhithe house, he'd felt a sick and unforgettable mix of anger, shame, pride and loneliness. The image was locked in his mind as if in some future anniversary gift, a locket containing the picture of the wife leaving her husband with a determined sadness, the husband abandoning his wife to some remorseless and unforgiving Duty.

The strange man who'd brought them there was still on his haunches against the opposite wall. He was making a lowing sound like an injured cat as Abigail walked away. A group of children were watching him curiously, while adults stood around shouting at each other and demanding to know of Horton what had happened.

'Give us room!' shouted Horton. 'There has been a terrible crime perpetrated in this house. I am an officer of the River Police Office, under the authority of magistrate John Harriott, and in his name I am securing the room from any entry. Who is the landlord of this place?'

A fat man with no hair and a bloodstained apron made himself known, and began to complain of the intrusion, but Horton shouted him down.

'Sir, there is no time to debate this matter. It seems the crime committed in this building has only just happened, perhaps even minutes ago.'

A female shriek went up at that, and a bubble of chatter.

'I must insist that no one enters the room behind me. I shall go in there myself shortly to secure what evidence there is. I need to get a message to the Police Office in Wapping immediately. Is there a boy or ticket porter here willing to take it?'

A dirty youth of perhaps fourteen presented himself. Horton decided to take a chance on him, however unpromising his appearance.

'Tuppence for you, lad, to take a message to John Harriott, magistrate of the River Police Office on Wapping Street. Message is: *terrible crime committed in boarding house between Rotherhithe and Deptford, possibly related to current investigations, require immediate assistance of four officers.* Repeat it, please.'

The youth did so, but not to Horton's satisfaction, so they tried again. When the youth had repeated it perfectly three times, Horton sent him away, saying he'd be paid when he returned with River Police constables. The youth looked like he was thinking about complaining about this proposal, but after another close look at Horton he appeared to decide on trusting him, and left.

Horton turned his attention to the young man from the *Solander*, who was still sobbing, his face hidden in the forearm laid across his knees. Horton grabbed both the man's arms and pulled him to his feet.

'Calm yourself, man. You must be calm.'

The young man's despair was painted onto his face. Horton made some rapid but, he hoped, accurate conclusions. The man had initially run out of the boarding house because he was alarmed by something, which also explained his reluctance to return when Horton had approached him. But this wailing despair was something else. It had the flavour of deeper fears, but also of a desperate sadness. His reaction had changed between leaving the boarding house the first time, and returning with Horton and Abigail. Which must mean something else had changed as well.

'Listen to me.'

Horton pushed the hubbub of the crowd around them away. His back was still firmly against the closed door of the room. No one could pass him. The other man's head was slumped and his shoulders were still bouncing with half-swallowed sobs, but he looked up then, and his brown-black eyes were cloudy and waterlogged.

'What is your name?' asked Horton.

The man looked momentarily confused, as if he couldn't remember.

'Nott . . . Peter Nott.'

The name was as plain as the man's clerical clothes but somehow in contrast to his face, with its deep tan and smooth, fat cheeks.

'Nott, do you know me?'

'You . . . you're a constable. You came onto the ship yesterday.'

'That's right. And as a constable I need to ask you what happened here.'

The eyes widened and the young man looked left and right, seeking out something. Somebody, perhaps.

'Nott, you must tell me.'

The eyes continued to search the hallway, looking at the surrounding faces as he answered.

'The door was open. I knocked on it, but there was no answer. So I went in. I found them asleep on their beds, but the room . . . The room was in a mess.'

'The first time you came in here, on your own?'

'Yes. The first time.'

'What made you run out?'

'That. Only that. The fact that the room had been ... *pawed over*. And they were asleep.'

'You saw no blood, Nott? The men were alive?'

'They were *asleep*. The room had been *searched*. But I have no doubt they were alive.'

'You were agitated when you ran out.'

'Yes, yes. I was. I had hoped to find them awake and undisturbed. When I found them asleep, both of them at the same time, while all around them their belongings in a mess ... I panicked, Constable. It did not seem usual. I even shouted to awake them, but they did not respond.'

'There was no blood, Nott? That first time you went in?'

'No blood, Constable.'

The eyes flicked around again, as if an army of assassins were lurking in the shadows.

'Do you know these men?'

'Yes.'

'Their names?'

'Bob Attlee. Tommy Arnott. They are men from the *Solander*.'

The names settled the matter. Horton ordered the landlord of the place to lock Nott in an empty room, and, wonder of wonders, the man did it, although there was no legal reason he should do so. Indeed, it occurred to Horton that if there were a parish constable or headborough in this crowd of people, the omnipresent question of jurisdiction would already have presented itself, and he'd have been arguing the finer points of it right now, rather than preparing to investigate the room behind him.

So he went back in. Here he is now, sniffing the air, watching the scene, turning it over and over in his mind.

It is perhaps a half-hour since he first entered the boarding house with Abigail. He wonders where she might be now, then forces himself to stop. He is overwhelmed by a growling sense of time rushing past, of trails going cold. If Nott is telling the truth, then the killer was in this place only minutes ago. Indeed, he might be in the house still. Might be in the *room* still, so little attention has Horton given it.

His first glimpse, with Abigail, had given a solid impression, but again the *frenzy* with which the room has been ransacked strikes him. The two dead men are lying in their beds, their throats in tatters, the sheets beneath and around them dyed a deep purplish red, the walls behind them splattered in an awful fashion. The scene in the room is of a mighty struggle, and yet the men lie serenely in their beds, as if dreaming of country meadows and apple-cheeked girls. Despite the dreadful purple that surrounds their necks like a ruff, they do seem to be smiling in their sleep. It would indeed have looked disturbingly unreal to Nott when he'd first come in: two men sleeping the sleep of exhausted children, while all around them is chaos. The echoes from Sam Ransome's chamber are resounding.

Horton tries to picture the scene as it developed. Did the men fight, and then calm themselves before retiring? Or did they struggle with their assailant, or more probably assailants, before he killed them and then laid them out in bed? But why the need for that final laying-down? And then there is Nott's claim that the men were only asleep when he first came in, that the slaughter happened between Nott leaving the room and returning with Horton.

How had the killer managed to make his escape, if the wounds were so fresh, without Nott having seen him? Horton tries to imagine the scene. The killer slays the men in their sleep, the blood fresh. But then he searches the room, perhaps for something essential to the case. That must have taken some time – judging by the mess, it was something that was hard to find. And then he left.

But that would mean Nott was lying about there being no blood when he first went into the room. And the blood was still fresh by the time Horton had arrived. How long would it have taken for blood to thicken? Minutes? Hours? Horton rather suspected the former.

And what happened between Nott first coming into the room, and then coming back with Horton? Had the killer really left, and then come back in that small sliver of time, and taken these men's lives with such haste?

Horton goes deep inside himself as he thinks. Abigail would have recognised the expression: slightly narrowed eyes, thinned lips, a few deep furrows in the brow, the occasional fingers through the hair, the slow walk, the bent head. Horton is *imagining* himself into the murder scene. John Harriott too has seen him do this, and it always makes the older man profoundly uncomfortable to see it.

He begins prowling around the room, taking some notes and (in a new departure) making some sketches. He has taken to carrying paper with him to write on wherever he goes. He is by no means aware of using any kind of technique. He takes simple steps. He assumes that some kind of answer to the question 'who did this?' is available in this room. Therefore, it follows that whatever kind of signs there may be in the room need to be protected from any potential disturbance, even though the room itself is disordered beyond all apparent pattern.

Another half-hour passes while he watches the room and takes it in. He stands in the centre of the floor. He does not know why. He sniffs. Again, he does not know why. He tries to concentrate on a meaningless mark in a corner of the room, up above him, where the ceiling meets the wall. He forces himself to look at that and not at the room itself.

He has managed, as far as is possible, to maintain the integrity of the room. And now he is standing in its centre, trying as far as he can not to see something, so that he might see something. He catalogues the things he sees.

The cups: two of them, almost identical, next to each of the beds, lying on their sides.

An open bag at the foot of one of the beds which reminds him of something. The sea chest in Ransome's room.

A swatch of red cloth hanging from the underside of the frame of one of the beds.

The view from the little window. It looks across the river to a windmill on the Millwall bank.

There is no money in the room. Whoever did this took it, or Attlee and Arnott had already spent it.

All these things and dozens more swirl around his thoughts. He picks up one of the cups and notes the dark sediment at the bottom. He picks up the other cup, and it is just the same. He checks the open bag, and sees that its contents are in a mess, as if they'd been stuffed back. He pulls the red cloth off the little splinter of wood it's attached itself to. He looks out of the window to the windmill.

He sniffs the air again. Something is missing. No smell of alcohol, and no smell of tobacco. Perhaps the only seamen's room in London without those smells.

He takes the cups and the cloth and puts them into the open bag, ready to take them back to the police office. He finds the key to the door on the inside, removes it and steps out into the hall, pulling the door shut and locking it. Ideas and connections are beginning to swirl in his mind.

From somewhere, he hears the sound of a violin.

KEW

Robert Brown arrives at Kew after a long day in the Soho Square library. Banks is insistent that he spend as much time with the Otaheite plants as possible, but administrative matters need his attention too. He had rather lost himself in his work, and had been alarmed to receive a message from Sir Joseph that his presence was required at Kew, and immediately. He is to attend Banks at the Great Stove, with all speed. Characteristically, there is no explanation for the summons.

It is another twilit evening of no little beauty. The river has the same dusty golden quality, the sunlight refracted through air thick with pollen and insects and edging the wavelets on the water's surface with gold. The herons sit along the riverbank like bishops in the House of Lords, monitoring the growing slumber of the stream.

Brown's carriage drops him at the gate into the Gardens, just at the edge of Kew Green. It is an odd thing, this little gate, hardly keeping with the splendours within. One expects to find a compact cottage garden, attended by two eccentric spinster sisters, rather than what is actually there. Brown walks through the gate into the Gardens, planted by Princess Augusta in the midst of the last century, now almost entirely the preserve of Sir Joseph. He walks through the Gardens to the Great Stove. Behind the Stove rises the solid boxy elegance of the Orangery and behind that the neat, unobtrusive Dutch House. In front and around those two buildings Kew opens out and sets the stage for the more eccentric construction projects of the King: an expanse of open ground, once containing the White House, knocked down as a precursor to George's building of the crazy, mercilessly mocked Castellated Palace on the bank of the river.

The King, prior to the return of his illness and the installation of his son as Regent, had spent much time developing Kew, both through construction and through acquisition. In this he followed the careful footsteps of his brilliant mother Augusta, for whom Kew had been both a mission and a hobby. Neighbouring estates had been gobbled up and replanted throughout the previous century, and even now Kew still has a fluid identity. Is it a pleasure garden? A working farm? A horticultural laboratory? For a while it was even a madhouse, the resting place for a King with a departed mind who has now himself departed for Windsor.

Madhouse, greenhouse, farmhouse, funhouse. Kew is all these things. As if in recognition of that fact Brown sees a small flock of sheep shuffling across the expanse of lawn where the White House had once stood, remnants of the merino flock which Sir Joseph Banks had smuggled in via Portugal twenty years before and which was, even now, transforming Britain's wool trade. Nature, Commerce and Empire were all stakeholders in this place, and Banks himself was, as it were, the Company Secretary, trading one off against the other in the name of Britannia.

For almost thirty years, Daniel Solander had been Joseph

Banks's amanuensis and philosophic inspiration, the quiet and popular thinker beside Sir Joseph's gregarious, ambitious and ruthless politician. Solander, no doubt, had advised both Banks and his friend the King on the botanical basis for these Gardens. He had also, again with no doubt, walked through these very meadows and copses, watching the great collections from around the world take root in this sandy soil beside the Thames. Here, all the world's flora came together, a botanical treasure trove of hoarded delights among which were those plants Banks and Solander had brought back with them on the *Endeavour* forty years before, the great Prime Movers of every botanical endeavour since.

Brown has now almost reached the Great Stove, the largest plant house in the Gardens. The wisteria which runs all along the eastern side of the Stove and which was exploding in magnificence only weeks before has now given way to a lush green cloud, and it quivers as if in excitement at what is happening inside. The Stove, erected by William Chambers fifty years ago, is heated by dry stoves at either end via flues in the wall, and by a great bark stove in the middle, based on a Dutch design, in which oak bark ground to a powder is mixed with the sawdust from elms and left to ferment, causing a natural heated mulch into which potted exotics can be placed. Two men are waiting outside the Stove even now, poor-looking fellows whom Brown takes to be the under-gardeners charged with maintaining its temperature. They nod towards Brown with the minimum accepted level of respect. He is, after all, only a librarian. He does not speak to them – Brown's sense of himself and his position in society is as carefully calibrated as any other intelligent Scot in London – and walks straight into the hothouse.

The change in temperature never fails to shock him, the great thick brick walls and expanses of glass storing the Stove's heat within. There has been a recent watering, and the air is heavy with the moisture and that sense of oppressive closeness which Brown can still remember from the tropical forests of New Holland. He is not in England anymore; he is deep within some strange green composite of a tropical world, where growth is rapid and change constant. Not for the first time, Brown finds himself wondering about how plants *grow* and what can be said about it more intelligently than the careful euphemisms of today's botanical texts. The thickness in the air and the quivering in the leaves could make one think that the forest itself had a soul, a watching mind as old as Time and just as pitiless.

Banks is sitting in his great wheelchair in the same place as before, when he'd planted the little sapling from Otaheite. He is leaning forward as if looking for it, and Brown does the same as he approaches, but cannot see where the plant is just now in this dim light.

'Sir Joseph,' he says, and Banks does not look at him, but does reply.

'Brown. I thought you would be here earlier.'

'I had business to attend to in town, Sir Joseph.'

'What on earth kind of business would you have in town that could be more important than what is happening here?'

But the question is quiet and, as Brown takes it at least, rhetorical. Banks is not particularly interested in Brown's business in town. He is, though, deeply and unaccountably interested in the shiny green tree close by where the sapling was planted. Brown looks at it, and in a snap judgement takes it to be another type of breadfruit. It is perhaps four feet tall, its leaves oval and shiny green.

'Was there something you wanted, Sir Joseph?'

'Yes, Brown, there was. This tree, here. What do you take it to be?'

'It appears to be *Artocarpus incisa*, Sir Joseph. The same species as was transplanted to the West Indies under your supervision. I do not believe one has been successfully grown in this country before now. I had no idea we had such a specimen at Kew. I'm astonished to have missed it, or not to have been informed of its presence here.'

'Indeed. But that is perhaps not the most interesting thing about this plant.'

'It is *Artocarpus incisa*?'

'Well, perhaps, Brown. Though if it is it's like no other *Artocarpus* I've seen before.'

'Indeed, sir? What are its distinctive differences?'

'One of fructification, and one of habit. It only has female flowers. The *Artocarpus incisa* is hermaphrodite, as you know; the male flowers appear first, followed immediately by the female flowers. Yet this tree only has female flowers; male flowers may yet appear, or they may not. In either case, it is very different. But the difference in habit is even more distinctive.'

'Yes, Sir Joseph.'

'Brown, this is the sapling from the *Solander* I planted. It has grown four feet in two days.'

FOUR

Oft have I wish'd, for such you love, that I
Were metamorphos'd to some curious fly;
Beyond the main I'd speed my eager way,
And buzz around you all the live-long day.
Nor would I be some ombrageous tree,
That shades thy grot, and vegetate for thee;
At thy approach I'd all my flowers expand,
And weave my wanton foliage around thy hand.

T.Q.Z Esq., 'An Epistle From Oberea, Queen of
Otaheite, To Joseph Banks Esq.', 1773

TAHITI

In the years which followed the death of the prince's brother, the island changed. There were wars, a great many wars, between different groups and even between different islands. Europeans continued to arrive and leave, bringing iron, alcohol and an ever-growing collection of new diseases, and as each year passed more and more of the islanders succumbed to whatever the Europeans carried with them, be it alcohol, guns or the invisible substances that crawled into their lungs and choked them. The Christian missionaries grew in number, then reduced in number, then all but disappeared, fleeing to other places in the face of the wars. They returned in the lulls between fighting, and continued with the work of translating their texts into the island language. When the fighting on the island grew particularly bad, there were times when the only missionary that remained was the oldest, tallest and fiercest of them. His sole companion was the young man who lived with him, who was shunned by all the islanders because of his English father and his poor, doomed island mother.

But the most important thing that happened was that the

prince stopped being little. He became a man. He was now the eldest son in his family, and (he supposed) a sort of chieftain. But his father endured and, whatever custom and tradition said about inheritance, it was his father who ruled the family and who paid tribute to the king, even while that king fought for his very existence against the forces ranged against him. The prince felt none of the ambition which had consumed his brother; he felt no desire to rule. His father was welcome to it, and in any case where was the future in ruling over a realm in which the subjects were, one by one, succumbing to death? Even the king's father had taken his name – *Pomare* – from the island words which meant 'night cough', in memory of the daughter who was taken by whatever European poison filled her delicate lungs.

The woods were filled with the dead. Their spirits choked the skies and the gods, if they were still there, became angry with the phalanxes of deceased they were expected to accommodate. The *haiva* danced and danced, not just in the prince's dreams, but throughout the living days and weeks and months, until even the men who took the role of *haiva* themselves died. The surviving islanders struggled on, in the face of war and disease, and as the years passed more and more of them began to find themselves attracted to the propositions of the Christian missionaries, who seemed to tell a tale which explained that this living world – which had once been so bounteous but was now so terrible – was in fact designed to be thus and was only an overture to the infinite pleasures of Paradise. The islanders, who had long been living on Paradise but now saw it poisoned, began to understand what the Christians were talking about.

The old ways endured, though, even while the king intimated that he might, one day soon, become a Christian himself. The people kept the *maraes* intact and tended them, they looked after their dead in the old ways, and the dark sect of *arioi* maintained their dancing, singing, sacrificing ways.

The prince himself had become attracted to a particular cult within the *arioi* to which he had been introduced by a young prince from a neighbouring fiefdom. Indeed, this cult occupied almost all his thoughts and helped explain his lack of interest in manoeuvring against his father. The cult convened at a *marae* high in the hills, where it was said the *tupapau,* the spirits of the dead, gathered for their own ceremonies. Given the thousands of deaths on the island, the prince sometimes thought, those ceremonies must be crowded indeed.

To reach the plateau where this *marae* was to be found, one followed a path along a river, where the rocks on either side grew and grew. You crossed the stream again and again to find the safest way, until eventually you reached an acre or two of nearly flat ground covered in fern. The air here was filled with a kind of dust, which some of the members of the cult believed was the effluence of the dead. When the prince asked his father what this stuff might be (without mentioning where he had seen it), he was told it was actually crumbling fungi blown from within the dead wood of trees.

On this flat ground, among the ferns, stood one particular tree. It was said by the cult's adherents that the tree had been there for centuries, but that was impossible; the tree quivered with young life. It was a bristling breadfruit tree, but one from which no fruit had ever been harvested. Instead, the adherents of this little half-secret cult cut the useless flowers and leaves of the tree and left them to dry down, which they did unfathomably rapidly. Using an old kettle which had been stolen from some visiting ship in the distant past, they then consumed the leaf of the tree as tea. No one knew who'd been the first to try this, but the technique was shown carefully to each new adherent, who learned how to boil the water, add the dried leaf and then pour it out into the little wooden cups they fashioned for the purpose.

Under the influence of this leaf they saw visions and experienced wonders, benign wonders of such beauty that they had been drawn to adapt the *marae* there in the centre of the island to celebrate the tree, its leaf and the wandering spirits which settled in that place. They promised each other not to tell anyone other than fellow *arioi*, and preferably younger *arioi*, of this magical place. They would meet there every seven or eight days, a group of up to a dozen young men and women, all of them *arioi* and island nobility of some kind. They would drink the tea and laugh and dance and sing, and the tree would quiver with delight and watch over them, far away from the beaches where angry men fired European guns at one another and European microbes hung patiently in the air, the malign spirits of distant islands.

RATCLIFFE

Colby Potter is dreaming. His body is flat and quiet on a dirty bed in a Ratcliffe boarding house. His friend Elijah Frost is dreaming on a bed at the other side of the room. It is four days since the two men left the *Solander* with Jeremiah Critchley and the other men in his group.

Colby Potter has been dreaming for four days.

He is walking down a lane lined with trees. It is a familiar lane, one connected with his childhood. It runs like an undulating river through a tunnel of trees. This is Oak Lane, the road he walked down from his father's cottage as a boy, trudging off to work in the school at the top of the hill, one of a small army of boys who cleaned and fetched and swept and dug around the grounds, invisible to the other children, more fortunate, who were busy learning to read and to write and to dispute.

Colby the boy is much as Colby the man will be: relaxed with his lot in life, a moderately well-fed child living with a moderately well-employed labourer in a house without women and without disharmony. In his dream his stomach is full of the glutinous porridge his father would make on the fire, warmed by the strange-tasting tea from Otaheite. His father, in the dream, had boiled water in an old iron kettle, nothing like anything of the implements that had really existed in their little Sevenoaks cottage. The man Colby dreams of the boy Colby wondering where this kettle had come from, and why it had been vaguely unsettling.

It is a sunlit Kent morning, the kind of morning which England bestows on its people as if in confirmation of the nationality of God. Colby is tired, and is becoming disconcerted by the realization that Oak Lane is longer today than it has any right to be, stretching away into a green distance through a tunnel of leaves, the sunlight striping the road like the back of a tiger. He thinks of his father, and as soon as he does so a picture leaps into his mind: his father cleaning the old iron kettle, rubbing its now-cool sides with a harsh cloth, and dropping the kettle onto the floor as smoke starts to pour impossibly from its ragged spout, filling the little cottage with grey impurities and the distant giggles of women.

The smoke disappears up the cottage chimney. Colby cannot see his father, because now he is watching the smoke as it streams up and out of the chimney. The head of the smoke peeks, dragon-like, from the chimney pot, sweeping across the forest trees in a full circle before locating what it is after, and then the head pulls the body of the smoke from the chimney and it rumbles the bricks as the house gives birth to it. A single smoke-serpent now, it pours down the roof and along the ground and into the trees.

Heading straight for Colby.

This is when what had been disconcerting becomes terrible. Each time he has the dream, during these four days, the fear is greater, because each time the smoke from the chimney grows darker, more knowing, and the girlish laughter which accompanies its progress rises in pitch and intensity. By now it is the cackling of a girl on the point of turning into a witch, still with some humanity but with a growing awareness of her own capacity. Colby hears it coming, and he runs down Oak Lane, through the tunnel of trees.

His breath is loud and repetive – in-out, in-out, in-out, a fearful desperate march to escape. The giggling of the female is a waltz: ha-ha-HA, ha-ha-HA, ha-ha-HA. And though he cannot see it, dare not look back, he knows that the smoke-serpent is undulating in time to this regular rhythm, a snake dancing on the air.

Colby knows, with a grim dismay, that he is being chased. He must stay in the middle of the road. He must stay out of the woods.

His father appears to his right, carrying an axe.

'Where are you going, Colby?' he asks.

'To work, Father,' Colby says, still breathing in march-time.

'If you come through the woods on this side, the way is easier,' his father says.

This is a lie, and it scares Colby.

A woman appears on Colby's left side. An Otaheite woman, her hair loose down her back, dressed in that strange bark-cloth they wore, a tattoo of a tree carved into her shoulder.

'Where are you going, Colby?' she asks.

'To work, woman,' Colby says.

'If you come through the woods on this side, the way is easier,' she says.

'You must choose, Colby, soon,' says his father, and points up the road. Colby can see that the road has split down the middle, a fissure that winds down the lane. 'Don't fall down the crack.'

Colby tries to stop, but can't. His feet are no longer in his control. He is walking, walking, walking, and the only thing he can do, the only thing that is left to him, is to choose. Right or left. Father or lover. Oak or ... What?

The Otaheite woman touches his arm, and the sensation of her skin is as hot as fire and as soft as silk. She leaves her hand there and he feels himself leaning her way, changing his direction, heading into the forest on her side of the road, forest which is no longer green and mossy but shining and rain-drenched and quivering with life ...

His father grabs his other arm, and shouts at him.

'Listen, Colby! Listen! You are in danger! You cannot see the danger!'

The woman's hand is soft on his arm, but it somehow pulls insistently, and his father's fingers are loosening.

'Colby! Colby!'

The fissure approaches. It is wide, as wide as the Channel, as wide as the Pacific, and soon he will fall into it. The woman presses her fingers into his arm and with that his father's grip loosens and disappears and now he is on the left-hand side of the fissure. It is empty and black in there, as dark as a mine. He is walking, but the woman's touch has gone. He looks to his left, and she is no longer there.

But there is something else in the trees now, something huge and hungry and angry. It smoulders inside the quivering trees, it screams and it shouts, its high voice that of a woman with murdered children. It streams through the trees, closer and closer, and Colby veers away from it, his insides turned to ash, and one step, two step, he falls sideways into the fissure, down into the blackness ...

Colby Potter is dreaming. He has been dreaming for four days.

ROTHERHITHE

Horton consults his list of the *Solander*'s crew as the men start to come into the Rotherhithe tavern. There are a total of forty-eight names, starting with the commander, Captain Hopkins. Almost two thirds of these names make up the sailing crew of officers and seamen, while the remainder are day-men, not on the watch, including four gardeners. Three of the thirteen able seamen are now dead.

Horton has asked for as many of the crew as possible to be sent to this particular tavern. The gardeners are already in Kew, and he will have to travel there to meet them. Hopkins is vague as to when and where the officers might be spoken to, and maintains a seaman's insistence that Horton come to the officers, and not the other way around. But he agrees to send the remaining crew and the day-men to meet Horton at the appointed place.

The tavern where Horton has been waiting is a small, old place, a fragment of an older time on the Surrey shore. The place has been made anachronistic by the new brickwork of Rotherhithe, which had begun to trace the outlines of the new dock system like ivy climbing a new wall. This old tavern is one of many which line Rotherhithe Street. The name of the place commends it to the recent past before men began digging the new docks into the land: the *Narwhal*. The tavern is a different type of whale, one with the magical ability to swallow up men sober and disgorge them drunk.

As they come in the men from the *Solander* look no different from any other gang of sailors recently returned from a voyage. Their skin is cracked and brown, and even a few days after their return they still dress with their open-necked shirts and scarves around their neck, as if they were beating to quarters off Barbados rather than shivering in a London early summer. Nor do these men show any sign of the fatal illnesses that can break out in a ship carving its way home from the Pacific; no flux or scurvy, no coughing or bleeding gums or fever or grey, anxious faces. They are robust and defiant, scruffy but strong, ennobled and empowered by being in a pack, unshaven, salty, and muttering.

He stands up from his table as the last of them comes in. Captain Hopkins has not accompanied him. He'd offered to, but Horton had refused, conscious of how easy it would be to fall in with such a man, and to forget that the captain, like the rest of his crew, is a possible perpetrator. No fraternising, even with officers.

'Men,' he says, putting an authority in his voice which he doesn't quite feel. They stare, neither acknowledging him nor quite ignoring him. There are fifteen of them standing there, which means a good number are unaccounted for. 'I am Waterman Constable Charles Horton of the River Police Office. No doubt you know why you're here. I wish to speak with each of you about Sam Ransome.'

'Ye can speak of him,' says one of the men, an older red-haired Scot. 'But don't expect nae nourishment from the words. The man was a waste of God's air.'

There are mutters of agreement.

'Then we'll start with you,' says Horton, and the Scot scowls at him. 'Your name?'

'Angus Carrick. Commonly called Red Angus. And who are ye to ask questions?'

'I have given you my name.'

'Aye, that you have. But I don't know ye from Adam, lad. On whose authority are you askin' us these things?'

The man is belligerent but clearly intelligent. Horton looks him in the eye as he speaks.

'You are here under the command of your captain. He himself is bound to assist me in my enquiries, since I investigate under the authority of John Harriott, superintending magistrate of the River Police Office, constituted by Parliament in the name of the King to prevent crime and misdemeanours on the river. Any man who does not assist willingly will be arrested and taken to the Police Office in Wapping, where he will be locked away and interrogated at my leisure. Does this make things clearer?'

The men say nothing to that, and Red Angus Carrick looks away.

Another man, tall and blond as a Viking, speaks up.

'Ask away, mate,' he says, quietly but firmly. 'There's little need for violent speech.'

Horton looks at him, and thinks that perhaps he was deceived. Where Carrick was sparky and resentful, this man looks both exhausted and resigned, though it is clear the other crewmen pay him significant respect. He is one of the two or three born leaders among the men of every vessel, the ones who transmit the wishes of the officers through their compliance but who also hold the possibility of mutiny in their hands. But he is also the sickliest looking of the whole bunch of them, obviously dog-tired. Perhaps he has been whoring and drinking his way up and down the river ever since the *Solander* returned.

'And I will use no violent speech. Your name?'

'Jeremiah Critchley, sir. Carpenter's mate.'

'Very good. Now, the rest of you, starting with Carrick: name, and position in the crew, if you please.' He sits down, and makes ready to tick the men's names off the list Hopkins has provided.

The Scot scowls. But then, Horton thinks, Scots do scowl, do they not?

'Cook,' he says, and one-by-one they follow him.

'Calder. Boatswain's mate.'

'Haddow. Sailmaker.'

'Bywater. Able seaman.'

'Dougherty. Butcher.'

'Forshaw. Surgeon's assistant.'

'Beasley. Able seaman.'

'Fitton. Able seaman.'

'Gilks. Cooper.'

'Flaherty. Able seaman.'

'Brooks. Captain's clerk.'

'Mackay. Quartermaster's mate.'

'Nunn. Sailmaker.'

'Craven. Able seaman.'

'Thank you. We'll conduct the interviews upstairs. If you don't mind, Carrick. The rest of you wait here until I call for you.'

The interviews are generally sticky affairs, but it is a stickiness to which Horton has become used in the months since he has been investigating incidents on behalf of John Harriott. Ordinary people do not recognise his right to ask them questions; they feel he is impertinent. Usually they demand (as Red Angus had) to understand under whose authority he shelters.

Even when he explains matters they seem to think the only appropriate place for an *interrogation* is a court room, under the eyes of a judge. This is the kind of questioning a thousand years of history has taught them.

Horton has therefore had to learn how to conduct these interviews, and has begun thinking of them as theatrical performances in which there are two players. For some subjects he affects a comradely warmth. With others, he adopts an officious asperity. But always he is playing a role. Captain Hopkins had been easy; the two of them had fallen into an open way of talking, as between two equals meeting at a coffee house. The crewmen of the *Solander* are another matter, and Horton finds he has to be constantly reminding them both of the power of his office and the justice of his investigation.

The first, Red Angus Carrick, is arguably the most difficult, not least because he will set the tone for the others, like the first act in a play. The room above the *Narwhal* is small and contains only an armchair and a side table. On the table Horton has placed a pile of paper and a quill with a pot of ink. He goes to stand by the window.

The Scot is a big man, but once he is seated Horton instantly feels more comfortable. He leans back on the windowsill, looking directly at Carrick.

'You had little time for Ransome, then.'

The Scot has relaxed, no longer playing out a role for his shipmates. His demeanour is now playfully grumpy rather than aggressive.

'Nae one of us had time for Ransome.'

'He had no comrades on board the ship?'

'We're all comrades, Officer Charles Horton,' says the Scot. 'At sea, a crew watches for itself. And for each other.' He sneers at Horton, in that universal look of contempt for the landlubber that all sailors share. Horton lets it pass. No lubber he.

'Friends, then. Did Ransome have any friends?'

'Why are you asking me this?'

'Because Ransome is dead.'

'Ransome was killed for his wages. 'Tis common knowledge along the wharves.'

'It is?' says Horton, navigating untruths as carefully as he can. 'Well, we need to be sure. There are some particulars of his death which are worthy of investigation.'

'Particulars?' sneers the Scot. 'You sound like a City clerk.'

Horton bristles finally.

'No, sir, not a clerk. An officer of the River Police. And a former lieutenant in the King's Navy, man and boy. I outrank you in experience and in office, cook.'

The Scot laughs, looking him up and down as if to test the truth of his claim.

'Lieutenant, eh? And why not captain, Constable Horton? Was it not to your liking?'

Impertinent but perceptive. Horton waits a moment, holding the Scot's eyes until they drop away.

'Did anything happen on the voyage which might have caused another crewman to have killed Ransome?'

'Ah, that's it then. You think one of us did for him. But not an officer, eh?'

'The officers will be interviewed.'

'Always us first, though, is it not?'

'Carrick, I am not here to argue below-decks politics with you.' Though I would have some things to say which would shock you, Horton thinks.

'Mr Horton, or whatever it is I call ye, this voyage wasn't like most others. Barely a bad moment, good winds, no storms, and no doubt I don't need to describe the attractions of Otaheite to an old Navy hand like *you*.'

'Humour me, Carrick. Describe the attractions to me.'

The Scot visibly warms to the question. His eyes look into a tropical distance as he speaks.

'Most beautiful place in the world. Green mountains with waterfalls coming down. Warm, soft sand. Rain which kisses you and then dries in minutes. Fish and veggies and drink like nectar. And the *women*, Horton. Ah, the women. You've never seen the like. They come to you each night, wearing nothing but a smile, and they stroke and play and ... Well, we're men of the world, Horton. But the women of England, even the women of Scotland herself – they'd poison every bitch on that island if they knew. '

Red Angus smiles in blissful remembrance.

'And Ransome? He enjoyed the fruits of Otaheite?'

'Hard to say. Hardly saw him once we were there. He was probably enjoying himself somewhere about.'

'You were left to yourselves on the island? What of Captain Hopkins?'

'Oh, he dinnae mind. We were there best part of five weeks, and we were given every third day off. The only ones who worked all the time were the plant collectors, the – what's the word – *botanists*. They were scrabblin' all over that place, digging up all sorts. We only went back to the normal watch when we left the island.'

'So men were left to their own devices much of the time.'

'Oh, aye.'

'Did you know Ransome before you left on the voyage?'

'No. Didn't know anyone, though. Was my first time in London, though think I'll stay now.'

'Why?'

'Wait for another trip south. I'm thirsty to get back there, Horton. You would be, too.'

Carrick does indeed look hungry for the place. Talking about it has made him so. Horton recognises the lust for voyaging in the eyes. He too used to feel the tug of warmer, distant climes. Still does, when the wind is in the right direction and Abigail is not nearby.

'You did not answer my question. Did Ransome have any particular friends on the ship?'

'Friends? It's not a bloody schoolroom, man.'

'Did he know Attlee and Arnott?'

Carrick looks at him for a moment.

'Attlee and Arnott?'

'Yes, Carrick. Did Ransome know them? Were they his friends?'

The cook thinks for a moment.

'Yes. Yes, I suppose they were Sam's friends. If Sam could be said to have any.'

'And were you friendly with Attlee and Arnott?'

'Bloody hell, man, why are you asking about them?'

'Because they were killed. Yesterday. Just down the street from here.'

It's a petty little thing, this sense of victory which sweeps through Horton at the revelation, but there is something to cherish in the way the cockiness sweeps out of Carrick's cheeks and for the first time he looks both impressed and afraid.

After that, the interrogation goes more smoothly. Carrick is compliant now, almost humble, but claims to have had no friendship with Attlee or Arnott, nor to have known where they were living once they left the ship, nor to have any idea as to why someone should kill them. Horton asks whether Ransome, Attlee or Arnott were particularly attached to drink or tobacco or any other intoxicant, but at this Carrick looks bemused and Horton does not pursue it.

'Well then, Carrick. That will be all. If you could just write down your name, age and place of residence while you're

138

ashore on the paper next to you, I would appreciate it. And say nothing of Attlee and Arnott on your way out.'

The Scot looks at him through narrowed eyes, and then forms his mouth in a tight little knowing smile. He turns, dips the quill in the ink, and does as Horton asks.

All of them have similar stories to tell. Didn't know Ransome. Didn't see him on the island. Want to get back there. All of them talk of the women of Otaheite. All of them go misty eyed with the memory. Some of them are crude. Some of them almost poetic. But it is clear to Horton that Otaheite and, more particularly, its women have exerted a powerful hold on these men of the northern hemisphere. More than half of them are already making plans to return. Some of them can write their own names. Many of them cannot.

The first few men look shocked and frightened by the news of Attlee and Arnott, the grinning insolence swept away like a broken mast. Carrick, it seems, did as he was asked, but soon the news sweeps out of the room and down the stairs, so Horton's revelation loses the capacity to shock. Even so one of the sailors before him, a man called Craven, looks like he may actually cry when Horton brings up the killings, and when Horton asks why he is so upset Craven alludes to a secret shared between Ransome, Attlee and Arnott. For the first time in the day Horton seizes on something. What nature of secret? But Craven shakes his head and cowers even further into his chair, as if he would roll himself into a ball like a guilty hedgehog, and claims to know nothing at all of this secret, only that Ransome, Attlee and Arnott spent a good deal of time doing things together on the island, and they'd never let Craven join them or even tell him what they were doing. Horton ponders this. Does Craven know something, or is he simply a weak, jealous man without friends in the crew? He decides he will pay Craven a visit at his lodgings to enquire further.

The final member of the group is the blond Viking, Jeremiah Critchley the carpenter's mate. He enters the upstairs room like a once-powerful prince going into a shithouse, his head lowered as he passes through the doorway, and sits in the armchair. He folds his arms and looks at the constable. His hands are enormous, and up one thick arm is a massive tattoo of a sea serpent, its tongue billowing fire. It looks fresh but amateurish. Once again Horton is struck by how exhausted the man looks.

'Like it?' asks Critchley, and Horton almost jumps, as if caught out staring. 'You'll not find it easy to get one of your own. Done on the island, it was.'

'Otaheite?'

'Aye, Otaheite, if you like. That's not what they call it, though.'

'They?'

'The islanders. To them it's just Tahiti. The "O" just means "it is".'

Horton leans back in his chair.

'You made some study of them, then? Learned their language?'

'Aye, I got some words.'

'In five weeks.'

Critchley smiles, a weak watery thing on such an impressive face.

'No officers, here, Constable? Only us pig-thick idlers and seamen? No chance of us ever understanding a thing, eh?'

'Captain Hopkins organised the men into groups for me. It seems sensible not to mix the officers and the ordinary men.'

'Well, Hopkins was always careful about things like that.'

'Ransome was a seaman.'

'That he was. Hardly saw him at sea.'

'And what of on land?'

'You mean on the island?'

'Yes. Did you fraternise with Ransome much on the island?'

Critchley looks away to the window.

'No, Constable. I didn't.'

The man is lying. Horton is sure of it.

'And what of Attlee and Arnott?'

'Aye, I knew them. 'Tis a tragic thing, that.'

'You know of their deaths?'

'Mr Horton, you've sent a dozen or more of my shipmates back down the stairs with fear in their eyes. They bloody told me, didn't they?'

The man's intelligence and confidence are clear. A natural leader, is Jeremiah Critchley. But something else too, dancing around behind the exhaustion. A suppressed nervousness, anxiety, even fear.

'How well did you know them?'

'Pretty well. They were good mates, both.'

'The circumstances of their deaths are . . . odd.'

'Odd how?'

'They appear to have been sleeping when they were dispatched. The killer did not even wake them.'

Critchley shakes his head.

'No doubt they were drunk, Mr Horton. They both liked a good drink.'

The man may be a leader, but he is a terrible liar. Horton's conviction that there is more to this than he can see immediately is growing.

'Were they close to anyone else on the crew?'

'No, sir. They kept themselves to themselves, pretty much.'

'Your shipmate Craven seems to think they shared a secret with Ransome.'

'Craven? You don't want to believe a word from that rat's mouth, Constable. He'd sell your liver for dog food if he could get a hold of it.'

'Indeed. Well, if you could just write your name, position and place of residence while ashore, Critchley, I'd appreciate it.'

Critchley looks at him, an appraising glance. He seems to be pondering saying something else, and Horton is conscious of being weighed, though for what he cannot say. For a moment, the Viking is about to speak, but then he gives a little sad shake of the head and turns to the task of writing on the paper. He stands to leave when he is finished, saying nothing else, lowering his head again as he goes through the door.

Horton snatches up the piece of paper, half-expecting some revelation or confession to be scribbled there. But all he sees is: *jeremiah critchley carpenter's mate the pear tree wapping.*

SOHO SQUARE

Robert Brown, it seems to Harriott, is a man who interests and then disappoints. When Graham had mentioned his name over lunch it had been familiar but Harriott had not been immediately able to place it. Some cursory research on his return to Wapping had clarified the matter. Brown is of course rather more than Sir Joseph Banks's librarian. He is Scottish for a start, which is for Harriott never a cause for recommendation. His background is Scottish Episcopalian, a Jacobite taint and another black mark. But he is without doubt a brave man. He had been the botanist on the *Investigator*, which had followed the track of the lamented Cook and mapped the coast of New Holland, botanising all the way, before coming to grief. Harriott, like many ex-seamen still fired by the maritime exploits of new discoverers, had been an appalled follower of the fortunes of that ship, whose captain Matthew Flinders had only returned to England two years ago, a decade after having left England, prematurely aged by long imprisonment by the French on Mauritius.

Brown, then, trails a good deal of reputation, so it is something of a disappointment to find, when the Scot enters the drawing room of Sir Joseph's Soho Square residence suddenly and unannounced, that he is an unprepossessing, thin, tall and sombre-looking fellow, dressed (as all these damned natural philosophers seem to dress) in a dark frock-coat and trousers and no wig. They shake hands and then sit opposite each other, as if in an encounter across generations.

Harriott is not alone. Attending him is Aaron Graham. A meeting which Graham had been reluctant to countenance over luncheon has become sharp and urgent since the latest deaths. Horton is even now interrogating the ship's seamen, permission for which has not been sought from Brown or Banks. Peter Nott, the strange young man from the *Solander*, is under lock and key in Coldbath Fields prison. Events are suddenly running ahead of polite requests for meetings.

Harriott finds himself both disappointed and relieved that Brown is not accompanied by his employer. He wonders what he would do if Banks were now to appear at the door of this drawing room. He has rehearsed dozens of imaginary conversations with Sir Joseph in the months since the Ratcliffe Highway murders. This is the closest he has come to having a real one.

'We apologise for disturbing you, Mr Brown,' Graham begins, to Harriott's irritation. He is by no means sorry for disturbing Mr Brown. There are unexplained deaths to account for, and the transactions of natural philosophy may have to wait.

'My thanks for that,' says Brown. 'We are indeed rather ... preoccupied with the new plants from Otaheite.' Brown's voice is soft and precise, with more than a hint of Scots. It has been seven years since he returned from his great voyage of discovery, but even so Harriott finds it difficult to see how a man who presumably spent hours, days and weeks beneath beating Southern suns could now be so pale, so smooth, so scrubbed clean. He tries to imagine this precise stick of a man hauling on a sheet in a tropical storm. He fails.

Graham continues, and Harriott lets him. This is his world, after all.

'Our gratitude to you for seeing us. May I introduce John Harriott, my equivalent at the River Police Office in Wapping.' Brown nods in greeting to Harriott. 'I should explain to you the reasons for our visit.'

'I understood that in your positions as magistrates you are investigating the demise of one of the crew of Sir Joseph's ship. Captain Hopkins informed me of this on Friday.'

The formulation *Sir Joseph's ship* seems interesting.

'Ah,' says Graham. 'You have not been kept fully informed, Brown.'

'I have not?'

'No, indeed. I'm afraid there have been two further deaths.'

Brown says nothing to that, but raises an eyebrow as if Graham has just presented a particularly interesting species of slug to him.

'Two crewmen of the *Solander* have been killed in Rotherhithe, Brown,' Graham says. 'They were discovered by a shipmate and Harriott's officer happened to be in the vicinity.'

'The same officer who discovered the first murder?' asks Brown.

'Indeed,' growls Harriott. Brown looks at him, and the moment is uncomfortable for Harriott. The man's cool brown eyes have a similar searching air to those of Charles Horton.

'He seems to have an uncommon knack for being in the right place,' says Brown. Harriott wonders for a moment if this is a joke or only an observation. He notes that Hopkins must have mentioned Horton in his note to the librarian.

'Constable Horton was following a member of the crew when the bodies were discovered,' says Graham, aware perhaps that Harriott is both irritated and disconcerted by Brown's dispassionate response. 'The man being followed is now being held by Mr Harriott here under some suspicion. Peter Nott is his name. He has been questioned, and claims to be the chaplain of the ship. What do you know of his character?'

'Peter Nott? I'm afraid I have never heard of the man. But, as you know, I have had little involvement with the practical side of the voyage. But wait – you consider the *chaplain* a suspect?'

Graham looks at Harriott for confirmation.

'Not quite a suspect, sir, no,' says Harriott. 'But he is unable to fully account for himself. The circumstances of the killings in Rotherhithe are odd, even bizarre. The deaths were bloody and violent and are, as of yet, unexplained. There is now some urgency.'

'Indeed?'

Brown looks expectant. A question hangs in the air: *and what do you want* me *to do about it?*

'I understand that Sir Joseph is the main sponsor of the ship?' says Harriott.

'He is. There are other backers, of course – including, I do believe, Mr Graham here – but the bulk of the costs were met by Sir Joseph. It is quite a large sum of money, I am led to understand, although again I must stress I have little involvement with that side of things.'

'Has Sir Joseph been informed of the death of Sam Ransome?'

'He has, Harriott. Although I find it unlikely he would have concerned himself much with the fortunes of the ordinary members of the crew once their employment had been ended.'

It is a brutal assertion, but Harriott sees the sense of it. Why indeed should someone like Sir Joseph Banks spend his time worrying about someone like Sam Ransome?

'The voyage was itself a success?'

Brown frowns, as if puzzled by the question.

'Oh, indeed so. Even now we are in the process of transplanting the seeds and plants to Kew. It is, as I say, a busy time.'

Harriott sees that the librarian has learned from his master. Brown is just exactly as impolite to him as he can get away with, and is making it clear with every sentence that passes that his time is limited, and Harriott is more than probably wasting it.

'My officer has investigated both the rooms of Sam Ransome and the two dead men in Rotherhithe,' Harriott says. 'In both cases, it appears the dead men had consumed something before they died. A kind of drink, which left a dry residue.'

Brown stares at him.

'Mr Harriott, I am bemused by your question.'

'It is a question of timing, Mr Brown. Your ship returns to London. Three of its crewmen die immediately. What started out as an odd coincidence with one death now looks like a conspiracy. We would like to uncover what that conspiracy might be.'

'And you believe you will find it at the bottom of a dead man's cup?'

Harriott's face reddens, and Brown sees immediately the effect of his words. He raises a hand.

'Mr Harriott, I apologise. I was horribly facetious. You must forgive me. The treasures of the *Solander* have crowded all human considerations from my mind these past few days, and I forget myself. Of course, we must help you and your officers conduct an investigation. What may I do?'

The man's charm is clumsy and sudden but effective. Harriott responds immediately to it.

'Well, here's the heart of the matter. I ... we,' indicating Graham, 'would very much like to meet with Sir Joseph and discuss the voyage with him. It may be that there are matters arising which will help us discover why these deaths have occurred.'

Brown frowns at this.

'It may not be immediately possible, Harriott. As I say, Sir Joseph is much occupied with matters arising from the return of the *Solander*. But I will of course pursue the matter with him. These latest outrages sound truly terrible. If there is a perpetrator attached to the crew, we will want to discover him as much as you.'

'And in the meantime, I wish to tell you that my constable will be interviewing your captain and his crew.'

'Hopkins? By all means.'

Brown is now all cooperation, and agrees to inform Sir Joseph and discover what he can of the dead men and Peter Nott. At no time, though, does he guarantee anything; he is consistently wary. The two magistrates prepare to take their leave of him. Standing, with one hand on his cane, Harriott holds on to Brown's proffered hand.

'I have been a student of your own voyage of discovery for some time, Mr Brown,' he says.

'Indeed?'

Brown answers cautiously, as if he had been cornered by enthusiasts before.

'Oh, yes. You have my admiration for the great bravery it must have demanded. Your personal sacrifices must have been beyond description.'

At the sound of the word 'sacrifices' something softens in Brown's austere features, and an emotion creeps in. Sadness, perhaps.

'My sacrifices led to my successes, Mr Harriott. Others were less fortunate.'

★

Brown watches the red-faced old man and his elegant colleague climb into the carriage out in Soho Square. The older man is clearly virtually lame in one leg, which (Brown supposes) makes his obvious determination to remain active either foolhardy or brave, or both. He had very much liked the old gentleman, although his request presents a conundrum for the librarian. Should he disturb Banks with this just now? The news of the recent deaths in Rotherhithe is shocking, no doubt, and despite what he said to Harriott it is perfectly obvious why the magistrates would connect Ransome's death with these new atrocities.

And then this matter of the ship's chaplain. Brown had been honest about his involvement with the practicalities of the voyage. He did not know the *Solander* had even carried a chaplain, but then he did not know it carried a carpenter's mate or a cook, either. He simply did not consider these things.

And in any case these assuredly terrible events seem like small things in the face of other matters. Robert Brown slept little the previous night because of concerns arising from the *Solander*, but they were not concerns related to murders or chaplains. These were botanical anxieties, and the biggest of them all was that strange plant he encountered the previous evening, the one which had sprung up several feet within days and which had danced in front of his eyes throughout his interview with John Harriott and Aaron Graham.

COLDBATH FIELDS

The great prison of Coldbath Fields sits on a hill at the northern edge of the City, surrounded on three sides by fields, and facing, on its fourth side, the final paved streets of the sprawling metropolis. Beside it runs a little trickle of water called the Fleet, now tamed beneath a culvert further downstream, but once London's second river. The fields around the prison are mainly owned by the New River Company, purveyors of a new kind of waterway, one trimmed by the hands of men and not the passage of water. The old river is made redundant as the new river emerges.

The carriage carrying John Harriott back from Soho Square stops at the prison gatehouse just off Bayne's Row. The place bears an immediate and pressing similarity to the magistrate's own London Dock, surrounded as it is by an enormous brick wall built barely a decade before that which encircles the dock in Wapping. One place processes goods, the other miscreants, but in both cases these transactions are masked from an outside world by a solid, impregnable wall. It is so high that a man on foot, or even in a carriage, has little impression of what is within. The only sound from inside the walls this morning is the occasional ringing of a lonely bell, though Harriott has been here at other times when a crowd has been gathered on the little patch of grass outside the gatehouse, screaming and shouting at their brothers and fathers and even mothers within, and the prisoners have screamed back such that the place was a very Bedlam.

Coldbath Fields is the great dock for ne'er-do-wells, a massive machine of criminality dubbed by Sir Francis Burdett, with his knowing talent for a controversial epithet, the 'Bastille'. Harriott has no truck with Burdett, whom he considers a slippery newt of a man capable of any iniquity, but he shares many of Burdett's concerns about Coldbath Fields. Behind that wall, he knows full well, lies an engine of corruption as depraved as any in the Empire.

Harriott had sent the *Solander*'s chaplain Peter Nott to Coldbath Fields following the events in Rotherhithe. He did this with some reluctance, as he always does. He does not trust anyone associated with this place: not the chief warder, nor the governor, nor any of the magistrates. He believes the warders take bribes in return for giving access to prisoners, and is certain that this has materially damaged previous investigations involving his office. The governor of the prison does nothing about this criminality, asserting that his warders are hardworking men. Harriott has been in continuing correspondence with him and the magistrates of the prison for months now, but nothing at all has been done. He has become convinced during the course of this correspondence that the governor and the magistrates know exactly what is going on, and therefore must be profiting from it themselves.

Coldbath Fields has always had a stink of corruption about it. Even at the time of its construction there were stories of magistrates pocketing money meant for building supplies. It is a place neglected by the authorities and the Home Office, despite its recent construction. It has become, very quickly, an embarrassment. Harriott has heard tales from men who were imprisoned there and from honest warders who have retired from the place in disgust; tales of a vast illicit commerce inside the walls, of basements hollowed out to store illegal items, of a shared undertaking between some of the prisoners and their keepers to smuggle and to extort.

But for short periods of incarceration, Harriott has no other options. The Police Office itself has no facilities for imprisonment. So Nott had been brought here yesterday, after a preliminary interrogation by Harriott in the River Police Office. Horton had secured the room in the Rotherhithe boarding house, which was now being guarded by a River Police constable. His note had been waiting for Harriott on his return from luncheon with Aaron Graham, accompanied by an impatient tyke who gave him a word-perfect message and then demanded money, claiming to have agreed a payment of a shilling with Horton. Harriott sent him on his way with tuppence and a clipped ear. He had then composed his own note to Graham, emphasising that with three bodies now to be accounted for the need was urgent for an audience with Banks, or if not Banks then his librarian.

Horton had returned from Rotherhithe with the chaplain as his prisoner. Horton and Harriott had tried to question Nott, but without success. He had arrived in Harriott's office in the late afternoon like a visiting foreign dignitary, albeit one who has received a bad scare. He was almost haughty in the way he spoke to Harriott, but the old magistrate saw immediately that this was a brittle superiority, and in the young man's eyes could clearly discern the fear of a lonely, anxious boy.

'What is this place?' Nott had asked, and Harriott had tried to explain the role of the River Police Office and his own position, but Nott had not seemed to understand. He was a strange vision, this foreign-looking fellow in the vestments of an English country vicar, his accent unplaceable. He essentially refused to account for himself in any way, but did throw himself upon the mercies of the magistrate. He claimed he needed protecting, though from what he did not say. He also claimed to have 'friends' in the metropolis who would help him if he could only make contact with them. Once again, he did not elaborate, even when pressed hard by an irritated old magistrate.

Eventually, Harriott's exasperation with the strange man spilled over and he told Horton to have him remanded to Coldbath Fields pending further interrogation. He and Horton had met again this morning at Wapping, arranging to meet at Coldbath Fields following their own appointments, Harriott's in Soho Square, Horton's in the Narwhal in Rotherhithe. Sunday or no, Harriott was not going to delay pursuing this increasingly odd saga. Three murders now, on either side of the river, a combination of the mysteriously serene and the frenziedly barbaric. Yet there seemed to be no motives for the murders, and the only suspect was this strange dark man who seemed full of fear, as if being pursued by demons only he could see. The viciousness and suddenness of the killings reminds Harriott vividly of the Ratcliffe Highway murders; the comparison is chilling.

Harriott climbs down from his carriage and limps up to the stone gatehouse which fronts the prison. On it are inscribed the words: THE HOUSE OF CORRECTION FOR THE COUNTY OF MIDDLESEX 1794.

The building may be young but the brick is already beginning to darken, and the scrub of land in front of the gatehouse, which must have been tidy eighteen years before, is now scruffy and overgrown. This morning it even has a sheep grazing morosely upon it, presumably left behind by one of the trains of livestock which make their way down the hill from here to Smithfield.

Harriott pulls with his usual impatience on one of the two gigantic door-knockers which are attached to the wooden gates. Nothing happens for a moment, but then the gate begins to open and the wicked old face of the chief warder appears. The man scowls when he sees who is waiting outside. He knows Harriott suspects him and the other warders of corruption, and his antipathy towards the old magistrate only serves to confirm Harriott's suspicions. Harriott scowls back, goes in, and the two old enemies walk into the gaol, the gate closing behind them.

The main prison building sits in the middle of the nine-acre site, encircled by scrubby patches of market garden in which a number of prisoners are half-heartedly digging. It is a staunchly solid stone affair punctuated by iron gates and iron windows, like a lunatic asylum from one of the thick Gothic romances Harriott's wife enjoys. The building is constructed around four quarters, and the warder leads Harriott to the first quarter on the left, where the prisoners on Charge – not yet tried but waiting interrogation or trial – can be found.

Nott is in a cell between a man accused of murdering his wife, and two petty thieves caught by one of Harriott's constables on Wapping Street picking pockets. The murderous husband weeps quietly to himself, while the thieves bicker with each other over some complicated tale articulating the depravity of Napoleon Bonaparte. As they approach the cell, Coldbath's old gaoler leans in towards Harriott and, apropos of nothing at all, tells him Nott already has a visitor. Harriott bristles.

'A visitor? I left no instructions that he be allowed visits.'

'You left no instructions that he not be allowed them either, *sir.*' There is no respect, only contempt, in the old man's voice and face.

The visitor, though, is Horton, who is standing in the cell.

Nott sits on the scruffy unmade little bed with his head in his hands, silent. When Harriott appears, Horton nods at him, saying nothing, as if he does not wish to disturb whatever considerations are going through the chaplain's distraught mind. He is watching Nott carefully, notes Harriott, who wonders what his constable is learning from the observation. Harriott instructs the warder to leave open the door of the cell.

'We shall be taking a turn through the gardens with this man.'

'A *turn*, is it?' says the warder. 'Not sure the governor would allow that.'

'Well, do feel free to consult with him. Now leave us.'

The warder scowls again, leaving the cell door open as ordered, and then walks away back up the corridor, screaming a terrible curse into one cell from which Harriott can hear a soft whimpering which sounds distinctly like that of a woman.

'Come with us, Nott,' he orders, waiting outside the cell. Nott raises his head from his hands and Harriott feels a sharp and, for him, unfamiliar wave of sympathy for what he sees there. He is reminded of Nott's scared eyes the day before, but today that fear is accompanied by something else. The man looks tortured and exhausted.

The prisoner stands, and looks at Harriott and then at Horton before stepping out of the cell. Horton steps out behind him. The magistrate and the constable walk on either side of the prisoner, out to the back of the gaol where there is tilled land and prisoners attempting to grow things in it. Harriott feels that in some way they are *attending* Nott; two curates walking down the aisle with the bishop. He looks at Nott's feet, and sees there an ancient but well-cared-for pair of leather shoes, exactly in keeping with the man's ecclesiastical bearing.

It is a pleasant day. There is a single empty bench at the side of the little plot. Half a dozen prisoners are digging in potatoes, under the eye of a fat, surly warder who shouts at Harriott as they appear from the building but whom Harriott magnificently ignores. The three of them sit on the bench, for all the world like old friends taking in the air in Hyde Park. Indeed there is something pleasantly bucolic about this incongruous piece of agricultural England, out behind the massive prison. Only the remorseless wall along the back of the plot lies between them and the pleasant hills to the north, up towards Hampstead.

Nott has lost his haughty air of the previous evening, Harriott is pleased to observe. He is forced to admit to himself that it is damnably hard for him to be firm with this man. Like all Englishmen, Harriott is acutely attuned to matters of class and respect. Nott is no common riverside thug. He seems a man of learning and morality, despite the things of which he is suspected, and Harriott speaks to him on this basis. Nott's priestly air demands another kind of respect again, whatever the beliefs of those doing the interrogating.

'You are comfortable here?' Harriott asks. Nott looks away from the men toiling in the soil, and turns his scared face to Harriott. Horton, the old magistrate can see, is keeping a watchful eye, as if recording every move of Nott's in some invisible ledger.

'Is it intended that I should be comfortable, Mr Harriott?'

The question is a good one, but is not meant sardonically. It is a genuine query. Again, that boy-like innocence.

'You are being held because of the events in Rotherhithe . . .' he begins, but Nott interrupts him, though without heat.

'Events which I witnessed, Mr Harriott, that is all. Why is the boarding house landlord not here? Or the women that stood in that hall? They all witnessed it as well as I. Yet I am here, and they are not.'

Horton smiles a little at that, Harriott sees. Is he smiling at Nott, or at the old magistrate trying to interrogate him?

'Nott, do avoid any impertinence with me,' he says, abandoning polite intercourse and adopting the air of the severe magistrate. 'You were the last person to see your two shipmates alive.'

'But I was not, sir. I most definitely was not. The last person to see them alive was he who killed them.' The 'he' is said with some reverence, as if Nott were talking of God.

'You are the last person we know of. And thus the main suspect for their deaths.'

Nott sighs at that. 'It is quite ridiculous, Mr Harriott. Why would I have killed them, in broad daylight, and then made such a fuss of it? Your constable here,' he gestures at Horton, and there is that flash of yesterday's haughty man with expectations of deference, 'he saw me. He saw the state I was in. Why would I behave in such a flagrant manner if I had just killed those men?'

'You were calm when we first encountered you,' says Horton. 'You only became upset when we returned to the room.'

'For reasons I have explained – they were not dead when I left them!'

'You may have concocted the whole story, for all we know,' says Harriot. 'You play-acted your upset to throw Horton off the scent.'

Nott exclaims at that. 'Stupendous! Your theory is ridiculous, sir!'

'Again I say to you, do not grow hot with me. I may be forced to return you to your cell and interview you there.'

'Hot, am I? I have been arrested and imprisoned in a gaol where the warders demand payment in return for sending letters. I have tried to write to my captain, but have been told that payment of a shilling is required. The gaolers here seek to profit from their inmates! What kind of place is this?'

'We will discuss this before long. But now I wish to ask—'

'We will discuss it now, sir! I have been maltreated and ignored, and I will put up with it no longer!'

Nott stands, and for an insane moment Harriott imagines he will stamp his feet like an enormous aggravated toddler. But he only steps off a pace or two, and then begins walking to and fro like a man wrestling with an enormous problem.

'Nott, be seated.'

'England is not supposed to be like this! Where is the liberty? The justice?'

There are tears in Nott's eyes now, tears of frustration. He bangs his fists into his hips as if to stop himself striking the old magistrate.

'Nott, be seated, immediately.'

'I am the son of an important man, Harriott! This is unacceptable!'

The insolent use of 'Harriott' causes the magistrate to bellow 'Horton, seize him!' but then Nott falls to his knees and starts to pray with a fierce intensity, his hands locked together against his forehead, his eyes closed, the words forced out as if his lips were tied together: 'I therefore, the prisoner of the Lord, beseech you that ye walk worthy of the vocation wherewith ye are called, with all lowliness and meekness, with long suffering, forbearing one another in love; endeavouring to keep the unity of the Spirit in the bond of peace. There is one body, and one Spirit, even as ye are called in one hope of your calling; One Lord, one faith, one baptism, One God and Father of all, who is above all, and through all, and in you all. But unto every one of us is given grace according to the measure of the gift of Christ.'

Harriott recognises Ephesians, and allows Nott to finish. It is a missionary's prayer, and the words calm the man down again. At the end, he drops his hands to his sides while his head remains bowed. Horton and Harriott wait for him to come to himself once more. After several minutes, he stands and returns to the bench, where he sits down again, his head still bowed.

Harriott looks at Horton, and nods. Time for the constable to take over. The magistrate is angry, and may shout.

'Nott,' says Horton, his voice gentle and almost inaudible. 'Are you now able to talk in more detail about the events of yesterday?'

Nott gives out a little sigh, as if the last drop of Holy Spirit is departing his body.

'Yes. I believe I am able to do so.'

'Good. So, once again, please. Your version of what happened.'

'I was planning to visit Attlee and Arnott, my former shipmates. I had not seen them since the ship docked, and I wanted to warn them.'

'Warn them of what?'

'Warn them of the death of Sam Ransome.'

'What did you know of Ransome's death?'

'Only what Captain Hopkins told me. After your visit to the *Solander*. Up until then I had not left the ship.'

'You believed Attlee and Arnott in danger?'

'I did.'

This is new, as Horton's glance to Harriott makes clear. The constable went on.

'Why did you believe so?'

'I cannot say.'

'Cannot, or will not?'

'I cannot and I will not.'

'Even at the expense of your own liberty?'

'It is not my *liberty* which is at question.'

Harriott cannot stop himself breaking in.

'You know what you are saying, Nott? You are admitting to knowing more of this business than you say, and you refuse to say what you know. This will end badly for you, sir.'

'I understand.'

Harriott has nothing to say to that. Nott speaks the words without energy or feeling, as if the stones at their feet were speaking to them.

'Why were you on the *Solander*, Nott?' asks Horton.

'I was born on Tahiti.'

'You mean Otaheite.'

'Such is how you like to say it. We say Tahiti.'

'We? You are a native?'

Nott looks up at that.

'A savage, you mean? An uneducated pagan without morality, one generation away from cannibalism, consumed with carnal lust? Is this what you mean by *native*, Constable?' The fire is back in his words, but they are spoken without heat.

'I meant only to ask whether you were born on the island.'

'Yes. To an Englishman and an island woman. I am, how do you say it . . . *mestizo*.'

'It is a Spanish word, not an English one.'

'It will serve the purpose.'

'Who is your father?'

'My father is Henry Nott. He is a missionary of some renown. He is a great man, Constable.'

'And he is still on the island? He did not travel with you?'

'No, I came alone.'

'Again I ask: why?'

'And again I reply: to search out my family.'

'The Notts?'

'Among others.'

'And have you made any progress in finding them.'

'None at all. The events on the *Solander* interrupted my search.'

'So, you knew of some danger Attlee and Arnott were in. You will not speak of this danger. And you decided to visit them yesterday morning.'

'Yes.'

'Describe what happened, Nott.'

'I left the ship, walked to their lodgings, and the boarding house landlord let me in. I knocked on the door, and when there was no answer I opened it and went inside. And I discovered them.'

Harriott has not visited the room in question and has no mental picture of it. But Horton seemed to think the disarray in the room was a key part of this case. The old bulldog holds himself back and decides to let Nott speak for himself. The results are surprising.

For a moment, Nott says nothing at all. He looks expectantly at Horton, waiting for the next question, and then at Harriott. When it doesn't come, he looks confused for a moment. His shoulders sag, and suddenly the man is whimpering, afraid, like a dog whose master is pouring cold water upon its back. Nott looks up at the wall which holds them in, but not with longing; to Harriott, it looks like fear that the walls will not be sufficient to keep out whatever lies beyond them.

'The room was wrecked. It looked like a gale had blown through it. Their kitbags were open. Their clothes, such as they were, were everywhere. But they were still in their beds. They seemed to be asleep. The place had been ransacked, and I feared for my safety. It was then that I ran out.'

'How long were you in the room?' Harriott does not know why he asks this question; it seems to come from somewhere else.

'Seconds. I touched nothing.'

'And there was no blood in the room at this point.'

'None, sir. Of that I am quite certain. I did not check the men, I assumed they were ... asleep.'

'That they slept through whatever it was that ransacked their room?'

'Yes.'

'And you contend that somehow, between you running into the street and returning with Horton, the men were annihilated.'

'So it would seem.'

'How is that possible?'

No answer.

'Nott, you seem suddenly alarmed.'

'Alarmed, sir?'

'Yes, Nott, alarmed. You appear as someone who expects a dragon to leap over that wall at any second.'

At that, Nott barks out a laugh, a sad and angry thing which startles Harriott.

'A dragon, sir?' says Nott. 'Perhaps not. But there are other monsters in the world.'

'What do you mean by that?'

'Only this. I did not kill those men, Mr Harriott. I have never killed any man. But someone did, and that someone must have the heart of a dragon to have done those things.'

'I believe you know the man who did it, if you did not do it yourself.'

'How so, sir? What possible reason can I have given you to have imagined that?'

Harriott cannot answer Nott's question. His thoughts are stuck in a muddy mess of exasperated disbelief. He looks to Horton for assistance, but his constable is watching the prisoners tending the pathetic little market garden, as if they might have the tools to unpick the strange chaplain and his meandering tales.

FIVE

Sure Friendship's there, & Gratitude, & Love,
Such as ne'er reigns in European Blood
In these degen'rate days; tho' from above
We Precepts have, & know what's right and good

Peter Heywood, in a l etter to his sister, Nessy, 1791

TAHITI

The prince had been dreaming of leaving the island for months when the latest British ship arrived. The young members of the *arioi* cult up on the plateau had been talking of little else while they sipped the tea made from the secret leaf. They complained about their parents and their constant squabbling. They mourned the thousands of deaths and the growing stink of decomposition which hung around the island's glades, where once had been only the fresh smell of green. They vied with each other to tell stories of the magnificence of Britain, where iron was so plentiful it was in every home, where everyone owned a gun, where you could buy intoxicating liquors on every corner. For people who had long believed that the Islands constituted the world, Britain was a story which only the gods could have dreamed into being. And the prince decided he was going to go there.

He felt like he had willed the latest ship into existence simply with the force of his wanting. He had made his definitive decision to leave weeks before while lying in the hut beside the same empty space where his elder brother had once lain. He had told no one about it. And yet here was the ship, an ugly dwarfish thing, with none of the brutal magnificence of the whalers or transport ships which had visited before. But it was still bigger, vastly bigger, than anything the islanders could conceive of building. In any case all he needed was something big enough to carry him away.

The prince climbed into one of the canoes which rowed out to meet the ship. These little flotillas had become customary with every new foreign arrival. Most of the canoes were there to trade, piled high with breadfruit, coconuts and in one case a pair of hogs, which the islanders knew the Britons treasured more than any other commodity. There were a few sightseers, mostly *arioi* like the prince, but their numbers were small; certainly far smaller than would have been the case a few years before, when the British visitors still had an aura of mystery and excitement about them. The prince knew his father would not be among the visitors. He had become violently anti-British since the death of his eldest son, killed, or so he believed, by the bad air from the *Britannia*. Some other islanders had similar prejudices, but they were generally mocked by the majority. How could 'bad air' kill someone? The idea was quite ridiculous. People who died did so because of the will of the gods. That was all the explanation needed.

It was not only familiarity that reduced the number of canoes rowing out to the new ship. This was as anxious a period of violence and unrest as anyone could remember on Tahiti. Even the king, Pomare, had fled the island, to nearby Moorea, where he sat and brooded. The remaining chieftains fought among themselves for control of the island.

The missionaries had sent an odd representative to the new ship. The lonely half-breed, adopted son of the missionaries' leader, rowed out in his own canoe and sat watching the vessel which had arrived, dressed in his strange dark European clothes, ignoring the splashing and shouting of the islanders who surrounded him. He saw the prince, and nodded at him, as if the prince's was the only friendly face in the crowd of canoes out on the water. The prince nodded back, but carefully. No one knew what he and the half-breed had been up to these past weeks, and he did not wish to reveal it.

The pale faces of the Britons looked over the side of their ship at the canoes below. The islanders who were there to trade held up their items from the water, shouting the English words for them as well as the words for the items they would accept in payment: 'Nails! Guns! Liquor!' The prince looked at the sallow faces of the Englishmen and saw in most of them the hunger he had seen in previous crews. One canoe contained four young girls whose fathers had rowed them out to the ship to be sold as whores. The prince watched as the eyes of the British sailors fell on the girls, who did as they were told and unwrapped themselves as they stood carefully in the canoe, their eyes empty, their smiles rehearsed. A whoop went up from the sailors. One of them even dived into the water near the canoe containing the girls. One of the other sailors hollered after him and the others cheered. It was a tableau terribly familiar from previous visits of European ships.

The prince wondered what the ship was here to do. Previous visitors had traded, observed, restocked or performed odd little experiments which bemused and amused the islanders. This one was of the experimental kind. Over the days that followed the ship's arrival, it became clear that this visitor's intentions would be as unfathomable to the locals as some of its predecessors had been. Dozens of men came ashore from the ship, and after they had established their tents at the back of the beaches which ringed the bay (as was customary for the British visitors), they began to collect, of all things, plants.

Gangs of British men plunged into the undergrowth, carrying a motley selection of boxes, barrels and bags which they filled with cuttings, saplings, seeds and soil. These they transported back to the beach. After a week, the British tents were ringed by dozens of wooden containers of various shapes and sizes containing every different type of island plant that could be imagined. The prince's father complained long and hard about the activity, telling all that would listen that the British were stealing the island itself. But he was laughed at by his fellow chieftains and nobles, who pointed out that the island was still well stocked with fruit and vegetables, with more than enough to spare for the strange appetites of the visitors. Did he think the British were going to tow the entire place away?

The prince, meanwhile, watched the sailors and the gardeners. One in particular caught his eye – a gigantic blue-eyed, blond-haired man. This man spent his first week whoring himself to distraction, but then, sometime during the second week, he began to disappear into the forest alone, exploring on his own. The prince followed him, unseen, as the blond giant meandered through the island's hidden places. The prince decided this was the man who would take him back to Britain, and towards the end of the second week of the ship's visit, he approached the giant, hoping he was friendly.

The man was inspecting a beached canoe, running his hands along the wood and whistling softly to himself. The prince, not afraid, exactly, but anxious lest he startle the stranger and ignite violence of some kind, walked along the beach as noisily as he could. The blond man heard him and turned to face him. The prince went up to him feeling as self-conscious as a boy lying with his first woman. He held out his hand in the way the missionary's son had shown him.

'Hello, British sir,' he said, the strange words angular on his tongue. 'How are you?'

RATCLIFFE

The Geordie Robert Craven does not see himself the way others see him. He is a curious soul, no question, but for him the world is a place filled with traps and ambushes, a place where information is the strongest shield against those who would hurt him. Forewarned is forearmed, as his father used to say, before going down in the cold North Sea in a fishing boat he'd bought from a Scottish stranger. Craven senior had liked the line of this boat and had been convinced by the stranger's patter, which promised greater hauls and enormous distances. In fact the flattering description belied the multitude of short-cuts the ship's builder had made and which now made the thing a death trap, the kind of vessel which old fishermen on the quay pointed at with the kind of hand signs normally reserved for avoidance of the Devil. Craven senior hadn't read the signs, hadn't got the information, was not forewarned and now his bones lay cold and unburied at the bottom of the North Sea. The lesson had never been lost on Robert Craven, his son.

So Craven has always sought information: who went where,

who said what to whom, who fancies whose job or hammock or woman. It would be wrong to say he sells this information for pecuniary gain, but he does distribute it with the care of a gardener laying out a flower bed, placing a single seed in each hole. Information begets information, he has long realised. With some care, a man who nurtures his crop of facts and gossip will always be forewarned and protected.

So he accepts the sneers, the dislike, the cold shoulder. All these are just the sufferings of a man who sees things clearly. Others cannot perceive a world full of men striving and fighting and manoeuvring, always seeking an angle, a way in, an opportunity. Only when a man sees this picture in full detail, from every side, can he hope to thrive and prosper and protect himself and his family.

But Robert Craven has no family. Any woman he has come to know has soon departed, unable to cope with his incessant questions and suspicions, his determined and relentless need to know where she'd been, who she was with and what they had had to say.

This need to know is what has driven him here, to a boarding house in a row of eight houses on Rose Lane, a half-finished meandering street just off the brand new thoroughfare of Commercial Road, at the north end of the hamlet of Ratcliffe. Behind the row of houses is a meadow which reaches down to a rope walk, more houses, a timber yard, a tar yard and then the river. It is a half-developed stretch of the riverside, a place to take breath between the crushed hive of Wapping and the new austere docks of the Isle of Dogs.

Inside the house, Craven knows, are Elijah Frost and Colby Potter, who, along with Attlee, Arnott and Sam Ransome he has begun to think of as Jeremiah Critchley's Crew. These were the six men he'd watched gather furtively soon after the *Solander* arrived in London, who'd left together and who'd then dispersed. Three of them are, Craven knows, already dead. Jeremiah Critchley is shacked up in Wapping but had not answered when Craven had visited the night before. Craven had waited in a nearby doorway for two hours before summoning up the courage to go in and knock on Critchley's door. There had been no reply, but careful listening at the door (an activity for which Craven has developed considerable facility) convinced him there had been *someone* in the room, their steady breathing plain to any careful listener.

It had been too late by then to walk to see Frost and Potter, the remaining members of Critchley's Crew. Frost and Potter had not attended the interrogations at the Narwhal the previous day. Like Attlee and Arnott, Frost and Potter were friends before the secret coming-together of Critchley's Crew to which Craven had borne witness. Craven has given some thought to the symmetry of Critchley's furtive little group: two pairs, and two loners (Ransome and Critchley himself). He has found himself wondering how such a grouping came about, since it didn't exist on the outward trip to Otaheite. Only on the way home did those six huddle together periodically, hissing at Craven whenever he approached like a cabal of witches hatching an infernal plot. Something happened on the island to bring the six of them together, it is clear. But what? And why those six?

He must know, because there is something important here, something which he has no doubt will be of some personal use to him. He feels no urgency to *warn* Frost and Potter, as he feels sure they will know of the deaths of Attlee and Arnott. He imagines that if the secret between the men is as big and as powerful as he has begun to imagine it is, then Critchley will already have been out here to talk to them.

He followed Colby Potter back here earlier today, having watched him leave the boarding house early this morning. He had taken up a position on the far side of Rose Walk from the boarding house, behind a pile of unused timber and coal which, in a tiny little economic miracle, had been left there and had not been touched by any greedy or needy hands ever since. The pile was close enough to the house so that any noise from the front door was clearly audible, and with each creak and slam Craven peeked around the edge of his hiding place to see who was coming or going. At about 8 a.m., Potter came out of the house and began to walk down the street towards Shadwell.

Craven had not seen him for some days, so was taken aback by the change in his former crewmate. Potter was pale and unshaven and walked with an empty shuffling gait as if obeying some lizard impulse in his brain. He took no notice of his surroundings. He simply pointed himself down the street and began to walk, his feet barely lifting off the ground, his eyes fixed to a point in the road eight or nine feet in front of him. He was thin and pale, a shocking transformation from the muscular, well-fed fellow who'd left the *Solander* a few days before, when his skin was still dark from the southern sun and his belly was full of the ship's comfortable rations.

Craven had followed Potter into Shadwell itself, and as the crowds thickened it became both easier to remain hidden and harder to keep his quarry in sight, although Potter's plodding gait made his progress easy to forecast. Craven could lose sight of him for a minute and still be confident of where he'd be when he next saw him. Then he lost Potter completely for a while, before realising that the man had stopped at a baker's to buy bread. Craven watched him through the window, mechanically counting out coins in the empty, desperate way of someone who knows they're the last coins he has. Then Potter came out of the shop, turned back towards the Ratcliffe house and began plodding again.

The two of them had returned to the boarding house after perhaps a half-hour in total. Potter had gone in, Craven had returned to his spot behind the pile. Then he'd continued his vigil, watching people leave the boarding house one by one, none of them Frost or Potter.

Another hour has now passed. Craven is bored and frustrated and realises that he must at least try to talk to his two shipmates. No one has left the little boarding house in the last hour, and the place has an empty watchfulness about it, as if it were waiting for its charges to return from their days. There may still be people inside, of course, but he will simply go in and, if it comes to it, ask for Potter and Frost and be shown to their rooms. God willing.

The door to the house is tidily painted and maintained, Craven notices, and it is unlocked. He steps into the hallway inside. Various doors lead off the hallway, and a staircase goes up to the first floor. It is well lit and open, not at all like the dark warren in which Craven himself resides in an older district of Wapping. There is not a sound: no cheery landlady doing the laundry, no snoring men in their rooms, nothing at all. The house feels completely empty, even though Craven is sure that in one of these rooms he will find two crewmen from the *Solander*.

Craven is neither a brave nor a cowardly man. He is simply one who follows a sequence of steps in life towards the goal of his own self-preservation and, with luck, his own advancement. So he feels no compunction in stepping into the house, closing the door behind him, and trying the doors one by one.

They are all locked. He knocks on each one, and tries its handle. The landlady or landlord must leave their front door unlocked during the day, and each boarder has his own key to his own door. The rooms at the back of the place must belong to the house's owner, and they too are locked. So, the residents and the owners are all out, or have locked themselves in. The ones on the ground floor, at least.

It is the same on the first floor. Craven tries all five doors and can get into none of them. Listening carefully at each one, he does not hear the front door of the house quietly open and close at the bottom of the stairs. He discovers another flight of stairs, small and cramped, leading up to, presumably, another set of rooms on another floor. He walks up these stairs, which are noisy, their squeaks masking another set of sounds which accompany someone walking up the stairs from below.

At the top of the house there is one door, and it is unlocked. He almost jumps when he turns the handle and the door begins to open, and he pulls it shut without thinking, slamming it shockingly loudly and then standing still, the handle still in his hand, listening for any whisperings from the house. There is no noise, only a watchful silence as if somewhere there is an audience waiting to see what is going to happen. Feeling stupid and somehow embarrassed, he knocks on the door.

'Potter? It is I, Robert Craven, your old shipmate. Are you in there?'

There is no reply, but from within the room he thinks he hears something like a quiet growl, which scares him badly and nearly sends him back down the stairs. But then he tells himself not to be stupid and that this is more interesting than he might have anticipated. Potter came into this house and hasn't come out, so he's in here somewhere, and this is the last room. With a little swallow, he opens the door and goes in.

Given his growing fear, the scene of tranquillity inside the room is a shock. Frost and Potter are both asleep on their beds. The little growl he'd heard was actually Frost snoring. They are dressed and lying on top of the bedclothes. On a table beneath the room's one window lie the remains of the loaf

Potter had bought this morning; there is no butter or cheese or ham. The two men had eaten the bread, unadorned and unimproved.

But there is a stench in the room, an unwashed and untended reek which comes from the men on the bed and the clothing which lies strewn around the room. The men's sea chests lie opened by their beds, unpacked and untidy. It is as if the two of them had returned from the *Solander* days before and had lain down on the beds and gone to sleep, without washing or putting away their things or doing any of the little things which travelling men do to their rooms to make them feel like a home, however transitory.

He walks towards Potter, and is struck again by how ill the man looks. His arm is hanging over the bed, a wooden cup still in his hand, the other arm placed across his chest. The man's cadaverous features are formed into an awful frowning grimace, as if Potter were face-to-face with a creature consumed with terrible hunger. His cheekbones are impossibly gaunt, his beard patchy, his shoulders and chest a sad pastiche of the vital strength that had coursed through the man only days before. He smells terribly, and looking down his body Craven notes the worst thing of all: his old shipmate has repeatedly soiled himself. Whatever it is that holds Potter in its grip will not even let him leave to relieve himself. In a sickening counterpoint, from a neighbouring room Craven hears a girl laughing.

The two men's beds are placed either side of a fireplace, and on the hearth Craven sees an old black kettle. The fire is still warm but was obviously lit some hours ago. He walks over to Frost and sees much the same thing as he saw with Potter: the same unwashed, unshaven face, the same horrific fearful grimace, the same hand trailing on the floor with a cup falling from it. But where Potter's other hand was placed across his chest, Frost's is by his side, and Craven can see that he is grasping, even in this unconscious state, a small leather pouch. He reaches out to take the pouch, but then he feels something tight and warm go around his neck and an enormous pressure is placed upon his windpipe. His feet scrabble backwards as an unseen assailant yanks on the cord around his neck, rupturing something inside his throat, until there is no air going in, and his fingers scrabble at the cord which is destroying him. He cannot get a purchase, the other is pulling too tightly, he is strong, so strong, and like his father before him Craven sinks into a purple-and-black doom, as surprised as it is possible to be.

KEW

Robert Brown knows of only one way to smother botanical anxieties – through systematic, remorseless observation. His life has been many things, but throughout he has been conducting a long conversation with the plant kingdom. As a child he had fled into the countryside to escape the hectoring echoes of his father James Brown, a rebel suspected of being a Jacobite, forbidden from preaching to more than four people in a room. Reverend Brown had got round this limitation in typically direct style by placing his congregation in groups of four in each room of the Browns' cross-shaped house, and then preaching from the stairs, his voice shouting so it could be heard in every room, and every room containing huddles of dark-clothed devout with pale faces and fire in their eyes.

Brown's father had interrupted whatever educational progress his son was making in Montrose in 1789 by moving the family to Edinburgh, where he was consecrated Bishop Brown in a secret and very illegal ceremony. He was still raging against the heretics and harlots when he died two years later of apoplexy. His son Robert could not have imagined a more appropriate death.

In Edinburgh the younger Brown attended some medical courses and, officially, was well on the way to becoming a doctor. But his passion was botany. The year his father died Brown produced his first *hortus siccus,* drying the best of his plants and displaying them, as if to prevent their own little deaths in the face of the big death of his father. Young Mr Brown had found his passion, a passion that was seeded in his mid teens and now filled almost every waking thought. He worked when he could and often went hungry. If he could have eaten the plants he studied, all would have been well; but man cannot live on botanising alone. So he was forced to sign up to the new Fifeshire Fencibles, and pursue his botanical obsessions while mending the broken limbs of Scotsmen who were putting down Irishmen on behalf of Englishmen.

Brown's entry into the botanical world was timely. At the end of the last century, many centuries-old questions were being answered: how plants procreated, how they nourished themselves, even how they should be classified. Theories tumbled over questions in a great rush as the old century ended. The great Linnaean system of a half-century's standing was beginning to give way to new ways of classifying based on natural affinities between species, led by the pioneering French, with their state-funded Jardin and their bureaucrat natural philosophers. Antoine-Laurent de Jussieu's groundbreaking *Genera Plantarum* made its way into the Brown book-box sometime in 1795, six years after it was published, and Brown spent many damp Irish nights absorbing the unity and elegance of de Jussieu, botanising when he could in the peat and on the heath. Ireland was wet and depressing. He frequently drank himself into a state of acceptance, and gambled away a fair proportion of his pay. The blissful botanising days above

Edinburgh receded into the distance. But then Joseph Banks came calling, and everything changed.

His consciousness of his debt to Banks is the single constant in their relationship, and it is why he finds himself acutely anxious about the recent behaviour of his mentor. Not least, he is concerned by the reappearance of Otaheite into the biography of Sir Joseph Banks. Brown is more familiar than he would wish to be with the stories of Sir Joseph's activities on the island. These stories caused immense scandal forty years ago and they still, even today, are capable of drawing flushed gasps from ladies at London dinner tables. Banks had gone to the island as a young man who already had a reputation as a womaniser. Scandalous tales of 'fishing trips' accompanied by expensive London courtesans opened the door for caricaturists to draw a direct, exaggerated line between Banks and his ageing mentor Lord Sandwich, a decaying rake and former member of the discredited old Hell Fire Club. When the young baronet returned from the South Seas trailing tales of glamorous and willing savage princesses there was a gleeful explosion of ink.

All that was forty years ago. Nonetheless for Brown, who has read widely on the subject of 'Banks, J.', the stories are vivid. Banks himself is seemingly unaware of the dangers of dredging up some of these tales. The older man's mind is elsewhere – in Kew, in fact. He has stayed down there these past several nights, close to the new plants, close in particular to the strange breadfruit tree (if such it is) which is growing at impossible speeds in the Great Stove. He has become a man obsessed.

So it is to Kew that Brown goes, and there is Banks again, hunched in his wheelchair before the tree, like one of Bishop Brown's devout knelt in a room at the bottom of the stairs. The tree has grown again, Brown sees – perhaps another two feet in less than two days. It will soon be the biggest thing in the hothouse. Its bright-green leaves quiver with moisture; one of the gardeners has just been in to water it. A branch is hanging down, notes Brown, and a leaf on the branch is almost touching Banks's fat, jowly cheek.

'Sir Joseph,' he says as he approaches. The old man starts and looks around, as if disturbed in some guilty undertaking.

'By God, Brown, you startled me,' he says. He knocks the leaf and branch away, and a small splash of moisture lands on the blue sash across his chest. The old man is dressed formally, notes Brown.

'Are we expecting company, Sir Joseph?'

'*We* are not expecting anything, Brown. *I* am due to meet with an . . . important individual later today. He is coming here to inspect the plant.' *And don't ask who it is*, is the unspoken instruction.

'Very good, Sir Joseph. I thought I might spend the day examining our new acquisition.'

'Acquisition?'

Brown nods at the breadfruit tree. Banks looks suddenly concerned and weighs something up in his mind.

'What kind of *examination* did you have in mind?'

'I would like to take some cuttings, and examine the leaves and the florescence under a microscope. The equipment I need is all here at Kew.'

Banks looks like he is going to object, and Brown finds this interesting. Why object to a study of such a natural phenomenon as this tree, which is (it seems to Brown) certainly a new species judging by its growth alone? What is Banks proposing be done about this?

But the old man does not, in the end, object.

'Examine as you will, Brown. But take care – do not damage the plant when taking samples.'

Banks sounds to Brown like an anxious mother leaving a child with a friend.

'No, indeed, Sir Joseph. I shall take every care.'

'See that you do. And ...' he looks up at the tree, and his face softens, 'let me know what you find out about her.'

He shouts for his attendant, who appears from behind a Jamaican candlewood tree and wheels the old man out.

Her.

Brown begins from first principles. The single astonishing fact of the tree is, of course, its growth. It is planted in the same earth as the other species in the Stove, so he believes its prodigious development cannot be attributed to any unique combination of salts or nutrients absorbed through the roots. No, somehow this tree must be taking in nourishment from the air at a rate of speed and in such quantities as have never before been observed.

A related thought occurs to him: why did the tree not grow like this on board the *Solander*? Could a tree go from sapling to giant so quickly in Kew and not show any evidence of such astonishing development on board the ship? Did it have to wait for some change in its circumstances before growing? There is something vaguely blasphemous about the thought, and Brown files it away for future cogitation.

The second fact, less astonishing but perhaps more pertinent to any classification, is the tree's florescence. It has only female flowers. Brown and Banks initially identified the tree as *Artocarpus incisa*, which is currently accepted as being of the class Monoecia Monandria, and the natural order Urticee. The tree is typically hermaphrodite, with male and female flowers. The male flowers form a long yellowish catkin with a single stamen. The female flowers gather into a globe with single perianths, each with a pistil. The fruit of *Artocarpus* is a berry, as large as a melon. It is this fruit which even now is feeding slaves and plantation workers in the Caribbean.

Brown makes a thorough examination of the tree, before taking any samples. He sketches it carefully – the bright green ovoid leaves, the triangular shape of the tree's growth, the deep brown, almost black bark. The colours should be hard to make out in the gloom of the Stove, but the tree's vitality transmits itself as if it is illuminated by some internal phosphorescence. He again carefully examines the female flowers. He wonders if this is a mutation – an accident of nature – but then dismisses such a thought. Hundreds of new species are still flooding into the botanic gardens of Europe from far-flung conquered places. It is far more likely that this is a new species, one with male and female plants rather than hermaphrodite ones, which has simply not yet been subjected to a botanist's investigation.

Brown has seen hundreds of new species, perhaps even thousands. He has drawn them, described them, taken cuttings from them, dried them and theorised about them. The thrill which accompanied the earliest discoveries has given way to a mild shiver of interest when a particularly unusual discovery makes its way to him. He has long ago decided that the world contains an almost infinite plenitude of natural wonder. Every European foot that treads on a far shore is almost certain to pick up dozens of new natural creations, for they litter the ground. The problem is one of classification, not of discovery.

There is a fresh excitement here. If this plant is a species of breadfruit, the economic implications will be enormous, as must already have occurred to Banks. The breadfruit tree has already transformed the economy of the West Indian plantations. It is fifteen years since William Bligh successfully transported the plant from Tahiti to Jamaica at the second attempt aboard the *Providence*, yet another journey sponsored by Joseph Banks himself. But a tree that grows this quickly could transform things again.

On the other hand, a tree without a fruit – which cannot

procreate – is useless as a means of feeding slaves. So perhaps this is indeed a curiosity, a mutation from the main branch of life, a weird and strange thing suitable only for a museum or a *hortus sicchus*.

He wonders if, anywhere within the samples from Otaheite, there may be a male plant of the same species. He observes that some of the female flowers on the tree are already beginning to dry out. They look like they could soon crumble.

He gazes on the female flowers for a while, the hard green leaves caressing his cheeks, the tree's dark odour filling his nose, his eyes prickling. Then he stands, and takes from his pocket the sharp little gardener's knife which his friend, Reverend José Francisco Corrêa de Serra, had given to him as a leaving present a week before the departure of the *Investigator*. Like him, it has been around the world, and its keen edge has bitten into all manner of wondrous and weird stalks, stems and branches. He uses it to cut into one of the younger-looking branches of the tree; no mean task, as they are *all* young. He hears what sounds like the shriek of a woman, almost as if she were in the Stove itself, and this so startles him that he accidentally cuts into the flesh at the end of his thumb, causing him to curse in a way which would have brought down righteous fury from his dead father. He sucks at the end of his thumb, his own blood metallic on his tongue. He looks about him, the severed branch in his hand.

He sees nothing, but walks around the inside of the hothouse to be sure. He even opens the door and shouts to one of the gardeners outside, irritated by the pain in his thumb. Had anyone heard a woman in distress? The man admits to hearing something, but could not be sure where it came from. Brown asks him to check the vicinity and the man complies, saying he'll bring word if he discovers anything.

Brown goes back into the Stove, and takes one last look at

the tree to confirm his findings so far. For a moment he imagines he is standing and staring at a savage on a New Holland shore, dark skin with white painted lines, and a bone through its flat nose. They were so fearful, those savages, so reluctant to approach and to converse, so different to the friendly, comforting Indian of Otaheite which he had seen described so often. But that fear, and their purple-black skin and penetrating eyes, made those New Holland savages all the stranger, all the more mysterious.

He takes his branch out of the Stove, and shuts the door.

There is a large shed which has been constructed in the Garden specifically for the landing, potting and cultivation of the plants from the *Solander*. In one corner of this shed, Brown has assembled a small version of his workbench in Soho Square, with paper, pencils, measurement devices, magnifying glasses and, most importantly, a microscope. Brown has been fascinated by microscopy since his days in Ireland, where he had acquired a single-lens microscope to help him botanise. It is still his favourite device, old-fashioned and in many ways little different to the original tiny devices made by Antonie van Leeuwenhoek in Holland a century-and-a-half ago. The excitement of seeing the tender skeletons of leaves and the rugged surfaces of seeds magnified dozens of times is still with him.

He cuts up the branch, chopping the leaves down, removing the female flowers and cutting the wood into serviceable chunks, which he proceeds to place under the microscope over the next three hours, a flower then a chunk of wood then a fragment of leaf, making notes and small sketches as he goes. The work of the shed goes on around him, and the Sun makes its way down towards evening, but Robert Brown pays no notice, absorbed once again in the work of identification and classification.

Around six, one of the gardeners shuffles up to him and coughs politely, then asks him if he has finished, for they wish to lock up the shed for the night. Brown looks at him for a moment, as if forgetting where and who they both are, his eyes round and open from their microscopic exertions. Then he smiles, tiredly, and says that yes, he will finish now.

He removes one more specimen from the microscope, and starts to slide the bits of tree into jars. The wood drops heavily into its jar, but when he picks up the leaves and flowers they crumble in his hands, suddenly dry and fragile. He has never seen a plant dry so quickly, and as he slides the fragmented material into the jar it reminds him of young green tea.

Nonsense, of course. Tea does not make itself.

He looks at the cut on his thumb, which had been forgotten during his work. His hands are stained green from his handling of leaves and twigs. The cut has scabbed over shockingly quickly, as if infected with the prodigious growth of the strange tree. He ponders this and barely notices the laughter from outside, where an unseen girl is running across the lawns of Kew.

ROTHERHITHE

As a young man – more a boy – Charles Horton had joined the Navy as a midshipman on the *Apollo*, a frigate out of Portsmouth. The ship was barely hours out of port and headed for Gibraltar and the Mediterranean when it encountered a pair of French ships off Brest. The subsequent fight, which was actually more of a protracted running-away on the part of the English and had almost led to the capture of the *Apollo*, saw the death of the vessel's captain and the precipitous promotion of its first lieutenant, John Willowhead, then in his mid twenties. When they'd finally extricated themselves from the attentions of the French, thanks to a particularly skilful and improvised manoeuvre on the part of their new young commander, the crew had sailed the *Apollo* back to Portsmouth, battered and bruised. Horton, like most of the crew, stayed with the ship and so did Willowhead, making post-captain after three more excursions.

Horton sailed around the world at least twice with Willowhead, a line of successful prizes enriching the captain and his officers and firing a fierce sense of pride among the frigate's crew. Willowhead was a man of no little learning, with a sardonic way of handling his men, and a ruthless appetite for combat. It was this hunger, Horton learned over time, which marked out men for successful captaincy. He recognised no such tendency in himself, and had for that reason given up any dreams of becoming a captain. Willowhead would do anything, go anywhere and fight anyone in pursuit of both a prize and of personal and national glory. Where possible, the two glories overlapped, but not always, and with most captains, including Willowhead, the personal was more resonant than the national. But he kept this leonine appetite in check through a careful allegiance to the safety of his crew. His cabin was crammed with books, his table was always pleasant and filled with direct, clever conversation. Horton was later promoted to lieutenant and transferred to the *Sandwich*, a newer and fiercer vessel than the *Apollo*, whose reputation receded along with her age. The last Horton had heard, Willowhead was involved in a skirmish off Japan, attempting to force the trading rights of that mysterious nation from the Dutch. But that had been a decade ago.

Captain Hopkins of the *Solander* strikes him as a man cut from similar lengths of robust but elegant sailcloth as Willowhead. He has a direct and unaffected way of dealing with other men, the consequence of an absence of fear but also the presence of respect. A third man Horton knew had that quality: Richard Parker, leader of the mutineers on the Nore in 1797, only two years after Horton had left the *Apollo*. If Willowhead had been his mentor, Parker had accidentally become his haunted inspiration. But Parker's quest for fairness and humanity in the Navy's dealings with its men ended with him hanging from a yardarm off Sheerness, and Horton in hiding from his shipmates, his future with Abigail bought with the betrayal of his fellow-mutineers.

Willowhead would not have done such a thing. This he has said to himself a dozen times a day for fifteen years.

Willowhead never had to, Abigail would respond.

Horton and Hopkins are seated in the Narwhal, each enjoying a pint of half-decent ale. Hopkins is angry but is trying not to show it. They are discussing the incarceration of Nott.

'You removed him from my ship without informing me, Constable.'

'We did, indeed. But there is no requirement upon the magistrate to seek permission from you, Captain. And he was not on your ship at the time.'

'No *legal* requirement, Constable. But a moral one, perhaps. You understand how it is on a ship.'

'I do, Captain.'

Horton is wary of this conversation. He half-suspects Hopkins of trying to open a fissure between the constable and the magistrate.

'And it is necessary to keep him at Coldbath Fields?'

'For now. He is not cooperating. I am hoping you may be able to persuade him to tell us why he was visiting Attlee and Arnott.'

'Can a man not visit his shipmates?'

'Has he visited any others?'

'Not to my knowledge. He's barely left the ship since we arrived.'

'Indeed? And why was he on board?'

'We needed a chaplain. Ours was taken ill before we even left London, and I had no chance to replace him for the outward track. Nott volunteered his services. The boy was keen to come to England.'

'Why?'

'I think no particular reason. His father is a man of some standing on the island.'

'A missionary?'

'*The* missionary. Most of his fellows have fled; the internal civil struggles on the island have become vicious in recent years. The missionaries were well-established, but the king has been struggling with rebels for years. He wasn't even on the island when we arrived; he'd removed himself to Moorea. I was worried about the unrest, but we had a pretty quiet time of it. The rebels subscribe to the old savage religion, and had made various threats towards the missionaries. Most of them fled to New Holland. Henry Nott, the boy's father, stayed. He is a remarkable man, but unyielding in his faith. Such unyielding men, in my experience, do not end well.'

'So the son is a half-breed?'

'Yes. His mother is an Indian.'

'The missionaries take wives?'

'Evidently. Though I imagine it was all very proper. No messing about in tents for Nott.'

Not like Sir Joseph Banks, you mean.

'The son seems to be of a somewhat odd nature.'

'Yes, he does. We were told by some of the locals to leave him behind. They seemed suspicious of him. I think he's a rather pathetic case, Constable. And any "oddness" he may be evincing will doubtless be partly rooted in his recent history. He travelled halfway round the world on his first ever sea voyage, and within days of arrival is locked up in a place which has the general reputation of being a shelter for vicious warders and corrupt magistrates. I'm surprised the lad hasn't done himself a mischief.'

'You mean, taken his life?'

'Oh, for the love of Christ, Horton. It's only a manner of speaking. I mean he is by no means a solid character, certainly, and you'd better be damned sure he's watched. I gave personal assurances to his father for his safety. I'm not a man who likes to give unmet promises. The boy looked like he was losing his mind.'

'You visited him?'

'Of course I bloody visited him! What decent captain would not? This morning.'

'How is he to return to Otaheite?'

'There are a great many vessels going that way just now. The French are sniffing round the island. They've got some idea that the current civil strife may give them an opportunity to move in. So we're sending men and supplies all the time. I'll get Nott back there. Once you release him, of course.'

'And assuming he is not guilty of the killings.'

'Oh, don't be ridiculous, Horton. He didn't kill anybody.'

Hopkins is furious, that much is obvious, but the fury is a cold one which he seems to be controlling. He speaks to Horton with the familiarity and respect of equals, which is generous of him, given they are by no means such.

'Tell me about the two dead men, if you please.'

'Very different to Sam Ransome. Hard working men, the two of them. Attlee is a Black Country lad, I believe, born and raised on a farm. Fine around the masts and in the sails, can do you a job anywhere. Arnott's from Grimsby. Fisherman's son. Doesn't say much, but works as hard as you like.'

'They were friends, then?'

'Indeed. Tight as anyone. Attlee does most of the talking, Arnott does most of the thinking, is what the rest of the crew would say about them.'

'And they were not particularly friends with Ransome?'

'No, Constable, I believe not. But as I have already said, there's not many on the *Solander* could claim to be close friends with Sam Ransome.'

It occurs to Horton that the captain talks about the men as if they were still alive. Hopkins drains the last of his ale.

'Shall we walk outside?' he says. 'I need to get back to my ship. We can talk further on the way.'

Without waiting for an answer, he gets up and walks to the door. Horton leaves the remainder of his own drink, and follows him.

The tide is falling and a few vessels at the edge of the river have already begun to settle onto the foreshore. It is grey and cold, less pleasant than the warm summer temperatures of recent days. Rotherhithe Street is busy, the shops and workshops and barrows all well-attended by shouting men and women, and everywhere the clanking wood-and-metal noises of the working river. The riverfront here has become as busy as Wapping's, with lumpers and watermen ferrying goods and people to and from the river, shouting at each other in words which sound as salty and alien as the incessant squawking of the gulls. A wind is blowing down the river and out with the tide. There are a few drops of rain in the air, but everyone ignores them.

Abigail will be somewhere like this just now, buying food and talking to friends. He wonders if her face will still hold that look of sad knowledge it held this morning when he left her, that terrible look which reflected back the awful images of the bloody boarding-house room of Saturday. That look will be added, like so many other things, to Charles Horton's melancholy store of guilt, which he carries inside him like a rock in his stomach.

'Will others die?'

Hopkins is not looking at him when he asks the question; he is looking out at the river. Sailing men, Horton knows, will always look out onto the water, whatever may be happening on the land.

'I cannot say, Captain, until I discover why the three who have already died were dispatched. That is the single thing I would wish to know: the motive for their deaths. If we have motive, we have a chance of discovery.'

'Have you *investigated* many events like this?'

'Myself, no. I understand killings within a crew are not uncommon, but these circumstances are unusual. Normally, such killings immediately follow the perceived affront. They come quickly and with passion – during the voyage, in other words. These events are rather different. Why should the men be killed only after they land in London?'

'Why, indeed?'

'Will you sail soon?'

'In a few days. The ship has been emptied of its cargo. It is still not entirely clear what will happen to her. She is formally owned by the Admiralty, and was only leased to Sir Joseph. Presuming he does not wish to fund a second voyage, we will no doubt be returned to the Navy and become His Majesty's Bark. There will be some errand that needs running to somewhere in the world.'

'Mr Harriott will have words to say if you leave before the murders are resolved.'

'I'm sure he will. I will do as I am told, by Mr Harriott, by Sir Joseph, or by Dundas himself.'

They reach the steps near the *Solander*, where the ship's yawl waits for its captain's return. A seaman sits inside, shivering slightly in the fresh air, bored but alert when he sees Hopkins appear at the top of the steps.

'I will visit Nott again this evening,' says Hopkins, walking down the steps.

'Is that a request or an instruction, Captain?'

'Neither. The man is a bloody innocent in a city full of rogues, and you've put him in the one place the greatest rogues can pick at his bones. I will visit him, Horton, whether you or your magistrate like it or not.'

'I do not foresee any problem with your doing so.'

'Do you not? Well, then, I am blessed. You know where to find me. Now, seaman, take me back to my ship.'

And Hopkins, who it transpires is even angrier than Horton had imagined, seats himself down in his yawl, and fails to say goodbye.

THE CHESHIRE CHEESE, FLEET STREET

John Harriott's day is taken up with Police Office business. He must catch up on other cases, and will be required to interrogate a half-dozen different men accused of a variety of offences. He deals with his correspondence first. There is a letter from Viscount Sidmouth, the new Home Secretary, requesting information on the murders in Wapping and Rotherhithe, stories of which have now entered the public realm. There is understandable concern in Whitehall that another situation of the same proportions as the Ratcliffe Highway killings is opening up on the damned river again. Harriott knows (for he is stubborn and bombastic but by no means stupid) how unpopular he was with Sidmouth's predecessor Richard Ryder. Now, a month after the shocking assassination of Spencer Perceval, there is a new administration to deal with, though Harriott rather suspects its dislikes and prejudices will be the same, even if the faces are different.

The letter from Sidmouth makes no mention of jurisdiction. Reading between its lines, however, Harriott can detect the whisperings of the Shadwell magistrates, who are no doubt maintaining that the first killing, at least, took place within their purview and that Harriott's interventions are an unspeakable outrage. Harriott replies carefully to the letter, telling Sidmouth of the incarceration of Nott and the investigations of Horton. Reading the letter back it occurs to him how sketchy and unsatisfactory are the results of their work so far. Three men dead, and all they have to show for it is one half-breed missionary locked up in the most unreliable prison in England.

So he folds up his first letter to Sidmouth and composes a second. It is a bland prevaricating missive that essentially says it is too early to say if there truly is a suspect, Nott's arrest notwithstanding, and that all efforts are being made to locate the perpetrators. *This is how Shadwell would behave*, he thinks with a grimace, and then wonders if he is not, after all, turning into a politician.

As well as the letter from Sidmouth, the pile of correspondence includes a curt and to-the-point note from Robert Brown:

Soho Square
Delivered by hand to John Harriott, Magistrate, Thames
River Police Office, Wapping

Sir,
Following our meeting, I have discussed your request with Sir Joseph. He is perfectly willing to meet with you, though his time is very scarce just now, taken up as it is with the new arrivals from Otaheite. He suggests that you join him and his fellow Royal Philosophers for dinner tonight at the Cheshire Cheese, Fleet Street, from 7 p.m., prior to this evening's meeting of the Royal Society. Please confirm by return your attendance.
I remain yours
R. Brown

The invitation is unexpected and generous and Harriott, still struggling to think like a politician, attempts to decode it. The Royal Philosophers are a well-known group of Royal Society Fellows and their invited guests who gather before every Royal Society meeting to dine copiously and discuss the latest discoveries and mysteries. For a man such as Harriott to be invited – a man with no ambitions or ability to be a natural philosopher, with none of the relevant reading or associations – is highly unusual. Why not simply invite Harriott to his house? With a rueful grimace Harriott remembers his only previous visit to the Banks residence on Soho Square. He sat, shivering, in a carriage while Graham went inside, refusing to take Harriott with him. He still feels aggrieved and embarrassed by the memory.

Perhaps Sir Joseph is seeking safety in numbers. The two men have never met before, but Harriott knows full well the capacities of Sir Joseph to manipulate events. He knows how he and Horton were used by Sir Joseph during the Ratcliffe Highway investigation. Now that unspoken knowledge sits behind this invitation, just as it had stood lurking behind his luncheon with Graham. Sir Joseph does not want a one-to-one encounter with the old magistrate. Perhaps he just wishes to avoid a row.

Well then, Harriott thinks. I will play the politician for another evening.

Just before seven, Harriott's carriage pulls up by the Cheshire Cheese. A well-dressed doorman helps him down and escorts him, with no little ceremony, into the tavern and through to a dining room at the back of the building. There he finds the Philosophers already assembled. Aaron Graham is already among them. Robert Brown is also there, and Graham goes across to speak in his ear before greeting Harriott. This rather confirms the magistrate's suspicion that the two of them have engineered tonight's invitation between them.

'My dear Harriott! A joy to see you. Brown said he had engineered an invitation.'

'A delight to see you too, Graham, as ever. I had no idea you would be here tonight.'

'Oh, I try not to miss these. They're always particularly good fun. Now, let me introduce you to some people.'

There are perhaps forty men in the room. Banks is already in his position as the presiding member, seated in gouty magnificence at the head of one of three long tables that have been squeezed into the little dining room. Graham manoeuvres Harriott skilfully through the room, chattering to various personalities as they go – 'John Harriott, magistrate, this is of course Edward Jenner, whose great work in vaccinations is so well known ... John Harriott, Thomas Young, who has broken new ground in the study of Light itself ... the Right Honourable Charles Abbot, of course, the long-standing Speaker of the House of Commons, may I present John Harriott, magistrate ... Robert Brown you already know, of course, and I do not need to list his many achievements ... John Harriott, magistrate, this is of course John Abernethy, the renowned surgeon ...' – the names a whirl of honours and prestige, some of them recognisable to Harriott, many of them heard for the first time and then forgotten. All the time they are making their way towards the President, Graham whispering in his ear betimes about Sir Joseph's personality and idiosyncrasies, in between presenting this surgeon or that baron or this discoverer of worlds. Harriott feels almost smothered beneath a blanket of Achievement, as if the successes and discoveries and inventions of the men in this room were some kind of heavenly score card against which his own struggles through life – Navy, East India Company, farmer, magistrate, inventor, bankrupt, magistrate, husband, father – look like a paltry harvest indeed.

Finally, they reach the head of the table, where the President sits silently, his wig of the old style (as indeed is Harriott's), his enormous belly encircled by the blue coat, the red sash and the one bright golden star so beloved by London's caricaturists. He is both surprisingly old and surprisingly formidable, and he is staring with enormous gloom into a large pewter tankard of porter. Various Fellows have edged towards him and then edged away again as his mood became apparent to them. But even in this gloomy state Banks is, without any doubt, seated in the very centre of the fray. There are other *significant* men in the room, perhaps a dozen by Harriott's reckoning; natural philosophers and nobles both. But these men only create their own little whirlpools of attention and deference. Banks is the still, brooding heart of the entire place, the sun around which the planets and moons revolve.

As they reach the head of the table, Graham leans in and whispers into the ear of the President, and Banks looks up and directly into the eyes of John Harriott. He glowers but now he also sparkles, the eyes filled with intelligence and the vestiges of what must once have been an extraordinary energy. Charm springs out of him like pollen from a zesty flock of Dutch flowers, the gloom lifted and blown away like steam disappearing from a great machine. He makes as if to stand but gives up almost immediately, grasping Harriott's hand and apologising for 'this blasted gout', and Harriott points out that he, too, is virtually lame and there is no shame in sitting, at which Banks positively glows with fellow feeling and indicates that Harriott should sit to his left, much to the visible annoyance of some of the other Fellows, who have had their own seating scheme in mind. Harriott does so, and Graham takes his own seat to Harriott's left.

'My dear Harriott,' says Banks. 'It is a great pleasure and honour to meet with you, sir.'

Harriott has rehearsed this meeting many times before. Sir Joseph Banks has been a persistent shadowy presence in his life these last months, a man of great power who seems to be able to craft circumstances to his own will. Harriott's resentment towards him is enormous and has, at times, almost overflowed. And yet here he is, being charmed by the old man (and yet, no older than he), resentment ebbing away like a receding tide.

'Sir Joseph. Your kindness and warmth towards me this evening is as welcome as it is unexpected.'

'Not at all. Graham here tells me much of the work you and he do in maintaining civic peace upon the hurrying currents of the river. I know of the sacrifices you have made in the service of the commerce, of the country, and, if I may say so, of myself and this society. You are a precious resource in our modern metropolis, my dear man.'

Harriott begins to see how Banks has risen so very high, and how he did it so very young. The man's charm is almost smothering, as if the air was being filled with it at the expense of oxygen. He cannot but help compare the events of his own life – with its adventures and shocking reverses – with the legendary dramas of the man's next to him. Both men have served Britain – and humanity – in their own way. But has Banks struggled like Harriott has? Has he had to scrabble around with the same financial helplessness? For there is the difference. It was money that made Banks so high, it was money that taught him this bountiful charm, and it is money that still keeps Harriott low. It is a sour thought amidst so much sweetness.

'We are of course dedicated in our work, Sir Joseph,' he says. 'But I make no comparison. You have discovered and catalogued entire worlds, sir. London may feel the benefit of my work. Mankind feels the benefit of yours.'

'Well, that is excellently put, Harriott, but I condemn it for its surfeit of praise. I have only lived to serve England.'

'Yes, sir. She is the mistress we all live for.'

'Indeed. And in these dark warlike days, it behoves us to remember her.'

'Indeed, Sir Joseph. Indeed.'

The food begins to arrive. One of the Fellows rises, a man Harriott does not recognise and to whom he was not introduced, but clearly a clergyman. He says a short prayer and blesses the food. Beef in steaks and cutlets is set on the table, along with mutton, potatoes and vegetables. A tankard appears at Harriott's arm, full to the brim, and in keeping with the general practice he downs the full pint with enthusiasm, at which point a replacement appears almost instantaneously. Graham encourages him to eat, and soon a plate piled high with meat, potatoes and vegetables is in front of him, along with a selection of sauces in bottles.

Banks eats little, but stares hungrily at the other diners.

'Curse this affliction,' he says, partly to himself, partly to Harriott. 'I have to eat like a young girl and drink like a governess. I would down this honeyed beer as you all do, but it would now kill me. Ah, me. Still. I have lived well, and fully.'

'We are indeed fortunate,' says Harriott.

'How so, sir?'

'We eat and dine well in this tavern, Sir Joseph. Many others do not. There are a great many poor and desperate men – and women – in Wapping, Sir Joseph, for whom this meal would represent a month's dining.'

'You are suggesting we are inconsiderate in our habits.'

'Not by any means. Your enjoyment has been well-earned by a life of dedicated service and, if I may say so, great personal courage. I merely point out that many men who may have very similar qualities have not risen so far.'

Graham chokes somewhat at this, and Banks looks at Harriott quizzically.

'Harriott, you seem to imply that I have been fortunate, while others have not.'

'Indeed, sir. That is not saying fortune is ill-deserved. But it is fortune nonetheless.'

'Do we not make our own destiny?'

'To a certain extent. But are we really able to say, Sir Joseph, that we are thus more deserving of any fame we achieve? I for one see Fortune as a fickle mistress. She has made me lame, she once washed away my farm in the waters of an Essex river, and yet she has also made me a magistrate.'

Banks considers this, and continues.

'I wonder, Harriott, to what extent this applies to countries as well as men.'

'Sir?'

'Take this country, this England. Its situation, for one: a temperate climate, well suited to horticulture and agriculture. Surrounded by sea, a natural defence against predators. A surfeit of natural resources, chiefly coal, which is even now driving huge changes in our wealth and our power. In historical times, forest covered the land, and we used the wood from that forest to build ships. In those ships we travelled the world, we discovered countries and we claimed them, we named them and we controlled them. We emerged onto foreign shores, and the natives saw us and were amazed, and we learned their languages and their habits. Some of them ate us. Some of them pleasured us. Some of them ran away. But the English took hold of the world. We sent them our prisoners, and we brought back their seeds and their bulbs and their plants and created little paradises of our own. Did you know, Harriott, that the word *paradise* comes from the Persian word for *garden*? We built paradises here on our damp and lucky little island, but we left behind our European diseases in those paradises we discovered. Diseases of the body, but diseases of the spirit, too: dissipation, greed, violence. All this, you say – and I agree, Harriott – depended partly on the Fortune of our situation. And if Fortune does indeed weigh everything and distribute her riches according to the weighing, I am caused to wonder what she makes of those foreign peoples. Were they lucky? Or were they quite as unlucky as they could be?'

He stops. There is a watchful expectancy around the table. Harriott realises that the whole group has been listening to this little homily. Some of the Fellows – the more ostentatiously attired ones, whom Harriott takes for Nobility rather than Philosophers – look mortally offended. Graham smiles impassively, presumably waiting to see how the room has taken Banks's speech before framing his own response.

'But surely, Sir Joseph, these other places have benefited from our knowledge of them,' says Harriott, carefully, but with patriotic feelings stirring in his breast.

'Perhaps so, Harriott, perhaps so. In what forms, would you say, do those benefits appear?'

'Well, sir, in Religion. Our missionaries have brought them the fruits of Salvation.'

Banks says nothing for a while, pondering a fork.

'I do wonder,' he says, after a moment, 'whether the Lord needed our missionaries to make himself known.'

The clergyman who had blessed the meal makes a small noise, as if he were swallowing a puppy.

'You see, Harriott, we found these peoples in a primitive state. Many of their practices were barbaric, and continue to be so. But they also existed in a state of innocence. The people of Otaheite, for example – we must remember with what wonder we first encountered them. They seemed both primitive but also, dare I say it, *blessed*.'

'But can we really say that of them, Sir Joseph? They sacrificed men, women and children.'

'They did indeed, and no doubt they still do, and you go right to the heart of the matter, Harriott. They were well-fed and they were healthy and yet they were implicated in the most profound evils. They fought and killed each other and in the recent past they may have eaten each other. We saw those things and they disgusted us, such that we were able, I think, to ignore their other qualities. Their innocence. Their happiness. The extraordinarily blessed circumstances in which they lived. That Island is so fertile, Harriott, that it feeds an empire.'

'How so, Sir Joseph?'

'Its breadfruit, Harriott. The breadfruit which Bligh took to Jamaica – in a ship called, mind you this, *Providence* – and which feeds the workers there and across the West Indies. The workers who harvest the sugar which fills the coffers of the banks in this great city we sit in tonight. That breadfruit we took from Otaheite, and in return we gave them missionaries, yes. But we also gave them disease. We poisoned their island with the flux and the pox. I do wonder what Milton would have made of such a transaction.'

The room has fallen quite silent. The clergyman looks like he may pass out. Aaron Graham has a fixed smile on his face, but it is the kind of smile he would make if a duchess's dog had appeared and starting bouncing its loins up and down on his leg. Robert Brown's face would look carefully blank were it not for one slightly raised eyebrow.

Banks looks around at them and suddenly laughs – an explosive bark of a laugh which punctures the sudden tension in the room like a musket-shot through a hot-air balloon, and the glee in his face is a miracle.

'Look at them, my dear Harriott! Look at their shocked faces! The President of the Royal Society has just questioned the beneficence of England's gifts! Look at Abbot! My dear sir, fear not. I am no apostate. We are English, gentlemen. We are members of the finest and longest-standing group of natural philosophers on God's earth. We wake every day and we advance human understanding. All God's people, from my Lord Liverpool to the meanest aboriginal savage in New South Wales, benefit from that work. Be proud, gentlemen! Be ecstatic! We are doing God's work!'

And with a *hurrah* the room raises its tankards and downs yet another portion of porter, and as the plates are cleared, cheese, wine and brandy make an appearance. Banks turns to Harriott. Harriott, whose time with Horton has wrought more changes in him than he'd care to admit, affects the same bonhomie as the rest of the room while watching the President carefully. The President now seems as cheerful as any man in the room, but the old magistrate can clearly see the lines of care drawn across his forehead, and thinks there was rather more to that little speech than the mere baiting of clergymen.

'This business on the *Solander*, Harriott. I understand you wish to discuss it with me.'

'Yes, Sir Joseph. Three men are dead. The first was apparently killed in his rooms by an unknown person, for reasons we cannot establish. Two other men were killed only this weekend past – they roomed together in Deptford, and were again murdered for reasons unknown. There are some grounds to believe the killings are connected, the principal one being, of course, that all three were crewmen on the *Solander*. We are holding one man on suspicion of being involved in some way, but there is no direct evidence to link him with the killings, and nor does he say anything to incriminate himself.'

'Who is this man?'

'His name is Nott. He is a man of the island, the son of a missionary. He acted as chaplain on the vessel on the return journey.'

'Chaplain?' Banks frowns. 'Hopkins made no mention of such an appointment to me. This chaplain is, I take it, the son of Henry Nott?'

'Yes, sir. You know the man?'

'I know him well indeed, Harriott. I have kept in contact with Otaheite as far as I can, and of course I needed to arrange matters for the *Solander* voyage. Anyone who knows Otaheite well knows Henry Nott – he is an impressive man, though still a missionary.'

Harriott does not pursue that. Not after what just transpired. Banks looks at him, as if anticipating some response. When none comes, he continues.

'The presence of his son in England is confounded odd, mind. Also odd is the fact that I did not know Nott even *had* a son. Who is the mother?'

'Why, I . . . do not know. Young Nott's appearance suggests his mother was an islander.'

'An *islander*? Nott with a native woman? I fear you must be mistaken, sir. That is by no means in Nott's character. Others have no doubt indulged themselves with the pleasures of Otaheite's women, myself among them.' Banks speaks directly, unembarrassed. 'And this man is of what age? He must be at least twenty years, must he not? Nott did not reach the island until fifteen years ago. It is out of the question that Nott can be father to this man you are holding.'

The obvious truth of this fact gives Harriott pause. It also causes him some embarrassment; for Banks to have so quickly understood this, when he and Horton had given it no mind . . .

'But why have you arrested this man?' Banks asks.

'Well, sir, this Nott, as he calls himself, was visiting the two men who were killed in Rotherhithe. He is, as far as we know, the last man to see them alive.'

'And yet you are here, Harriott. Which suggests to me that you do not think this man was the killer. Whoever he truly is.'

'I do not believe he is of that character, no, sir. And I do not see his motivation for committing such a crime.'

'Yet his background has been called into question.'

'By this conversation, certainly.'

'There are no other avenues of investigation?'

'We are doing all we can. But I would be remiss in my work if I did not seek to ask *you* if there might be any indication of trouble aboard the ship.'

'None that I know of. Hopkins is assisting you?'

'The captain? Yes, sir. I have met the man myself.'

'He is a first-class fellow. His voyage transported more live plants and cuttings than any other in history. He followed my instructions to the letter. I am delighted with him.'

'You cannot think of any reason why someone should want to kill these men?'

'Well, let us examine the circumstances. The deaths occurred in London, not on the voyage itself. That in itself is worthy of note, is it not?'

'How so?'

'Because they did *not* happen during the voyage. Believe me, Harriott, it is a trivial matter to kill a man on board a ship. But to kill *three* men – well, now that would draw some attention. And the deaths happened only days after arrival?'

'Yes, sir.'

'So it is perhaps safe to deduce that the motivation for the deaths was something which happened either on the voyage, or on the island itself. But why not kill the men on the island if it were the latter?'

'It is an excellent question. I do not have an answer.'

'Hmm.'

Sir Joseph's face is one of fierce concentration.

'Does anything link the three men?' he asks.

'Nothing we can guess at. The captain sees no obvious connection.'

'How were they killed?'

'We believe the first man was strangled. The second or third deaths – their throats were cut.'

'Hmm. An interesting combination: a calculated killing, and then two passionate ones.'

'Not necessarily, Sir Joseph. The second or third deaths also had something calculated about them. Nott claims to have seen the murdered men alive and asleep, but the room around them ransacked. He ran away, and by accident encountered my officer, who returned to the room with him. There, they discovered the men dead, their throats cut and the blood fresh. The men were found in bed, as if they'd been killed in their sleep. We are unable to establish how the blood can have been so fresh if the rooms were so thoroughly ransacked after their deaths, nor can we understand how they would have stayed asleep during the ransacking if they were not dead.'

'And you only have this so-called Nott's word for the first part of this episode.'

'Indeed. It is why I am holding him under a charge.'

'So, either Nott killed them – in which case, why? Or someone killed them between him fleeing the room and returning? And the men never woke as they were attacked.'

'It is a conundrum, Sir Joseph. We do not yet have the answer to it.'

'Nor do you know exactly how or why the first man was killed.'

'Indeed.'

'Your job is a difficult one, I think, Harriott.'

'There have been difficult episodes within it, certainly, sir.'

Harriott does not know why he says this. A slight frustration at the relentlessness of Sir Joseph's questioning, perhaps. He also struggles with how odd it is, conversing with a man who has occupied so many of his thoughts for such a long time. They share a history, the two of them, deriving from the previous year's Ratcliffe Highway murders investigation. But neither may mention it, or the way it ended. It is as if a third man sat between them – or a statue, perhaps, covered in a shroud. Banks, who had been staring into his tankard in concentration as Harriott explained the events in Wapping and Rotherhithe, now looks up in surprise and, Harriott sees, some irritation at the impertinence of this magistrate.

'Difficult episodes I am sure,' says Sir Joseph, and his voice is low and somewhat threatening. 'We all of us have participated in events which we would not have chosen. But our duty should always be at the front of our minds.'

'Duty, Sir Joseph? I am a man who has had a long and hard attachment to duty.'

'So I am led to understand. And sometimes duty enforces its own silence, when to talk would damage the institutions we seek to preserve.'

'And sometimes silence acts as a seedbed for its own corruption. For if a man be not allowed to speak, he may turn resentful.'

'Do you know of such a man, Harriott?'

'I know only men who know their duty, Sir Joseph. But not all men are the same.'

'Indeed not.'

Banks looks long and hard at him. The charm is still there, dancing in his brow, but it is dancing with a cold and steely partner now.

'What do you need of me, Harriott?'

'I would like to see your records of the *Solander* voyage – any papers on the crew, the contracting of the ship, and correspondence. The more access we have to your records, the greater the chance of establishing some connection between the three dead men, and perhaps a motivation for their deaths. I would also like my officer Charles Horton to be able to interview the gardeners who went on the voyage. Captain Hopkins has informed him that these men are now in Kew, under your immediate supervision, and it is for you to release them for interview.'

'You shall have all of it. As two men who speak of duty, I would have you understand that I am at your service in this regard.'

'And I would have you understand, Sir Joseph, that I know my duty, however resentful it may occasionally make me.'

'I understand you completely. And now, some brandy?'

'I would be much obliged.'

From Harriott's left, Aaron Graham, who may have been holding his breath throughout this entire exchange, lets loose a long, audible sigh of relief.

SIX

If the universe bears a greater likeness to animal bodies and to vegetables than to the works of human art, it is more probable that its cause resembles the cause of the former than of the latter, and its origin ought rather to be ascribed to generation or vegetation than to reason or design.

David Hume, *Dialogues Concerning
Natural Religion*, 1751

TAHITI

The two young princes – the one of the island, the other of England – climbed ever higher into the centre of Tahiti, sweating in the morning sun. The day was still and hot and clear, as all the days had been since the arrival of the English ship. They had been walking for almost an hour, since the prince had met his friend at the point where the thick green forest met the open plantation land down near the sea.

'I have a great surprise for you,' the island prince had said the previous evening. They had been sitting near the Englishman's tent watching girls dance in the fire light. The Englishman, like all his countrymen, watched the girls hungrily, his eyes half-closed, his palms rubbing together as if under their own volition. 'Meet me tomorrow morning, and I will show you something which will change the way you think and feel.' The prince had been serious-faced and sober, and his friend had laughed distractedly, his blue eyes dancing along with the girls. This island had already given so much. How could there possibly be yet more?

It had been three weeks since the arrival of the English ship.

The men from the northern hemisphere were now well-established, their little encampment just above the shoreline a busy conjunction of the island's different worlds. Prostitutes and fishermen came to sell their wares, desperate as their fathers had been for the iron which the English brought with them. Even the whores could be paid for in nails.

Since their first meeting, the prince and his new friend had spent many hours together, walking and discussing and exploring. The Englishman could not believe how accomplished the prince was with his own language, and took the opportunity to be taught a few island words. The prince had been preparing for this friendship, and the opportunities it brought, for months. He had been trained in the English language by the lonely half-breed, who was shunned by the islanders and had for company only the fierce old missionary who had adopted him.

The half-breed and his stepfather came to the English encampment every day to warn the sailors of the dangers of the island's syphilitic whores and to offer their redemptive services to the depraved and lost souls of the visitors. To start with, they were ignored. Increasingly, they were verbally abused or even worse. The prince had come across the young half-breed at the back of the beach the previous evening. He had been staring out to sea, tears in his eyes. The prince saw in those eyes the same longing he felt: to be far away from here, over the blue edge of the world, on the way to the northern island paradise of England.

'So, Prince of England. Tell me about your own kingdom,' the prince had said one night, almost a week after their first meeting. The two of them were sitting in a tree, watching the bay of Matavai in which the Englishman's ship was anchored, surrounded (as it always was) by dozens of the island's canoes and fishing boats. The Englishman had laughed, a big delighted laugh. He was no prince, but his savage friend's little joke enchanted him.

'Ah, my *kingdom* is a cold green land of rain and storms,' he had said at last, his big open face lit by the fires from the beach, his hair bleached almost pure white by the weeks at sea. 'There are mountains and valleys and birds that whistle down from the skies. My people work underground, digging jewels and coal from the ground and singing while they work, and when night falls we gather against the windy rain and drink a sweet nectar that kills memories and lights up dreams. We are a fierce sailing people, builders of boats and smelters of iron, and we travel the world seeking adventure and pleasure, the far horizon our only boundary.'

The island prince had watched his new friend during this pretty little speech, and at the mention of horizons and discovery the Englishman had looked out onto the ship and the bay and had lifted his chin into the soft warm breeze, as if to smell the shores which lay over the edge of the world.

'And will you take me to your kingdom when you leave?'

At this the Englishman had looked less pleased. He became furtive and fidgety.

'If you so wish,' he had said, but he did not look at the prince. 'But enough of this. I need a woman!'

The prince had laughed, and had shouted down to the ground, and four of his finest concubines had appeared and began to dance below them, turning and turning, their clothes falling to the ground.

For the next three days, the prince kept returning to the same subject: the Englishman's kingdom, and his desire to see it. Each time the subject was raised, the Englishman became short with him and changed the subject, until it was obvious to the prince that his new friend was not ready to carry him away from the poisoned island. Not, that is, unless the prince could give him something in return.

So he'd appeared at the encampment last night with a

proposal, and now he was taking his English friend to the place high in the hills, the plateau where no Englishman, not even the missionaries, had ever been. They walked along the river, as the prince had done dozens of time before, the walls of the hills growing tall beside them. They came upon a waterfall, and they crossed the pool below it and then climbed even further, the trees around them coming in closer and closer until, quite suddenly, they emerged through the treeline onto the open plateau.

At the centre of the open ground was a single tree. It was a breadfruit tree, thought the Englishman, who knew something of botanical matters. Its leaves were green and shining, and it stood fifteen feet high and elegant. It seemed to occupy the clearing as if the place was made for it, and the birdsong which surrounded the two men was at once deafening and as sweet and organised as a choir.

To the right of the tree was a slightly raised table of flat stones – a *marae*, like several the Englishman had seen around Matavai bay, constructed from rock and coral piled up to create a more-or-less flat area raised two feet off the ground. The *marae* were both churches and cemeteries to the islanders, the sacred ground on which they acted out their own religion. When the Englishman had asked his friend about such matters the prince had become quiet and secretive, as if embarrassed or even fearful.

At one end of this particular *marae* stood a kind of altar, a flat rock lying atop two smaller rocks. The prince stepped up onto the stone platform, indicating that his friend should by no means follow him, and thus quietly consecrating the space on the flat top of the construction. He walked to the altar, making strange movements with his hands and his head which, the Englishman supposed, were the equivalents of genuflecting.

As he approached the altar, the prince knelt down and laid his head on the floor, his hands out in front of him, prostrate. Then he sat up on his knees again, the ritual apparently over, and removed a flat stone from beneath the altar. From inside he pulled out a bag made from *tapa*, a material made from tree bark, about the size of a coconut and seemingly just as full. He also picked up two wooden cups from the cavity. Then he stood, backed away from the altar, and stepped down from the *marae*.

The prince walked a little way to the edge of the clearing. The Englishman could see that the ground here was scorched, as if many fires had been lit. The prince began to gather twigs and branches from the treeline, and soon had the beginnings of a little fire on top of the scorched ground. Then he went into the trees, telling the Englishman to wait.

After only three or four minutes, he returned, carrying something which caused the Englishman to frown with surprise: an iron kettle, obviously from the northern hemisphere and very old. The prince had filled it with water. The Englishman began to ask where on earth this relic of his own land had come from, but the prince shook his head and pressed his finger to his lips. *Be quiet. No more questions.*

The prince opened the *tapa* bag and with enormous care – *infinite* care – he dropped several pinches of the stuff inside into the kettle. The Englishman glimpsed something that looked like tea within, dried and fragrant, but then the prince closed the bag again. He placed the kettle within the flames, and then they waited.

After only a few minutes, steam began to rise from the ancient kettle's spout. Steam and something else: a strange aroma which made the Englishman's eyes water and his nostrils dilate. With the same ceremonial care the prince poured water and the infusion from whatever had been in the bag into the cups from beneath the altar. Then, finally, he handed one of them to his friend.

The Englishman gazed down into the liquid in the cup. He could see various bits of organic material, fragments of leaf and triangular shapes that looked like the tops of some strange flower. He breathed in the aroma and his head spun, momentarily, in one great circle around itself, like the leaves circling in the hot water. He looked up and saw the prince watching him and was surprised, even shocked, to see the expression on the savage's face. For the first time the Englishman thought the prince looked like a king, a great king from the far side of the world, skilled with hidden knowledge and enormous wisdom. The Englishman remembered the joke about his own fabricated royalty and felt not so much ashamed as suddenly terrified lest this king should ever be offended.

The wooden cup was in his hand, hot in his palm. He held it up to his nose, and something flashed before his eyes – *a beautiful young woman, running away* – and then he drank it, and everything changed.

He sipped, then gulped, then swallowed it whole, the leaves and seeds accompanying the water down his throat and into his stomach, and then his head exploded with light and the trees were full of everything and the world was a golden coin which he held in his hand, and he fell backwards onto the earth as the island prince watched, a surprised look on his face, shocked by the strength of the Englishman's reaction to the leaf.

The tree in the clearing rustled in the breeze, and waited for its newest acolyte to wake up.

SOHO SQUARE

A couple of years after his return from New Holland, Robert Brown became ill. He had fallen ill many times in his life, but this had felt different. He was overcome by a terrible torpor, a sense of nothing being to any purpose. Worse, this dissolute sense of indolence was accompanied by an intermittent but profound deafness. When this came over him the world was smothered in a dull hum which, with a terrible irony, seemed to grow louder during the evening and kept him awake, such that his torpor grew worse due to lack of sleep.

It was a difficult time for other reasons, too. Sir Joseph was proving a mercurial patron. He seemed uninterested in Brown's plans for a major work on the botany of New Holland, and barely supported the younger man's *prodromus*, for which the Scot ended up paying most of the costs of production. As a result only 250 were ever printed. Sir Joseph's own journey to the far side of the world had bought him enormous fame and bountiful connections. It seemed to Brown, who had made as big a journey, that he had returned to general indifference and penury. He was on the point of returning to Scotland and resuming a medical career when Jonas Dryander died, and Banks offered him the post of librarian.

Today, he is a person of some consequence. His *prodromus*, he has been told, is viewed with awe by France's finest botanists. His positions with Sir Joseph and the Linnaean Society bring with them a certain standing in society. Nonetheless that old sense of torpor had been returning, along with those thoughts of returning to medicine.

But everything had changed with the previous day's examination of the alien tree at Kew. A new kind of energy is now pouring into him. He did not sleep the previous evening for thinking of the impossible tree. A new species of course, but so much more than a species. A potential economic miracle, a breadfruit tree which is alien and astonishing, a plant with such capacity for growth that it throws into question many of the experimental botanical discoveries of the last thirty years.

This morning he stays in Soho Square to research the matter further in the Banks library. He starts at the beginning: with the papers from the original *Endeavour* voyage, principally Sydney Parkinson's sketches of breadfruit and the descriptions of them by Sir Joseph. He re-examines the papers from the *Bounty* and the ship that followed her, the *Providence*, which successfully took live breadfruit from Otaheite to Jamaica twenty years previously, as the *Bounty* had been intended to do. There is no record in any of the documents available to him of a tree such as the one he saw yesterday. Nor is there anything in the records of Sir Joseph, Lieutenant Cook or Parkinson.

He has placed the dried specimens from last night on a shelf above his desk, and now he gets up and examines them again. There seems to be nothing special about them, here in their component parts, no great revelation to be had. He takes down the microscope he keeps here in the library and then thinks better of it. Today is for following a paper trail, not for further hours lost with his eye to a microscope. He opens one of the jars, the one that contains the dried leaves and flowers which looked to him like tea the previous evening, and the odour from within nearly overwhelms him. His head spins for a moment in a great leap around the place, and the odour flies up into the room such that he believes for a moment he can almost *see* it, this bizarre concoction of smells which causes his nostrils to quiver with life. He feels light-headed and dizzy, and tries to remember if he ate breakfast.

'You'd best sit down, Brown. You look somewhat uncertain.'

Sir Joseph wheels himself into the library, and Brown snaps awake. The first thing he hears is the sound of a girl giggling in the street outside. He goes to shut the window.

'Leave it open, Brown. The air is particularly pungent in here, and I am still recovering from last night. I indulged myself rather more than is good for my health.

'Indeed, Sir Joseph? And you are not to visit Kew today?'

'Not today, no. I had to be in London for the Royal Philosophers dinner last night, and will attend to matters here. These are the specimens you examined yesterday?'

'They are.'

'May I look?'

Brown feels an unaccountable resistance to showing the material to Sir Joseph, a feeling which he observes with some detached interest, as if another part of him were gazing down into the room through a microscope. There is no earthly reason he should feel possessive towards the specimens. A headache is beginning to form just behind his left eye, in a familiar place, and something like the old lassitude has crept up upon him. The entrance of Banks has brought back unwelcome maladies.

'As you wish, Sir Joseph.'

He says it with some insolence, and Banks notices this with a raised eyebrow followed by a scowl.

'I will take care, Brown, not to damage your specimens.'

He holds each jar up to the light and looks within. After a few minutes of examination, he begins asking questions, and it is these questions, Brown realises, that he was hoping to avoid.

'The flower is that of a breadfruit tree?'

'It is, Sir Joseph. As far as one can tell from a tree that is still so young yet possessed of such prodigious growth, the flower is of a piece with breadfruit. The female flower, that is.'

'Hmm. And the flower grows as fast as the rest of the plant.'

'Indeed it does.'

Brown watches the economic calculations whirl through the old man's brain, and feels thinly disgusted.

'How did you dry the material?'

'I did no drying, Sir Joseph.'

'You must have done. The contents of this jar are quite desiccated.'

'Yes. But I did not dry them. They became like that within hours of being cut from the tree. Perhaps even quicker – I did not notice how dry they were until the end of the day.'

'They dried like this inside the shed yesterday? At Kew?'

'Indeed, Sir Joseph.'

And now Banks, like Brown had done, opens the jar with the dried stuff in it. Even from the other side of the desk Brown can smell the extraordinary scent. Banks, for his part, widens his eyes and sits back in his chair, holding the jar away from his face before, after a few seconds, gradually bringing it back in towards him.

'My God. Extraordinary,' says Banks.

'It is.'

'I am reminded of nothing as much as the smell of the hemp plant, *Cannabis sativa*, which I understand is used in India in some forms of religious ritual. Cannabis, of course, has male and female plants with their own flowers. Unlike the *Artocarpus*.' Banks replaces the lid on the jar.

'Yes, I can see the resemblance,' says Brown.

'It had already occurred to you?' says Banks.

'In the matter of the flowers, yes. In the matter of odour, no, Sir Joseph. Just now, watching you open the jar, I was reminded of something, but your knowledge is wider than mine.'

'I wonder if it can be consumed.'

'That is perhaps something to be tested.'

'One would need to make it into a form of tea, I would imagine.'

'Perhaps so, Sir Joseph. Though it would be a dangerous effort.'

'But not one without precedent. I remember reading of Robert Hooke's experiments with an Indian tea made from hemp; *bhang*, I believe they call it. He wrote about the experience. It is in the Royal Society library somewhere. There may even be a copy in here.'

Sir Joseph closes the jar and puts it back on the table.

'And the male flowers? There continue to be none?'

'None, Sir Joseph.'

'So this cannot be *Artocarpus incisa.*'

'No, Sir Joseph. The lack of male flowers, the prodigious growth . . .'

'Indeed. But how useful is a breadfruit tree with no fruit?'

'Not useful at all. But no doubt this is just a matter of finding the male plant and bringing them together. As I understand it, no male plant has been found. This seems particularly odd, given how thorough the botanists were in their collecting.'

'You spoke to the botanists about this?'

'I have had some conversations. I need to have more.'

'Perhaps that is something I should do directly. They may feel more obliged to be complete in their report.'

'Is there a suggestion that the botanists are somehow dishonest, Sir Joseph?'

'No, Brown, there is not. But this plant is important. We should do everything in our power to learn as much about it as we can.'

And with that, Sir Joseph leaves.

WAPPING

The day after the Royal Philosophers dinner Harriott has a heavy head. He has not drunk so much beer and wine in a single evening for a long while, and the morning is taken up with a good deal of staring out of the window from his ancient chair, trying to piece together his conversation with Banks and tease out the meanings. He does not relish such quiet introspection at the best of times, but with a headache and a stomach which is murmuring in protest at its mistreatment this is by no means the best of times and he is capable of little else.

Banks had seemed preoccupied during their conversation, certainly, but a man with as many wheels turning as Sir Joseph is bound to be preoccupied. He had been warm and welcoming towards Harriott, and there had been little of the tension Harriott might have expected. This morning he'd received word from Robert Brown that Horton might visit him at Soho Square to arrange interviews with the *Solander* gardeners and inspect the documentation relating to the voyage to Otaheite. Sir Joseph has been as good as his word already, but however hard he pushes his addled old head Harriott cannot recall a single sentence from the President's pronouncements the previous evening which might help Horton move the case forward.

There remains an unacceptable void at the heart of the case, a dead space, as if no one with any authority truly cared that three men are dead, two of them in very unusual circumstances. Harriott knows these were ordinary men, by definition unexceptional, and in that sense possibly disposable to men like Sir Joseph Banks. Perhaps he is being unfair, but it seems to John Harriott – who has always valued ordinary men, and rather thinks himself one of them – that he could end this case immediately, turn it into another file in the River Police archives, and it would attract no comment.

These worrying thoughts are interrupted by an unwelcome arrival: Edward Markland, one of the three magistrates from the Shadwell police office and, in Harriott's eyes, the most intelligent but also the most devious. Despite the proximity of their offices, and the frequent uncomfortable overlaps between their investigations, the two men have never shared a dinner or indeed a conversation other than one pertaining to a particular case. They circle each other within London's chaotic legal systems like impotent lions fighting over a barren pride.

Markland is shown in to Harriott's room by the servant and extends his customary smooth greeting.

'My dear Harriott, a pleasure to see you. I take it you are in good health.'

'I am, Markland, thank you. Won't you take a seat?'

'Thank you, I will. And Mrs Harriott does well, I trust?'

'She does.'

'I have still never had the pleasure of her acquaintance.'

'Really, Markland? Well. Is this a social visit, or a business one?'

Markland marks Harriott's impoliteness with a smiling pause and some business with his hands, which brush off invisible fibres from his silk breeches. He looks up with his routine smile and calmly delivers his bombshell.

'I came to tell you we have had reports of a particularly vicious set of deaths in Ratcliffe. Three dead, one strangled, two slashed throats. The circumstances bear some uncanny resemblances to the killings you are yourself investigating in Rotherhithe.'

He stops and waits for a Harriott explosion, but he does not know of Harriott's thick head, which is only capable of a dull irritation this morning. Last night's alcohol seems to have leached away any capacity John Harriott might have had for explosion.

'You are well informed as to Rotherhithe,' he says.

'It was in the newspapers this morning, Harriott. It is not a state secret.'

'You believe the same person or persons may be responsible for both slaughters?'

'I do rather think so. Two of the dead men were crewmen on the *Solander*.'

This second bombshell is accompanied by that same fixed smile. Markland looks like a boy watching a cat in a box into which he has just dropped a mouse.

'You are certain of this?'

'Of course. The woman who owns the boarding house where the incident took place told us as much. Now, you are investigating two separate incidents, one in Wapping, one in Rotherhithe. The first should of course be the responsibility of *my* office, Harriott, and the second – well, the second is a moot point; you are investigating in any case. Now, I hear you have made little or no progress on either of your cases, which of course I do not believe. You have the most effective men here, as you are sure to state. That one clever fellow we had dealings with before. Naughton, was it?'

'Horton.'

'Ah yes, Horton. Well, I am here to suggest we cooperate on these incidents. I suggest that Horton investigates the murders in Ratcliffe, along with those already under investigation. We would take joint ownership of the, well, what should we call it? The *operation*, perhaps. We can combine our resources, Harriott.'

Hangover or no, Harriott sees immediately what Markland is up to. The fame of the *Solander* and its sponsors, and the infamy of the existing murders, mean that a successful investigation will bring enormous political capital. But there is no one in the Shadwell office with the detective capacities of Charles Horton. So he is to be co-opted. It is clever and, Harriott supposes, it is a kind of compliment to his River Police Office.

'Are the detailed circumstances of the Ratcliffe murders the same as those which preceded them?' asks Harriott. 'Are you sure they are connected?'

'Oh, you can be assured there is every reason to think so. In addition, we have a witness who saw the killer.'

Harriott almost smiles at that, but is not so oppressed by last night's excesses that he forgets himself. The Shadwell magistrates are always good at trawling for *witnesses*. Whenever they investigate a serious crime, they approach it the same way: ask if anyone saw anything. As a result, every woman and man with a grudge against any other woman and man comes forward to assert that yes, they saw who did it, it was him or her or them who did it, arrest them now, they've had it coming to them for a long time. The Irish and Portuguese in particular are favourite targets for these witnesses. Every murder Shadwell investigates is accompanied with a sudden but temporary incarceration of large sections of both those communities.

That said, there is something unusually *certain* about Markland this morning. The fact that it is he who has come with this proposal, and not his fellows Story or Capper, says something. Markland is clever. He would only make this move if he thought there was personal gain in it for him. He cannot gain from Harriott making a mistake, for they both know that Harriott has no reputation to speak of in Whitehall and that the new Home Secretary is just waiting for the old man to die or retire before putting someone in the River Office more compliant and willing. Perhaps, Harriott thinks with a start, Markland himself.

The servant knocks on the door, firmly but politely, and Harriott tells him to come in, at which Markland looks momentarily put out before reattaching his unflappable face. The attendant whispers in Harriott's ear.

'Constable Horton has returned, sir. You asked to be informed of his arrival.'

'Thank you, Upson. Tell him I will be done here in a few minutes.'

The attendant leaves and shuts the door, and Harriott turns back to his adversary.

'Your idea has merit, Markland. It may well be that the murders in Ratcliffe are by the same man, or they may be by someone different entirely. Either way it makes sense for Horton to establish the truth of it and judge the bearing, or otherwise, these killings might have on the existing cases at hand.'

'I am glad you see the sense of it as well.'

'I must speak to Horton and it may also be necessary to put more men on the case.'

'I can find men.'

Harriott is sure this is true. But he has seen the calibre of the men Markland employs.

'But Horton must lead the investigation.'

'Of course. Your faith in him is well known and, it is said, well placed. He is discreet and effective.'

'He is, sir, he is.'

'Then I may leave it with you, Harriott?'

'You may, Markland.'

The Shadwell magistrate rises, and approaches Harriott's desk, his hand out. Harriott struggles to his feet, ignoring Markland's entreaties to remain seated, and they shake on the arrangement. Markland holds onto Harriott's hand firmly as he speaks.

'We have never spoken of the Ratcliffe Highway investigation and its conclusion. It ended in some doubt. Perhaps one day we could discuss it over some dinner.'

Harriott smiles.

'Perhaps, Markland. Though I must warn you, there is very little I am permitted to tell you.'

Markland's smile slips again at that, and Harriott's grows wider.

'Well, Harriott. No doubt there is good reason for the secrecy. Good day to you.'

Markland opens the door, and on the other side of it Harriott sees Horton, who nods at Markland curtly and almost rudely. Markland, for his part, stops and takes his hand, gives it a shake and says something which causes Horton to frown and stare at him, and then Markland has gone.

'Come in Horton, come in,' says Harriott, sitting down again with a sigh of relief.

'Sir, Mr Markland just congratulated me on joining his operation,' says Horton as he comes into the room. He looks confused and perhaps a little upset.

'Did he now? How very characteristic of him. Well, here's the fact of it. More murders have come to light. In Ratcliffe, this time. According to Markland, the men killed were crewmen on the *Solander*. He's suggesting we incorporate the Ratcliffe deaths into our own operation, with myself and

Markland as co-authors, as it were. You're to lead the investi-gation, of course. Some of Markland's men may also join you.'

Horton begins to speak, but Harriott raises his hand in some irritation.

'I know, Horton, I know. You work better alone. But this is a political matter. You will have to rely on me to keep Markland and Shadwell at bay, but this Ratcliffe situation may well help us unlock things on a particularly sticky case.'

Horton now looks miserable. Harriott has little time for this.

'Pull yourself together, man. And go and look at these bodies.'

RATCLIFFE

On Harriott's instructions, Charles Horton heads for Ratcliffe. Like his magistrate, he is becoming frustrated with this case. There seem to be countless threads, but they tangle themselves in his hands. He has still to interview the gardeners in Kew, and had intended to travel there today, before this new interruption. He believes there is more, a lot more, to discover about Peter Nott's involvement in the affair. He has tried to speak again with Jeremiah Critchley, who lives at the Pear Tree in Wapping. He has walked past that place dozens of times since it formed a central part of the previous year's Ratcliffe Highway investigations, but he has never once gone in before now. Reacquainting himself with the house – and its landlady, Mrs Vermiloe, a key witness in the 1811 inquiries – was uncomfortable and frustrating. He has knocked on Critchley's door four times now, and has received no response. The door is always locked and Mrs Vermiloe, now a legal expert, has refused him entry without a warrant from his magistrate. Harriott has now promised this, but not before Horton looks into whatever new horror has been perpetrated in Ratcliffe.

That name – *Ratcliffe* – rattles in his head, speaking of earlier horrors and secrets, as if the word itself haunted him.

In a different time and place the chance to investigate fresh bodies in a case which seems to be generating more and more of them would be irresistible to him. So why this great reluctance? Is it because more bodies will just mean more threads to thicken the knots he is already failing to unpick? No, not that. Edward Markland is the problem. He goes to meet the Shadwell magistrate with no enthusiasm and with that constant sense that his past is waiting to snatch at his clothes and pull him down. Markland is a dangerous man. In the past he has alluded to knowledge of Horton's past – of the mutiny in the Nore, of Horton's purchase of his freedom with information on his shipmates. It gives Markland a power over him, and one such as Markland is not to be trusted with power. When talking to Markland he feels like a man tied and bound in a room full of spiders.

He walks along the river, deliberately avoiding the route through Shadwell. Thirty minutes of walking brings him to Rose Lane, and the boarding house which is his destination. There is a small crowd of people outside the house. Horton pushes through them, not without stirring some complaint, and goes inside.

The stench in the hallway is terrible: shit and death, the odour roiling through the air like the pollen of doomed plants. Markland, despite Horton's roundabout efforts at avoidance, is there. He is accompanied by two of the Shadwell constables, Hope and Hewitt, a partnership of particular viciousness. Their presence depresses Horton immediately. If this is the standard of investigation Shadwell has conducted so far, Horton has little hope for it.

'Ah, Constable,' says Markland. He does not offer a hand, but smiles like he might at a new manservant. 'We have been waiting quite some time for you. I fear you must inspect the scene immediately so we may clear it. The smell is almost overwhelming.'

Horton looks around him.

'Where are the residents of the house?' he asks Markland. He ignores Hope and Hewitt, and feels rather than sees the scowls with which they have welcomed him.

'Removed to ... well, somewhere,' says Markland. 'The landlady alerted the local constable yesterday evening. There was a man here, she says, who went upstairs and then left in a great hurry. She went to investigate and discovered the bodies. We emptied the house then so we could secure it. I believe this is the kind of procedure you think important.'

'It is vital to secure the scene in case of evidence, yes. But have your own men not investigated the evidence?' At this he does look at Hope and Hewitt who look back at him as if ready for a fight. He very much hopes Markland answers no.

'Oh, they surely have,' says Markland. 'But as I explained to your magistrate, I believe you have unique experience of this kind of thing.'

So Markland has no faith in his own officers. His deal with Harriott is to secure his own reputation and to avoid the incompetence of his own men. Horton sees the truth of this immediately.

'We have names for the men?'

'Well, of course, Horton. For two of them, in any case. The landlady furnished us with those. Elijah Frost and Colby Potter. The third body is unidentified. I believe Frost and Potter were crewmen on the *Solander*.'

Horton does not respond to this. He tries to remember if Frost or Potter's name came up in his interviews with the crew. He rather thinks neither did.

'Did the landlady describe the man she saw running away?'

'She did indeed. A tall blond man with blue eyes. Unusual. I do believe she found him rather handsome.'

Horton thinks: *Critchley?*

'The room is upstairs?'

'On the top floor. There is a small room up there. That is where the murders were transacted.'

'I shall head up there immediately, then.'

He makes for the stairs, and Hope and Hewitt make as if to follow him. Horton stops on the bottom steps and turns around, speaking directly to Markland.

'If it pleases you, sir, I'd rather inspect the room on my own.'

He does not look at Hope and Hewitt, but the savagery coming off them almost breaks through the stench coming from the top of the house. It has a sour reek all of its own. Markland frowns for a moment, irritation breaking through his smooth exterior, but then smiles that empty deliberate smile.

'Very well. Officers, await Mr Horton down here. Now he has made an appearance I shall return to the Shadwell office. Horton, I'd appreciate a report this evening.' He places a hat on his head, and taps his elegant cane on the wooden floor of the hallway, before disappearing out of the front door. Horton turns and heads up the stairs, still not looking at Hope and Hewitt, still sensing their intense wish that they be allowed to take him in hand and inflict careful injury upon him.

The stench deepens as he climbs to the top of the house, such that he covers his nose and mouth with a handkerchief. The final flight of stairs is almost beyond endurance. There is a terrible buzzing of flies in the air – it has been warm this past night and day. The door into the room at the top of the stairs is open, and he steps inside.

He is struck immediately by the similarities with the room in Rotherhithe, but also by the obvious differences. The similarities, first: two men have had their throats cut while, apparently, lying asleep on their beds. Flies buzz around the open necks of both men, and around the thick bloodstains which cover the walls, again a clear echo of the room in

Rotherhithe. Both men's sea chests have been pulled out from under the beds and opened. Both men are holding little wooden cups at the bottom of which is the same residue Horton found in the cups in Rotherhithe.

Then, the differences. The third body, for one: lying on the ground, face down, a thick leather lace lying around its neck, the obvious instrument of death. There is a lack of any other mayhem in the room, too, as if the killer performed no search this time, finding what he was looking for (assuming, of course, he was looking for *something*) quickly and efficiently. Or perhaps he knew where to look.

As he did in Rotherhithe, Horton stands still for a while, not consciously watching anything. The room gives up no other secrets, but it suggests a narrative to him just as the Rotherhithe room had done. Something about the way the third body is lying, as if the man had been looking at the bodies on the bed, and someone had come up behind him . . . Yes, he can perhaps tell a story of the third death. So did this man discover the two other men sleeping, as Peter Nott claims to have done? Or were they already dead?

He kneels down and turns the face-down man over, and recognises him immediately. It is Robert Craven, one of the crew he'd interviewed in the *Narwhal*. The man who'd intimated that Attlee, Arnott and Ransome had shared a great secret. Had they shared it with the two dead men in this room? And had Craven discovered it?

After perhaps thirty minutes, Horton shuts the door and walks back downstairs. Hope and Hewitt are waiting for him, and begin to speak, but he walks past them to the door in the street and, turning back on the way out, says only this:

'You can clear the room now. Call the coroner. I'll report to Markland.'

If Hope or Hewitt had a gun at this point, Horton is sure he'd be feeling a lead ball in his back. Instead all they have is enraged silence, so Horton gets out of the house alive, his head churning with possibilities. He says nothing about Robert Craven.

By the time he gets to the Shadwell office, Markland has already departed, a casual neglect of duty which Horton finds frankly astonishing. John Harriott would be waiting behind his desk, blustering and impatient. Therein lies the difference between the two men.

Still he does not go home. Not yet. His brain is fiercely alive and aware, and he needs to let it run its course lest he spend the entire evening discussing the case with Abigail. Her exposure to the scenes in Rotherhithe is still a fresh wound to him; he has no wish to return home this evening with more tales of slashed throats and unhinged slaughter. So he stops in at the Prospect of Whitby for a pint of ale and a think.

A man he recognises is sitting in the corner of the tavern: Angus Carrick, known to the rest of the *Solander*'s crew as Red Angus. He'd been the first man Horton had interviewed in the Narwhal. Carrick is working his way through a huge plate of herring, and a jar of whisky and a glass sit alongside. It is a quiet night, with only a few drunken workers from the dock keeping him company.

Red Angus scowls at Horton as the constable sits down. He downs a half-glass of whisky with barely a flicker of a grimace before slamming it down on the table.

'You again,' he says.

'Me again.'

Horton waits and watches the *Solander*'s cook.

'Please join me, Constable. You're welcome to make free with my comp'ny.' Carrick sneers sarcastically, and then starts again on his plate of herring.

'I've been to Ratcliffe.'

'Have you, now? Bugger all in Ratcliffe, is there?'

'More than you'd imagine.'

Red Angus looks at him, his mouth full of fish. It is a long, appraising look.

'You playin' with me, Constable? Havin' a little joke at my ill-educated expense?'

'Why do you believe that?'

'Because ye've a smug air about you, Constable. An air of knowing more than the rest of us, and of wonderin' when and where you're going to put us all in our place.'

This shocks Horton. Is he really like that?

'Tell me about Robert Craven,' he says.

'Why?'

'Because he told me about a secret that Ransome had, with Attlee and Arnott.'

'Craven told you that?'

'Yes.'

'Well, ask him about it, not me. Wasn't much happened on the *Solander* Craven didn't know about it. Oh, he's no killer, mind. But he's a quiet creepy little sod. Always watching and listening. Bit like you.'

'You strike me as an unusual man, Mr Carrick.'

'Mr Carrick? No one's called me Mr Carrick since my ma died.'

'What would you prefer I called you?'

'I'd prefer if you fucked off.'

'Well, I've got a job to do.'

'Aye, ye have. And I canna help you do it.'

'Can't or won't?'

'Both.'

He pours out another huge shot of whisky from the jar, and downs it.

'You Scots like your drink.'

'We Scots like to forget what you English have done to us. Whisky is a great aid to forgetting.'

'Who might have wanted Attlee or Arnott dead?'

'I haven't the faintest idea. They were good lads, as I say.'

Horton sees with interest that he's considering the matter. There is a quick brain behind those bristling red whiskers.

'One of us *could* have done it. But I don't know why we would. None of us had any particular time for Ransome, but none of us had any particular grudge with him neither. And that goes double for Attlee and Arnott. Of the men you had speak to you in the Narwhal, I'd say Critchley was the closest to Attlee and Arnott.'

'Jeremiah Critchley?'

'Yes. Come to think of it, he was tight with all three of them, he was. Ransome too. We assumed they were all buggering each other. On the island, they were forever disappearing into the night.'

Horton leans forward.

'Disappearing?'

'Now, don't get excited, Englishman. There was a lot of *disappearing* went on in Otaheite, believe me. The women, you see. They'd fuck you seven shades of blue and then they'd fuck you again, and then their mothers would fuck you, all for a few nails and a bit of old iron that might be lying around. Some of us was almost sick of it by the time we got back. '

'So where did these men disappear too?'

'No idea. But they went off together more than once. Potter and Frost, too.'

Carrick ponders.

'Bloody hell. I think they've rooms over in Ratcliffe.'

Horton stands.

'Enjoy your herring, Red,' he says as he leaves.

GERRARD STREET

Brown asks himself whether he is really contemplating this.

He is sitting at his desk in his apartment at the Linnaean Society in Gerrard Street. This is where he lives and, for a few days every month, works. The Linnaean Society may pay the bulk of his upkeep, but it is Sir Joseph Banks who takes up the bulk of his time. In his drier moments Brown has contemplated asking Banks if he should move into Soho Square, perhaps in a bedroom next to Sir Joseph's own, so he can be on hand at all times of day or night to tend to the old man's needs.

It took him no time at all to find a record of the Robert Hooke experiment to which Sir Joseph referred. It is collected in a book in Sir Joseph's library, filed under Hooke (there is a copious amount of material filed under Hooke). The book was published in 1726, and is already very old, and well-used. It is called *Philosophical Experiments and Observations of the Late Eminent Dr. Robert Hooke and Other Eminent Virtuoso's in his Time (with Copper Plates).* The book collects many of Hooke's more obscure lectures and experiments, and on page 210 Brown found the relevant lecture.

He has read this account a dozen times now, but feels no nearer to preparing himself for what it is he is considering. Following in the path of old Hooke is one thing – a kind of blasphemy, but a blasphemy that Hooke himself would have had no hesitation in committing. Newton himself had spoken of standing on the shoulders of giants, and while Hooke would not have used such a messianic turn of phrase he would have recognised the need to repeat experiments that had gone before. He probably would have added that the shoulders Newton was referring to were frequently those belonging to Robert Hooke.

It is more that the world has changed since those early adventurers. Newton had stuck a bodkin down the side of his eyeball as part of an investigation into optics. Hooke had been the Royal Society's first curator of experiments, in which role he had gleefully imagined dozens of investigations which combined the insanely practical with the wildly creative: depriving dogs of air, using telescopes as telegraphs, investigating the vibrations made by a musical chord. But it is as the father of microscopy that Brown has long worshipped his forebear, the creator of the *Micrographia*, the describer of hidden worlds which leapt with unrestrained passion and horror up to the naked eye under Hooke's lenses.

The *bhang* (or "*bangue*", as Hooke had it) experiment is typical of the man. Hooke knew that *bhang* had already been consumed by Indian natives, but he couldn't have known how the substance would affect a European. Even so, the experiment was performed on himself, recklessly and fearlessly. How can Brown hope to follow him?

One answer springs to mind: because Brown has sailed around the world.

And that is true, isn't it? Hooke may have been creative and brave, but so little of the natural world was known and understood in the late seventeenth century, so much remained to be named and discovered and described, that Hooke could begin his investigations in the immediate environment around him. He could describe an entire world by looking at a flea. But there has been a century-and-a-half of noticing since then. Men need to look further and further afield for new discoveries. Brown himself had drained all the mystery out of the hills around Edinburgh by tearing up plants and describing them. Everything on those remembered hills was now *known*. The *not-known* is further and further away, on the far side of the world, where a host of flora and fauna without names or description remains to be discovered. It is men like Brown who are cataloguing that host.

Brown wonders to himself how Hooke would have managed on an ocean voyage. It is a presumptuous thought; almost, again, a blasphemous one. Yet had Hooke ever set foot on an oceangoing craft? Had he indeed ever been on a body of water wider than the River Thames? Had he ever felt his vessel climb then fall down mountains of water, the breath of death blowing through its sails, men screaming and shouting in a mad mixture of terror and delight?

Brown does not think so. And it is this thought that gives him the strength to nudge open those same doors as his illustrious predecessor.

He makes careful preparations. He instructs one of the servants at Gerrard Street, a young boy named Leary, to wait outside his door, with instructions to check upon him every half-hour and to come in immediately if Brown calls out. He has paper and quills prepared to write with, for he intends to describe the experience of taking the leaf even as he is experiencing it, unless he passes out and is unable to do so. Leary is to watch him if he passes out, and tell him anything he sees. The boy can read and write, but Brown prefers to rely on his eyes and memory than on his literacy.

A kettle is boiling on the little fire in his room. He lays out the paper and quills next to the book containing the Hooke lecture, in case there are parallels which occur to him. He takes the kettle from the fire, pours it into a pewter cup he has ready for the purpose, and as he drinks, he begins to read:

An Account of the Plant, call'd *Bangue*, before the *Royal Society*, Dec. 13 1689

It is a certain Plant which grows very common in *India*, and the Vertues, or Quality therof, are there very well known ; and the Use thereof (tho' the Effects are very strange, and, at first hearing, frightful enough) is very general and frequent; and the Person, from whom I receiv'd it, hath made very many Trials of it, on himself, with very good Effect.

'Tis call'd, by the *Moors, Gange*; by the *Chingalese, Comsa*, and by the *Portugals, Bangue*. The Dose of it is about as much as may fill a common Tobacco-Pipe, the Leaves and Seeds being dried first, and pretty finely powdered.

This Powder being chewed and swallowed, or washed down, by a small Cup of Water, doth, in a short Time, quite take away the Memory and Understanding so that the Patient understands not, nor remembereth any Thing that he seeth, heareth, or doth, in that Exstasie, but becomes, as it were, a mere Natural, being unable to speak a Word of Sense yet he is very merry, and laughs, and sings, and speaks Words without any Coherence, not knowing what he saith or doth.

Brown takes a jar containing the desiccated leaf of the Otaheite tree and opens it. Once again that heady, pungent, numbing odour leaps from the open jar, and causes him to hesitate at the brink, to ask himself if this is wise and prudent. But he reminds himself of his responsibility to Knowledge and

Understanding (the initial capitals resound in his mind), and pours the water onto the leaf.

The odour instantly intensifies, as if a cloud of smoke were being sucked down into a hole, turning into a solid column rather than a diffuse miasma. Brown begins writing.

The leaf and its tea

The Leaf is dried and has broken down into many smaller parts, and now strongly resembles a tea leaf from China, though none of the normal preparation required for tea has taken place. The Leaf has simply taken this form of its own accord. The odour of the dried material is strong and reminds one clearly of Cannabis sativa, *though with an earthier undertone.*

When boiling water is poured onto the Leaf, this odour intensifies even further, and sniffing the steam from the water causes my Head to spin slightly, as if from a sudden combination of Drink and Tobacco. Removing the head from the steam causes this Sensation to quickly pass, leaving the Head very clear and capable of rapid Thought, as if refreshed by a dose of clear cold Water. I am now about to drink the Tea, and will attempt to write down my sensations and any other items of Notice as they occur to me.

The effect of the leaf

The Tea from the Leaf is bitter and foul tasting, and . . . its effect is sudden. It has burned my tongue badly, but the pain is as if from a distance place. My head fills light . . . filled with light . . . and the room . . . suddenly huge.

Young Leary hears Mr Brown shout from inside the room, and hesitates for a long while. His instructions had been quite clear: to enter the room if he hears a shout, *of any kind*, Mr Brown had said, and his eyes had been emphatic on the point because, more than anything, Mr Brown had looked scared. Leary, who is barely sixteen, has never seen any of the bookish men who congregate at the Linnaean Society look scared. Angry, yes, and frequently impatient, and certainly not beyond smacking their dry botanical hands around the back of his head, but never *scared*.

So he enters the room reluctantly, as per Brown's instructions, and finds the librarian lying with his head down on his desk, a pewter cup hanging down by his side in one hand, the other hand holding a quill which blindly carves out odd patterns on the paper laid out on the desk. There is a rich dizzying odour in the air. Leary rushes to the side of the man, and Brown then sits uprights and grabs him by the throat.

'There is light ... light ... pouring out of me ... pouring out of the walls ... spinning ... my Father shouting.'

Leary struggles and eventually Brown lets go, his eyes rolling back into his head as he falls back in his chair. Leary stumbles back a step or two, and then Brown arches his back as if from a great convulsion, and shouts more of that insane gibberish.

'An Island ... there ... a boat ... a figure in white standing in a boat ... cliffs, the sea ... scared ... a tree ... roots go deep down the mountain ... into the island a tree ... holds the Island together.

Leary grabs a cloth from the sideboard and drenches it in a bowl of cool water. He does this automatically, as if a cool cloth to the head could cure the ills of the world, his memory full of the sweat-drenched face of his mother as she expelled his dead little sister and with one final arch of her own back departed this world. Brown screams, and leans forward in his chair, holding his stomach, his head down on the desk again. He speaks as he does so, and Leary is conscious that he should be remembering the things Brown says. He wishes he could write them down, but feels Brown gave him no permission to use the quill and paper on the table. Leary instead concentrates on remembering what he sees and hears. Brown has dropped the pewter cup but the other hand still scrabbles frantically at the paper, the quill scratching like rats beneath the floorboards. But the marks he makes are only swirls and lines, not letters. He mutters while the strange random characters pour from the quill.

'Something is chasing me ... chasing me through the trees ... I can hear her coming ... Oh my *Lord* ... there is pain and ... *infection* ... I feel my blood in my veins ... something else ... something else in my veins ... it is sharp and ...'

He screams again, and then falls back, allowing Leary to mop his forehead once more. Gradually, Brown's face smoothes out and relaxes, his breathing steadies and a smile breaks out over his face like sun over a calming sea. Within only two minutes he is peaceful in the chair, staring at the ceiling, the quill forgotten at his side, his fingers picking out shapes in the air above his face, as if organisms danced in the space above him.

'I can see ... inside *everything*,' Brown whispers, rapturously. 'Inside ... my eye is a microscope ... there, at the heart of everything ... inside the Cell itself ... there, small ... invisible ... in every cell the same thing ...'

Hooke: After a little Time he falls asleep, and sleepeth very soundly and quietly; and when he wakes, he finds himself mightily refresh'd, and exceeding hungry.

Minutes pass, and then an hour. Brown's fingers continue to dance in the air, but gradually they slow and eventually drop to his side. Brown's eyes close, and he sleeps, leaving his young attendant to carefully resoak the cloth, over and over again, his mother's voice whispering back through the years.

Three hours afterward

I have sent Leary away. Several hours have passed since I drunk the tea made from the leaf. Leary woke me from a sleep after much trying, he says. He believed me almost dead, so hard was it to wake me. At first I did not want to wake up, and I shouted at him for disturbing my dreams (I do not remember doing so, though Leary assures me this is true). He was scared and said he would go and fetch help. But then the effect of the leaf seemed to cease, suddenly, as if dying off from lack of sustenance. It was an extraordinary sensation of falling away, as if my head was filled with a light-infused smoke which then, without warning, disappeared, leaving me awake and refreshed but also in a state of profound thirst and hunger, both for food and drink but also for more of the tea.

Hooke: And that which troubled his Stomach, or Head, before he took it, is perfectly carried off without leaving any ill Symptom, as Giddiness, Pain in the Head or Stomach, or Defect of Memory of any Thing (besides of what happened) during the Time of its Operation. And he assures, that he hath often taken it, when he has found himself out of Order, either by drinking bad Water, or eating of some Things which have not agreed with him.

It is now three hours since I took the Tea, and I can report strange contrary feelings of great physical renewal combined with intense thirst for more of the leaf. My former feelings of lassitude and torpor, which plagued me some years ago and had in recent days been returning, have entirely gone. Also, my mind seems to be operating with a renewed clarity, and even my vision seems sharper and clearer than it had wont to be. And yet I take little comfort in these advantages, for they are accompanied by this sharp hunger and thirst for more of the leaf, which I am struggling to overcome. For there can be no doubt of the intensity of the experience of the leaf, and until I know a good deal more about it I am not prepared to indulge myself.

Hooke: He saith, moreover, that 'tis commonly made Use of, by the Heathen Priests, or rambling Mendicant Heathen Friars, who will many of them meet together, and every one of them dose themselves with this Medicine, and then ramble several ways, talking they know not what, pretending after that, they were inspired.

Four hours afterward

I remember only impressions of the visions which followed my initial consumption and preceded the deep sleep I fell into: a boat heading towards an island, and a preacher, no doubt my Father, standing on a staircase and shouting, from passion, from fear or from revelation I cannot recall. Most powerful of all are two images: being chased through an alien forest by someone who wished evil upon me; and a bizarre theory, as it were, about the internal structures of plant cells and their unity, a thought which has never before struck me but which cries out to be investigated. And everything suffused with an intense light, a bright white cloud which surrounded me even while I dreamed. I did not succeed in writing down any words while the vision had me in its grasp, but Leary ran in and was able to tell me some of the things I said. His recollections are strange and fragmentary but seem to confirm what memories I have. What I did write during the vision is incomprehensible, the hand an alien one, as if I were possessed of another's personality.

Hooke: The Plant is so like to Hemp, in all its Parts, both Seed, Leaves, Stalk, and Flower, that it may be said to be only *Indian* Hemp. Here are divers of the Seeds, which I intend to try this Spring, to see if the Plant can be here produced, and to examine, if it can be raised, whether it will have the same Vertues. Several Trials have been lately made with some of this, which I here produce, but hath lost its Vertue, producing none of the Effects before-mentioned; nor had it any other Operations, good or bad, since I receiv'd it with this Account I have related; imagining I had met with somewhat like it in *Linscotten's* Voyages, which the Reader may peruse at his Leisure.

The effect of the leaf is, of course, extraordinary. But also extraordinary, I think, is the suddenness of its cessation. Apart from the clarity of my physical senses and this raw hunger for more, there are no other after effects. Nothing remains of that strange dreamlike state. I wonder if perhaps the dose was too small (but I must not allow myself to intensify it), or if there are perhaps other ways of consuming it which will prolong the effect – the Chinese smoke opium, and I have even heard tell of the Indians making bhang with milk, which seems to intensify the experience. It is perhaps significant that Hooke talks of a dose of bhang being 'enough to fill a Tobacco pipe' – did he in fact attempt to smoke the Cannabis sativa?

Hooke: I have formerly given an Account of the Effects of the Roots of *Hemlock*, accidentally eaten by some young Children, which, at first, had an Operation on them much of the like Nature with this Vegetable; and possibly the last Effects might not have been much differing, if they had not made Use of Medicines, to recover them out of the Trance, before the Period of its Operation, tho' that be uncertain, and wants Experiences to ascertain it. Whereas this I have here produced, is so well known and experimented by Thousands; and the Person that brought it has so often experimented it himself, that there is no Cause of Fear, tho' possibly there may be of Laughter.

Five hours afterward

It is now five hours since I took the tea, and my body and, as it were, my appetites are returning to their normal states. The old headache behind my eyes has begun again, a familiar but unwelcome acquaintance. And I seem to have persevered in the face of the gnawing hunger which came on when I woke up; it no longer seems to me that I need to take more of the tea, even though it remains in my power to do so. The odd thing is this: I miss the hunger. It seemed to be of a piece with that extraordinary sense of clarity which accompanied it, as if one could not exist without the other. I wonder if there is not perhaps some greater truth in this.

Hooke: It may therefore, if it can be here produced, possibly prove as considerable a Medicine in Drugs, as any that is brought from the *Indies*; and may possibly be of considerable Use for Lunaticks, or for other Distempers of the Head and Stomach, for that it seemeth to put a Man into a Dream, or make him asleep, whilst yet he seems to be awake, but at last ends in a profound Sleep, which rectifies all; whereas Lunaticks are much in the same Estate, but cannot obtain that, which should, and all Probability would, cure them, and that is a profound and quiet Sleep.

The hour is now late. The fire is out and the lid is back upon the jar. My body and my mind feel as heavy as a wet sail, and I can write no more. I shall retire to bed, and consider these findings in the morning.

SEVEN

And may not light also, by freely entering the expanded surfaces of leaves and flowers, contribute much to the ennobling of the principles of vegetables? For Sir Isaac Newton puts it as a very probable query: 'Are not gross bodies and light convertible into one another? And may not bodies receive much of their activity from the particles of light, which enter their composition?'

Stephen Hales, *Vegetable Staticks*, 1727

TAHITI

Up on the high plateau the young prince sat and took in the view. It had never been particularly impressive. The trees obscured everything almost all the way around the clearing, but by positioning himself just *so* he could see across towards Tahiti Iti, the smaller of the two peaks which formed the island.

He was feeling nostalgic. Today was the day he would leave the island. Down in Matavai Bay the English ship was waiting. His blue-eyed friend Jeremiah would be there as he had promised, waiting on the beach by the big wooden boat in which the English went from ship to shore. Together he and Jeremiah would sail to that dreamlike country in the north, where men built towers which climbed to the sky, and great vessels rode the waves, and fierce fishermen grappled with whales. Where *sugar*, that sweet drug of the prince's longing, was so plentiful people would pour it out like rubbish into the streets.

It was because of this vision of England that he had introduced Jeremiah to the leaf. They had shared it now on a half-dozen occasions. Most recently other Englishmen had taken it with them. Jeremiah said these others had learned of the leaf, though he never said how. He said they needed to be given their own share of the leaf to be taken home, to ensure their silence. So yesterday the prince had lain down with the six Englishmen on the *marae* and taken the leaf on the island for the last time. The prince had given them all a small pouch as a token of his loyalty and friendship, and this was no small thing; the cult of the leaf strictly forbade taking the leaf down the mountain. He had made each of the Englishmen promise him to take the leaf with them off the island immediately and not to speak of it, because of his concerns that the cult members he would leave behind (who were, after all, only his friends) would be discovered by the other islanders and their secrets exposed.

He had other concerns, too. Since that first time with Jeremiah, he had been startled and a little frightened by the nature of the leaf's effect on the Englishmen. For he and his island friends, the leaf brought visions of light-drenched peace. Drinking it was like lying down in the woods on a beautiful day with no work to be done and no worries to intrude. The leaf provided an escape from the pestilential present of Tahiti.

It was not the same for the Englishmen. For Jeremiah and his countrymen the effect was violently rapturous, and unexpectedly addictive. Since that first time Jeremiah had pestered him on every meeting for more of the leaf, and at times this pestering had been coloured by desperation. And Jeremiah was strong, in body as well as character. Not all the other Englishmen were like him. Some of the other five had looked like hungry dogs when they came back up to the *marae* after their first time.

Each of the Englishmen had assured him that they would take the leaf with them from the island. They assured him that they would take him as well. Was he not their friend? The prince, now so steeped in his original crime that there was no going back, became reckless and said he would find more of the leaf and would bring it with him, tomorrow, when the ship left. Their eyes had glittered with a strange animal greed which he did not recognise; all of them were now consumed by an endless longing for the leaf. The prince realised, of course, that this gave him enormous power over them, for only he knew where the leaf came from.

Which is why the prince was here, now, at the *marae*. The space beneath the little stone altar had been emptied, and what remained of the leaf which had been in the *tapa* bag beneath the altar was now in his own pouch, compressed and ready for use. This would mean there'd be none left for the cult, but they would not have to wait for long. The tree guaranteed a plentiful supply. His new friends, and particularly Jeremiah, would be delighted to see the full pouch, and delighted to see him. They would accept him as one of their own, and at the end of the great voyage they would introduce him to the wonders of England.

But first, he must say goodbye in the accepted fashion. He walked over to the *marae*'s altar and prostrated himself before it. He followed the established ritual of the cult – a new ritual by the standards of the island, invented by self-conscious young men and women only a generation before. He said a small prayer to the island gods before standing and walking over to the true object of veneration, the thing which had brought the cult members up to this point all these years.

Not the *marae*. The tree.

He hailed her in the traditional way, from a respectful distance:
Thank you for letting us see You.

We who live upon this place are delighted, for we share it with You.

In this form You are shown to us, and in this form we understand You.

We thank You for the gift of this Home, this Island, and for the gift of the Life which you have breathed into us.

And we thank you for the Leaf, without which we would never have known You.

Those who went before us are now as one with You. They swim in your Dreams and speak of us here. Soon we will see them, and once again we will be part of You.

He was standing by the tree now. He put his hand against the tree's bark, then his forehead, then his other hand, and he leaned into the tree and whispered the refrain of the Saying:

Thank you for showing yourself. Thank you for being here.

This is what they always whispered before they took the leaf and lay down to swim in its delights, beneath the gaze of the tree. His eyes were closed and his head was pressed into the bark, the words of the Saying in his ear, and his lips moving. So he was shocked by the sudden sound of someone walking up behind him, but this shock was over in an instant because hands grabbed his shoulders, pulled him back from the tree, and then smashed his forehead into its trunk, and for a while he saw no more.

When he recovered and opened his eyes he was tied to the tree, his back against its bark, his hands bound behind him. His head hurt abominably and there was something sticky in his eyes. He moved his feet and something scraped against them. He looked down. A great pile of branches and twigs lay all around him, carefully arranged, some of them leaning against the tree, some of them even against him. He was held against the trunk by a rope – an *English* rope – which encircled his chest and his legs. The tree quivered in the breeze, and he realised with horror that it was now early evening, and he was in danger of missing the ship. Perhaps he had done so already. He began to shout for help.

An Englishman stepped into his field of view, one he had

seen before down at the beach. The prince felt an immediate
and quite stupid relief. If an Englishman was here, it meant the
ship was, too.

'Please, sir, please ... the ship ... I want to go to the ship.'

The Englishman smiled.

'You speak my language well, savage. How on earth did that
come about? And what of this?'

He held up the pouch that had been at the prince's side. He
spoke slowly and deliberately so the prince would understand.

'Is there any more?'

The prince shook his head.

'Are you sure, boy?'

'No. It is all gone.'

'Gone where?'

'With my friends.'

'Who are your friends?'

The prince shook his head at that.

'Let me go first. I will tell you. Let me go.'

The Englishman laughed. He took a strange box with a
cloth in it, which was the machine the English used to make
fire. He struck it four times, and on the fifth time the cloth
ignited, and he held it near the wood, and the prince understood.

'No!'

'Who are your friends?'

'I ... no ... Jeremiah.'

'Jeremiah?'

'Yes, Jeremiah.'

'How many others?'

'Others. Jeremiah.'

The Englishman said a word the prince did not understand,
a hard word. He looked at the fire in his hand as if wondering
what to do next. The prince felt a screaming in his mind, but

then a leaf of the tree stroked his face and he felt a kind of peace steal into his chest. He heard a girl laugh. Where was she?

The Englishman said the same strange word again, and dropped the charcloth onto the sticks. They caught alight immediately and the fire jumped towards the prince, and suddenly there was smoke all around him, and then the first flame touched his leg, pain flashed through him and he screamed. The fire jumped up towards the tree, and more flames touched his skin and he started to burn.

But then four or five branches of the tree dipped down towards the flames and caught fire, and a creamy smoke rose from them and encircled the trunk and the burning prince. The smoke poured into his nose and eyes and ears and mouth, and when it touched his brain the world exploded with light and he danced his way into the infinite while, back on Earth, his body burned.

WAPPING

Jeremiah Critchley is burning. He burns with desire and he burns with fear. It is all he can do to keep from running down to the river and throwing himself into the stream, letting himself die and be washed out into the estuary, clean and gone and safe. But instead he cowers like a frightened animal inside this sparse room, his back against his sea chest, a chair propped against the door to stop it being opened, fear grasping at the edges of his mind. And always: the rampant desire for one more, just one more dose of the wondrous leaf.

He had taken shelter in his boarding house, the Pear Tree in Wapping, two days ago. The chair has been in place against the door since then. Jeremiah Critchley is not a cowardly man. To many of those who know him he is something like a god, a great blond-haired, blue-eyed Viking hero of enormous strength and boundless courage, the first to leap into battle, the last man standing, the leader when those who are paid to lead have abandoned the fight. If any of his former shipmates could see him now – soft, shivering, foul-smelling and tearful – they would assume he had a pusillanimous womanly twin, a pale shadow of the real Jeremiah.

There is a knocking at the door, and he hears the muffled sound of Mrs Vermiloe, the landlady, thumping around on the landing. He'd charmed her from the first minute of his arrival, flashing his white teeth and flirting with her, making her giggle and blush even though the sight of this fat, ugly and old coquette made his face hurt. 'A room with a lock is what I need, my dear,' he'd said to her, and she'd protested, saying locked rooms weren't allowed, ever since that business with John Williams last year, and she wasn't having rooms she couldn't get into, not her. He'd smiled even more widely and looked even more deeply into her pale rheumy eyes and she'd giggled like some witch's doll of a girl and had given him this room with the lock. So he could take the leaf and not be disturbed.

He'd indulged himself too much since their return. He knows that now. He'd made cup after cup of the stuff, plunging each time into that same light-filled pool of feeling which he'd swam in that first time up on the *marae* in Otaheite, that poor dupe of an island boy beside him. His hands had shaken the first time he'd prepared the leaf himself, after weeks and weeks of waiting on the return voyage. So many times he'd been tempted, so often he'd wondered about finding some corner of the ship where nobody went and taking some of the tea. But there was no such corner, on the *Solander* or on any ship. He'd issued dark warnings to the other five about not taking the tea while they were on board, so they would not be discovered and be forced to share what leaf they had. The young savage who'd supplied them had never appeared on the beach the day they left Otaheite. They only had what he'd given them. They must conserve it. Yet there he was, struggling with his own compulsion, the voyage home stretching out into a grim eternity.

But they'd done it. They'd made it back to London undis-covered. And oh, that first taste of the leaf, alone in this room, had been wondrous indeed: as intense, perhaps even more so, than that first time on the *marae*. He'd fallen back on his bed and into the same blissful sleep, and he'd bathed in the light and swum in the infinite just as before.

Three more times he'd taken the tea in the first two days. Three more plunges into that delightful pool, although the last time he'd felt something else in the sleep, something swimming in the purple dark beneath the pool of light, something aware and watchful and hungry. But by the time he awoke he'd for-gotten it. And then he'd told himself to pause, to rest. He was disciplined, was Jeremiah Critchley. He knew when to stop, when to take a rest. He'd wondered how the other five were feeling, what their experiences had been, what they'd seen in their own visions (and whether they'd felt that thing lurking in the dark).

Then the note had come: attendance required at the Narwhal in Rotherhithe. There he'd learned of the deaths of Ransome, Attlee and Arnott, and a purple-black shadow had fallen over the enjoyment of the leaf. Three of those who'd returned with the leaf were dead. The connection was obvious, and terrifying, and incomprehensible. Only six men knew of what they'd done on Otaheite, and what they'd brought back with them, and now three of them were dead. Leaving him, Colby Potter and Elijah Frost.

So, he made the obvious assumption, and wondered if Potter and Frost would be after him next.

He'd taken the leaf again on his return from the Narwhal, and this time the vision had been truly terrifying: Potter and Frost chasing him through an oak wood, accompanied by a woman with bare shoulders and a tattooed tree down her arm, the two men laughing and shouting as they hunted for

Jeremiah, who ran and ran, the wet leaves smacking into his arms like a forest of wet clothes. He'd plunged into a river, and the two men had grabbed him and pulled him out. He was unable to resist, because he was suddenly small, as small as a ten-year-old child. Shouting triumphantly, they carried him to the strange woman, who bent over him smiling, opening her mouth, showing her sharp teeth, which closed on the skin of his throat . . .

Then, nothing.

He woke from that dream covered in his body's own expulsions, an awful mixture of sweat, blood, piss and shit. His fingers had dug great pits into his stomach and chest as he'd clawed at himself. Fear rumbled within him like boulders rolled down a hill.

He'd decided to make his way over to Ratcliffe. If Potter and Frost were behind the killings, he was not going to wait for them to come to him like some frightened woman. Day before yesterday, that had been – a fine day for a stroll. He'd cleaned himself up and, with some struggle, had resisted taking the tea again. He'd felt clearheaded and strong as he walked up New Gravel Lane, despite the searing memory of the night's visions. He'd stopped in at a tavern for a plate of food – by God, he was ravenous – and a pint of ale. A redheaded girl with flaming eyes had sat down with him and had taken no time at all to offer herself to him. Women had been offering themselves to Jeremiah since he was thirteen, but for the second time that day he had refused to indulge himself.

He had left the tavern and turned onto the Ratcliffe Highway, walking its full length until he reached Ratcliffe itself. Frost had told him how to find the boarding house before they'd left the ship. He'd told Jeremiah to come and visit when he could, and they'd shaken hands and exchanged hearty goodbyes, the hunger for the leaf in their eyes but still a good dose of fellowship in their chests. The five of them had been firm in their friendship: Critchley, Potter, Frost, Attlee and Arnott. Ransome was another case, a damned idiot hanger-on who was only part of this little group because he'd stumbled on Attlee and Arnott on the island when the two of them had been waiting to meet Critchley, and had refused to leave them. He'd worked out they were up to something, and had become so insistent and annoying that they would have had to murder him to keep him away, and that would have attracted all the wrong kind of attention. Critchley, despite himself, had decided to let the fat idiot into their little secret.

So had Potter and Frost turned on their old friend Critchley? And had it been the leaf that turned them?

At the boarding house in Ratcliffe he'd encountered another woman, older than the redhead in the tavern but younger, firmer and altogether more prepossessing than Mrs Vermiloe. She'd been mopping the floor of the hallway when he arrived. She wouldn't let him in while the wet floor dried, although Jeremiah knew this was just a ruse to keep him talking to her for a while, for he saw that same sly smile in her eyes when she caught sight of him, that little spark of hunger which he'd seen so many times before. She laughed and blushed and swirled her hips while they talked, and as much as offered herself to him there and then, though with considerably more wit and discretion than the redheaded girl in the tavern. He was careful to leave the option open, not so much because he desired her but more because he wanted her to like him and help him and women could turn from giggling admirers to spitting cats in a heartbeat.

He asked where he could find Potter and Frost, and she'd said upstairs, though she didn't know if they were in, she never heard a squeak out of them night or day, they were the easiest boarders she'd ever had. He'd thanked her and given her half a wink to acknowledge her offer and to leave open his acceptance, and he'd headed up the stairs. He wasn't scared of confronting his two former friends. Even on his own he was more than their match. But when he entered the room, fear did barge back into his life, a fear as bright and resounding as the terror he'd felt during last night's vision, its teeth sharp and unceasing.

Frost and Potter were dead on their beds, their faces both in a terrible grimace. Their throats told a savage story, the blood thick and purple on them, a stench already beginning to swell in the space, flies buzzing in anger and hunger. He heard a girl laugh from somewhere in the house, and it was chillingly incongruous, the cold ghost of another world where such violence was an object of mirth.

But most bizarre of all was the sight of Craven – poor, despicable Craven – face down, his neck purple from the ligature which still twined itself around the top of his shoulders, like a sleeping snake. Craven's position was in keeping with his name and reputation, but what was more disturbing to Jeremiah was the fact that Craven was there at all. And even while the fear gurgled through him Jeremiah found himself walking over to Frost and Potter's disturbed sea chests, already ransacked but now to be ransacked again, for even in the extremity of surprise and horror Jeremiah Critchley still hoped to find any remnants of leaf among the dead men's belongings. There were none.

Then he ran out of that place, past the landlady who shouted in anger and disappointment and asked what he thought he was up to. He ran through Ratcliffe, back down the Highway, back down New Gravel Lane and then into the warren of streets which contained the Pear Tree. He ran through the door and up to his room, and he locked it and he put the chair against it. And there he'd stayed, watching the door, through evening and yesterday and last night and up to this morning and now. Men had come to the door, knocking on it with increasing exasperation and shouting his name, but he'd ignored them. He was the last one alive. They would believe him the killer.

He hasn't given in to the need to take the leaf since his return, because he fears what he might see. The blood on the walls of the Ratcliffe boarding house has already made its own shapes in his mind: here a crow, there a dog, here a ship, and there an incarnadine tree splattered on the white wall of the room above the opened throat of his friend Colby Potter. He fears knowing what the leaf might do to those shapes in his mind, how they might themselves start to swim in the dark beneath the light, and he wonders if he might not go mad.

And now there are more pressing needs. His chamber pot is full, the piss and shit of almost two days filling the room with an awful stench. He is hungry, so enormously hungry that his stomach has stopped chirping and farting and now he feels it is beating, a great beating void of emptiness that cries out to be filled. He is thirsty, his mouth as dry as the stones of the Otaheite *marae*.

Am I to die here? Am I to just sit here and die?

He decides the answer is no. He pulls himself to his feet and a swirl of exhaustion hits him. His knees feel suddenly old and useless, and the mighty Viking Jeremiah Critchley nearly falls onto his face in his little Wapping bedroom. But then he gets hold of himself, straightens his back and pictures the red-headed girl in the tavern and starts to remember who he is.

He takes the small leather pouch, still almost full, and hangs it around his neck, beneath his shirt, just as it had hung during the long journey from Otaheite. He removes the chair from the door, and unlocks it. He stands for a moment with his hand on the door handle, but then reminds himself who he is once more, and opens the door.

The landing is quiet. From somewhere in the house he hears Mrs Vermiloe singing, a wavering tuneless ditty about a packet sailing down the Ratcliffe Highway, and he heads for the stairs after locking the door and placing the key in his pocket. He thinks again and for the last time of the redheaded girl, and as he steps out into the street, where the normal swirl of humanity goes about its normal business, he wonders what to do about Frost and Potter and Craven. Is there anyone he should tell? None of the men have wives or even parents as far as he knows. He worries about drawing attention to himself by reporting it to the authorities, whatever those authorities might be. And then he remembers the landlady and the fuss he'd made about her and the way he'd run out into the street, and remembers how blame could attach itself to him, and then he feels a knife press into his side and the warm breath of a man in his ear.

'So there you are, Jeremiah,' a voice says. 'Keep walking and don't look back, if you know what's good for you.'

They walk out into the street, in amongst the warm grubby well of humanity, and the stranger's knife is hard and insistent against the small of his back. They turn into New Gravel Lane, and Jeremiah thinks of escape, but his body must tense in anticipation because the stranger's knife is pushed into his back, only breaking the surface but enough to make him shout, and there it stays, the stranger hissing: 'Move suddenly and this goes into your liver.'

They reach a storehouse and go inside, and the pressure on the knife in his back eases for a moment, just before an enormous pain blooms in the back of his head and he falls down into a grey fog.

Sometime later he surfaces back into the light, feeling something pulling him to his feet, something steady and insistent that has got him to his knees and is now forcing him to stand

and then has him off the ground. Rope, a thick rope, round his neck, lifting him from the floor, gravel strewn in piles beneath him as he is raised, up and up and up, the air emptying from his lungs and spots of purple light appearing before his eyes, one after another until they all merge together into a velvety blackness, and Jeremiah dies.

COLDBATH FIELDS

Horton is waiting with the chief warder in the gatehouse of Coldbath Fields. One of the warder's underlings has been sent to collect Peter Nott from his cell. The chief warder claims to have become fascinated by the missionary's son.

'Is it normal – is it *right* – for our missionaries to be fathering half-breeds with savages?' he asks Horton. 'Is it not the case that our missionaries are in the business of bringing God to these animals? Not fucking their women and raising their brats.'

'You would have our missionaries be Catholic priests, celibate and robed?' says Horton, as much to pass the time as anything. The warder believes that Peter Nott is the natural son of a missionary, as indeed did Horton, until John Harriott passed on what Banks told him over dinner. Henry Nott cannot be the natural father of Peter Nott, or whatever the young man's real name is. Which means the chaplain is either lying or has been adopted by the old missionary. Either, supposes Horton, is possible. The chaplain is clearly of mixed parentage. So is his father a native, or his mother?

The question will have to wait, for now Nott must be

released. It is clear that Nott cannot be the killer they are look-ing for. Frost and Potter and Craven were killed while Nott was under lock and key. Harriott has no reason and little right to keep Nott in Coldbath Fields, but he does want to question the *Solander*'s chaplain. The man has been deliberately obtuse in his evidence, and may even be obstructing justice. Harriott's orders had been to bring Nott back to Wapping to answer for himself, but Horton has suggested a different course. His mag-istrate has reluctantly agreed.

'Papists?' says the chief warder. 'No, no. But why can't they take English women with them to satisfy their needs? Lying with all these dirty pagan whores. What's it doing to their good Christian souls?'

'The East India Company has long had a policy of encour-aging its officers to marry local women and sire children with them. It is thought it strengthens connections with the indige-nous peoples.'

'Strengthens connections'? A strange euphemism indeed!'

'Our overseas possessions increase with every year. We need the locals in these places to work with us, not against us. We must therefore fraternise with them closely, and that will inevitably lead to relations as between husbands and wives, and offspring descended from both cultures.'

'And what about good old English stock, eh? How do we preserve that? Are we just going to end up a mongrel nation of half-breeds and half-savages?'

'The Romans shared their Empire – and themselves – with peoples far and wide.'

'And look what happened to them. I'm a man of learning, I am, Constable. I've read my Gibbon.'

Horton wonders if this is true, and decides it may well be. One can always be surprised by the knowledge of even the most dissolute of men.

A junior warder appears, bringing Peter Nott into the gate-house where Horton waits. The chief warder smirks at the chaplain.

'Well now, young *sir*. It seems you're to be let out, back into the big wide world.'

Nott stares at him and does not answer. Horton rather admires the young man for this, even if it is done with the same kind of affected disdain the young man had once tried on Harriott. The chief warder is angered by Nott's reaction, which only increases Horton's admiration.

'Now, my advice to you would be don't go sticking it into any English girls,' says the chief warder. 'And watch out that any *Romans* don't try and stick it into you. Take him away, Constable. He's nothing but a complaining woman. I'm glad to be rid of him.' The chief warder, Horton notices, speaks of Coldbath Fields as if it were some kind of private gentleman's club of which membership is a desirable commodity.

Horton nods at Nott, who stares at him and then walks to the door. As they are stepping out, the chief warder shouts something more.

'And 'ere's your letter, *missionary*.' He throws it at Nott, who scoops down quickly to pick it up before Horton can read the address. 'Next time, pay the fucking fee.' And he grins at Horton, a brown gap-toothed smirk of defiance, brazen in his corruption, firm in his prejudices, happy in his work.

Outside, Nott looks around him in some confusion, clearly not knowing where he should go next. Horton's carriage is the only vehicle waiting in the street. A small knot of children are staring at the horse, contemplating some mischief or other. The carriage driver is eyeing them with endless wariness.

'I am going back to Wapping,' Horton tells Nott. 'You may accompany me in my carriage.'

'I am free to do as I please?'

'You are. The charge has been lifted.'

'Then I will not return to Wapping. I have business in town.'

With that final prim little assertion, and without saying goodbye, Nott begins to walk smartly down the hill towards Clerkenwell. Horton watches him for a moment, and then walks over to his carriage, through the knot of children. He speaks to the driver, and then selects the tallest of the children, a gangly youth who is almost as tall as Horton, and gives him a coin and his hat. The youth climbs into the carriage and puts on Horton's hat. The carriage leaves, passing Nott on the road who glances at it as it passes, seeing a constable-like shape within.

Horton follows Nott down into London.

It had been a struggle, persuading Harriott to release Nott. But Horton had impressed upon him the need for some drastic action to move the case along. There are only two leads: Nott, and Critchley. Horton had gone to Critchley's rooms at the Pear Tree this morning. This time the door was unlocked, but Critchley was nowhere to be seen. The room was in a primitive, awful state, the chamberpot overflowing, the bedding rancid and stained with sweat, piss and even excrement. Beside the bed Horton had found another cup, with another layer of residue at its bottom. So whatever the men who'd died were taking, Critchley was taking it too. And now Critchley has gone.

That leaves Nott. Horton had persuaded Harriott to release the chaplain, but only to allow him to be observed. Horton would keep an eye on him, in case he might incriminate himself or some other. Already, Nott is heading away from Wapping, Rotherhithe and the eastern part of the metropolis. He is heading south and west. Horton's hopes begin to rise.

There is an art to following, and it is one Horton has been

developing these past few months. Prior to the Ratcliffe Highway murders, he had done little following. A good deal of *waiting* and of *watching*, usually on the water, but very little actual following. He thinks back to jurisdiction again, and wonders if the land-bound constables of Shadwell ever follow suspects or witnesses. He decides almost certainly not. The men of Shadwell have little interest in the innovations of detection which Horton finds so fascinating.

But he has not yet followed someone quite so important to him as the *Solander*'s chaplain. Losing sight of Nott now would be a disaster. He has assured his magistrate that he will discover today who Nott really is. Questioning the man further is, Horton believes, pointless; he has a stubborn, somehow alien resistance to interrogation. That had become clear when Harriott tried to get answers from him in the garden of Coldbath Fields. Nott is hiding something, clearly, and the obvious mistake both Horton and Harriott had made about his parentage is as wincingly painful to Horton as it was to the old magistrate. Discovering why Nott is really in London is a puzzle both men want resolved for reasons as much personal as professional.

They stay on the Westminster side of the Fleet. Nott had turned first of all into Coldbath Square, in front of the prison, and then had asked for directions from a young woman carrying a baby, pointing at the letter the chief warder threw at him. So, he had decided to deliver the letter himself. The woman pointed to the right, and Nott headed off down Great Bath Street, then Eyre Street, then across Liquorpond Street. Meux's Brewery, which brewed the porter that John Harriott and the Royal Philosophers had enjoyed the previous evening, appears on their right.

Following at its most basic means keeping your quarry in sight but making sure he doesn't see you. The balance to those two things is the essence. However, that balance changes around every London corner. Some streets bustle with people, and in those streets one must keep close to one's quarry, running the risk of being seen. Other streets are almost empty, and here the follower must hang back, sometimes hundreds of feet, lest he be spotted.

Then there are the people on the street. London's streets are full of watchers – standing, sitting, talking in groups, looking out of windows, boot polishers and barrow boys and hawkers and porters and all. Any one of them can take pleasure in shouting at a suspicious-looking follower, merrily asking 'Wot you up to, guv?' in the full knowledge that the follower is up to no good and, more to the point, does not wish to be identified. This cheery sabotage has interrupted a dozen or more of Horton's pursuits, and always ends in an embarrassing piece of street theatre whereby he tries to pretend not to be aware of the quarry or the saboteur, and turns the nearest corner and disappears.

Compared to these earlier episodes, following Peter Nott is relatively straightforward. The streets they are walking through are neither busy nor empty. They are at the northern and relatively prosperous (by Wapping standards) edge of London, where rambling streets go up and down gentle hills and are surrounded by recently built houses and older warehouses, manufactories, churches and taverns. Smart squares with cobbled streets and new pavements abound. Nott walks somewhat at random, and stops occasionally to ask directions, heading broadly downhill and south, towards the river and into town.

Nott continues into Leather Lane, Horton close behind. There is a growing sense of the metropolis here, of buildings clustering together, of noise and crowds and an intensity which was missing in Clerkenwell. Up ahead streams the great thoroughfare of Holborn, but to get there they must walk the entire length of Leather Lane, past George Yard and then past the biggest institution they have seen since they left Coldbath Fields: Furnival's Inn, the ancient Inn of Chancery. The Inn's massive buildings stretch back from Holborn to Greville Street, enclosing a space that resembles the prison from which Nott has just been released, even down to the tidy little gardens and fields inside. This particular prison, though, contains clerks and solicitors, not thieves and murderers, and they are chained to depositions and not walls. Thomas More himself had learned the law within Furnival's, and did he but know it there is something of More in the starchy and prissy missionary's son who now walks beneath the walls of the Inn. Nott hurries past, head down, as if trying to hide from the eyes of the lawyers and their students watching him from above.

Now they reach the wide stream of Holborn, the thoroughfare of lawyers which connects London with Westminster. A stream of carriages and people pours in and out of the City, to and from Westminster, racing eastwards down the hill to the culverted Fleet or back up the hill towards the theatres, salons and shops of the West End. And here Nott stops, as if in awe of what he is seeing, and Horton stops with him, seeing the thin little black-garbed figure halted before a tide that sweeps across him, a visiting Moses struggling with the immensity of the Red Sea. Moses was a foundling, it occurs to Horton. Perhaps Nott is one, too.

Nott walks in a small circle for a while, as if afraid to plunge into the waters of traffic, but in fact he is just bouncing off passers-by, trying to get one of them to stop and tell him which way to go: south to the river, east to the City, or west to Westminster. Horton itches to see the address written on the envelope Nott is holding, the destination towards which he travels.

Finally, a shabby-looking fat man relents to Nott's pleading

and listens to his question. Again, the gesturing and the point-
ing to the envelope. Again, the finger indicating the direction.
And then Nott is off again, turning right onto Holborn.
Westminster it is, then.

Following now becomes particularly hard. Anyone walking
along Holborn has to share the street with the dozens of carriages and post-chaises which jostle each other, seeking a quick
way through the crowds. Horses whinny and stamp, their
heads knocking into the rears of the vehicles in front of them,
while drivers hurl cheerful insults to each other. All the while,
people of every description swirl around the carriages, in
between them, in front of them, behind them, in a lethal dance,
and all simply to get to the other side of the road. In this madness, Nott seems for a while to be frozen with fear, taking only
a few steps in and out, being pushed and sworn at by others
more familiar with the rhythms of the insane thoroughfare.
Finally he begins to move more steadily, making his way west.
They squeeze through the point where the road is part-
blocked by an island of buildings in front of Staple's Inn, and
from here the going is easier, as the road is narrower and
forces the carriages to move more slowly and take more care.
Gray's Inn goes by on their right-hand side, and then the
buildings which ring Lincoln's Inn appear to their left. They
ride the stream through this valley of the law, suspended
between the City and Westminster, a machine of equity and
tort which processes lords, bishops, merchants and industrial-
ists alike.

Soon after passing Lincoln's Inn, Nott stops again, and
again those walking beside and behind him visibly curse him
for interrupting their flow. But he is busy comparing the
address on his envelope with the sign on the little street off to
the left. He turns into it, and Horton follows: Little Queen
Street, a narrow place with poor-looking dwellings on either

side which, Horton believes, are certainly boarding houses of some kind, no doubt accommodating students of the law and clerks from the great Inns.

At the end of Little Queen Street, Nott turns right into Great Queen Street. Suddenly a more prosperous type of metropolis leaps into view, a place of some refinement, elegance and wealth. Great white Palladian villas line both sides of the street, and clean steps lead up from the pavement to solid black front doors festooned with as much brass as a fighting brig. Nott walks down this row of houses and stops in front of one about halfway down. Horton crosses the street, anticipating Nott going in. There is a neat little coffee house almost opposite the door Nott has chosen, and he plans to take a seat and wait to see what happens.

Nott knocks on the door, which after a moment or two is opened by a servant who is barely visible from Horton's viewpoint. Nott speaks to the man for some time, growing increasingly pleading and showing the letter he has carried all the way from Coldbath Fields. Eventually the servant must relent, because Nott is let in. A minute or two later, the servant appears at the door and walks down to the street, hailing a ticket porter and giving him a note, presumably to be taken to the absent master of the house with news of the visitor. The porter, a neat youth with shiny shoes and an eager demeanour, races off down the street towards Drury Lane and Bow Street.

Horton orders himself a coffee and settles down at a table in the window of the coffee house. If following is something he has had to teach himself to do, waiting is something that comes naturally. There has been a good deal of waiting in Charles Horton's life, and it is something he does very well indeed. A pot of coffee, a cup, a milk jug and a sugar bowl are deposited on his table, and he pours the coffee and adds several spoonfuls of sugar and no milk. The street outside is busy but its aristocratic air, a haven from the fierce battles of Holborn to the north, gives it a refinement and a kind of peace which is entirely absent from the City. The smell of the West End is strong in the air, a fresh smell of money and manners. The coffee is potent, and his eyes widen a little at the first swallow, the liquid hitting his stomach and his brain almost at the same time with that familiar broadening of awareness. He thinks about the current investigation, and then forces himself *not* to think, pushing back the connections and hypotheticals and conjectures into the dark back corners of his brain, allowing them to continue mixing and fermenting, determined not to let them out into the light before they are ready. He worries, of course: about Abigail and about Jeremiah Critchley, who is still out there in the metropolis. How does he fit in? Was it indeed him in Ratcliffe?

He waits for an hour, consuming three more cups of sweet coffee, so that his hands are shaking and the unusual vessel of his imagination is rambling gleefully all over the six deaths and those faces. Ransome, Attlee and Arnott had been smiling terrible smiles on their death-beds, but the men in Ratcliffe were different. Their faces were full of fear. He is thinking so hard on this that he almost misses the arrival of the master of the house, who appears at the western end of Great Queen Street and walks up to the house and then up the stairs and into the door, magnificent in a bright-blue tailcoat, white breeches and elegant hat.

It is Aaron Graham.

WAPPING

It is to Aaron Graham's immense credit that he makes his way with such speed to John Harriott's office in Wapping. He can have been in no doubt about the flavour of the reception. When he is shown into Harriott's office it is like being introduced to a typhoon. Harriott's unspoken resentment towards Graham has been building like water in a mine and now comes out in a crashing wave. The revelation that the Otaheite missionary – if such he is – has been attempting to correspond with Bow Street feels like a final confirmation that Graham's interests do not coincide with Harriott's. The older man believes that, once again, he has been manipulated, and this takes his rage beyond the bounds of decent manners.

Graham, for his part, is embarrassed beyond words by the situation and spends much of the immediate minutes after his arrival apologising with rehearsed precision, rolling out assurances and conciliation like golden gifts to an angry god. Horton had preceded Graham to Wapping, bearing the news of Nott's visit to Great Queen Street. Now he watches the two men reduce themselves to their essences: Harriott's rage against Graham's balm. For a while he wonders if he might be seeing the very end of their friendship, and he finds himself wondering if such an outcome would upset him. He rather thinks it would not. He remembers Graham's visit to his own apartments during the Ratcliffe Highway investigation, and his helpless anger at Graham's machinations. Harriott's rage today feels something like justice.

Eventually, though, Graham's immense charm begins to work its way through the Harriott cataclysm. Horton reminds himself that rage will always wear itself out. Better to let it break its waves upon you than seek to shout back at it. He can see Graham following this strategy, and thinks how much he could learn from this shameless diplomat, if he cared to do so. Harriott sits down eventually with a final resigned yelp of dis-enchantment. His rage has been such that even the uselessness of his lame leg has been ignored. Graham prepares to exploit the moment.

'Harriott, please, allow me to explain.'

'I have no interest in your explanations, Graham. If they are of the same flavour as your usual excuses and flattery, they will be both pretty and unbelievable.'

Graham looks like he might become angry himself at that, but stops himself. Horton can see him do it – can see the lips tighten, the eyes narrow, and then the sigh which accompanies his resignation and acceptance.

'Please, Harriott, please. Let us not say something we come to regret.'

'I regret a great many things, Graham. Not least the friend-ship of a man who seems to take me for either a fool or a mere instrument of his own ends. I have nothing I need to hear from you.'

'You must listen to what Nott has told me.'

'Why?'

'Because it will explain what he wishes to speak to me about. And it will exonerate me of any of the suspicions you lay at my door. Please, John, allow yourself the chance to find the truth of the matter. Your anger has an incandescent quality which may burn out more than you wish.'

'I am tired of this, Graham. I had hoped to discuss my conversation with Sir Joseph with you, but now I fear I may not trust you with any thoughts I had from it.'

'You become too hot again, John. You became somewhat too hot when conversing with Sir Joseph, as I recall.'

'Well, Graham, we do not all posses your bottomless wells of patience and – what is it the French say – *sangfroid*. Ah yes. Cold blood. I do believe your blood is pretty cool.'

'And I do believe your own blood could benefit from a drop in temperature.'

'Oh, well, say what you will. Horton will listen to you. I am done with you.'

And with that Harriott swivels his chair away to the window. Graham looks appalled at this. For once, the Bow Street magistrate is lost for words. He looks at the back of Harriott's chair for a moment, then looks at Horton. It is a measuring look, and Horton sees that despite everything Graham remains calm and alert. Once again Horton reminds himself not to underestimate this fellow, who hides his enormous ability beneath a fashionable carapace of elegance and wit.

'Well then, gentlemen. Here it is. Peter Nott has approached me in an unexpected capacity. You know, Harriott, and you may know too, Constable, how I once acted as an advisor to a man accused of being a mutineer on the *Bounty*. A man called Peter Heywood.'

At that, Harriott's chair turns round again to face Graham. He says nothing, but stares intently at the other man as he continues to speak. Graham's words are so unexpected that they beg to be heeded. Heywood is a name which was rarely out of the newspapers twenty years before. Even Horton, then a mere adolescent, is shaken by the name. Graham continues.

'Heywood was a young officer, barely a boy, on the *Bounty*, and claimed that he had not intended to throw in his lot with the mutineers led by the blackguard Fletcher Christian. He was seized from Otaheite by the *Pandora* in 1791, and brought back to England for trial. I had some acquaintance with his family, and they asked me to help prepare his defence, which I agreed to. The defence was partially successful. Peter was found guilty but thrown onto the King's mercy. He was pardoned, and returned to the Navy, where he has rebuilt his career with a good degree of success.'

'All this we know, Graham,' says Harriott, and his tone is softer now. 'All this every Englishman knows.'

'Indeed. But you do not know this. Peter Nott, you see, claims that Peter Heywood is his father.'

No one says anything to that.

SOHO SQUARE

Horton is sent on to Soho Square while Harriott and Graham travel to Bow Street to interview the chaplain. He is by no means happy about this. Nott and Critchley hold the keys to the case, he believes. But Harriott is adamant that any available information at Sir Joseph Banks's residence must be pursued, and quickly. Banks has given his permission, and another day cannot be allowed to pass without some action being taken on it. Horton, however, sees the truth. Harriott is snared on the story of Peter Nott as firmly as a trout on a hook, baited with the bright myths of the *Bounty* and William Bligh. There is no force in the world that will keep John Harriott from finding out more about that epic from two decades ago.

So Horton goes to inspect the papers relating to the *Solander*, in a foul temper and with his mind elsewhere. Normally, he cherishes these trips west, in the same way as a farmer's wife might cherish a trip to Bath: they fascinate and enthral him, but also throw into relief the great qualities of his own part of town. They might knock you down and rob you in Wapping, but they wouldn't smile while they were doing it.

Today, though, the brittle charms of the West End only serve to irritate him. His purpose seems random and redundant. Banks's house sits in the corner of Soho Square, but he catches only glimpses of it as he is shown through to the room at the back. The house is wider than it looks; its relatively narrow frontage on the square widens out into a spacious, elegant interior which sprawls through to Dean Street at the rear. There, in a library surrounded by books and red cedar boxes, he meets Robert Brown, Sir Joseph's librarian, who has made the *Solander* papers ready for him. Brown seems tired and distracted, and not a little resentful at Horton's presence. It is clear to Horton that they're not much used to officers of the law digging around in their archives at Soho Square. Neither man wants to be there: Horton's head is full of the questions he would be asking Peter Nott even now, while Brown's attention is barely on his visitor.

Brown shows Horton through to a little room off the library. In the room a small pile of ledgers and a box have been placed next to a nondescript table and chair. A window looks out onto a brick wall. So, my prison for the day, thinks Horton, and the frown which has framed his face since Wapping deepens. Brown seems unembarrassed by the Spartan nature of the provision.

'This will be sufficient, I take it?' he asks. His eyes have dark shadows beneath them, as if he hasn't slept.

'Yes, Mr Brown. This will be adequate. I may spend the day in here should I need to?'

'That is my instruction. I will not be here; I am going to Kew today. But if you need anything you may ask the servants for it. Though I imagine everything you require will be in here. There are no other papers.'

'Thank you. Sir Joseph was also going to arrange for me to talk to the *Solander*'s gardeners.'

'Was he? He has made no mention of it to me.'

'Will it be possible?'

'The gardeners are all living and working in Kew for at least another week. Can you get down to Kew?' This last question asked as if Horton were a child, not used to travelling alone.

'I can take a carriage there.'

'I will mention your request to the head gardener, and to Sir Joseph if I see him. When do you plan to travel?'

'Today, if possible. This afternoon.'

'Well, it is difficult, but not impossible. Shall we say four o'clock at Kew?'

'That will suit perfectly.'

'I shall tell them to expect you then, unless you hear otherwise.'

'My thanks to you, Mr Brown.'

The librarian nods his austere Scottish nod, and makes to leave, but then stops.

'How many men have now died?' he asks.

'I believe six. All crewmen of the *Solander*.'

'Is such a slaughter ... *usual* when a ship returns?'

'By no means, Mr Brown. I have seen nothing the like of it.'

'And you have no sense as to what lies behind it?'

'At this stage, none whatsoever. Do you have any ideas?'

'Me? Why, no, none at all. But these new murders – six deaths is rather more than three.'

'It is indeed.'

'Were there any shared features between the deaths?'

'Why do you ask such a question, Mr Brown?'

'I am a natural philosopher, Constable. A botanist. I am rather skilled at categorising plants by viewing their affinities and appearance, and finding shared characteristics. It is perhaps a skill you could make use of.'

'Well, then. Of the six men killed, five were found on their beds, as it were asleep. One had been strangled, the other four had had their throats cut. Their sea chests and kitbags had been searched but nothing of any apparent value was taken. Three of the dead men were marked by a strange smile upon their faces. It seems to me they were killed in their sleep, but it must have been a profound sleep indeed. And all five of these men were holding cups of one kind or another, at the bottom of which seemed to be the residue of some kind of tea. Mr Brown, are you perfectly all right? You look like you should sit down.'

'No, I am ... I am perfectly well. Please. Continue.'

'The final man seems to have been killed in a different way – strangled with a ligature rather than with hands, probably from behind, probably by someone entering the room behind him. He was standing, not lying upon a bed. He was, presumably, awake.'

'You have a suspect?'

'One, a Jeremiah Critchley, the ship's carpenter. He seems to have been close to the other men, but he is not to be found at his lodgings, which leads us to suspect him even further. My fellow constables are searching for him now.'

'What do you know of this Critchley?'

'Very little. I will examine the papers here, and then I will speak to Captain Hopkins – once I have spoken to the gardeners in Kew.'

'Very well.'

'And how do you *classify* these deaths, Mr Brown? Do they seem capable of ordering?'

'I see you have already ordered them, Constable. As you say, five of the deaths seem to belong to one genus, the sixth to another. I suppose your challenge is to work out which family of death the members of the genus of five belongs to.'

'I know little of such things. My wife is the botanist and natural philosopher in our household.'

'Ah, indeed? An enthusiast?'

'Yes, sir, a great enthusiast. Our rooms are filled with books on the subject.'

'She sounds like an interesting woman.'

'She is rather more than that, Mr Brown.'

'Well, then. I think you have all you need, and now I will leave you to your work. Good day, Constable.'

'One more thing, Mr Brown. Would you have any idea what might have been in the cups the men had drunk from? Did something come back from Otaheite which might have caused them to sleep so deeply?'

The librarian's austere Scottish face looks momentarily tortured, like a priest wrestling with a crisis of faith. Horton knows he is going to lie before he says anything.

'I cannot imagine what that might be, Constable.'

'There has been no discovery which might explain these matters?'

'Not to my knowledge, no. Now, I must really be leaving for Kew. I will alert them as to your plans. Good day, Constable.'

'Good day, Mr Brown.'

Horton watches Brown leave and shut the door behind him. He then ponders the odd conversation he has just had. He sets it in his mind and, as it were, walks around it, considering the way the light falls on each curve and line, trying to pick out the unity of a whole. Brown had seemed disturbed even before the conversation began, and shaken in particular by Horton's description of the murder scenes. He had clearly lied about whatever had come back with the *Solander*, which opens up intriguing possibilities. And then that odd little interlude on *classification*, which seemed to speak to matters of which Horton knows little. He must talk to Abigail of it tonight.

He hadn't seen her the previous evening. By the time he reached home it was after ten, and Abigail had gone to bed.

She'd left him some food on the table in their little sitting room, and a carefully tended fire was still burning. He'd looked at the books on the shelves which surrounded the little room, and felt unaccountably sad at the sight of them; he associated Abigail's intellectual interests with their failure to have children, as if she was filling an empty space which existed between them. She herself would have recognised such an explanation, but would not have mourned it as her husband does.

He'd looked in on her before sitting down to eat. She'd been lying on her side, her blond hair lying across her face and one hand placed on the pillow in front of her, the other arm lying along her side. He could see the shape of her legs beneath the bedcovers, and could hear the soft sound of her breathing which soon, he knew, would break into bestial snores which she would not hear and did not believe in. For now she was at peace, and Horton felt a wave of fearful affection wash over him. He'd traded friends and shipmates for a life with this woman. The fear came from knowing he would do it again, and from knowing he still could not protect the life which lay before him. The head which lay on that pillow was a fierce and unique one; a hot and kind and brave and soft heart beat beneath that stretched out arm; and it was this being which he'd placed in harm's way only three days before. The horror of that moment sat with him like a pox of the soul, but it was only part of the horror that was always there, the horror that someday he would be parted from his wife and thus his humanity, and that horror rises up before him like a gigantic Pacific wave.

Life doesn't have to be hard, Charles.

That's what she would say. And she would smile. And he would not believe her.

The papers in Soho Square tell the story of the *Solander*, but in a fragmented and oddly half-baked fashion. It is clear to

Horton that Sir Joseph Banks is not one for keeping detailed records; there are several bits of handwritten stuff in among the papers with a scribbled 'Sir Jos— B' at the bottom of them, the handwriting almost illegible, the spelling execrable and the grammar worse. Sir Joseph is a man of words, but spoken ones. Writing clearly bores him to tears.

The papers confirm that Banks paid for the trip virtually out of his own pocket. The stated purpose of the voyage was to 'botanise in Otaheite and take the oportunity to bring back as many Samples of the Island's plants as posible, at a time of recent Uncertainty among Islanders which may lead to future Missions being impossible.' Horton knows little of Otaheite or the 'recent Uncertainty', but he suspects Harriott does. The old man keeps a close watch on Britain's far-flung Empire, and reads newspapers and journals assiduously.

The ship itself was acquired in Whitby by agents working for Banks. It seems that up to this point Banks had been running the project singlehandedly, but now he had appointed Captain Hopkins to be in charge of things: to sail the collier, already renamed the *Solander*, round to the Thames for a fit-up, and to supervise the mission from that point on.

Hopkins had been recommended to Banks, it seems, by William Bligh; there is a letter from Bligh to Banks among the correspondence. Horton imagines the conversation now taking place in Bow Street between his magistrate and the man who claims to be the son of one of Bligh's cursed mutineers. It is odd how these stories are winding around each other.

Government House, New South Wales, 1807

> *Sir Joseph,*
> *It was a delight to receive your missive, and I was flattered*
> *to discover your willingness to promote my application to be a*

Fellow of that great Society which you preside over. My
unbridled thanks for your attention and solicitude.

You described your great new Project to me, and asked me
to consider if I knew of any captains who might suit the
purpose of running it. A name has sprung to mind. He is
Thomas Hopkins, a fine man who was made post-captain
some four years ago but who is not, to my understanding,
currently in a position of command on any vessel. Hopkins is a
capable man who rose through the ranks with great distinction,
but there are dozens of such men. What makes Hopkins
particularly appropriate for your voyage is, I think, his
experience of Otaheite. He was a Lieutenant on the Pandora –
the ship that was despatched to bring back those evil men who
mutinied against me on that ship we both know so much about.

This recommendation may smack of obsession on my part, I
realise – sending a man to you who was one of those
instrumental in my revenge against those who rose up against
me. But this would be a mistaken assumption. Hopkins is a
man of parts, and can do the job you require of him with
discretion, speed and ability. I commend him to you.

My thanks again for your generous support in my
application.

I remain
Yours
William Bligh, Governor

Horton feels an odd disjointed sense of something at this
point; here he is, inside the nest of the great Sir Joseph Banks,
searching through his letters and files like a French spy, furtive
and hurried. And he is reading a letter from one figure of fame
to another: Bligh to Banks. A letter sent, what is more, only
months before Bligh himself was seized by a second rebellion,
on land this time, and incarcerated for two years by his own

soldiers. What would the correspondents from the *Chronicle* or the *Times* give for access to such a treasure trove?

Hopkins has never mentioned his previous voyage to Otaheite. The captain lives, he knows, in Putney, which is not that distant from Kew. Horton wonders if he has time to speak to the Kew gardeners and then to visit Putney on his way back to London. He believes he might.

He has been looking at the papers for two hours, and they have revealed little. He tidies up the desk and then leaves, shutting the door on the room and telling one of the servants that he has finished for the day, but to leave the papers in the room lest he need to investigate them further. Then he goes out into the square and hails a carriage to take him to Kew.

COVENT GARDEN

John Harriott's memoirs, *Struggles Through Life*, were published in 1808 to the general approval of his friends and the general indifference of everyone else. He had tussled with the book for years, until it began to serve as a metaphor for the life it set out to describe: an enormous undertaking, almost a backbreaking one, begun with little understanding of its size or its likely effect on him or his family, which then became an ordeal in its own right, such that the act of finishing the damned thing became more important than the thing itself. Such has been John Harriott's life, and such was the document of it.

By the time he'd reached the end of this mighty effort, he was out of energy and desire. He could manage only two pages at the very finish in which to encapsulate his philosophy, such as it was. In the four years since he published the memoirs he has begun to feel this to be an opportunity squandered. So he has been working on another book, which he has called *The Religion of Philosophy* and which has attracted some interest from printers in the City. In that book he has tried to expand on the sketched personal philosophy outlined in the *Struggles*:

The greatest pageantry or show, that human magnificence can exhibit, would not tempt me to any particular exertion to view it; yet I would still toil in any cause of humanity, or climb up a burning mountain to view any great operation of Nature, as enlarging my views, and giving new energies to my adoration of the Great Omnipotent.

In others words, John Harriott has ceased to struggle in the world of Money, but is still prepared to take on the world in the cause of Humanity. Sitting above him he still sees a Creator, the Great Omnipotent, but this deity is one increasingly distant from him, as are the liturgies and rituals of the churches, established or otherwise. He has flirted with ending his own life in recent times, such has been his exhausted capacity for despair, and a man who has contemplated his own self-inflicted doom has little truck with the apocalyptic rules of an established church.

To put it yet another way: Harriott still has need of Heaven, but has no belief in Hell.

Of all the types of churchmen he has come across, Harriott finds missionaries the most perplexing. Like most Englishmen, he had followed with interest the establishment of the London Missionary Society towards the end of the last century. He'd felt a definite pride, again like most Englishmen, when that Society sent its first shipload of missionaries to the East. But these were patriotic feelings, not spiritual or evangelical ones. John Harriott is a man who has lived with Indians, who still dreams of a certain squaw and the way the North American sunlight fell on her long shining hair. Such a man cannot believe in the damnation of pagans, as missionaries must believe, and thus cannot entirely believe in any personal duty to bring the Word of God to them. These savages are God's creation as much as he is; that is John Harriott's view. They celebrate the Great Omnipotent as much as any bishop.

All this informs his reaction to the revelation that the odd young man from Otaheite is not, in fact, the natural son of the most famous missionary archetype of them all, Henry Nott. He must now look at the young man in a new light. He had thought he understood this so-called Nott's strange intensity and fervour, because he thought it came from a spiritual source. The discovery that the man's demons may be of a more earthly stripe makes him rather more interesting to John Harriott.

Harriott rides in Graham's carriage back to Bow Street. The atmosphere in the carriage is quiet and even elegiac, as if the two magistrates are in mourning for their former friendship but still have hopes of establishing a new one. Neither is exactly angry any longer. Harriott's months-old resentment of his friend has been burned out by his explosion in Wapping. Graham was upset so much by what Harriott had said that it has caused him to look in upon himself in a way he normally tries to avoid. Thus both men are pondering their inner selves on the ride west from Wapping, like two overdressed philosophers.

Peter Nott has not been precisely incarcerated in Bow Street, but he is being watched. Graham had taken him from his house in Queen Street to the Police Office, where an officer kept watch on him during Graham's visit to Wapping. When the two magistrates arrive back at Graham's office, Nott sees Harriott and springs from his seat to protest.

'Mr Graham, sir, why is this man here? This is a matter between you and myself. Is there no privilege between a client and his representative?'

Graham bridles at that, even as he takes off his hat and moves behind his desk.

'Nott, I am by no means your *representative*. I am a magistrate of the King, as is Mr Harriott here. And you remain implicated in a series of vicious murders. You have still given no good account of your presence at the deaths in Rotherhithe. If you want my help – and I am by no means assuring you that I can or will give it – then I suggest you moderate your temper, and tell Mr Harriott here what you told me this afternoon. Leave no detail out.'

Nott's face looks perplexed, and Harriott recalls the sympathy he felt towards him in Coldbath Fields. The man is such a confused bag of passions.

'But much of what I told you was highly personal!'

'If you wish me to arrest you, Nott, and return you to Coldbath Fields on a charge I will do so,' says Harriott. 'You are obstructing our investigations, and I will have no more of it.'

Nott frowns that frustrated little frown again, the one Harriott had seen in the prison the previous Saturday, and sits himself back down.

'Well then,' says Graham. 'Harriott, please take a seat. Nott, please speak. Myself and Mr Harriott may interrupt with questions. Proceed.'

Nott looks at Harriott, still with that same look of frustration Harriott can remember in the faces of his own children when they were on the boundary between childhood and adulthood. And yet this man must be twenty-five or more. Finally, resignation falls into the childlike man's eyes, and he begins to speak.

'I told you, Mr Harriott, that my father is the missionary, Henry Nott. And this is true – Nott is my father. But he is an adopted one. When he came to Otaheite, he discovered me living in poverty with my mother, a native of the island. He saw instantly that I was of mixed parentage – a half-breed. My mother told him my father was an English sailor who had been on the island ten years before, a man she called Peter and after whom she'd named me.'

'You had no memory of your English father?' asks Harriott.

'Impressions, sir, that is all. I was barely an infant when he was taken away, as my mother told me.'

'Taken away?'

'Yes, sir. I am coming to that.'

Nott looks as miserable as a man can look. He speaks to Graham.

'May I have some water, Mr Graham? I am confoundedly thirsty.'

Graham calls an attendant and tells him to fetch water, then nods at Nott to continue.

'Over the months that followed, Henry Nott spent a great deal of time with me. He taught me the English language and the catechism, and he often said to me I was the great experiment of the English mission, an attempt to prove that a native could learn English and become a good Christian. His fellow missionaries disapproved somewhat, I think. They were uncomfortable with my . . . well, perhaps we should call it my personal history. They questioned Mr Nott's relationship with my mother. There had been some unpleasantness early on in the mission when one of their number had professed his love for a native woman, and they'd expelled him from their community. I think the other missionaries were worried that Mr Nott might follow the same path.'

The attendant returns with some water, which he places down in front of Peter Nott. The young man takes a swig from the glass, and returns to his story.

'They need have had no worries about Mr Nott. He was as firm and unyielding as an old breadfruit tree. He showed no interest in my mother. To her shame and mine she did offer herself to him. All his interest was in me and me alone. He was delighted with my progress, and I began to accompany him on his trips around the island, when he attempted to preach to the islanders.

'It was a difficult time for the missionaries. The old king and his son had no interest in the Christian religion, and still practised the old ways: sorcery, taboos, human sacrifice, all were still common on the islands. These have been dark years for Otaheite, Mr Harriott. The population has collapsed. Many have died from diseases brought by the Europeans, and not all those diseases were carried by the act of ... of fornication. Some were carried in other ways. All were lethal.

'Henry Nott believed the islanders could be converted, and he saw me as the first convert, the first savage on the island to come to the Lord. But of course I was a blank page. I wasn't even ten years old when he began teaching me. I did believe in the Christian stories he told me, and more than once I felt the Holy Spirit moving through me. My mother was terribly upset. She felt I was being stolen from her. And, eventually, I was.

'When I was about twelve, Henry Nott came to my mother with a proposition. He wanted to adopt me, to make me his son. He believed I would never become a true Christian while living in her hut by the beach. He wanted me to come into the Christian mission and be a permanent part of it. He had not spoken of it to me, and she initially resisted with awful rage. But then he offered her currency. He brought nails and even tools to her, and she saw that these could make her rich and powerful and then she acquiesced. Henry Nott bought me, and I became his son.'

Nott's hand shakes as he picks up the water glass and drinks from it. His eyes are wet. Whatever his feelings towards missionaries, and however difficult he'd found this young man in recent days, Harriott feels a yawning sadness for him. He'd seen this kind of thing before – the strange half-life of the half-breed, caught between two worlds, native to neither and alien to both. And what an extreme example of the type Peter Nott is: a Christian savage with two fathers, abandoned by one, converted by the other.

'I never saw my mother again. The missionaries never really accepted me. But I lived with Henry Nott. He continued to teach me, and from that point on I began to think of myself as English, whatever the other English thought of me.

'Yet I always knew Nott was not my real father. My mother had spoken of *that* father many, many times. She said he had come from England on a great ship years before, and that this ship had taken from the island a great quantity of breadfruit. She said the ship had left but had then returned, and that some of the men from the ship had decided to stay on the island, and that the others had left again. My father was one of the ones who had stayed.'

Harriott looks at Graham, and the Covent Garden magistrate nods silently and then holds up a hand and points to Nott. *Wait. Hear it all.*

'She said she had two years with my father, and she talked of those two years as if she'd been in Paradise, though God forgive me for the blasphemy. Otaheite is not Paradise, despite what you may have been told. Sometimes I think it is ... well, sometimes I think it has more of the other place than it has of Paradise. At the end of that two years, my mother said another ship came from England, and men from the ship came and found my father and took him away. She never saw him again.

'I told this story to Henry Nott as soon as I had the words for it, so I must have still been a young child. I remember he was much taken with it. It became like a puzzle for him, and one night he came to me and told me that he believed my father's name was Peter Heywood, and that he was a bad man, and he taught me a new word: *mutiny*. He said the ship which came to the island was called the *Bounty*, and that the men on that ship had taken against their captain – that's when he taught me the new word – and put him off the boat, that they'd come back to Otaheite and some had stayed. He said my father was taken away two years later on a boat called *Pandora*, and that he had been hanged.'

'He lied!' says Harriott, astonished at the missionary's behaviour.

'Yes, Mr Harriott. He lied. But I only found that out much later.'

'How?'

'A ship came from New South Wales, I think it must have been seven or eight years ago. I remember it was called the *Porpoise*. She was on her way back to England. I spoke to several of the crew and I told one of them that my father was Peter Heywood, the dead mutineer. And this man laughed and told me, no, Peter Heywood is not dead, he was pardoned by the King himself, and is once again a Navy man, alive and thriving.

'I confronted my father with this story, shouting and crying and disrespectful, and I remember he hit me and I remember what he said when he did so: "You are my son now, Peter, not Heywood's. The man is a rascal and a devil and a mutineer. No boy should want a man such as he as a father."

'But I became determined that one day I should meet my father. My *real* father. I was a dutiful son to Henry Nott and a dutiful missionary. I stayed with him in Otaheite even when many of the other missionaries fled to New South Wales, when the fighting between tribes on the island became fierce and dangerous. But I dreamed of coming to England and of finding my father. I think Henry Nott knew of these dreams, and it saddened him, but the man is made of such firm unyielding stuff that he never said a word.

'I waited years. Ships came and went, but there was always

some reason why I could not get on them and away; either my own cowardice, or the captain was unwilling, or I was away from Matavai Bay when the ship anchored. But finally the *Solander* arrived, and with it my chance. I went down to the ship the day it arrived, and immediately went to see Captain Hopkins to tell him of my wishes. As it happened, the *Solander* was in need of a chaplain, and I offered my services in return for a voyage to England, and the captain agreed.

'I told Henry Nott what I intended. He didn't say much in reply, but wished me well and begged me to write with news of what I discovered. I gave little further thought to him, although the next day several of the island women came to see me to say goodbye, in the stiff formal way they had taken to speaking to me, and they told me that they'd heard weeping from my mother's hut the night before.

'When we sailed, I stood in the stern and waved goodbye to my island home, and wondered if I would ever see it again, and wondered if I cared. It was a terrifying voyage for me, even though I'd travelled between the islands on canoes. I'd never seen oceans or waves the like of those I saw on the voyage to England. And everyone I met and spoke to, I asked about my father. And then I heard about Mr Graham.'

Harriott looks at Graham with an eyebrow raised, for this is the part of the story he is most astonished by. John Harriott is like most Englishmen of a maritime bent and of a certain vintage; for him, the tale of the *Bounty* has the status of myth, as powerful and resonant as the actions of Achilles for an Athenian general. William Bligh is a specific kind of hero to a man like Harriott: brave, diligent, earnest, a stickler for rules and duty and discipline. If Harriott had captained the *Bounty* he can see no part of Bligh's behaviour which he himself would not have mirrored. To discover, therefore, that his good friend Aaron Graham was instrumental in securing the King's pardon for one of the mutineers is rather like that same Athenian general discovering that Achilles did not in fact chase Hector down but merely took all the credit.

For Harriott, Heywood's subsequent success in the Navy – reaching the exalted levels of flag-captain, no less, and having had the command of half a dozen ships – is a confused mystery, an insult to simple morals and fierce loyalties. Moreover it reveals to Harriott the truth of English institutional matters. For while Bligh has had to fight to protect his reputation from the smears of those attached to Heywood and even those, Lord help us, friendly to the blackguard Fletcher Christian, Heywood has himself thrived under the patronage of powerful friends. Even Christian himself, it has long been rumoured, has made his way back to England for a peaceful life.

Graham looks back at him and almost appears amused at the serendipitous coincidences they are discussing.

'I advised Heywood in his court martial, Harriott. I was a young lawyer at the time, fresh back from Newfoundland, making my way in the world. As I have said, Heywood's family were known to me and they asked me to conduct his legal strategy. We were successful, as you now know. Or at least successful enough to secure a pardon.'

'You *defended* the man,' says Harriott. 'A mutineer.'

Graham looks uncomfortable.

'I *advised* him and his family, Harriot, that is all. I did not speak for him during his court martial. And he was only ever an *alleged* mutineer. There was insufficient evidence of his motivation to say he was actively involved. He was only fifteen years old when the *Bounty* left England. A mere boy. He was taken up in the excitement of the events.'

'Excitement, Graham? The men mutinied against their rightful captain!'

'Indeed they did, Harriott. But not all of them mutinied with enthusiasm, and not all of them knew what they were about. I convinced the court martial that Heywood was caught up in events outside his control, and was too young to do anything other than be taken along with them. I was believed.'

'He was found guilty.'

'By the court martial, yes. But not by the highest authority. The King pardoned him.'

'For reasons of justice, or for reasons of patronage?'

Graham looks uncomfortable at that, and Harriott sees clearly a truth about his friendship with Graham. The Bow Street man does not hold the same rigid standards of propriety and duty as Harriott does. He lives in a world where acquaintance and social connection are as important to a man's life as sunlight and rich soil are to a plant's. Harriott can still vividly recall the story of the *Bounty* mutiny and remembers how the facts of that case were slippery things, liable to run away from themselves and blend one into another, until the truth of events was as impossible to read as the wishes of a woman. It is that slippery world which Graham inhabits, and Harriott has long known it. He must make his peace with it, or end the friendship forthwith.

Harriott turns back to Nott.

'So you came back to London. Why did you not contact Mr Graham immediately? Why wait until you were in Coldbath Fields?'

'I was afraid.'

'Afraid of what?'

'Afraid that he might refuse to help me. I had come all this way and the risk of being denied overwhelmed me.'

Harriott thinks this unlikely. He thinks Nott is lying. He wonders why.

'Why, then, were you visiting Attlee and Arnott?'

'Because they were my friends, Mr Harriott. They were

among the kindest of the crew towards me. Their deaths are painful to me in the extreme. But I did not kill them.'

There is silence while the two magistrates digest what the young missionary has told them. Harriott's mind is a whirl, but of an abstract kind which doesn't ask who, what, where and when, but sticks rather on a disbelieving *how on earth?* and gets no further. Nott's story is epic and preposterous, but has an internal consistency to it which cannot be denied. His age, the dates he gives – he *could* be Peter Heywood's son.

Or the whole thing could be the fantasy of an ignorant island woman who once lay with a European sailor and spawned a half-breed son. For all they know, Nott's father could be a Spaniard or a Frenchman or a Portuguese.

And yet he can see in Graham's eyes, at least, the spark of belief, and it occurs to him that Graham knew Peter Heywood, and perhaps sees some resemblance to his old client in Peter Nott.

Nothing is said for a while, but after a short time Nott bows his head and, so quietly that Harriott can barely hear it, he begins to pray.

KEW

Robert Brown has a comfortable carriage ride to Kew, a time to reflect on the experiment with the leaf, but also to consider what the officer from Wapping has just told him. He takes little notice of what passes outside the carriage window, although it is yet another glorious spring day, and he is heading west, where Westminster puts on its best summer frock and colourful hat and flashes its skirts at the passers-by.

He is enormously tired. It was a restless night punctuated by dreams he can barely remember. It is an odd feeling: the old torpor that had been creeping up on him is quite gone, as is the thudding pain in the head. It now occurs to him, as a blackbird screeches in a plane tree to the right of the passing carriage, that his hearing is clearer than he can ever remember it being. But this newfound feeling of healthy wellbeing is accompanied by a dour handmaiden – this aching tiredness. He probably should not have gone to bed when he did. Only routine had told him to do so. All that met him was broken rest and disturbing dreams, the details of which have long subsided.

He has with him his sheets of notes from the experiment with the leaf, on which he has also scribbled extracts from Hooke's lecture. He consults them again, and is struck for perhaps the twentieth time how odd they seem. He has little memory of the effect of the leaf itself, other than sharp feelings of enormous pleasure which he tries urgently to suppress, though he does not know quite why. He sees from his notes that in the immediate aftermath he did remember things: the boat to the island, his father shouting from a staircase. He does not remember those things now, and if they were not written down he would not consider them. He has appended other notes based on Leary's account of his behaviour during the experiment itself, but these are frankly obscure: a great deal about light, and something about the island, and that strange reference to an organism at the heart of things. He thinks of Hooke and Democritus, and wonders whether he has not had some kind of a revelation.

So, he has much to report to Sir Joseph: the effect of the leaf, both during and after its consumption. But also this strange tale the Wapping officer has to tell, of the dead men all holding cups which contained a residue, possibly of some kind of tea. The coincidence is stark and almost certainly no coincidence at all. He had deflected the constable's questions on this, because he could see no way of answering honestly which did not enormously complicate matters with Sir Joseph. Had the sailors on the *Solander* experimented with the same leaf he himself has taken? But how can they have done so, when it was taken from a tree in Kew?

Ah, but then that tree was taken from Otaheite, was it not?

And of course it is obvious. The tree in Kew is a cutting, not grown from seed. The original tree is still in Otaheite. The sailors must have discovered that tree, and then discovered the effects of the leaf which came from it. He must discuss this with Sir Joseph before another encounter with the Wapping constable.

But he never has the chance. Events rather overtake him.

Sir Joseph is waiting for him in the Dutch House, the elegant structure that sits almost at the river's edge on the north side of the Gardens. He sits in a small room overlooking the formal gardens of the house and the temporary shed which has been constructed for the *Solander* gardeners. It is quite clear that Sir Joseph is waiting for Brown. There is an unusual restlessness about him, and Banks is not a man who can easily hide his own impatience.

'Well? Anything to report?'

Brown thinks this question very odd, and wonders if Banks knows of his experiment. He thinks back to his last conversation with Sir Joseph, and remembers it was the President, not he, who had brought up Robert Hooke and his experiment with *bhang*. Brown ponders the possibility that he has been somehow manipulated.

He describes the events of yesterday to Banks in full, though he does not mention the presence of his father in his dreams, nor the oddest parts of his leaf-inspired vision: the tree on the island and that intimation of an organism, something within the cells of things themselves. Banks is impatient to hear particularly of the physical effect of the leaf.

'How do you feel now?' he asks.

'I am tired from broken sleep, but other than that I feel quite well.'

'How "well"? You are somewhat prone to illness, Brown, I need not remind you. If you can ignore the tiredness, which after all springs from an ancillary effect of the experiment – I speak of your lack of sleep – if you can ignore that, tell me how it is you now *feel*?'

Sir Joseph's tone is peevish and hectoring, and for a moment Brown toys with the idea of refusing to answer, of asking how exactly this kind of undertaking fits into the responsibilities of a librarian. But, of course, he does no such thing.

'I feel enormously well, Sir Joseph. My head and my hearing are clearer than they have been for a long time – perhaps since my childhood. And I can feel a great energy in my body which perhaps was not there before. Alongside this tiredness, as I have said.'

It is acutely uncomfortable discussing his wellbeing with his employer, but Sir Joseph seems oblivious to the sense. His eyes are bright with excitement.

'Call my manservant, would you?'

Brown goes out and comes back with the manservant. Sir Joseph hands the servant an envelope.

'Have this sent to Windsor immediately.'

'Yes sir.'

The manservant leaves.

Windsor.

The two of them go down to the Stove to see the tree. Thoughts are crashing into each other randomly in Brown's head as he pushes Sir Joseph's wheelchair, like disconnected particles in a hot soup. He asks Sir Joseph if he might be impertinent enough to wonder what was in the letter sent to Windsor. Sir Joseph grunts and says all will become clear, irritated by the question but not angered by it, for he seems to be experiencing a childish giddiness which Brown has never seen before.

It is noticeably darker inside the Stove, and it is immediately obvious why. The Otaheite tree is now almost full-grown, or least it would be if it hadn't outgrown the height of the Stove itself which, Brown knows, is some thirty feet. The top of the tree is bent over and has begun to spread along the roof of the Stove, obscuring the light from the other plants, which as a consequence look pale and unhealthy, as if their vitality had been sucked up out of the soil and into the tree.

They walk up close to the tree, and Sir Joseph leans forward and points.

'Look, Brown.'

Brown can see what he means immediately. There are copious female flowers hanging down from the trees, at varying rates of growth. The biggest are drying out and turning into something like an unfertilised hemp flower-top, but bigger, more substantial, almost like a fruit in itself. There are still no male flowers. Really, the classification of the tree remains a complete mystery.

As does the ability of children to get in here, thinks Brown, irritably, as the sound of another girl giggles up from some corner of the hothouse. He notices Sir Joseph is gently smiling at him.

'You seem exercised by something, Brown.'

'Oh, nothing sir. There always seem to be *children* in here. I must speak to the gardeners about it.'

'I'm by no means sure the gardeners can do much about these children. You see the flowers, of course?'

'Of course.'

'I have confirmed your findings. There are no male organs of reproduction anywhere on this tree.'

'So, this must be an entirely new species, one which has male and female plants. But this blinds us to the more problematic conundrum.'

'The tree's precipitous growth.'

'Indeed, yes. How can a living thing consume enough material to grow so quickly?'

'It seems to be having a detrimental effect on the other plants, as well.'

'Quite so. Might this tree in fact be parasitic? Parasitic on the entire flora?'

Brown's question hangs in the air, almost obscene in its size and implications. The two men watch the tree for a while, like two Spanish explorers standing upon a peak in Darien, gazing on an undiscovered sea, only the distant giggling of a girl to disturb their reverie.

Horton arrives at Kew in the late afternoon. He is already in a state of mild wonder at the beauty of the place in which he finds himself – indeed, he has been in some astonishment ever since they passed through Mortlake. He has seen a great many places in the world, from Newfoundland to Batavia, but nothing with half as much precise and ordered splendour as this corner of England. The river, which he is used to thinking of as a muddy, noisy, rushing stream, a highway for shipping and a breeding ground for the ugliest of crimes, has here turned into a polite, green, whispering thing, watched over by herons and caressed by willows, hemmed in by terraces and artful temples. The air is full of the material of plants – tickling pollen which shines in the late afternoon sunlight, picking out the sunbeams which fall onto smart little houses, brand new villas and grand mansions alike. A rich man's playground, no doubt, but a playground decked out with the most exquisite taste in the world.

The feeling lasts as he climbs down from the carriage at Kew Green. His name has been left by Brown with the soldiers at the gate, and he is accompanied into the Gardens by a red-coated soldier, who glares at him.

'Wot are you, then?' the soldier asks as they walk through the grounds.

'A waterman-constable. Of the Thames River Police Office.'

'River Police? What you supposed to catch? Fish?'

The soldier laughs at that, his harsh Essex accent incongruous against his traditional uniform and the elegant balance of
the surroundings – although here that balance, so stark outside
the Kew walls, is thrown awry by the odd buildings, like the
enormous Pagoda that rises above the trees to the south and
there, upstream and on the edge of the park, the crazy wilful-
ness of the Castellated Palace.

The soldier leaves Horton outside an ugly shed which looks
like it has been freshly constructed. Abigail should be here, he
thinks. He imagines her darting around the gardens, counting
leaves and pistils and stamens and telling him which class was
what and what species was that, and his eyes would droop and
she'd laugh at him, saying he took no interest in anything that
wasn't a man who'd done something terrible.

He goes into the shed, and spends an hour or two talking to
the gardeners within, who are coming to the end of the work of
categorising and transplanting the wonders from Otaheite.
They use the word 'wonders' a lot for things which, to Horton,
look like the kind of plants you might just as easily have found
walking the meadows up towards Highgate. He can see why
Hopkins had not recommended he talk to them immediately.
They are lost in their own botanical worlds, and claim to have
seen nothing, spoken to no one and heard little about anything
other than plants, plants, plants. When he tells them the names
of the dead men, they look at him blankly. When he asks them
about Critchley, they don't know the name, although a couple
of them recognise the physical description of the blond Viking.
They are all effusive in their praise of Captain Hopkins, who
had willingly turned his ship into a veritable floating plant
house, his carpenter able to find stowing places for every new
discovery the gardeners brought onboard. Horton remembers

that Jeremiah Critchley was the carpenter's mate, but even when this is pointed out to the gardeners they don't recall the name.

So, it turns out to be a frustrating trip, and evening is now falling. He leaves the shed, and wanders back towards the gate, in front of the Orangery to his left, and spies a great hothouse over to the right in which he can just pick out a shivering greenness. A carriage arrives at the gate; despite being plain and undecorated, it manages to look enormously opulent. He is about to walk over to see who is arriving, when he hears that unwelcome Essex voice again.

'If you've finished with the gardeners, Mr River Police, I've got orders to escort you back to Kew Green and get you a carriage.'

The soldier must have been waiting and watching all this time. A careful man, is Mr Brown, thinks Horton, and saying nothing he turns and walks back to the gate, the soldier beside him smirking annoyingly.

Sir Joseph and Brown are waiting as the plain-but-expensive carriage pulls up near the Orangery. Banks sits in his wheelchair with Brown behind him, and the librarian can see once again the clear marks of enormous excitement and stress in the shoulders and hands of the President. But they wait patiently as the doors to the carriage are opened by two footmen to reveal an elegant fellow who looks like nothing less than a well-to-do artist. Brown recognises him as Thomas Monro, physician to the Bridewell and Bethlem madhouses. Brown had heard tell that Monro had been asked to examine the King since the return of his illness the previous year.

Monro steps down and walks up to Banks, who greets him with a handshake. Monro nods at Brown, who is busy making connections and pondering on the insanity of what Banks has been planning.

Monro frowns at Banks, and gives a *get-on-with-it* nod. An impatient man, then, one well used to having his own way and being attended to by those around him.

'Come with me,' says Banks, and the librarian pushes the wheelchair towards the Stove.

Going through the door of the hothouse, they are once again assailed by a cacophony of scent. The tropics rise up to meet their jaded English noses. The wheelchair is wheeled between green walls of flora, the growing treasure chest of material plundered from a world which bows beneath the power of a British navy and British exploration.

In the middle of all this is the tree Banks had planted a few nights ago and which now quivers enormously and with a desperate energy, and Brown imagines for a moment that the tree *bends* towards the old man in his wheelchair, like a giraffe bending down to view a dog.

Banks indicates to Monro.

'Here it is. Here is the leaf which I believe will cure His Majesty.'

And there it is, stark as day, the thing that has been creeping up on Brown all day long, the knowledge that Sir Joseph has always had his own agenda. He was manipulated into the experiment with the *bhang*. Perhaps they were all manipulated. Perhaps the voyage of the *Solander* was always about this one moment, when the doctor to a mad old king was offered a cure.

'The Regent suspects,' says Monro, his first utterance.

'No doubt,' says Banks. 'But you are the King's doctor.'

'The latest in a long line of doctors, most of whom have done their best to kill him. I only keep him alive. I strongly doubt this ... *plant* will cause any significant change.'

'The plants of Otaheite are like no other plants in the world.'

'You are the expert, Sir Joseph. I am only an instrument.'

'Then good. Come with me. We will make a draught from the leaves of the tree, and I wager that we will see an improvement.'

Monro nods, and taking over from Brown, he wheels the old President away.

DEPTFORD

Harriott and Graham are sitting in a neat drawing room inside a neat house at the edge of the enormous Royal Dockyard at Deptford. They are waiting for Peter Heywood, post-captain and hydrographer and, more to the current purpose, rehabilitated mutineer, who is currently at Deptford supervising the fitting-out of a new ship, HMS *Douglas*, of which he has the command. Despite Heywood's trappings of military power, for Harriott they are still in the business of attending on a wicked miscreant. Why, wondered Harriott as they made their way downriver to Deptford, had Graham assisted the mutinous little monkey at all?

'Because his family asked me to,' Graham had replied.

'But that is no reason to aid a scoundrel,' said Harriott.

'It is every reason in the world, my dear Harriott.'

'Are we to believe such men, just because they claim their innocence?'

'Of course not. But we must agree that every man has recourse to the truth of the matter, even in a court martial. Do you not accept that?'

A grumble from Harriott.

'So, if a man has recourse to the truth, and if the machinery of state is ranged against him, it seems right to my eyes that he be given the chance to defend himself. He must have access to legal counsel who will advise him. Such has been the way in our criminal courts for almost a century. And if counsel is advising him, that counsel must work tirelessly on the assumption that he *is* innocent. No other course is open to him.'

'Which rather suggests you never believed he was innocent.'

'It does no such thing. As it happens, I did believe his guilt was by no means clear, which is not to say he was innocent, but I do not live in a world of certainties, Harriott, and am quite comfortable with a little ambiguity. But what if he were innocent? What if he were wrongly accused, and had his career taken away from him and his life destroyed? Is it not better that a guilty man escape justice than an innocent man be ruined?'

'No, sir, I do not believe it is. That may be the difference between us. I am prepared to allow that my view is pig-headed, just as yours is dangerously lenient.'

'I thank you for that.'

'So, you defended him because you thought he *might* be innocent.'

'Just so. In addition, he has a charming sister.'

'And in any case, the court martial found him guilty. It was left to the King to pardon him.'

'Indeed it was. As I said, Harriott, I am comfortable with a degree of ambiguity.'

A flurry on the stairs and in the hall suggests the imminent arrival of an excited boy, but when Peter Heywood bursts into the room it is an experienced naval officer who presents himself.

'Mr Graham! Wonder of wonders, Mr Graham here in Deptford! You are welcome, sir, most welcome, a delight to see you. And you, sir, I do not believe we . . .? Ah, Mr Harriott, a pleasure to meet you, sir, a pleasure to see you both. Atkins, please, some sherry and at the double. Please, gentlemen, please be seated and let me know your business here. My, what a wonder. What an extraordinary surprise!'

Peter Heywood is a man of forty years, but looks at least fifty. His hair is almost uniformly grey, and he is barely as tall as Harriott, five foot four or perhaps five. He is in full naval uniform, as if coming back from or preparing to go to an official function. He is thin, much thinner than most naval captains of Harriott's acquaintance, who have a tendency to run to fat and as a consequence always look rather breathless and clammy. Heywood looks cool and considered, despite his excitement at the magistrates' arrival. And it cannot be denied: he looks like Peter Nott. The younger man has a fatter face and darker skin and hair, but his eyes look out from Heywood's face.

Heywood makes idle chit-chat with Graham while the manservant fetches the sherry and pours each of them a glass, and then he raises his in a toast.

'To Mr Aaron Graham, magistrate, sailor and saviour,' he says, smiling. 'My gratitude to him remains as bright as it was twenty years ago. Your health, sir. And yours, Mr Harriott.'

The two magistrates return the toast, and sip their sherry which, Harriott notes, is very good indeed.

'So, Peter. Captain Heywood. You appear to have prospered,' says Graham, in his best twinkling fashion.

'Beyond all hope and expectation, Mr Graham,' replies the captain. 'Since you rescued me from infamy and despair, I have risen but I have also, I trust, served His Majesty well. I am about to take a new command, on a ship now being finished here.'

'I am delighted to see it, Peter,' says Graham.

'Are you gentlemen on some species of tour?' asks Heywood. 'I can think of no other reason for your surprising arrival, other than happenstance.'

'No, Peter, not a tour,' says Graham. 'We were rather hoping you could help us with an investigation Mr Harriott here is undertaking.'

'Oh, indeed?'

'Yes. There has been a series of deaths among the crew of a ship which recently arrived in London from Otaheite. Mr Harriott, as magistrate of the River Police Office, has been undertaking to seek out the truth of these events.'

At the word *Otaheite* Heywood's expression changes. Gone is the boyish enthusiasm and rather theatrical bonhomie with which he'd greeted Graham. Now, they are in a room with a serious-minded, competent and successful naval commander who is on his guard. Harriott can see that Graham also recognises the sudden change.

'I trust, Graham, that there is more to this appeal to me than a mere wish to probe my memories of that island.'

No more *Mr Graham*, then. Now Heywood is an equal to the magistrate.

'There is a good deal more to it than that, Peter ... Heywood. The ship in question is the *Solander*. You have heard of it?'

'Of course. Any naval captain in London just now would have heard of it. There is a good deal of upset still among certain parties within the Admiralty that a Navy captain was supplied for the voyage, as it was privately funded by Sir Joseph. There are some who say that Sir Joseph made enough use of Navy men forty years ago.'

Harriott is suddenly very grateful for Graham's presence. This is now a dangerous conversation between two very capable men, in which temper must be kept and norms followed.

Words are likely to be sharp while smiles remain fixed. It is not an ideal situation for bluff old John Harriott.

'Well, then, Heywood. One of the ship's passengers is known by the name of Peter Nott. He is a half-breed, the child of an island woman and, he says, an Englishman. He is the adopted son of the missionary Henry Nott. He claims *you* are his natural father, Heywood.'

'My God.'

Heywood stares at Graham for a moment, forgetting himself, and then stands and walks to the window. His hands go behind his back. He must look like this on the quarterdeck with a French ship off to starboard, thinks Harriott, waiting to pounce upon her in the name of King and Country. Ah, but no. Heywood is a maker of maps, not a battler. For a while the captain says nothing at all, and his still back and perfectly unmoving hands give no suggestion as to what he is feeling. But the gesture itself speaks of ... what? Anger? Despair? Surprise? Delight?

None of these, Harriott sees as Heywood turns from the window. None of these at all. *Amusement.*

'Well, this day brings a second package of wonder. First they show me round my ship. Then you come, and tell me of my son. How perfectly ... *bizarre.*'

'You knew about your son?' Harriott asks the question, cannot help himself. Something about Heywood's light manner and easy smile as he sits back down has infuriated him beyond measure.

'I knew I *had* a son, Mr Harriott,' says Heywood. 'I knew I'd *fathered* one. But I did not know he was alive or that he even knew of me. But you know how it is. We have all fathered sons in foreign lands. There are probably bits of us Navy fellows walking around three or four different continents.'

Harriott had known, of course, that such a response was

possible. Heywood is right. Naval men of a certain stripe are relentless sowers of English seed. But he still feels a wave of anger, sparked no doubt by his sympathy for the pathetic figure now sitting under a sort of lock and key in Bow Street, whose eyes are so like those of the man opposite him.

'Sir, I find your response to this news alarmingly distasteful,' he says, despite himself. 'Your suggestion that I might have . . .'

'Oh, well, Mr Harriott, I apologise. After all, I was only making fun of the situation. Do sit down, sir, you are old and your leg is clearly lame. No? Well then, stand if you wish. Now, what do you expect me to do with this news you bring?'

Graham looks down and frowns, and speaks without looking up again.

'Peter . . . Captain Heywood. Your attitude is surprising to me.'

'Really?' The smile on Heywood's face is that of a society beau kicking a beggar outside his club. 'How so, Graham?'

'You feel no responsibility towards this young man?'

Heywood laughs, then, a rich salty captain's laugh.

'Graham, how am I supposed to feel any *responsibility* for a person I do not know, have no intention of meeting, and have no interest in. He could be *anybody*, Graham. Your story is preposterous – my son, from Otaheite, the adopted son of an English missionary, back in England to find me? And what? Affect some reconciliation out of the pages of a Gothic romance? Am I to make him my lieutenant? Do we sail the oceans together, storming ships and chasing women like some half-baked buccaneers? No, Graham, I feel no *responsibility*. I feel nothing at all. I slept with half a dozen women on that damned island – we all did. One of them bore a brat. Now that brat wishes to call me *Father*.'

Graham says nothing, but looks up at Heywood with an expression the like of which Harriott has never seen on the face of clever, witty, urbane, fashionable Aaron Graham. His fellow magistrate looks like he has stepped in something profoundly distasteful, and his Saville Row shoes are thus ruined.

'You will not meet him?' asks Harriott at last.

'I will not,' replies Captain Heywood. 'I am a busy man about to set sail again for seas far and wide. I have no need, nor time, for a son.'

'Then, Captain, we will not keep you from your duties any longer.'

Harriott waits for Graham to stand, but for a moment he does not do so. Then he asks a soft, strange question.

'Were you indeed on the deck, Peter? When it happened? Were you one of those who mocked their captain as they forced him down into the boat?'

Heywood's amused look cracks somewhat at that, and Harriott spies some apprehension there. The dislike he has developed for the former mutineer is as sharp and clean as a new needle.

'Do you doubt what I told you?' says Heywood.

'I didn't,' says Graham. 'But now . . . I wonder.'

He stands, and walks out without saying another word. With a final look at Heywood, which he tries to invest with a lifetime of contempt, Harriott follows.

PUTNEY

Captain Hopkins lives in a new house built on the fringes of Putney Common, and Horton arrives there a little before nine o'clock in the evening on his way back from Kew.

It is not a fancy or particularly elaborate house, but it stands on its own on the edge of a wood and is, in its way, as fine a place as a naval man could expect to take possession of, subject as he is to the whims of the Admiralty, the unreliability of his agent and the vicious stabs of Fortune.

The house sparks in Horton an almost unbearable envy. Were it not for other matters this smart little house could belong to Abigail and him. She would be inside, washing and cleaning and reading and sewing, and he would be returning from a long ocean voyage, his heart full of joy at the prospect of seeing her, his purse full of gold and silver, and they would shut the door on this little house and not come out again for a week.

But it is not Abigail who answers the door. Far from it. It is a fat wholesome woman who chirrups with delight at this unexpected visit but must inform the constable that – for shame! – her husband is not home, but she really must insist he take some tea with her, despite the hour. Horton hesitates – the carriage is waiting outside and, more to the point, Abigail is waiting far, far across town. But this chatty little captain's wife may be able to offer more than just tea this evening, so he accepts.

They talk and talk for some time, or rather she talks and Horton listens. He takes heed of her tales of the deeds of her majestic husband, his diligence and his immense concern for the men under his command, many of whom have been to this house. At least those of the officer class have; she has never met any of the *ordinary* seamen, and she supposes these men are quite brutal in their way, but the officers are always immaculate in their manners and prodigious of their praise of the captain's house and household. And yes of *course* he spends a lot of time on board ship just before and just after a voyage; really, she has hardly seen him at all. And had Horton met all the officers, and had he met in *particular* that odd little chaplain, the half-breed, she's never seen a half-savage Christian before and she doesn't know what to make of it, but he was a quiet thing when her captain brought him here, a quiet thing indeed, but she'd fed him and watered him and he'd blossomed like a little exotic flower. Was the constable interested in botany, because really it was *quite* the most interesting thing in the world, she and all her lady friends agree, and, oh, pardon me, come again, what did you say? Yes, of course I understand, the hour is late, and perhaps it is not entirely proper for you to stay much longer, but it is indeed charming to have a man visit, oh bless me, I am blushing, now do let me show you out, yes, yes, I can see, that is a nasty tear in your coat, yes, you will have to get that seen to, and yes, I do happen to know someone who I use for the captain's repairs, really that man is always tearing this and that, it's like he goes a-voyaging with a lion in his cabin, there's a lovely clever little man up on Clapham Common that I take all my repairs to, no, I've got no eye for it at all, I know, I'm a terrible wife, no really I am, yes, Clapham Common, on the far side, not where all the rich men live, the other side, yes, Constable, it's been a delight, careful voyage home, I'll tell the captain you were here, goodbye, goodbye!

LONDON

The thirst hits him on the way back from Kew, somewhere around the little hamlet of Nine Elms. It is an overpowering thing, and he actually gasps when it sweeps over him, gasps so loudly that the carriage driver's head twitches around and looks behind him before facing forward again, the horse's breath rising like steam into the midnight darkness. Inside the carriage, Brown wrestles with the torment as if it were a wriggling serpent, his head aching as badly as it has ever done and, even worse, that old torpor creeping over him like a black cloud, such that he falls back into the carriage cringing with hunger, with pain, with anxiety and yet with lassitude, as if some internal demon was merrily combining his humours with no regard to propriety.

He thinks of the leaf sitting there in the jar in his Gerrard Street room and the thirst hits him again, like a needle in his stomach and a poker in his head, and for several minutes Robert Brown is transmuted into a tense, shivering ball of need, aware of only his forward direction towards where the leaf can be found, the substance that will resolve this desperate desire, miles up ahead on the other side of Westminster Bridge.

He argued with Sir Joseph for long hours at Kew, argued and cajoled and pleaded with him, but Banks remained immovable. He had researched the leaf for years, the President said, it was entirely safe. He had corresponded with that vast network of captains and botanists and ambassadors and soldiers which he'd assembled over the decades. For forty years he'd assembled a great record of the strange rites and rituals of Otaheite, a dark melange of human sacrifice and sorcery and demons, his fascination with the place whetted by the *Endeavour* voyage so long ago, but deepened and sharpened since by that relentless Banksian correspondence, by which every visitor to Otaheite, be they from Britain, France, Spain or wherever, had received a letter from Sir Joseph Banks, enquiring of their experience of the local rituals. And of course he had given endless thought to the great medical matter of the Age: the sanity of the King.

'The King, who is my friend,' Banks said, as if that explained and forgave everything.

In recent years, the news from Otaheite had become more and more alarming. The natives were constantly at war with each other, such that the security of the island itself and Britain's presence upon it was called into question. Even the missionaries had left, or almost all of them. The last remaining was Henry Nott, with whom Banks had maintained a regular decade-long correspondence, at least as regular as the patterns of shipping on the far side of the world would allow. Nott had become, almost by default, the Banksian representative on the island, an ambassador of natural philosophy, despite his austere religion. Nott had known more of the island rituals than any man alive, and he'd told Banks about the stories of a strange tree and the leaf which came from it; how it was said that this leaf had magical properties, and could restore clarity of thought and sense, as well as supplying an immensity of pleasure.

And so Banks had crafted a plan within a plan. He had been plotting a final botanising expedition to Otaheite for years now, as the news of the brutal tribal wars grew worse and worse, and as the rumours swirled of France's interest in securing the island for her own possession. So now he took his opportunity: send a ship to the far side of the world, bring back the botany of the island, and also bring back a cutting from that very tree, and see whether it would grow. And, by God, how it had grown!

Banks had kept the true purpose of the voyage secret from everyone, even the ship's captain. He'd told one of the gardeners where the tree was and what to do to take a cutting from it. The gardener had done as he was told, and had thought nothing of it, for Banks had told him to collect dozens of other specimens, as he'd told each gardener, so the secret of the tree was kept.

Brown quivered just like that ominous tree in the Stove quivered, though not with growth but with a raging disappointment. He had been the test case for the leaf, the one who would check its safety, and Brown shouted then, shouted for the first time in the odd, pitted relationship he shared with his mentor. Banks said nothing, as if giving permission for Brown's loss of control, but then his librarian said 'You do not know what you have done.' At that Banks too lost his temper, asking Brown if he was or was not a Briton, was he not prepared to put all aside for the sake of the *King*, to save his country from the gargantuan appetites of the King's son, who is a man, said Banks, with a mouth, a wardrobe and no morals whatsoever. Brown, helpless to argue with Sir Joseph's fierce patriotism, gave way before it.

Banks had used him before, when he'd put him on the *Investigator* and sent him around the world. That is what Banks did. He used lives – his own included – for the furtherance of two ideals which orbited each other like twin planets: man's knowledge of the natural world; and Britain's domination of it.

But the *King*, he said to Banks, you cannot surely know enough about the leaf to give it to the *King*. Banks looked at him and asked how much Brown knew about the King's illness, and Brown said he knew very little, and Banks said *exactly*, because *very little* is what the army of doctors who surrounded His Majesty knew. Modern British medicine had exhausted itself on the steep hills of King George's mysterious illness. Everything had been tried, and still the man who had once debated planets with Herschel was an idiot, a vegetable, barely even a human, and at what point did the King's friends have to decide that *any* solution was worth the candle, despite its danger? That moment had passed years before, Banks claimed. If the leaf was dangerous well, then, it was dangerous. It could not make the situation any worse.

Brown tried one more argument. The deaths of the crewmen, he said. The dead men had taken something before their death, something unexplained which had seemingly transported them. The constable investigating those deaths had asked Brown directly whether the men could have brought something back from Otaheite. The question was a sharp one. It suggested the constable was close to uncovering truths about the voyage. Was it not possible that the men had consumed the leaf, or something similar to it, something which had put down roots in southern soil but which had delivered its effects to the other side of the world?

Banks paused at that. The news surprised him. He pondered it for a few moments, and his stubborn old face turned to Brown's.

'Did what they consumed kill them?'

'No, Sir Joseph, they were . . .'

'Well, then. No more of it. Some of the crew found the leaf, and now they are dead.'

'But killed by whom?'

'It is of no concern to me, Brown. Some ignorant men dabbled in matters beyond their comprehension. They are now dead. The King's health is still the matter of paramount concern.'

'And what of the Wapping constable?'

'He is Harriott's officer?'

'Yes.'

'Then I can address the problem. It will soon go away.'

Brown said no more. As midnight approached he left the old man. Silence had descended between them, and neither could bring themselves to look at, let alone speak to, the other. He took a carriage home. And now here he is, quivering with fear and with hunger and with thirst, his head squeezed in pain and the longing in his chest swamping all other remembrance.

His carriage passes, at last, over Westminster Bridge. The dark hulks of Westminster Hall and the abbey float above and beyond the river, dark polygons against the sky which grow in size and definition as the carriage reaches the other side of the bridge, and then turns right into Parliament Street and makes its way up towards Whitehall. Eventually, the Admiralty passes on the left, and Brown looks up at it and, even in his despairing thirst, wonders how much is known in *that* building of the schemes of Sir Joseph Banks.

The streets are almost deserted. As they pass round the Charing Cross and into Cockspur Street, two dark figures run in front of the carriage. Street children, headed back to St Giles after a night of begging and picking pockets. Brown scarcely notices them, as the minutes stretch out into infinities. Why is the coach going so damned slowly?

But eventually they reach Gerrard Street and Brown shoves some coins into the driver's hands, not checking them carefully at all, his habitual parsimony a victim of this pungent addiction. He lets himself in and up to his room, and then must go through the agony of lighting a fire (the servants have not done so, as the June evenings have been particularly clement) and waiting for it to catch, then putting the kettle on the fire and waiting for it to boil and then, finally then, he can put hot water in the same cup he'd used the day before (there is still a residue from the leaf in the bottom of the cup but Brown does not care) and add leaf from the jar, more than before, much more, but his need is so great, the leaf's aroma stinging his eyes and sharpening his need – *come on, come on, come on.* Then he is drinking the tea, the water scalding his lips and mouth and throat, but no matter, because now . . .

Light explodes. His hands fall to his side, spilling boiling water onto his thigh where it will burn the skin as a memento of tonight for tomorrow's consideration, and he falls backwards in his chair to the ground, his head slamming into the rug but by now he is already under, deep under, in a long, dark well . . .

His father is shouting from the staircase. There are people in every room of the house, whispering and praying. One of them is his mother, he knows, but she will spare him no attention while his father shouts from above.

'There is no authority but the Lord!'

He hides beneath the stairs, directly beneath his father, and in his hand he holds a plant, its roots still full of soil, its leaves bright and alive.

'There is no law but the Book!'

The green leaves of the plant are the only colour in the hallway, which is dark: dark wood, dark floor, dark walls, dark dark dark. He wonders where he can hide this plant, because he knows his parents will not allow it in the house, for reasons he cannot be clear about. He just knows. His father takes a step down the stairs, moved by the force of his own assertion, and so Brown pushes even further back into his hiding place, in case his father is on the way down, but then the wall behind him gives way and he is falling away and down.

He lands beside a waterfall in a green place, the air hot and humid, the ground soft and warm, as if great fires had been lit beneath it. He is still holding the plant, but now he can see, as it were in miniature, a tiny breadfruit in among its leaves. He is examining this carefully when he hears a girl's laugh. He looks into the trees that surround him, and the laugh seems to be coming from all of them, from behind and beneath and within every tree. He stands and steps into the forest.

The leaves caress his face, and branches stroke his arms, the roots tickle at his feet as he walks through the enchanted forest. Everywhere, there is laughter, as if a troop of princesses were accompanying him through the forest. Soon, he comes into a clearing.

At one side of the clearing there is a stone platform with an altar upon it. He realises he is at the top of a hill, and all around he can see the ocean, a deep blue ocean as still as glass. But the clearing is empty, apart from the altar, as if a great fire had burst through here and claimed all the flora. There is only a scrubby grass covering the land. The laughing has stopped, and he steps forward into the centre of the clearing.

He stops, and looks around himself, but then he feels the plant in his hands begin to shake. He looks down upon it and realises that the plant has begun to grow before his eyes. Its stem extends, its branches multiply, strange flowers burst from buds and fruits appear by the second, growing from peas to grapes to oranges to grapefruits to pineapples in size, until the plant becomes too heavy to hold and he drops it on the ground. Still it grows, the branches twirling around his legs and up his body and beginning to squeeze, until one of them reaches his shoulders and then his face and plunges down his mouth, while others enter his ears, his nose, his eyes, and he hears that girlish laughter again but now it is within him and filled with an unquenchable sadness and anger, for it is full of poison, a poison that would eat the world.

EIGHT

*The most active poisons which are known do not so
quickly destroy the life of an animal as the want of
air, or the breathing of it when it is rendered highly
noxious. It will appear in this work, that those very
plants, which, influenced by the light of the sun, repair
the injury done to this fluid by the breathing of
animals and by many other causes, may, in different
circumstances, poison so much this very element, as to
render it absolutely unfit for respiration, and, instead
of keeping up life, to extinguish it in a moment.*

John Ingen-Housz, *Experiments Upon Vegetables*, 1779

WAPPING

The storehouse on New Gravel Lane has been used for a great many things in its time, but in the main it has always been gravel that is kept there. It is brought down from the higher land above Wapping to be taken on as ballast in ships – mainly colliers from the north-east – returning empty to their home harbours. It is this gravel that gave Old and New Gravel Lanes their names. Other stuff might be left in the storehouse – tar, rope, sailcloth, even the odd barrel of rice or tobacco surreptitiously left out of a manifest and redirected here rather than to the new brick-and-glass warehouses of the dock – but gravel is always piled up all around. It is above the piles of gravel that the dead body swings, hanging from a rope which is itself worked by a metal winch and crane which can be turned through 360 degrees to unload onto the street via a shuttered opening high up on the wall. The crane itself is attached to a small platform running along one side of the storehouse, two-thirds of the way up the wall, and accessed by an unsteady-looking ladder.

Standing beneath the swaying body are three men: Edward

Markland, and two of his constables. Harriott recognises these men but cannot recall their names, although he does associate both of them with an unpleasant stench of violence. Markland has the two of them sketching, Harriott is almost amused to note. Charles Horton's methods are catching. He looks at his constable as they walk towards the little group, but Horton's face is turned upwards to the swinging body above them.

'Critchley,' he mutters, quietly, to the magistrate. Harriott says nothing in return.

'Ah, Harriott,' says Markland. 'At last. I was beginning to give up hope.'

Markland steps away from his two officers, and notices Horton's presence.

'And Horton! What a pleasure.' The scowl on Markland's face makes it clear that the pleasure is entirely in his words. 'Two of London's finest investigators in one storehouse.'

'Oh, *three*, surely,' says Harriott, who even in his gloom has a ready propensity to bait Markland. In this case, his sarcastic tone works its magic almost immediately. Markland's scowl deepens, while Horton stares intently at the feet of the body above them.

'Should we perhaps bring the poor fellow down now?' Markland asks.

'A moment, if you please,' says Horton. He walks over to the rickety ladder and with only a small hesitation begins to climb up to the platform above.

'Ah, the indefatigable Horton,' says Markland. 'Does he recognise the body, perhaps?'

Harriott ignores Markland's question, smothering it with questions of his own.

'When was the body discovered?'

'Earlier this morning. The thing is, we're not at all sure how long it's been here. No one's been in the storehouse for days.

They only came in today because a collier's ready to journey back to Newcastle and needed ballast.'

'We should seek out a physician, to tell us about the condition of the body.'

'On his way, my dear Harriott, on his way.'

'Who reported it?'

'The foreman of the storehouse. Fellow named Miller. Hope and Hewitt have questioned him intensively.'

'Have they? I assume you consider this case linked to the deaths in Ratcliffe?'

'Yes, I do, rather. It is why I sent for you. The body is unidentified, of course. But the coincidence seems strong.'

Harriott says nothing about the identity of the dead man. Horton has begun winching the body down to the men below, though slowly, as if experimenting with the winch. Harriott can see him imagining himself into the man who'd done this, working the winch as if with another's hands. The tall, blond-haired body is slowly lowered down onto the pile of gravel. Horton looks down anxiously as the feet, legs and then back touch ground. Hope and Hewitt step towards it.

'No, if you please,' Horton shouts from above.

The two Shadwell officers glare up at him, then look to their magistrate. Markland, in turn, looks at Harriott.

'Your constable enjoys giving instructions to my men, Harriott.'

'You asked for his help, Markland.'

'I did no such thing. I suggested a mutually beneficial cooperation.'

'Well, then, let Horton be Horton. Your men may disturb some vital evidence.'

Horton, meanwhile, is scrambling down the ladder like a small boy desperate to be the first to finish a race. His shoulders knock into Hope's as he approaches the body, and

Harriott sees murder in the Shadwell man's eyes. Horton does not notice. He squats down on the pile of gravel. He loosens the rope round the dead man's neck, and they all see the vivid bruise which marks his strangulation. Horton looks at the body's fingers, which are bloody, the nails coming away.

'He struggled,' says Harriott.

Horton nods. 'He was lifted up while still alive,' he mutters. 'The neck is unbroken.'

The Shadwell men say nothing. Hope and Hewitt look almost bored.

Horton looks through the man's pockets, and from inside the coat he pulls a scrap of paper, carefully folded. He opens it and reads its content. He looks at Harriott, then hands the note to Markland. He begins to read it, and after a moment starts to read it aloud.

I assume all the Guilt in these terrible Undertakings. The Deaths are all upon me, and I have decided to go to seek my Peace with God, or whatever awaits me on the other side of the Grave. Otaheite has left a terrible Scar on my Mind and a terrible thirst in my body. We did a terrible thing on the Island, and the stench of it has pursued us back to England. We killed a young man there, a chieftain's son, under the influence of some Godless ritual which he had introduced us to. I know nothing of the Gods of that place, but I know Nightmares have haunted me ever since we departed the Place. The Things I saw there I will take to my Grave, but anyone who saw them with me bears the same Madness of Spirit as I do. If they say they do not, they Lie. It is this Madness which has caused me to take the lives of those I was close to, and though I know Forgiveness is unlikely to be waiting for me, I die in Hope. At least the Nightmares will now cease, unless the terrible Truth is that Nightmares pursue us into the Hereafter.

I commend my Soul to God and my Memory to my dear
Mother, may God bless her Soul.
  Jeremiah Critchley, Carpenter's Mate

Markland hands the note to Harriott, who reads it carefully before handing it back.

'Poetic,' says Markland.

'I find it mawkish and irritating, I will admit,' says Harriott.

'Nonetheless,' says Markland. 'It does seem to bring the case to a satisfactory conclusion.'

'I must say, this is as unsatisfactory an ending as I could have imagined,' says Harriott. 'I'm reminded of Williams.'

Markland looks exasperated.

'How so, unsatisfactory? I find the mention of Williams distasteful, Harriott.'

'Do you?' says Harriott. 'Well, there it is.'

The dead man's body is now laid out on the gravel, although there is still some tension in the rope which causes his head to be lifted off the stones, as if Critchley had been woken from sleep suddenly and had raised his head to look at them. The neck is a livid purple and oddly misshapen, and his skin is blackened by the dust in the air.

'So, this is the last murder, and this is the killer?' asks Harriott, rhetorically, and not without sarcasm.

'But of course,' says Markland.

'There is no "of course" about it, Markland,' says Harriott. 'This is all rather neat, is it not? The theatrical death, the emotional suicide note, all left here for us to find.' He finds himself looking to Horton, recognizing how sceptical the constable will be. But Horton's gaze is fixed upon Critchley. Well, then, he must supply the scepticism while his constable travels back from wherever he is.

'Why must you always complicate matters so, Harriott?'

asks Markland, and his voice has grown peevish. Hope and Hewitt stare at the dead body as if they would happily kill it again. 'Why can it not be taken at face value? This man killed his fellow shipmates, and then killed himself.'

'Why, Markland?'

'Why what?'

'Why did he kill them?'

'Because, as he says, he was mad.'

'Mad enough to kill them, but sane enough to give us this artful little note.'

'The note seems mad enough for my needs, Harriott.'

'And why the elaborately staged suicide?'

'It gained our attention,' says Markland.

'Well, precisely, Markland. It *gained our attention*.'

A stream of watery sun comes through an upper window and frames the man's dead, blackened face in weak light.

'He looks almost happy,' says Horton.

WAPPING

Critchley's note sits on Harriott's desk, blackened by the dust from the storehouse. Horton had placed it there after staring at it intently as he stood by the room's mantelpiece. He'd placed it down carefully on the desk, which was when Harriott had told him of Markland's intentions.

'Markland is closing the case; at least, that part of it to which he can lay claim. He thanks us for our cooperation, but he believes Critchley's note explains all.'

John Harriott is back at his customary position, seated in his great chair, looking out at the window overlooking the river. Charles Horton's own position has, he notes, also become somewhat customary: standing, arms behind his back, in front of Harriott's desk. Being quiet.

'Markland only has formal responsibility for the three Ratcliffe deaths, and this one, of course,' Harriott says. 'Sam Ransome and the Rotherhithe incident are still ours.'

'Yes, sir.'

'Are you listening to me, Horton?'

'Yes, sir. No. I mean . . .'

Finally, Horton looks up, and Harriott realises that indeed the man has not been listening to him.

'Did you hear what I said about Markland closing the case?'

'Sir, this note was not written by Critchley.'

'What?'

'I can't be certain until I retrieve my papers from my home, but this handwriting does not appear on any of the notes I took from my interviews with the *Solander* crew.'

'Your notes.'

'Indeed, sir. Critchley did not write this. Nor did the captain.'

'The *captain*? You suspect the captain?'

'He has questions to answer, I believe, yes.' Horton says nothing of night-time visits to Putney houses. Not just yet.

The old magistrate ponders things for a moment. He has become somewhat inured to these sudden wrenching manifests of new information from his constable. He has decided he finds them invigorating and infuriating in equal measure.

'Well, Horton, you appear to have made vastly more progress on this case than I had realised.'

'Not really, sir. Would you excuse me for a moment?'

Harriott almost laughs at that.

'By all means,' he says, and his sarcastic tone is unnoticed by his officer. Horton leaves the office, just as the manservant appears at the door. He announces Aaron Graham, who follows him into the room. He greets Harriott. His face is pale.

'You spoke to Nott?' asks Harriott.

'I did, last night,' replies Graham, seating himself in one of the chairs at the desk.

'How did he take the news?'

'The news that his father wants nothing to do with him? That he is an unashamed blackguard with no sense of responsibility? That the man he travelled halfway around the world to meet does not want to meet him? He took it as well as can be expected, Harriott. Which is to say, not well at all. I have never seen a man so destroyed. He looked like he would take his own life. I put a man to guard him last night, and I spoke to him this morning. He was still at Bow Street when I left to come here.'

A silence falls between the two magistrates, broken when Harriott speaks.

'There have been further developments, Graham. This morning we were called to a warehouse. A body was found.'

Harriott tells it all, and shows Graham the note on the desk. The Bow Street magistrate reads it, with what looks almost like resignation.

'Gods, this case has more turns in it than the maze at Hampton Court,' he says at last. 'So, Critchley was the killer?'

Horton reappears at the office door.

'If you please, Mr Harriott?' he asks, and Harriott calls him back in. He is carrying a piece of paper, but when he sees Graham in the room he folds the paper and puts it in his pocket, a move which saddens Harriott. It seems his constable has no trust in the Bow Street magistrate. Graham notices Horton's action but, being Graham, affects not to notice.

'Graham, Horton firmly believes that Critchley was not the perpetrator of these murders.'

'Indeed?'

Horton clears his throat, and speaks directly to Graham.

'Mr Graham, is it not the case that Peter Nott wrote a letter to you and delivered it when he was released from Coldbath Fields?'

'It is, yes.'

'Do you still have the letter?'

'On me? No, I do believe I ... Well.'

Graham has put his hand inside his jacket, and pulls out an

envelope, the same envelope Horton saw Nott carrying through London. Graham looks at it as if it were an artefact from the stars, and then smiles a rather sad smile of self-awareness.

'Do you know, gentlemen, I do believe I have not changed this coat since yesterday. My, I must have been distracted indeed.'

'May I see the letter?'

Graham hesitates slightly, and looks at Harriott, who nods, so Graham hands it to Horton, who opens it and starts to read. The hand is careful and has some elegance, as if written by a diligent juvenile afraid of making a mistake.

Magistrate Aaron Graham
Great Queen Street
London

Mr Graham,

I am writing this Note on a matter of particular Delicacy, and from a place of enormous Danger. It may be that this Note does not find its way to you, and that I die in this Place never having talked with you. If that were so it would be an enormous Cruelty on the part of Providence, for I have endured a sea voyage of almost endless Distance for the single purpose of finding You. To see this Note delivered I may have to put it into the hands of some undoubted Criminal, who will deny God's work and throw it into some open Sewer between this Place and the no-doubt gilded Streets on which you live.

But if this Note does reach you, I beg of you with all my Heart to heed its Call and to come and retrieve me. For I believe I am in the greatest Danger here, and perhaps even greater Danger on the outside, without the protection of a great Man like yourself. Please be sure, Mr Graham, I do not say this in an idle offhand way. My very Life is at stake.

To the Matter, then. I feel great Reluctance in setting this down on Paper, and you will see why when I explain. My name is Peter Nott, and as far as the World is concerned I am the son of the great British missionary Henry Nott, of Otaheite. But Henry Nott is not, in fact, my Father. He adopted me as a young child. He has always showered me with Devotion and with Care. But my real name is Heywood. My real father is Peter Heywood.

I have travelled to England to seek out my real Father and to make my Peace with him. You know better than anyone the Circumstances under which my Father was taken from me, and it is on to your good Mercies I now throw myself.

I have done terrible Things to be able to reach you, Mr Graham. And I now find myself in a most terrible Place, a kind of Hell on Earth which encases me and which may eventually kill me. But I know you are a Legal man, a man who knows of Courts and Charges and the like. I know how you helped my Father and I pray – even now I am kneeling as I write this – I pray that you will find it within yourself to help me also. If you turn away from me, the Pit is open, and the Lies I have told purely to make my way to you will devour me, as sure as they will devour the desperate, evil Men who share this place with me.

I pray to the Lord that this letter finds its way to you, and I pray to his Son that you have the Charity to help me.

Yours

Peter Nott (otherwise. Heywood)

'He was terrified,' says Horton as he finishes. 'Why did you not mention that he was terrified?'

Harriott begins to splutter at his officer's impertinence, but Graham holds up a warning hand. Harriott sees for the first time that Graham will take a good deal of impertinence from

Charles Horton. Whether from guilt or respect or a complicated compound of the two, he does not know.

'Of course he was terrified,' says Graham. 'He was locked in Coldbath Fields. He gave this note to the warden to be delivered to me, but the warden demanded payment, which he was unable to provide. So he delivered it himself when he was released.'

'But there is something else here, is there not?' says Horton. 'An admission of a kind of guilt. *I have done terrible things to be able to reach you.* What things?'

'Are you saying Nott may be the killer?' asks Harriott.

'Well, sir, the handwriting matches.'

At this, the two magistrates rise out of their seats, as Horton lays down the letter alongside the suicide note from the storehouse.

'By God,' says Graham, who is able to see the notes more easily. For Harriott, they are upside down. 'Nott wrote Critchley's suicide note.'

'Yes, sir,' says Horton. 'But he did not kill everyone. He was in Coldbath Fields when the Ratcliffe murders were perpetrated. We do not know exactly when Critchley was killed. But Nott must have either been in the prison or under the watch of Mr Graham's officers, even then.'

'So why did he write this note?' asks Harriott.

'Well, that would seem to be the question, wouldn't it?' says Graham.

ROTHERHITHE

Peter Nott stands on the stairs at Rotherhithe, opposite the *Solander*, waiting for a wherry to row over and pick him up. When one arrives, the waterman inside gives him a strange look, but then shrugs as if to say one man's money is as good as another's, even if the man is a half-breed dressed like a rector.

He'd walked from Bow Street this morning, exhausted from lack of sleep, playing over that awful final conversation with Aaron Graham. He had listened to Graham's story of the encounter with Peter Heywood, and he'd said little, only asking certain questions about the appearance of Captain Heywood, the place in which he lived, his family settlement and suchlike.

When Graham had finished, he'd asked Nott if he had understood what he'd told him: that Heywood would have nothing to do with him, and that there was little if any recourse to the law for the purpose of challenging his decision. Nott was free to go wherever he wished, but perhaps Graham might recommend the London Missionary Society, who after all were employing his father and would no doubt wish to assist the man's son. The words *father* and *son* had been spoken with small hesitations on either side of them, as if the words no longer quite meant what they once did. At the mention of the society, Nott had only smiled, remembering how the Otaheite missionaries had reacted to the news that one of their number was to adopt a savage, even one with English blood in his veins. That blood, which had marked him out as different since his birth, now feels like a kind of poison.

Graham had left Nott to his rest, and Nott noticed how the magistrate placed an officer at the door of the small room of the Bow Street office which had been his home for the previous three days. Graham had made it clear that Nott was a free man and could come and go as he pleased, and had said nothing about how long he would be welcome to sleep at the Police Office. So the constable was not a guard, then. Nott realised with icy amusement that Graham half-expected him to destroy himself.

He had slept not at all, although the constable watching him had fallen almost immediately into a slumber after Graham left. His snores echoed through the door of the room in which Nott lay, wide awake, trying to picture Peter Heywood, looking at his hands as if they might give a clue to the hands of his natural father, while all the time the notion that he had damned himself to no purpose clattered at the back of his brain.

Graham had looked in on him this morning, saying he was free to wait out the day here in Bow Street, or do otherwise, as he pleased. Nott had thanked the magistrate, and then had waited for him to leave. He had nodded to the officer who'd been watching him, walked out into the street and started making his way towards Rotherhithe.

Along the river, of course. Graham had explained where his father was – downstream from here, out towards the open ocean. So every step down the river was a step towards his father. He crossed the river at Blackfriars, making his way to the Surrey shore, the same shore where his father dwelt, and continued his journey downstream, as if being taken out to sea on a falling tide.

It took him almost three hours to reach Rotherhithe, and then he stood for a while, looking out at the ugly ship which had brought him here, across thousands of miles towards a hopeful destiny. Which, it had turned out, was instead a sordid rejection.

The wherry reaches the *Solander*. He pays the waterman what is left of his wages as ship's chaplain, then climbs up onto the deck. Nott has the ship to himself. She is deserted, her hold empty, no one even left to guard her. He walks back to the stern of the vessel, and stands there for a long while, his legs tired from the walk, looking downstream once again, his mind as empty as his hopes.

After a long while, he hears his name shouted up from the water. He looks down and across and sees Captain Hopkins arriving in a boat, waving fiercely. The captain disappears behind the side of the ship for a moment but soon Nott can hear him climbing up, and he turns away to face the river again as the captain walks up behind him.

'Well, *this* is a surprise,' says Hopkins. 'When did they release you?'

The question confuses Nott for a moment. When was he released? And from what? The prison had happened to another person, one for whom a meeting with his father was still a possible dream.

'They released me soon after your visit,' he says.

'Did you speak to Graham?'

'Yes, Captain, I did. And he did indeed know of my father.'

'And? What then?'

Nott says nothing, his eyes flat and set.

'Ah. I see. Well, Nott, 'twas likely to end thus.'

'It did not seem so to me.'

'So, what now?'

'Now, I will tell them of our arrangement. I will tell them that you told me on Tahiti of my father and told me how I could reach him, in return for my cooperation in your own transactions.'

It is now the captain's turn to be silent for a moment, but Nott does not turn to see his face. He feels a great calm.

'That would not be wise, Nott.'

'Perhaps not. But it would be right, Captain. And I am very much minded to do what is right, after having done so much wrong.'

'Have you forgotten what we said? Of how your father would hear of all this?'

'Which father?'

'The one you will be returning to.'

'Ah. Well, perhaps.'

Hopkins puts a hand on his shoulder now, and gently turns him around so the two are facing.

'You spied for me, Peter.'

'Yes.'

'You are complicit in all that has happened.'

'Yes.'

'You led me to them.'

'Yes.'

'You wrote the note, in your own hand.'

'Yes.'

'If you do not hang, you will be abandoned by the only father that remains to you.'

'Yes.'

But being abandoned already, what of it?

Nott turns back to the river. Behind him, the captain picks up a coil of rope from the deck.

It is Peach, once again, who rows Horton out to the *Solander*. They are become like an old married couple, hating each other yet forced to live side-by-side. Horton does not smile at the thought.

The squat, solid little ship occupies all his attention as it grows bigger and bigger. The noise and clamour of the river are barely more than background. Even the sound of Peach's oars in the river water is louder, to him, than the men shouting up from a lighter to the side of a ship which looks like it has been half torn to pieces on its journey here from the Baltic or Newfoundland. There is only he and Peach and the wherry and the *Solander*.

He sees, straightaway, that somebody is on the ship. He would have expected at most a cursory guard, given that the ship is empty. But there is a shape moving around inside the captain's cabin, pacing apparently even within the neat confines of that space, which he'd inspected so long ago and yet just the other day.

As the wherry passes beneath the cabin, Horton sees the pacing stop, as if whoever is inside has heard the precise *slap-slap-slap* of Peach's oars in the water.

Peach ties up the wherry alongside the *Solander* and Horton grabs the ladder.

'Wait for me here.'

'Aye-aye, *Captain*,' says Peach with his customary insolence. Horton ignores him and begins climbing up onto the deck.

He steps over the rail, and there is Captain Hopkins, standing on the quarterdeck beside that strange plant house. The whole ship has an emptied air about it. The holes along the edges of the decks and in the planking running beneath the rails (made, of course, by Critchley) are now devoid of their half-barrels and their strange Pacific plants. The *Solander* has been so comprehensively retooled as a ship for botanising that Horton wonders if she will ever be good for anything else.

'Constable Horton. First a night-time visit to my wife, and now a day-time visit to me. Perhaps I should formally adopt you as my cousin so you can move among my family without disgrace.'

Hopkins's tone is light, but there is a fierce aggression underneath. Horton thinks it has perhaps always been there, that fierceness.

'I meant no disgrace by my visit last night, Captain,' he says. 'I was returning from Kew, and wished to speak to you of what I learned there. It seemed to make sense, as it was on the return journey.'

'Oh, yes, no doubt it made a good deal of *sense*. And did you learn anything from my lady wife?'

'Learn anything? I did not *question* her, Captain.'

'You did not? You strike me as someone who is always *questioning*, Constable. Whether or not your interlocutor is aware of it.'

Horton says nothing to that, and simply waits.

'Do you wish to *question* me, then, Constable?'

'I wish to discuss matters with you, Captain, yes.'

'Well, perhaps we should seek out a more appropriate location. Follow me to my cabin.'

He turns, abruptly, and Horton walks behind him.

The cabin is as neat and tidy as when he first visited. The log is open on the desk, as if Hopkins had just been adding to it. The captain shuts the log as they go in, but leaves it upon the desk. He sits in the chair, but does not offer the bed as a seat to Horton, who stands with his head slightly bent and does not acknowledge the slight. It seems bizarre to be standing in this enclosed space when the rest of the ship is so empty.

'Jeremiah Critchley is dead,' says Horton.

Hopkins makes a church roof of his fingers and presses the point of it to his lips. His eyebrows go up and he stares at Horton. Then he breathes in and out through his nose in something like a sigh, and looks down at the surface of the desk and the log upon it.

'Sit down, man. I can't talk to you with you looming above me so.'

Horton takes a seat on the bed and watches Hopkins carefully. The captain unmakes his church roof and drums the fingers of one hand on the log, as if pondering evasive manoeuvres in the face of a French attack. Eventually, he speaks, but without looking up, his fingers still *thrum-thrum-thrumming* on the log.

'He was killed? Like the others?'

'Not quite like the others. He was hanged, though he may have been dead already. There is a suicide note.'

'You have it?'

'Aye.'

'May I see it?'

Horton takes the note from his pocket, unfolds it and hands it to Hopkins, who takes it from him without looking at him and reads it and then reads it again. Then he makes that same breathy sigh through the nose.

'My God. What a bizarre tale.'

'What do you make of his assertion to have killed the other men?'

'Well, it seems insane to me. Critchley was a hard-working man, respected by his fellows and by the officers. I saw no sign of any such madness in him during the voyage. If it was insanity, it must have come on quickly, or he kept it well-hidden.'

'You assume insanity? He rather suggests it was guilt. That they killed a chieftain on the island.'

'I know of no such event. Not a whisper of it reached my ears.'

'But such a thing is possible? The men were left to themselves sufficiently?'

'Well, yes, perhaps. But to move from a sense of guilt over a dead savage to murdering his fellows? Insanity, surely.'

'Perhaps.'

Hopkins hands the note back to Horton, and looks at him then, his eyes clear and unflinching, no guilt in them whatsoever, just defiance and that continuing fierce anger, daring Horton to continue.

'Your wife was very kind last night.'

Hopkins's nostrils flare slightly at that, and Horton half-expects to see a whiff of smoke emerge from them.

'She is an exceptional woman,' the captain says.

'She mentioned your close relationship with Peter Nott – how you helped him on arrival, inviting him to dinner and suchlike.'

'He visited our house for dinner, yes.'

'You did not mention this before.'

'I did not mention that our ship's chaplain came to my house for dinner? No, I did not. There were a great many things I did not mention to you, Constable. None of them seem in the least bit relevant to the matter in hand.'

'Did you know of Nott's reasons for coming to England?'

'Well, I assumed his *reasons* were to do with a wish to see something of the world before returning to his home, but the tenor of your question implies I was mistaken.'

'He came to find someone.'

'Really? Who?'

'You visited him in Coldbath Fields?'

'Who? Nott? You bounce around like an anxious cat, Constable.'

'Yes. Nott.'

'I did visit him, yes.'

'Soon after your visit, Nott wrote to Aaron Graham, the London magistrate. Asking for help with finding someone. Did you tell him about Mr Graham?'

'No, Constable. I told him nothing. I know nothing about this *search* you say he was on.'

'And have you seen Nott since his release from Coldbath Fields?'

'Neither hide nor hair. In fact, I was going to send a note to you asking where I might find him, to learn whether he was well or no. He has not had a particularly comfortable time of it, thanks to your interest in him.'

'Well, perhaps if you see him, you could let us know.'

'I live to serve the River Police Office, Constable. Now, will that be all? I have some matters to clear up before I return to Putney.'

'I think that will be all, Captain.'

Horton stands from the bed and leaves the cabin, ignoring Hopkins's furious eyes and stepping out onto the quarterdeck. He walks over to the rail and sees Peach waiting there below, and sees a more resentful but still potent fury in the eyes of his fellow waterman-constable. When he left this morning, Abigail's eyes had been bright. He could do with some warmth from those eyes right now.

He looks back at the open hold and ponders a final search. But the ship is empty, and he has angered Hopkins enough. He decides to leave, and so doesn't see the dead empty eyes of Peter Nott, lying lifeless against the hull of the *Solander*, waiting for Horton to depart so his captain can drop him over the side and into the rushing Thames.

GERRARD STREET

So this is what it is like to Die.

He is on a ship, and something is looking for him. She is laughing as she looks, this something, but it is not a laugh that brings any cheer. It is full of spite and vengeance. She means to do him a great harm when she finally comes across him.

He is on the deck and she is in the hold. He runs from starboard to port, bow to stern, and she follows him, because he can hear the stamp of her feet and her cold heartless laughter every time he changes direction, tracking him, waiting for him. On every fifth turn, he wakes up, his breathing like that of an endless runner, his body soaked with sweat, and his eyes stare madly around his little Gerrard Street bedroom again, before she pulls him back down into sleep, back into the nightmare.

Starboard to port.

Bow to stern.

Up and down.

Am I dead? Am I in Hell?

While he runs and wakes and sleeps, he feels the leaf in his stomach, tearing away at him, flooding into his cavities and organs the way that terrible tree had crept into his mouth and nose and eyes. He knows that this is more than just a poison. It is a terrible addiction. Even while it tears at him, he thirsts for it. He knows that on wakening he will need it again, that the kettle will be there in the fire and the leaf will be there in the jar, and Robert Brown will be consumed by his need, consumed beyond all understanding.

As the hours pass, the dread rhythm begins to slow. Finally he is plunged into an empty purple-black sleep, as if at the bottom of an endless ocean.

As morning breaks, Robert Brown awakes to the biggest struggle of his life.

He is clear-headed when he wakes. No headache, no torpor, only clarity. There are just three thoughts in his head. The biggest, by far, is the need he feels for the leaf. The need towers over him, throwing his sense of himself into shadow, blocking out all other externalities. But within it are two other smaller thoughts which have their own intensity and their own urgency. One is that he must destroy what remains of the leaf in his room, lest it destroy him. The other is that he must save the King.

He rises from the bed, and prepares to make some more of the tea, to fulfil his own desire. He can hear his father, shouting from the staircase. He can hear a girl giggling. He takes the jar containing the leaf in his hand and pictures himself filling the kettle with water, pouring it into the cup, adding the leaf, drinking it and watching the light explode again, and he takes the jar and making a noise which is unrecognisable to him he hurls it through the window and out into Gerrard Street. There are two distinct crashes of breaking glass: one as the jar goes through the window; another as it hits the street outside, sending the leaf down into the shit and dirt and litter of London. A man shouts in anger. Brown falls to the floor and can do nothing, not even respond to the urgent sound of young Leary banging upon his door.

Get up, you pathetic worm.

The voice is his father's, the rebel bishop, still shouting from the stairs, though now shouting incontrovertibly at *him*.

Get up, get up now.

I cannot, Father. I am too weak. My legs will not support me.

You disgust me. You chose your King and now your King needs you. He's no Stuart, and he's no King of mine. But he is your King, Robert. So get up. Get up now.

The truth of this is manifest. Brown stands.

Now get the manservant, clean yourself up and remember who you are. You are a man of means and of standing. You are not some piss-stained Chinaman smoking opium in a basement. You are Robert Brown, Fellow of the Royal Society. No preacher, more's the pity, but you always were suspect in that department. You might burn in Hell for what you don't believe in, but you won't burn in Hell for cowardice. Now. Do it now.

Shivering with addiction, the rebel bishop's voice thundering in his temple, Robert Brown calls Leary to come into the room. The boy's eyes look astonished as he speaks to him, to tell of the arrival of Sir Joseph Banks.

Brown somehow manages to dress himself in a moderately seemly fashion, and before long appears in the library of the Linnaean Society, where Banks is waiting. At his first sight of the librarian Sir Joseph is the old Banks again, firm in action and decision. He can see that something is very wrong indeed with Brown, who looks feverish and exhausted and near collapse, and immediately calls for a tonic and a damp towel.

'Sit down, Brown, sit down. Put this towel on your head and *sit down*. Tell me what has happened to you.'

Brown manages to construct a kind of narrative about his experiences of the previous night: the terrible thirst; the vivid dreams of chasing and being consumed; the bouncing around between consciousness and senselessness. And he describes his struggle to wake and to find himself once more.

'And you feel it now?' asks Banks. 'This desire to consume more of the leaf?'

'Sir Joseph, with every part of my being,' says Brown. He remembers his earlier vision of the world being broken down into little cells. 'Every part of me yearns to consume more of that terrible substance, and every part of me knows that it will bring death.'

'My God,' says Banks while Brown takes a swig of the sweet tonic which has been brought for him. 'Have we done an unthinkable thing?'

You, not we, says Brown to himself, his old self returning by the minute. *I wanted nothing to do with this insane scheme.*

Banks barks for Leary.

'Fetch me some paper and a quill, at once. And call a carriage. You need to carry a note for me.'

Leary looks at Brown, angering Banks, who may be in the Linnaean Society and not on his home ground but is by no means used to having his orders questioned. Brown nods as Sir Joseph shouts: 'Get to it, boy!'

It takes only ten minutes for Banks to compose a letter to Monro at Windsor, and to dispatch Leary, who quivers with fear at the mention of his destination. Even in his weakened state Brown is forced to encourage the servant and to make it clear that the matter is of profound urgency and is related to the health of the King. Still looking uncertain, Leary pulls on a coat and disappears, leaving the two men to stare at the floor of the Linnaean Society library. Brown feels desperate and hungry and ill. Banks gives no indication of feeling anything at all.

Brown wonders if they will sit like this, waiting, until Leary returns to tell them either that the King is unchanged – that Monro has not got round to giving him the leaf yet – or that some change has occurred, some awful shift in the King's state which, if it is anything like the state in which Brown now finds himself, would have implications of such awful grandeur that his sick stomach gives another immense churn as he thinks of it. But then Banks speaks.

'Describe, please, again for me – the effect of the leaf.'

It is a simple request, but Brown feels the weight of what is required of him. A dispassionate observation, as would be required of a botanist coming across a new species in the fields around Edinburgh. He tries to pull himself together, to move out of this fog of thirst, to use the clarity of the thirst to express himself.

'An immensity of pleasure, at first. Accompanied by insight. Or at least the appearance of insight. I believed I could see into the interior of things, into the stuff of matter itself, its particles and its building blocks. I believed I saw how everything living was composed of tiny essences, almost like tiny organisms themselves, alive and multiplying. And everything was subsumed in this terrible harsh light. I believed I heard my father preaching. And, as the vision continued, I believed I was being chased by a female, who was angry with me and wanted, in some way, to consume me.'

'The vision sounds terrifying.'

'It was, Sir Joseph.'

'And yet you have this desire to repeat it.'

'I do. It is indeed a terrible thing, Sir Joseph. A substance which pleasures and destroys all at the same time.'

Banks stares at him, and Brown feels for a moment that he is himself a specimen, a strange plant growing on an unfamiliar hillside.

'I am not a man of words, Brown. You know that. Words are slippery things which are difficult to dream up and easy to misunderstand. But I would like to find words to apologise to you, Brown. To you, and to my friend the King.'

Brown says nothing, nor does Banks seem to expect it.

'I first heard of the leaf – or at least rumours of it – from a man who accompanied Cook on his final visit there. He'd been on the *Endeavour* with me, also. He told me that a story had lately grown up on Otaheite, a story of a place where a tree grew. A strange and unique tree. The leaves and buds of this tree, when dried and drunk in boiling water, inspired an awesome vision. I was put in mind of *bhang*.'

'Yes, Sir Joseph. And of Hooke.'

'Indeed. As you know, I have long been as interested in the customs of native peoples as I have in the botany of their far-flung shores. It fascinated me what this man said, that a whole culture had grown up around this tree, had as it were accreted itself to the strange religions and practices of the island. Have you heard of an island sect called the Arreoy, Brown?'

'I have read of them in Lieutenant Cook's log, sir.'

'We did not know what to make of them, Brown. We didn't know if they were minstrels, priests, mummers or murderers. They travelled the island and seemed to have an enormous power over the local people. But to what extent their practices were part of the accepted religion I was never able to ascertain. As a young man, I was drawn to them, drawn to their self-indulgence and their . . . well, they *consumed* life, Brown. They lived it with a freedom and an intensity which almost devoured me. But there was a terrible dark side to them. They believed their power was transmitted to their children. So to keep their power to themselves they destroyed a great many of those children. Mothers destroying newly born babes. Even the powerful ladies who were non-Arreoy were consumed by this belief. They believed it was their right to do with their children as they wished, even if it meant destroying them. Bougainville called the Island *la nouvelle Cythère*. But every Paradise has a Hell. Or perhaps that is just an old man's thinking.

'As I told you, I corresponded with a great many others over the years, to learn more of this leaf. And I admit this correspondence grew more urgent when the King became unwell, with an apparent frenzy of mind which no treatment could assuage. The leaf began to seem to me a possible remedy. Perhaps even a cure.

'The King has long been my friend, Brown. He is a difficult, prickly, insecure man, but he is capable of enormous kindness and a touching loyalty, much like that of a child. He has elevated me beyond all expectation. We have together embarked on a great project to ally the theories and discoveries of natural philosophy with the growth in Great Britain's power and prestige. Our great nation dominates the face of the Earth and the surface of Knowledge like no other. And I will take some credit for that, Brown. I will claim that it was my friendship with the King and my tireless efforts to develop the Royal Society which brought Britain to this happy state. And I did not want that to end.

'So I arranged for the leaf to be brought here. And I placed you directly in harm's way, Robert Brown. You have my apologies: as the President of the Royal Society, as a friend of the King, as a man and, I trust, as a friend.'

'Thank you, sir. Your honesty is evidence of your sincerity.'

'I feel deep and complete responsibility for your current state, Brown,' Banks says, now looking at the floor, his massive chin sunk into his swelling chest. 'But I think your addiction can be either managed or overcome. We can grow the leaf, and we can give it to you as required. It is a medicinal process, nothing more. But you do not want that, do you?'

'No, Sir Joseph.'

'No. Because the addiction isn't the problem, is it? Your current unwell state, awful as it is, is rather beside the point.'

'Yes, Sir Joseph.'

'It's the *visions*, Brown, is it not?'

Brown nods, his throat dry, unable to speak anymore.

'My God, man, your face when you described what you saw in those dreams. You looked as a man must look when he is confronting his own death, for the final time in this world. You were *pursued* in your dreams, Brown, I think. No. I know.'

The great clock in the corner of the library makes a huge mechanical noise as it turns through the hour. Brown has long before disabled its chime, but its workings still have the capacity to disturb quiet thoughts within the library.

'We seek knowledge, you and I,' says Banks, and turns his face to look at the bookshelves as he speaks, gazing upon Britain's intellectual harvest. 'We harness the world within observation, experiment and description. We seek out new frontiers and we pull them into our circle of understanding. We collect, catalogue and classify. But not everything that is can be classified, Brown. It is something enormous for a President of the Royal Society to say, but perhaps only one such as I, with access to a century-and-a-half of secrets, can admit to the stark truth: there are more things on this earth than are dreamt of by our natural philosophy.'

Brown watches, and waits. Banks is silent for some time, and then he turns his old eyes to his librarian, who is disquieted to see the evidence of tears on the old man's cheeks.

'You see, I think I know who was pursuing you. I think I pursued her myself, once. I think she has been looking for me.'

WAPPING

It is mid afternoon. Abigail is once again considering whether there is any hope of eating supper with her husband today when her fears are confirmed by a knock on the front door. It will almost certainly be a message from the River Police Office, carrying the familiar news that Charles Horton will not be returning home at a normal hour and she must make do with her own company.

Contrary to the beliefs of her husband, however, making do with her own company has never been a chore for Abigail Horton. She will open another book on natural philosophy – perhaps even her recently acquired copy of Davy's *Elements of Chemical Philosophy*, which she has been much anticipating – and while away the empty hours until her husband's return by dreaming of the undiscovered frontiers of the natural world, where miracles occur and revelations abound. Unlike her husband, Abigail is a comfortable but firm believer in the Creator (in this, she is much more like her husband's superior, John Harriott), and she believes that she celebrates Him by glorying in the array of his creation.

She opens the door, and outside is a broad, dark-haired smiling man dressed in shipshape breeches and tailcoat, holding a very naval-looking hat in his hands.

'Mrs Horton, is it?' he asks.

'It is, sir.'

'Splendid. Mrs Horton, my name is Captain Hopkins. Of the *Solander*. Perhaps your husband has spoken of me?'

Charles had said something of the man, she believes. He seemed to like him very much.

'Why yes, Captain. Charles has mentioned you to me.'

'Splendid. Well, Mrs Horton, I am soon to be taking off on a new adventure. New oceans, new discoveries, that sort of thing. There is a particular place I have been waiting to visit. You know what we sea captains can be like. I very much hoped to leave a small token for Mr Horton. It has been such a pleasure conversing with him.'

'Well, how kind.' The man's charm is palpable. Abigail has never met a sea captain before, but she thinks this man might be the very model of one.

'Not at all. May I leave my gift here for him?'

'Well, he is sure to be at the River Police Office, if you would like to . . .'

'Oh, I don't wish to disturb him there, and besides I must be on my way. Here it is.'

And he hands over a small leather pouch. Actually, not leather; it seems to be made of something like tree bark.

'May I enquire what it is?' Abigail asks, feeling rather that this is a rude question.

'Oh, of course. It is some tea, from China. Rather beautiful tea, the best I have ever tasted. It has an extraordinarily uplifting quality. Best taken in boiling water without any milk, I find. Quite delicious. It is a small thing, but I hope it will be taken in the spirit in which it is given.'

'Well, this is very kind.'

'Oh, it is nothing, nothing at all. And do feel free to try it yourself, should the constable be a long time returning. No doubt he is busy with some difficult case. And with that, good lady, I will be on my way. Another new world awaits this captain!'

He puts his hat on his head, gives a jaunty little salute, and walks off into the early evening. Abigail watches him go, shakes her head slightly, and goes back inside.

THE THAMES

Nott is the key. There is something about the relationship between Nott and Hopkins which is at the heart of all this. Their stories were already intermixed, even before Horton learned from Mrs Hopkins of the chaplain's evening visit to Putney. With Markland closing the Ratcliffe case, pinning all the blame for the murders on the dead Jeremiah Critchley and claiming credit for a tidy case quickly dispatched, there are no other options. Finding Peter Nott has suddenly become critical; certainly, in the short term, more critical than spending an evening with a terribly neglected wife.

So Horton spends the day scouring the riverside. He tries to seek out as many of the *Solander* crew as he can, officers and seamen, in boarding rooms across Wapping, Limehouse, Ratcliffe, Rotherhithe, Deptford and Southwark. A good number of the men have already moved on, to new adventures or old haunts, and in more than one place he is greeted by an angry landlady or landlord complaining about the absence of due rent. He bounces around a dozen inns and alehouses, almost running between each of them, spiralling ever closer to the Police Office, where Harriott will be waiting with a keen interest in what happens next.

In the Town of Ramsgate he finds Red Angus Carrick, tucking into another plate of herring. The Scotsman is almost merry at the sight of him.

'By God, man, you look like you've been runnin' all year.'

'Do you know where Peter Nott is?'

'The half-breed? No, why would I?'

'Do you know who would know?'

'Same ways, no.'

'Well, then.'

Horton turns to leave, to try perhaps one more alehouse or one more lodging before surrendering to Nott's disappearance and heading for the Police Office with empty hands, but Carrick stands and pulls him back by the arm.

'Slow down, man, slow down! I've questions for ye.'

Horton looks at him. Being pulled back has stilled what was a kind of mania in him. Now he feels terribly tired and terribly in need of seeing Abigail. He sits down opposite Carrick with a thundering sigh, and asks for an ale from the landlord. Carrick sits down and pushes his herring away.

'Potter and Frost,' he says. 'Word is, they're dead.'

Horton only nods, too tired to speak. Carrick sits back in his seat.

'Fucking hell.'

'That's about the size of it,' Horton says, and his beer appears beside him. He swigs a third of it at a draft, feeling the alcohol swirl into his bloodstream, calming him and waking him and sharpening him again. Two more gulps, and the pintpot is finished, and he's ready for Harriott.

'Do you know who did this?' asks Carrick, and Horton is reminded of a story of a Corsican *vendetta* he once heard from John Harriott. Carrick looks murderous.

'Aye. I believe I do.'
'Who, man? Who?'
'Soon, Carrick. Soon.'

It is clear, or at least the visible parts are clear. He'd found a fragment of red cloth beneath one of the beds. On his way back from Putney, he'd visited the Clapham tailor mentioned by Mrs Hopkins, who'd confirmed that Hopkins had taken a red coat to be mended the day after the deaths. The rooms of all the dead men had been searched, even Critchley. The signs were there at Critchley's room at the Pear Tree just as they had been at Sam's, at Attlee and Arnott's, and at Potter and Frost's: the sea chests and bags had all been opened and ransacked. But money had been left behind.

Three of the men were found dead with smiles on their faces, implying some state of rapture, of one kind or another, on the point of death. Two others had looked terribly afraid, and though they didn't smile their faces had also suggested a species of transport. All these five had apparently consumed something, possibly a kind of tea. It was likely they were asleep – or, more accurately, they were under the influence of whatever was in the cups – when they were killed. The odd, ruptured timescale of Attlee and Arnott's murder can thus be explained. If they'd been asleep or unconscious when Nott burst in on them, and if the killer had been in the room *while Nott was there*, it was possible for the two men to have been killed after Nott left the room for the first time, and for the killer to make his escape. Just a few slashes to the throats, that was all the butchery that the situation required. The killer must have hid beneath the bed when he heard Nott coming in, and must have caught his coat on the frame when he was down there.

Finally, Nott had a closer relationship with Hopkins than

either admitted to. He had dined at Hopkins's house, and Hopkins had visited him in Coldbath Fields immediately before his release. And Nott had written the letter that incriminated Critchley, days before the murders themselves – unless, thinks Horton, Hopkins demanded he write Critchley's note while visiting him in Coldbath Fields.

But why did Nott write the notes? How could Hopkins possibly have compelled him? Without an answer to that, all Horton has as evidence is some rudimentary analysis of handwriting, a scrap of red cloth and the word of a Clapham tailor.

But there is more information waiting for him in Wapping.

A familiar carriage has drawn up outside the River Police Office: Aaron Graham's, its horses breathing heavily as if it had just arrived after a fast ride.

He finds Harriott seated at his desk, with Graham standing by the fire, looking into the flames. The Bow Street magistrate looks up at Horton as he enters and nods almost imperceptibly. Some might say rudely. Horton nods back, and Harriott greets him from the desk.

'Have you found Nott?' he asks, with some urgency.

'No, sir. There is no sign of him at all.'

'Then I fear he is lost.'

'Lost, sir?'

'Lost, Horton. Mr Nott left a note at Graham's residence in Covent Garden. I have just read it. Graham, can I assume you are comfortable with Horton reading the letter?'

'By all means.' *Not very jaunty tonight, Mr Graham*, thinks Horton as Harriott hands him the letter. It is in the same hand as the note he had read this morning.

There is no date on the letter, none of the formal addressing of place or recipient. It just begins.

I have made two terrible Mistakes. One has hurt only Myself. The other has led to the Deaths of many Men. The first Mistake was to come to England to find my true Father, only to learn that to Him I am as Nothing, as insignificant as a Gull shot from a Pinnace. The second Mistake was to put my Trust – indeed, my very Soul – into the hands of a man such as Captain Hopkins.

For it is Hopkins who has killed these Men, but not without an Accomplice. I helped him. 'Twas I who spied on the men for him, 'twas I who led him to them. Hopkins promised me he would help me find my father and this he did, leading me to you, Mr Graham. In return, I promised I would reveal what it was Critchley and his fellows had discovered on Tahiti.

Critchley it was who made the acquaintance of a young chieftain of Tahiti, a young man I knew well. It was this prince who showed Critchley one of the great Secrets of the Island. There is a marae at the top of the island, a secret place, and there the prince showed Critchley the thing which the islanders had long concealed: a leaf, which when consumed as tea sparks intense dreams, blasphemous visions that consume men's souls.

Gradually, others discovered this secret: Ransome, Attlee, Arnott, Potter, Frost. They all consumed the leaf, and at the last they all took a portion of it with them back to England. I offered Hopkins this information on the island – though I did not reveal the men's names. I also gave him the details of where more leaf could be found, in return for a passage back to England.

Hopkins consumed the leaf for the first time on the island, after I revealed its existence to him. It had the expected effect. He was enthralled by it, its delights possessed him. From that moment we entered a terrible dance. He demanded to know which of his men possessed the leaf, while I dangled this information before him as a means of ensuring his assistance when we reached London. He dealt out his knowledge in the same way, telling me nothing of use about my father, buying my loyalty and my silence with promises of help. We were tied together in terrible mistrust, all through the weeks of that trip home. The thirst was strong within him, but he showed nothing of it to the crew, and I saw the horrible capacity of the man, his ability to suppress his deepest desires. He did not touch the leaf again on the journey home, knowing as he did it would have incapacitated him, and I do believe the man's will is so strong that he has not yet taken it again since our arrival in London. He must finish his business first, and he has collected even more of the leaf, in the darkest way imaginable.

When we docked in London, I gave him Ransome's name, may God forgive me. When it came to it, I would do anything. In any case, none of the men in that crew ever showed me any kindness, months on the water with not a kind word or a warm glance from anyone. So who was I to stand in the captain's way? He told me that there was a magistrate in London who had helped my father and who would know who he was and how to find him. I was desperate to know this man's name, but in return Hopkins demanded more names, so I gave him Attlee and Arnott. How easily I gave up these men to their doom! Then remorse overcame me, and I rushed to warn them, but I was too late, too late, he had already discovered them, and in his diabolical way he managed to kill them even while I was outside that terrible house. Finally he visited me in Coldbath Fields, in that awful prison, and warned me I would spend the rest of my days in such a place if he were to tell anyone of my involvement, that I was an instrument of death as much as he, that he would remain silent as to my crimes – and give me the name of the magistrate – if I would give him the last names. And so I did, and then he demanded I write that terrible note, his final extraordinary lie.

And I did it. One can only understand Eternity if one is a missionary's son, Mr Graham. But my shame is eternal. I did all he asked me to. And I found you, and you found my father, and only despair awaited me.

You cannot know how my sadness and my shame wrap themselves around me like dark smoke. I feel the heat of Hell beneath my feet, and I know that Satan awaits me – as a murderer, as a liar, as a cheat, and worst of all as a man who has abandoned the good name of his father. For Henry Nott is my father, my true father. A good man. A Christian man. A man whose name I have been given and have besmirched. I must travel back to him, and seek his Forgiveness.

KEW

The carriage conveying Brown and Banks from town arrives at the gates of Kew, and the gigantic form of Sir Joseph is eased down to the ground by the offices of Brown and the driver. One of the soldiers in the gatehouse comes out and helps as well, and they lift Banks into his chair.

'We are going to the Stove,' Banks tells the soldier. 'And we are not to be disturbed.'

'Yes, sir.'

'I mean it, Sergeant. No one is to come close to the hot-house, whatever may occur.'

The soldier frowns in puzzlement. What on earth could happen in a hothouse?

'Yes, Sir Joseph. I understand completely.'

'We will make our own way there. Please remain here. Come, Brown.'

And the librarian pushes the President through the grounds of Kew, marvelling at how the old man can apparently command an army.

'How are you now, Brown?'

The question is asked as they pass almost underneath an enormous willow, its contours English and familiar, its leaves and branches silent. Brown takes a second or two to register this question. A precise answer is expected, he knows.

'I feel an enormous longing, Sir Joseph.'

'Longing for the leaf?'

'Yes, sir.'

The need burns within him. The Stove is now before them, and it is almost full dark. The hothouse is an enormous glass-and-brick container full of a thrusting, urgent life. The tree is inside, and it has consumed the place.

That girlish giggling again. Brown no longer looks for young women playing in the trees. He only looks at the Stove. Inside it, in front of him, is the source of all that he craves. Banks is looking at him with real concern.

'Can you do this, Brown?'

His father, shouting from a staircase.

'I believe so, Sir Joseph.'

'Then fetch an axe. Two, if you can find them.'

PUTNEY

'Trim,' says John Harriott as the carriage pulls up before Captain Hopkins's house. A good sailing term, thinks Charles Horton. Indeed the house is even trimmer than it had seemed when he'd visited on the way back from Kew and Mrs Hopkins had welcomed him with chatter and tea. It is set back from the road just a little way, and half a dozen plane trees line the drive, like a mansion in miniature. Horton notices the top-right window of the house is open, and when he steps down from the carriage and looks up at the window, a piece of net or muslin flutters in the evening breeze, and a whiff of something pungent, acrid and yet sweet floats down to them through the darkness. There is an enormous stillness about the place, and Horton knows they are already too late.

Graham knocks on the door, taking charge, just as he has taken on a heavy personal responsibility for whatever has happened to Peter Nott. He has been quiet, almost silent, during the ride to Putney, and there is something funereal about the way he walks up to the door and bangs, carefully but loudly, on its ship-shape brass knocker. The percussive racket echoes on the trees beside the house and for a moment there is no response, but after half a minute they hear a scratching at the door, and Mrs Hopkins opens it.

She looks carefully around the edge of the door, as if expecting highwaymen grown bold at this time of night. When she sees the well-dressed Aaron Graham her mouth makes a little 'o' and Horton can see her brain beginning to whirr in a different direction, seeking to triangulate the appearance of three apparently well-to-do men on her doorstep at this hour of the night.

'Mrs Hopkins?' asks Graham, softly so as not to startle her. His manners remain immaculate, even in his current state of emotional extremity.

'Why, yes, sir, Mrs Hopkins it is. But ...' Then she recognises Horton and her eyes do a strange thing, relaxing at the sight of a familiar face but widening at the same time because Horton's reappearance here must mean something grand and perhaps terrible.

'Mrs Hopkins, my name is Graham. I am the magistrate at the Bow Street Police Office. With me is John Harriott, magistrate of the River Police Office, and his officer Charles Horton, whom I believe you have already encountered. Mrs Hopkins, we are here to see your husband.'

'Why, sir, of course, but I ...'

Graham is smoothly insistent.

'May we come in? Is he inside?'

'Why, yes, I think ...' Even as she speaks she backs into the hall and Graham follows her, then Harriott and finally Horton, who closes the door behind him.

They stand in the hall, and the house is silent. *Why has he not come down?* thinks Horton. *He must surely have heard us.* He prepares himself, though for *what* he does not know.

Mrs Hopkins is fluttering, her eyes hopping from one man

to another, her evening turned upside down. Three strangers in her hallway! Graham seizes her attention again.

'Mrs Hopkins, it is imperative we speak to your husband immediately. Can you please go and tell him we are here? Perhaps Harriott and I will wait in the drawing room – Horton, please wait here.' Graham looks at the door, and Horton nods. *Watch the way out.*

'Of course, sir, through there, through there,' says Mrs Hopkins, making her way to the stairs. 'I will go and get him, of course, but he is resting, he asked not to be disturbed, please be patient, by all means be seated, sirs.'

She is halfway up the stairs, now.

'You, sir, look particularly uncomfortable on that poor leg, do please take a seat.'

Harriott scowls at her as she reaches the top.

'I shall just be a moment, do please wait.'

She disappears onto the landing. Harriott makes his way down the hallway, looking to see if there is another way out, and they can hear her knocking on a door upstairs and then opening it, and then they hear her saying something quietly but urgently, and then there is a silence for a while, and then she screams.

Graham is the first up the stairs, and Horton is about to follow him, but then remembers his own lame magistrate. Harriott shouts at him as he limps back up the hallway.

'Go, man. Go!'

Horton chases Graham up the stairs, onto the landing and through the only open door he sees. Within, Graham is already standing over the figure of Captain Hopkins, who is lying on the bed on his back. That sweet acrid smell he'd detected outside fills the room. Hopkins is dressed in trousers and a white shirt, open at the collar, and his hand lies across his chest. In it is a pipe, now almost burned out, but sitting on the naked flesh of his chest, where it has burned a deep purple scar, the smell of which mixes with whatever was in the pipe to create a rich, sickly, awful odour which Horton will never forget.

But that terrible smell is as nothing to what is on Hopkins's face. His head is thrown back on the pillow, as if in some extremity, his back arched and his shoulders pushed down, such that Horton only really sees the man's face when he reaches the side of the bed. The eyes are wide and sightless, the nostrils flared open, and the mouth is tensed broadly open, the captain's yellow teeth exposed in a terrible grin.

Horton, naturally, waits for the coroner, allowing the two magistrates to return to London in the carriage. It is already well past midnight. Abigail will have gone to bed long ago, another few hours will make no difference to him. Harriott says he will send word to the Surrey coroner and magistrates and will, if needs be, supply officers from Wapping to take over from him, and Graham makes similar undertakings. Then they are gone, leaving Horton with a dead captain, a widow who is somewhere in the house weeping gently into some embroidery, and the rustling Putney dark.

Hopkins, it is clear, had become reckless with the leaf described in Nott's letter. He had waited to consume it, but then had indulged in a deadly innovation. He had attempted to smoke it in a pipe rather than just drink it as a tea. What difference this makes to the intensity of the leaf's effects Horton can only surmise, but it has clearly led to the captain's death. The smile on his face is a grim exaggeration of those peaceful smiles on the faces of his dead crewmen. While those had been made terrible by the circumstances – bloodstained throats, empty lungs, livid necks – the captain's grin has its own essential horror. It is as if Hopkins's body has been possessed by an external force, a gleeful malignancy which was too much for his human heart to bear. Despite the stillness of the body, Horton cannot escape the feeling that at any moment the hands will rise from the captain's chest and will seek out his throat, squeezing the air from him as the mad grin widens before his eyes.

After some time, Horton hears a noise from the landing, and then the voice of the captain's wife speaks through the half-open door.

'Constable Horton?'

He rises, and steps out into the landing. The exhausted woman still holds her embroidery in her hands, and she will not look at the door to the captain's room. She raises her eyes to Horton's and they are red-raw and desperate.

'Some tea, Constable?'

Horton, despite himself, struggles with a smile.

'No, Mrs Hopkins, thank you. I will take no tea.'

'I may have some. Is that permissible?'

'Perfectly permissible. The coroner will be here soon.'

'Thank you.'

She turns away from him, and heads down the stairs.

The coroner arrives after another two hours. By this time there are threads of grey in the sky as dawn approaches. The coroner pronounces Hopkins dead and arranges for the two men who have accompanied him to carry the body out to their carriage. Mrs Hopkins stays out of the way, hiding somewhere in the house and now silent, her weeping ended. When the two men lift the captain's body it is stiff, as stiff as a mast, and they are forced to carry it out still holding the pipe, as they can by no means force the fingers open. As the coroner prepares to leave, another carriage appears at the end of the driveway, sent by Harriott to bring Horton home.

He goes to find the widow. She is in a neat, tidy sitting room at the back of this neat, tidy house, gazing out onto the pearl-coloured light which is beginning to pick out the individual plants in the neat, tidy garden. Her embroidery sits upon her lap, now forgotten.

'Mrs Hopkins, I must now take my leave.'

'Of course, dear. Of course.' She continues looking into the garden.

'Is there anything you need?'

'No, dear. It is perfectly all right. My husband has been on many a journey and I have waited many a day and night for him to return. Now he has left on a final journey, it is for him to wait for me, wherever he may be. As he has often said to me, I say to him: I don't know how long I'll be, dear. You'll just have to be patient.'

She smiles a sad human smile, which she turns onto him. It goes a good way to erasing the memory of that awful grin of her husband's.

'In any case, he has left me a delightful memento.' She looks into the garden, and Horton thinks he can detect the leaves of a tree moving outside the window. 'A beautiful tree, from the far side of the world.'

Horton says nothing to that. He wonders if he might need to visit the widow again before long.

'Goodbye, Mrs Hopkins.'

'Goodbye, my dear.'

London is waking up. He can almost see it coming back to life, street by street, light by light, window by window. His carriage crosses Westminster Bridge, as Robert Brown's had done, and starts to make its way towards Whitehall. Two figures which would have been familiar to Brown appear from behind the corner of some great Government building, where later today the machinery of Empire will be winding its way towards another day of battle with Napoleon. The figures shout something at

Horton's carriage and then they cackle harshly before disappearing into the shadows once more. Little London organisms, cells of humanity, bouncing randomly in the urban soup.

There is still a long way to go, and for a while Horton sleeps, dreamlessly and fitfully, waking every now and again when the carriage bumps against some London feature in the road. Finally, the carriage starts to make its way down the Ratcliffe Highway, past the tall masts down below in the Dock, like the trees which surround Captain Hopkins's little Putney cottage. The Highway is already busy with lumpers and traders and craftsman ready to begin stoking the engines of Trade, and at some point Horton will join them, but for now he needs to sleep, perhaps for the whole day.

Down Old Gravel Lane turns the carriage, down the hill towards the river, in between the shops and workshops and inns and boarding houses, from which men are streaming into the morning light. At the end of Old Gravel Lane the carriage turns right, down Wapping Street, then right again into Lower Gun Alley, and he is home.

Harriott has already paid the driver, for which Horton gives silent thanks. As the carriage begins the tricky business of turning round in the narrow alley Horton opens the door of his lodging and climbs up the stairs, trudging with exhaustion but also careful not to make too much noise in case Abigail is asleep. He opens the door to their little flat, goes into the sitting room, and sees the burnt-down fire, the kettle on the side, the pouch. He smells the pungent, acrid smell, weaker than in Putney but the same as all those days before in Sam Ransome's room. Coming further into the room he sees his wife lying on the floor, a cup in her hand, her chest rising and falling, rising and falling like a little frantic bellows, and a high, dog-like whimpering coming from her throat, and he shouts and falls down upon her, his guilt rising up to meet him like that Pacific wave.

NINE

Meanwhile the mind, from pleasure less,
Withdraws into its happiness:
The mind, that ocean where each kind
Does straight its own resemblance find;
Yet it creates, transcending these,
Far other worlds, and other seas;
Annihilating all that's made
To a green thought in a green shade.

Andrew Marvell, 'The Garden', 1651

PUTNEY

Last night, she said, she dreamed of today's burial.

'He was smiling inside his coffin. That terrible smile which you described and which, in some strange way, I'd already seen. The coffin was covered in earth, almost instantly, and then some time seemed to pass, and a tree sprung up above the coffin. I dreamed I could see the roots of the tree twining around the coffin until the wood cracked and splintered, and then the roots went inside and began to twine around *him*. I heard her laughing again. Oh, Charles. She laughs with such joy at the pain he suffers, but when she looks at me she smiles, and then she leaves. The worst of it was, I wanted him to suffer. I wanted those roots to tear him asunder.'

Abigail laid her head on his chest, her fine blonde hair brushing his chin like a spider's web blowing in the breeze. She shivered slightly at the memory of her dream. She had slept and dreamed for much of the time since that terrible early morning when he'd discovered her lying on the floor. Whenever she woke she asked for more of the tea. She cried and shrieked and slapped his face and tore at him with her nails, but it was no good. The leaf was gone, perhaps thrown into the river by the desperate captain and now somewhere out in the estuary, causing silver-grey fish to dream of walking. He had visited the captain's widow, too. With an axe.

Abigail screamed with frustration this morning, too, but with less violence. The quality of the dreams she described had changed also. Her dreams were nothing like those which Robert Brown had described to him two days before, when he'd visited the librarian in Soho Square.

It had been an instinct, that visit, but he'd been sure that Brown could tell him something of the leaf and of its effects. Brown had looked shockingly pale and haunted and Horton had been convinced, immediately, that he'd come to the right place. Brown had been appalled at what Hopkins had done, and after some prodding had admitted that he too had taken the tea, and that he had been subject to the same enormous longing and those dreams of a terrible woman pursuing him through a lush landscape.

'How is she terrible?' said Horton as Brown related his experience.

'She wishes me harm. I am convinced of it. Why, I cannot say.'

'And she is pursuing you?'

'Without doubt.'

Horton frowned. 'Abigail's dreams have been disconcerting. But she always describes the woman's presence as protective.'

Brown had looked amazed.

'The woman does not chase her?'

'No. She has spoken of a woman, but to Abigail she is like a fierce friend, one who will always protect her but is at the same time disturbing.'

Brown said nothing to that.

Hopkins is buried at St Mary's Church, despite the

strongest representations from magistrates Harriott and Graham that he should be given an unmarked grave as a vicious murderer. But the leaf stolen from the dead *Solander* crewmen remains unfound, and Peter Nott is still missing. The Surrey magistrate argued (with the connivance, Harriott later discovered, of Edward Markland) that there was no firm evidence to commit Hopkins's name to an eternal damnation, and until Nott was found that was likely to remain the case. So Hopkins's widow got what she wanted: a church burial for her beloved captain. There was little either of the two London magistrates could do about it. Horton feels none of the anger that Harriott expresses about this turn of events. The man is dead, after all.

He goes to the burial for no other reason than to see who else will be there. He still wishes to find Nott, and half-believes the strange missionary's son will make an appearance himself, and demand that the Christian burial be ended. He wonders to what extent Hopkins's death was self-imposed; whether he realised that smoking the leaf would be fatal. Traditionally a man committing suicide to evade justice is buried at a crossroads with a stake through the heart. But Hopkins after all was a sea captain, and captains are not buried like common men.

Horton waits outside the church during the funeral service, pondering on forgiveness and the eternity of sin. The enormous weight of his own guilt – the whole sorry parade of mutinies and betrayals – is such that it feels as if the church tower had fallen on him. He remembers Abigail's light head on his chest that morning, and wonders how such a memory can be so redemptive.

Hopkins's coffin is carried from the church by four old shipmates. No one from the *Solander* is there. Horton rather suspects that Red Angus Carrick has put out the word that the old captain is not to be mourned. As the coffin makes its way to the open grave, followed by the widow and her family (Mrs Hopkins looks calm and distracted, as if pondering on when she might follow her husband on this final journey), a carriage arrives at the church gates, and Horton sees Robert Brown get out of it. He walks up the path, and greets Horton with a nod which the constable returns. Then his eye rests on the coffin, and there it stays, as if the casket contained arcane knowledge needing careful interment.

The constable and the librarian watch the coffin being lowered into the earth. Nearby an ancient English oak waves his branches in the spring breeze, his leaves brushing the head of the vicar. The captain's widow throws in a handful of earth, and then the little burial party turns away, leaving the gravediggers to complete their work. When they have smoothed out the earth they too leave that place, and only the ancient oak remains to stand guard.

AUTHOR'S NOTE

There was no ship called the *Solander* and Sir Joseph Banks financed no trips to the South Seas at the end of his long and distinguished life, although he maintained an extraordinary network of collectors and gardeners which continued to populate the beds and stoves at Kew well into the second decade of the nineteenth century. The design of the *Solander* is based on the great ships which preceded her – notably the *Endeavour* and the *Bounty* – but she is fictional, as is her crew and mission.

What is more, it is highly unlikely that such a botanising mission would have been sent to Otaheite in 1812. As I suggest in the book, this was a time of great upheaval on the island, with chieftains battling for supremacy while the titular 'king' Pomare II sat it out on the neighbouring island of Moorea.

The depiction of Tahiti itself is one part imagination to one part history. Otaheite (as the island was known in England until well into the nineteenth century) held such a grip on the imaginations of Britons that a clear picture is hard to paint. The fact that Tahiti fell under French imperial sway a couple of decades later means we are left with contemporary accounts of the pre-French 'first contact' from the late eighteenth century. Prominent among these is the account of Banks himself, but there are also accounts from missionaries and amateur explorers. Banks is notable for being one of the few Europeans who made an attempt to understand the strange (to European eyes) mysteries of Tahitian culture and religion on their own terms. Others viewed the islanders as savages, albeit savages that they wanted to sleep with. Even those who dubbed the savages 'noble' did so on the basis that the islanders were different: alien, exotic, almost not-human. What is not in doubt is that the Europeans flooded the place with their own poisons, both physical (dysentery, syphilis) and cultural (alcohol and guns).

There will be those upset by the opening scene of the book. It is of course an imagined scene, but that does not have to mean it is an implausible one. Joseph Banks is one of the great heroes of English science and imperial history. He was a man who contained worlds, who saw the bonds between scientists as being at least as strong as the bonds between countrymen, a friend of the King and an architect of Empire. But he was also a man of enormous appetites whose accounts of his sexual activities on Tahiti shocked England for a generation or more, and to whom gossips attached countless tales of spurned women and expensive courtesans. Banks's account of his adventures on Tahiti is like a message from another world, a world which preceded modern morality, in which licence and licentiousness spawned both the astonishing gluttony of the Prince Regent and, within a few years, the public morality of the Victorians.

The Banks project in Kew is drawn from history. Sir Joseph did indeed use Kew as a horticultural engine of Empire, and believed strongly that nations would gain power by gaining mastery over plants. He was not alone in thinking this; it was something of an Enlightenment view, shared equally by Carl Linnaeus and Thomas Jefferson. The story of Sir Joseph's quest for a cure for the King's illness is entirely my invention. However, there can be little doubt that the man would have moved mountains if beneath them he might have found a curative for George III's demons.

The book is set during a period which stands at the end of a hundred years of enormous advances in botanical understanding. Reproduction, respiration, classification, photosynthesis, inheritance, the development of species over time – all our modern understanding of these concepts arrived in a rush, fully- or part-formed, at the end of the eighteenth century. Robert Brown himself occupies a distinguished place in the pantheon of the great botanists, alongside John Ray, Carl Linnaeus, the de Jussieus and Adanson. However, at the time in which my story is set his reputation was yet to soar, in England at least (his *Prodromus* on his New Holland botanising was widely admired in France) and his discoveries of the inner worlds of cells were still some years away. His analysis and description of the bread-fruit (*Artocarpus incisa* in 1812, *Artocarpus altilis* today) is, I hope, appropriate for a skilled botanist at the beginning of the nineteenth century. Needless to say, the breadfruit tree described within does not exist in nature. If anyone knows of a tree with the qualities described here, I suggest they contact their nearest botanical garden immediately.

Lastly, the story of Aaron Graham's defence of Peter Heywood against the charge of mutiny is true. It is also true that Heywood had a 'wife' on Tahiti who was left behind when Heywood was brought back to England to face charges, though his son is my invention. Henry Nott was indeed the senior missionary on Tahiti at this period; again, his adoption of a son is fictional.

For more on the core characters of *The Poisoned Island* – Horton, Harriott and Graham – please see the notes to the novel which precedes this one, *The English Monster*.

ACKNOWLEDGEMENTS

The poem by Peter Heywood at the start of Chapter FIVE is from 'Correspondence of Miss Nessy Heywood,' E5. H5078, the Newberry Library, Chicago. I found it in Caroline Alexander's excellent *The Bounty* (Harper Perennial). Sources for the other quotations used in the book are provided within.

I came across the 'Hindostanee Coffee House' and Dean Mahomet for the first time on http://www.georgianlondon.com, an excellent blog maintained by the historian Lucy Inglis.

My thanks to the staff of the Kew Gardens library and herbarium; the staff of the London Library; my editors at Simon & Schuster, Jessica Leeke and Mike Jones, who by their efforts made this book much better than when they found it; my agent, Jim Gill; my friends Dan Dickens and Josie Johns, who read the manuscript and made wise suggestions; my wife Louise; and the two people to whom this book is dedicated, my amazing children, Jack and Lily.

Reading Group Discussion Questions for

THE POISONED ISLAND

1. Rather than focus on the well-documented role of explorers claiming new territories, *The Poisoned Island* revolves around botanists. How do you think this shapes the story?
2. In the novel Banks is said to use people's lives 'for the furtherance of two ideals [. . .] man's knowledge of the natural world and Britain's domination of it' (p.326). Can you find other, more compelling motives in the novel? Are these maxims still prevalent in modern life or can you think of any alternatives which are more relevant to today's society?
3. Horton's wife Abigail is not the typical Georgian wife; she is not a subservient partner and is intellectually curious beyond the usual boundaries of an 'accomplished' female. Discuss Abigail as both a predecessor of modern women and a Georgian wife. Where do you think she best fits?
4. 'Every Paradise has a Hell'(p. 360). This applies most obviously to Otaheite and the drug related murders. However, the author constantly reveals imperfections in every character, relationship and setting. Which situations in the novel can you apply this to?

5. The author vividly describes both Georgian London and far flung tropical islands. Which setting do you find the most convincing and evocative?

6. The novel deals with the contentious issue of the British colonial period. How did the often brutal or exploitative interactions between the British and the natives affect you as a reader? (Can you compare it to the wars and savagery enacted by the islanders on one another?)

7. In *The Poisoned Island*, Horton pioneers many procedures and methods which we now consider integral to the detective. How does he compare to detectives in popular culture? Can you see any parallels between the River Police and the organisations featured in television and novels today?

8. Peter Nott is the ultimate outsider. Separated by race and upbringing from both islanders and foreign visitors he is vulnerable to the manipulations of the murderer and comes to a tragic end. Discuss his characterisation. Do you pity him?

MEET THE AUTHOR Q&A:
LLOYD SHEPHERD

**In what way is this novel a companion to your first novel,
The English Monster and how does it stand alone too, for
readers new to you?**

I certainly think both novels can be read as standalone stories,
with their own narrative arcs and resolutions. I did intend that
to be the case.

But writing stories within a 'series' does allow the novelist
space and time to develop characters and themes. For
instance, I think the relationship between Horton and his wife
Abigail is given more colour in *The Poisoned Island*, and that
sense of our deepening awareness of them probably depends
on having read *The English Monster*.

Horton is himself a character I'm very conscious of 'colour-
ing in' over time. In terms of historical records, the real Horton
is barely more than a couple of entries in a couple of ledgers.
I've been able to get to know the fictional version more deeply
by revisiting him. That work began in *The English Monster* and
is continued in *The Poisoned Island*.

Thematically, where *The English Monster* deals with the very worst kind of human exploitation – slavery – *The Poisoned Island* focuses more on the exploitation of nature by the Great Nations of Europe, as Randy Newman called them. Of course, such exploitation has a tragic human dimension also, and I've tried to show that in the book.

The Poisoned Island features both real and imagined characters – can you tell us about these, illustrating the period in which you're writing?

It's actually a bit more complicated even than that!

There are 'real' characters, or at least characters based on real personages, but obviously a great deal of their depiction is imagined. Sir Joseph Banks, for instance, is in the book both a caricature and a reflection of the real Banks. There is no suggestion that the real Banks was involved in the kind of royalist machinations suggested by *The Poisoned Island* – at least none that I'm aware of. Nonetheless I like to think that if the Regency world had been as I describe it in the book – with a good deal more to it than the contemporary natural philosophers could imagine – then the real Banks would have done something similar to my fictional Banks.

Robert Brown is also a figure drawn from history, but with considerable biographical liberty taken – and again I would hope his motivations in the novel would be similar to those facing the real man in such circumstances. If he were here with me I would like to ask him, directly, about the influence of his father. But I've had to imagine that.

And there's the rub. When you're writing historical fiction, you are of course attempting to get the *history* as right as possible, but it can only ever be an imagined approximation, no matter how much research you do. Dates and kings and prime ministers have to be in the right order, that much is obvious. But how people felt and thought and reacted – they are either going to be very educated guesses, or at least partly imagined.

So all the 'real' characters in the book – Sir Joseph Banks, John Harriott, Aaron Graham, Henry Nott, Robert Brown and the others – are, though based on real people, at least partly my creation.

And then there are the characters who have very few biographical bones to hang a story upon: most of all, Charles Horton. He's very much a fictional character, though there was a 'real' Charles Horton working at the River Police Office during this period. I've invested him with all the concerns of 'detecting' crime which were becoming current at the time.

The key characters who are completely 'fictional' are Peter Nott and Abigail Horton. Peter is my attempt to try and depict what must have been an increasingly common phenomenon: the rootless half-breed, parented by colonial invaders and exploited aboriginals. As the British Empire expanded, these people began to become more and more common. It must have been an extraordinary experience.

As for Abigail – she's a piece of wish-fulfilment on my part. It's unlikely a woman of her background would even have considered seeking access to the natural knowledge Abigail thirsts for. Women were not expected to hold such interests, nor was there any sense in which they were entitled to knowledge. They were entitled to almost nothing at all, and were essentially the property of their husbands. This is a theme which I'm exploring in the third novel in the series.

The inspiration for Abigail was another incredible woman, whose birth came two years after the events in *The Poisoned Island*: Ada Lovelace, the only legitimate child of Lord Byron, and the self-styled 'poetical scientist' who paid a key role in Charles Babbage's invention of the Analytical Engine.

This is a novel about empire and exploitation. 'The Poisoned Island' refers not only to Tahiti, but to Great Britain as well. Can you explain?

I was interested while writing *The English Monster* in the idea that a nation's crimes might return to haunt it. That theme is expanded in *The Poisoned Island*, but also I wanted to personify the impact of those crimes in the person of Sir Joseph Banks. In the book he's an old, gout-ridden, near-decrepit figure, barely able to walk, trying to complete one final nation-changing intrigue. He's poisoned by his past, in many ways – his dietary appetites have given him gout, and his sexual appetites are (as we discover) returning to haunt him.

And of course there's the matter of the tea, which is of course a symbolic 'poisoning' of Britain by Tahiti, the island it has ravaged. The introduction of pathogens into unprepared primitive societies by European powers has always struck me as a very primeval sort of crime – anyone who wants to know more about it should read Jared Diamond's *Guns, Germs and Steel*. I liked the idea of a 'pathogen' that could go the other way.

Horton is an extremely intriguing character. What or who was your inspiration for both him as a person and his singular methods of detection?

I needed somebody to be the personification of the coming changes in policing: the move from hue and cry, from witnessing, towards discovery and detection. In many ways, John Harriott, Horton's boss, was a lead player in that move, but I always needed a younger man, a spirit of the age who could put Harriott's own beliefs into direct practice. But for such a man to be so different, so against the common herd, he would need to be a singular person. The template for such a man is pretty clear, I think – our modern idea of the male detective, a damaged loner, unable to interact quietly with people because he cannot help observing them. But I wanted him to be more than that, which is why I gave him Abigail, who is both his conscience and his redemption.

The Poisoned Island is very much about disease – of the body and of the spirit – dissipation, greed, violence. Obviously, there is a murder investigation at the heart of the story – but on a wider scale, how does this play out in the novel?

There is a disease, but it is the disease of addiction, and from that all else follows. This is why I was intrigued by the metaphor of a 'leaf' which is like cannabis, ie: like a drug we now associate with addiction. Brown's sudden addiction to the leaf is shocking to him, as he does not have the personal or cultural coordinates to place it. We of course recognise it as addiction. And so many characters are addicted to one thing or another – even Horton is addicted to something, in his case the explanation of mysteries. And England, of course, is addicted to resources, to trade, to power. Everything stems from that original addiction; and, in the case of Hopkins, it is the most destructive addiction of them all.

Turn the page for an exclusive excerpt from

Lloyd Shepherd's upcoming novel

Coming in 2014 from Simon & Schuster UK

I wander thro' each charter'd street,
Near where the charter'd Thames does flow,
And mark in every face I meet
Marks of weakness, marks of woe.

In every cry of every Man,
In every Infant's cry of fear,
In every voice, in every ban,
The mind-forg'd manacles I hear.

How the Chimney-sweeper's cry
Every black'ning Church appalls;
And the hapless Soldier's sigh
Runs in blood down Palace walls.

But most thro' midnight streets I hear
How the youthful Harlot's curse
Blasts the new-born Infant's tear
And blights with plagues the Marriage hearse.

William Blake, *London*

DEAL, SPRING 1814

From his room at the top of the tallest hotel in Deal, with the help of an eyeglass stolen from an inebriated officer of the Rum Corps more than a decade ago, Henry Lodge can see the *Indefatigable*. She is resting at anchor out on the Downs. The sails on her three masts are down, and he reckons her at more than 500 tons, square-rigged, with three decks.

There are perhaps twenty ships out in the Downs. The April air is clean, just washed by spring rain, and there is no mist from the sea. The vessels clustered between the Goodwin Sands and Deal's beach look calm and settled. Local boatmen row from beach to ship to beach again, busy water ants with oars and strong arms. Henry Lodge supposes he will have to go out into one of those boats, and as always the thought fills him with fear.

But there is no doubt. She is a transport, freshly returned from New South Wales via Canton, just as the messenger had said.

Since his own return from New South Wales, Henry Lodge has performed his little pilgrimage to Deal a dozen times. He pays a man a retaining fee to watch the ships that come and go to and from the Downs, and to alert him when one of the new arrivals is a returning convict transport. The money required for this undertaking is not insubstantial, but it's also affordable. He is, after all, by now a man of some means.

The operation runs like this: his fellow in Deal learns of a new arrival. He then dispatches a messenger, post-haste, to the hop gardens Henry Lodge owns around Canterbury. It is a ride of some twenty miles. The system has become so well-worn that Henry can be in Deal within a day-and-a-half of a new transport arriving. This is more than enough time; the vessels out on the water move at oceanic time, where a day is an hour, and a hurry would look to the observer like massive animals turning into an invisible wind.

The *Indefatigable* has the same air of worn-out ordinariness as all the transports, particularly when set against the gilded splendour of Naval vessels which predominate in these waters. An exhausted woman is what she is. A silent, disregarded female approaching the end of her disappointed road.

He closes his eyeglass and takes it with him downstairs, where a boatman is waiting to take him over. The man is unpleasant and crude, and shouts at Henry as he struggles to get into the boat, reluctance biting into his bones like the gout which has, in recent months, slowly been making its jagged presence felt.

He hates these boats. They remind him of the worst weeks of his life, shivering inside the sinking wreck of the listing Naval frigate HMS *Guardian*, icebergs hidden in the mist, ice spurs slicing through the cold depths – including the one that had torn into the side of the frigate and removed its rudder with seemingly diabolic intent. Between them and Cape Town: endless miles of empty ice-cold sea. He was not yet twenty, a convict-gardener, sent to New South Wales to try and scratch a harvest from the thin rocky soil.

He had survived that disaster, rescued by, of all things, a

whaler. With war billowing out from Paris and Europe shivering, it had seemed another petty miracle, as ordinary and as wonderful as an ice mountain with designs on a rudder.

How many more times will I do this? he asks himself now as they make their way across the glassy water of the Downs. *How much longer will I care to watch?*

He keeps an eye on the *Indefatigable* as they row towards her. Slowly the other vessels move away from his perspective, as the transport rises from the water, becoming bigger and altogether more impressive the closer they get to her. He imagines the three decks within, the bulwarks between male, female and sailor quarters, the tiny cots in which the convicts are chained. He imagines furtive wanderings between decks underneath tropical skies, female prisoners called to the hammocks of sailors and marines, pressed into service as journeying whores, each sailor given individual permission by God and the King to take his pick of the women on board.

These are childish imaginings. The decks of the *Indefatigable* will have been cleared of bulwarks and chains over in New South Wales. Space will have been cleared for cargo on the return voyage; tea instead of girls. He imagines the piles of unwanted ironware on the quays of Sydney Cove growing higher with each visiting transport that discards its chains just as it discards its human freight.

He asks himself, as he has done times beyond counting, how a man with such a runaway fancy can possibly have become rich. He remembers why he makes these pilgrimages.

Now they are alongside the *Indefatigable*. The boatman calls up to the deck, and a head pops over the gunwale.

'Visitor from town!' the boatman calls in his oaky Kentish accent.

'What kind of visitor?' replies the seaman, in a West Country voice.

'One who visits all the transports.'

'What's his business?'

The boatman looks at him. It is a well-worn routine, this. He shouts up to the gunwale himself.

'I am a representative of James Atty & Company, the firm which built this vessel. I am to come aboard to ascertain her seaworthiness and to determine when she will be ready to voyage once more.'

It is a practised lie, and one day it will fail. One day, the *real* representative of a shipowner will be in Deal waiting for his transport, and however quick Henry Lodge may be in getting to Deal with the correct intelligence on the ship's ownership, he will face embarrassment when another seaman's face stares down at him and informs him that the owner's agent has already been aboard.

Not today, though. Today, the sailor disappears for a moment, and then reappears with instructions that they may climb aboard. With goutish difficulty and no small amount of self-disgust, the man of means makes his way up onto the deck.

He is introduced to the master, who has as much common humanity as a bleached piece of driftwood on Deal beach, but he listens to Henry's second story, which he produces only once he is on board and only in the hearing of the master. He is a representative of the Home additional information (for a small fee – always a small fee with such men) about his passengers. Five men returned to England, two of whom were former convicts. The master gives the names, and the man of means pretends to note them down.

Any women?

The master frowns. Why would this man be interested in women? But yes, there were three women among the passengers. Two were wives, and one has been abroad.

Their names?

Simpson, Gardener, Broad.

The Gardener woman is still on the ship, with her sick husband and her three children. But Henry Lodge barely hears this. The name *Broad* resonates like an anchor dropped on a quayside.

The Broad woman. She is no longer on the ship?

'It's Broad who is abroad,' smirks the master. She'd been in a great hurry to leave.

Did she converse with any of the other passengers?

The master frowns. Something about the Broad woman discomfits him, and seeing this only excites Henry Lodge further. She'd been a quiet passenger, says the master, though she'd spent as much time on deck as she could. She'd had little to do with the crew or with the other passengers. The crew avoided her. She'd taken a bit of a shine to two children who were traveling with their parents.

Did she bring anything with her?

She'd had some goods shipped with her from New South Wales, at considerable expense. The goods had already been unloaded, onto a vessel bound for the Thames.

What was the nature of these goods?

The master has no idea. They were boxed. He suspected something botanical or herbal.

You did not investigate the goods?

Again, that uncomfortable frown. No, the master had not investigated the goods. The woman had made it quite clear that they were not to be touched, and she had a way of making sure people obeyed her wishes.

What do you mean by that?

The master did not mean anything by that. Mrs Broad was just very forceful, is all. Henry smiles, and asks if he can speak to the children who'd conversed with this mysterious passenger. The master, who appears relieved at the focus of the interrogation turning away from him, shows the man of means below decks.

The small number of passengers who have returned from New South Wales are accommodated alongside the officers' quarters below the quarterdeck, but the family to which he is directed have moved away from these rooms and taken up their own space between cargo and the cabins. Henry sees why instantly. There are two boys and a girl, watched over by a haunted-looking mother. The father lies in a hammock, the stench of illness coming off him. A doomed family, shunned by the crew lest the father's illness carry beyond his own body.

Seeing this family accommodated like this, in a space which a year before would have been filled with chained convicts, men or women or possibly both, revolts him. It is as if the ship will not let them go.

He asks them about the woman, and the mother says yes, such a woman was onboard, her name had been Margaret Broad, and the boys said she had worried the crew, who thought her a witch. And so the master's discomfort is explained.

And now Henry Lodge must sit down, for his heart is racing. He collapses onto a sack of Canton tea. The children look at him, curious but patient. The mother looks at her sick husband. Henry tries to imagine the woman he seeks waiting here belowdecks, gazing at her cargo, cursing anyone who came near it, alarming the crew with her hostile presence.

His waiting is over. Margaret Broad has returned to England.

But where can she be now?

Part One: Madhouses

For you shall understand, that the force which melancholie hath, and the effects that it worketh in the bodie of a man, or rather of a woman, are almost incredible. For as some of these melancholike persons imagine, they are witches and by witchcraft can worke wonders, and do what they list: so do other, troubled with this disease, imagine manie strange, incredible and impossible things.

Reginald Scot, *The Discoverie of Witchcraft*

CHARCOT: Let us press again on the hysterogenic point. Here we go again. Occasionally subjects even bite their tongue, but this would be rare. Look at the arched back, which is so well described in the textbooks.
PATIENT: Mother, I am frightened.

Jean-Martin Charcot, Charcot the Clinician:
The Tuesday Lessons

WAPPING

She feels a prodigious and fearful sorrow when she closes the door on the little apartment in Lower Gun Alley, though Abigail Horton has of late become so suspicious of her own feelings that she is wary of this clenching sadness. For much of this past year she has been aware of two Abigails in attendance behind her eyes: one acting, the other watching and judging. She feels, and then the other part of her watches her feeling, and draws its conclusions, as if a mad-doctor were in residence. Increasingly, the conclusions of this watching Abigail are ominous.

She barely sleeps, and when she does her dreams are so terrible that most nights she wakes with a cry of fear which startles her husband Charles awake, and she must once again face that morbid expression of guilt which descends on him. The one she has come to loathe.

She walks down the stairs and out into the street, peeking round the corner of the door like some cowardly lurking footpad. Her husband must not see her leave, for he will stop her and she will not able to resist his crushing responsibility. And she knows that he has a veritable invisible army of small boys watching the streets of Wapping, reporting back anything interesting or odd. He is a constable, after all – one with responsibilities for the peace. Perhaps the peace of this street has been bought with the peace of her own marriage bed. She wonders if Charles pays the boys for watching the comings-and-goings so assiduously, or if they feel they are taking part in some kind of game.

The street is clear, at least of any faces she recognises. She closes the outside door and locks it, little activities for her hands as her mind scurries through its two-headed dance of dismay and observation. With her heavy canvas bag she walks down Lower Gun Alley, for all the world like some seaman headed down to the London Dock to catch a ship to Leghorn or Guinea or Arabia.

Lower Gun Alley gives out onto Wapping Street, and if she were to turn right here she would find herself at the River Police Office, her husband's place of work. The street is crowded with people, and the thick early morning fog has lifted. She looks left and right again, but the gesture is ridiculous. She would not notice Charles, or one of his small boys, or even the other constables of the Police Office out here on this crowded street. She must hope that she blends into the crowd as easily as they would. She turns left and walks away from the Police Office, away from Lower Gun Alley. Away from Charles Horton.

There is a good deal of panic in her head as she goes. She has barely left their rooms for six weeks now, ever since her anxiety had deepened, suddenly , like the dark-blue sea water off a reef. Charles has taken to buying the food and drink that she prepares for them. When necessity has forced her out into the street she has found the crowds oppressive. The new brick walls which now lace their way through Wapping, holding in the new spaces of the London Dock, have become to her like the walls of a prison, holding her and all those on the streets in a state of isolation from the Metropolis, squeezed in against the river, unable to flee. A madhouse on the water, with its own streets, its own watching eyes, its own stenches and mysteries.

This feeling of imprisonment has been acute, because it is flight she dreams of. Not flight from Wapping, or even from Charles, but from the woman in the forest, the one who pursues her and fills her head with unclean thoughts as she comes. A savage woman promising violence and revenge and despair for those who oppose her.

She catches the glance of a small boy who is staring at her. He is standing in the door of a shop, chewing on something indescribable, wearing a man's hat which looks like an upturned bucket, his clothes scruffy and dirty as his face. But his eyes are sharp and watchful, and she sees in them that something about her – her scurrying walk, her bag of clothes, maybe even her frantic face – has caught his attention.

She hurries on, the urgency in her as great as it is in the dreams. If the boy finds Charles and tells him what he has seen, Charles will know immediately what she has decided to do, for she has spoken of it before. He will chase after her, perhaps with a carriage. He may even guess at her destination; Charles is mystifyingly good at such guesses.

Things start to change as she nears the top of Old Gravel Lane, the Ratcliffe Highway in front of her. She turns around to look back down the hill towards the river, to look for attentive small boys or even pursuing constables, and the flow of people running up and down the Lane seems to blur into one stream, with only one person left distinct and clear, standing down by the wall of the Dock, staring at Abigail with those dark Pacific eyes.

The woman from her dreams is standing on Old Gravel Lane.

Abigail does not quite scream, but the noise she makes in her vice-tight throat is loud enough to draw the attention of several bystanders. She turns, and the chase begins.

The two Abigails behind her eyes squabble over this new development. The woman has never appeared to her in waking life before. But what if, asks that calm doctoring voice, what if she isn't awake at all? What if this is all just another dream? Abigail has enough of herself left to vanquish this thought, to push it back into the mists for future consideration. But it doesn't quite disappear.

The woman is not real, says her mind.

The woman is chasing me through London, her mind replies.

Her body takes no view on the question. It just propels her, half-running, half-walking, across the Highway and north towards her destination. She has no money for a carriage, and it is perhaps four miles from Wapping to Hackney. The only currency she possesses is a letter, and that can only be used for admission when she reaches the end of her journey. It cannot help her fly from whatever it is that pursues her.

There is nothing pursuing me, says her mind.

She will destroy me if she catches me, her mind replies.

She looks back every few minutes, and every time she looks the woman is there, standing out clear and prominent in the blurry street scenes, always still and staring, never apparently moving. But always there.

North of the Commercial Road, open fields and wasteland present themselves as options for flight, but she avoids them, not wishing to be caught out on open ground by her pursuer. So she pursues a more zig-zag route than she would otherwise have chosen, keeping to the streets, to the blurry crowds, which slow her down and shout angrily at her as she barges her way north, her heavy bag knocking into stomachs and shoulders, her own body tiring with every hurried step.

But as she nears Bethnal Green, the roads begin to open out on both sides, as the metropolis starts to loosen its grip on the landscape. Rope walks and tenter grounds give way to open fields and farms. The Hackney turnpike stands at a crossroads, facing three or four clusters of houses which developers have built in anticipation of the inevitable encroachment of London.

She looks back as she passes the turnpike. The woman is closer now, and she is running, her arms rising up in front of her, and most frightening of all: twigs and branches and leaves poke out from her clothes and her hair and even her skin, as if she were becoming a tree, an echo of the most awful flavour of her nightly dreams.

Despite her exhaustion, Abigail runs now, her husband forgotten. Luckily for her, the building she seeks is obvious, the largest building in the neighbourhood, its crowded lines rising up above the fields to her left, its elegant front facing eastwards across the road. She smells something tropical and green coming towards her as she bangs on the porter's gate and screams for entry, desperately waving the letter she has carried from Wapping, the one which guarantees her security.

A huge man with a simple face opens the gate and with a final desperate lunge Abigail Horton enters Brooke House, a private madhouse for the deranged.

Turn the page for an exclusive excerpt from

The English Monster, Lloyd Shepherd's first

novel, featuring the Ratcliffe Highway murders.

21 JUNE 1585

The ancient road began at the Tower and ran east to west along a terrace of gravel. To the east it disappeared into the flat treeless horizon of the estuary, merging into the earth just as the earth merged into the sea at the muddy edge of England.

As it left London, this road, which in only a few years would become a highway, formed the northern boundary of a dreary region of swampy land. The great river, as it bent south then north again, formed the southern edge of this semicircle of marshland. It had been drained and flooded, drained and flooded half-a-dozen times in the previous fifty years, while England burned Protestants then Catholics and then Protestants again. This place could not seem to decide if it was of the river or of the earth. The ancient name for the misbegotten half-land was Wapping. No one could remember where the name came from.

In recent years small wharves and little clusters of houses had appeared along the riverbank at Wapping. The rich men who funded the buildings decided that houses and wharves would do a better job of keeping out the river than the sea walls they'd been building for decades in their vain attempts to reclaim the land from the waters. And, more to the point, a wharf generated more profit than a wall.

During the days men made themselves busy around the dozens of boats that moored up along the wharves, the vessels settling down into the riverbed when the tide went out and rising again as it flooded back in, washing up against the wood-and-brick pilings. The pickings were not rich. London's most lucrative trade still headed further upstream towards the wharves that operated within the city walls, but a new grey economy was emerging here downstream at Wapping.

Beyond this sliver of moneymaking and building, back behind the wharves, between the river and the road, were the marshes. The occasional flood still occurred, sweeping away families and livelihoods as well as the property of the men of business. This dank, oozing landscape, unpromising and undeveloped, was the result of the river's inundations. The ground was low, lower than sea level in some places, rising up to the bluff along which the road ran to the north. A man could stand there in the marshes, his feet sinking into the mud, and look to the backs of the wharves and warehouses along the river and imagine that they were floating on water.

There was a gap in the riverside development, and in this gap stood a group of gallows. The gallows lived on borrowed time – already there were complaints that this place of execution was dragging down the land value of investments. Could it not be moved downstream a bit, perhaps to Ratcliffe, somewhere benighted and undeveloped where men of business were not trying to attract custom? But for now the gallows still stood. On this midsummer's eve there were six river pirates hanging there.

The gallows were right at the water's edge, set in amongst the wharves. The six unfortunates hanging from the ropes had been caught after leaping aboard a barge in the river. It had been their sixth attack in four weeks and it was to be their last. The local lightermen and watermen had banded together to bait a trap for them, putting out stories that a barge with wool intended for France and Spain would be travelling downstream that day. When the pirates had clambered onboard, a group of twenty river men hidden beneath sails had emerged and captured them, but sadly not before the pirates, or at least, reported most of the ambushers, the apparent captain of the pirates, whose knife had flashed more quickly and more viciously than those of his crew, had sent three of the Wapping lightermen into the embrace of the old river, their throats slashed and their eyes empty. Eventually the men overcame the pirates and after some cursory discussions with what passed for the authorities in this new outpost they decided upon a customary punishment. The pirates were hanged at Execution Dock, where they would be left for three tides as a signal to others (and perhaps an offering to the river) before being cut down and disposed of.

The river was already rising for the first of these three tides when the leader of the pirates heard a clatter of hoofs on the mixture of mud and stones that constituted the main street here in Wapping, running along the curve of the river behind the wharves. A mighty carriage, it sounded like. The clatter stopped, and he heard the sound of a carriage door slamming. A few minutes later, some squelching footsteps as a man approached. The pirate kept his eyes prudently closed as the footsteps stopped, perhaps directly in front of him. Within two hours, the river would be up to the chins of the men on the gallows, before falling back again.

Carefully, the pirate opened one eye halfway. He saw the swaying feet of his dead shipmates on either side of him, and opened the eye a little further. His visitor was standing on the foreshore, dressed in the Dutch style, all sombre black and white, the clothes effortlessly wealthier than the new gay and gaudy fashions that were rippling out from the English Queen's court.

The visitor cleared his throat and spat. The pirate heard a small splash in the water, and his careful eyes caught the sun as it glittered on a thick lump of green phlegm which appeared and spun around in the water as it commenced its journey down to Tilbury. The visitor glanced up and behind at the gallows, and the pirate closed his eyes quickly. He resolved to keep his eyes that way as the visitor started to speak, in rich aristocratic tones with just the hint of a clammy Dutch accent.

'Quite a view they've given you. Desirable waterfront property, I'd say.'

The pirate said nothing, obviously. The creaking of the gallows was the only sound as he and his men swung gently in the soft summer breeze. Miles and miles upstream, it was a beautiful evening among the willow trees and reeds at Runnymede and Richmond, where the aristocrats played at court and love and wrote poetry to each other. The sun was setting in the opulent west. But here, to the east of the metropolis, the dominant colours were greys and browns. Mud and water, not trees and flowers.

The thought seemed to make the visitor positively cheerful. He put his hands behind his back and actually rose up on his toes at the vista before him. 'Someday all this will be very desirable property, captain. When my father built his wall here, he had a vision of a new suburb, with the river kept out and the land turned into meadows and orchards. He wanted this to be the prettiest part of London. And all within sight of that dreadful Tower.'

It occurred to the pirate to wonder why the Dutchman was speaking when, as far as the man knew, there was no one there alive to listen to him.

The visitor spoke again, and even with his eyes closed the pirate captain had the impression that the Dutchman had turned his back on the river and was facing him. Almost as if he were speaking to him. Perhaps he was practising an address.

'You'll be the last, captain. The last crew to be hanged on this so-called Execution Dock. It's keeping the developers away, this grisly habit, and this land is valuable. A hundred years, maybe two hundred, this'll be the busiest port in the world. Trade is coming, captain. Trade. Not petty thievery or the ridiculous swapping of bits of unmade cloth for bits of food 'n' drink. The world's wealth is out there waiting to be bought and sold, and unlike most of my countrymen I predict that the buying and selling will happen here, in London, not in Antwerp or Rotterdam. Wapping's going to flourish. It's going to become the hub on which the world turns. You'll go down in history, captain. The last pirate to be hanged at Wapping. My congratulations.'

Another movement, and then the sound of the visitor walking back to his carriage. The slamming door, the 'hai!' of the coachman, and the snap of hoofs and wheels on the road back into London. And then only the sound of the creaking gallows again.

The tide rose, and later it fell. It rose and it fell three times. When the locals came to cut them down, they were disconcerted to find only five pirates hanging from the gallows. The sixth – the *captain* – had gone.